Also by Suzan Holder

Shake it Up, Beverley

ROCK 'N' ROSE

SUZAN HOLDER

One More Chapter
a division of HarperCollins*Publishers* Ltd
1 London Bridge Street
London SE1 9GF
www.harpercollins.co.uk
HarperCollins*Publishers*
1st Floor, Watermarque Building, Ringsend Road
Dublin 4, Ireland

This paperback edition 2022
1
First published in Great Britain in ebook format
by HarperCollins*Publishers* 2022
Copyright © Suzan Holder 2022
Suzan Holder asserts the moral right to be identified
as the author of this work

A catalogue record of this book is available from the British Library

ISBN: 978-0-00-852210-0

Printed and bound in the UK using 100% Renewable Electricity
by CPI Group (UK) Ltd

For my very own rock n' roll guys – Nod and Django XX
And remembering Swinn and Pete – who both lived for the music they loved.
Love & Music Live Forever!

Chapter One

Daisy was grappling with an uncooperative dummy on the floor of her shop, Blue Moon Vintage. The mannequin was all knees and elbows, and trying to get a Fifties-style floral dress over the head and onto its angular body was proving impossible. Daisy realised she should have waited for Nana Rose; the two of them would surely be able to wrestle the blank-faced dummy into submission in no time. But Nana Rose was late, again. This had been happening more and more and Daisy had to admit her grandmother's behaviour was starting to worry her.

Daisy gave up the struggle to re-dress the dummy and went to peer out of the shop window again. Blue Moon Vintage nestled between a newsagent and a chemist on an ordinary high street in a small Welsh town. It used to be a traditional gentlemen's tailors, full of polished wooden fittings, large full-length mirrors and a temperamental old till. When it had come up for rent Daisy had leaped at the chance to move her online vintage clothing business into a bricks and mortar store.

Not for the first time, Daisy was beginning to regret her impulsive nature. The shop was her way of trying to fit into her home town; it had always felt such a struggle. No one else dressed like Daisy or liked the kind of vintage stuff she was into. She now realised that wasn't the best premise for opening a retro business but being naturally pig-headed she'd quickly signed the lease and used all her savings on the deposit. Her mother Lilian had made it very clear she didn't approve – nothing new there then – and had pleaded with her to think carefully. Unlike Lilian, Daisy much preferred to throw caution to the wind and act on impulse, but since her bank account had gone into the red and the bills kept piling up, she couldn't help but recall an argument she'd had with her mother about the value of vintage.

'Vintage?' Lilian had sniffed as though the very word brought a bad smell to her nose. 'You can call it whatever you like, Daisy, but if it doesn't sell it will be "jumble" and no one *ever* made a living out of selling jumble!'

Whatever her mother's misgivings, Daisy had worked hard to ensure the shop looked gorgeous. It might indeed turn out to be a folly – but at least it was a pretty one! The double bay windows were always stunningly dressed in a colourful assortment of yesterday's fashions and framed by baby-blue painted woodwork. Daisy had invested in a beautiful painted shop sign that sat above the windows: silver lettering on a dark-blue background spelling out the name against a half moon crescent in an Art Deco style.

There was even an old-fashioned bell over the recessed shop door that dinged when customers came in – not that they came in very often. It might not be a money spinner, but Blue Moon Vintage always *looked* wonderful.

The sight of Daisy's anxious face peering out from between the silk and taffeta dresses on display was now rather ruining this image. Where had Nana Rose got to? Daisy had been trying not to join in with her mother's increasingly frequent worries about Rose's deteriorating condition. Lilian was a worrier, that's what she did. Daisy tuned it out most of the time. Okay, so Nana Rose was slowing down a bit, getting a little confused every now and then – she was well into her seventies after all, and everyone knew she was a bit of a 'character'.

Daisy and Nana Rose were as close as could be; Daisy's addiction to pre-loved fashion, rock 'n' roll music and vintage Americana had been completely inspired by her grandmother. It was not a love that was shared by Daisy's mother Lilian, however... not at all. She'd almost flipped her lid when Daisy had splashed out on a refurbished juke box the first week she opened. 'Why can't you just put the radio on?' she'd said, and Daisy had tried to explain, yet again, how she was completely missing the point.

The point being that Daisy was constantly dissatisfied with life in sleepy Llandovery and yearned for a life more like the ones she saw in old movies and heard about in her favourite songs from the Fifties; Blue Moon Vintage was her way of trying to experience that lifestyle.

Daisy caught sight of her own reflection in one of the many mirrors on the wall and thought how her straight-

3

laced mother would probably think she looked ridiculous. Her blue and white gingham blouse was knotted at the waist just above the waistband of her dark-blue pedal pushers. The red ballet shoes she wore matched her scarlet lipstick and, just for good measure, she'd tied a silk scarf patterned with yellow daisies around the ponytail in her long dark hair. She was aiming for the look of a Fifties Hollywood starlet on their day off but presumed her mother would think she looked more like an old-fashioned cleaning lady. Lilian didn't really have much of a sense of style, unless you considered knife-sharp creases in the front of your jeans as stylish. Who in their right mind ironed creases in their jeans?

Daisy went over to the brightly coloured retro juke box that housed all of her and Nana Rose's favourite music tracks. She'd rung her grandmother's home a dozen times this morning already, but the landline was continually ringing out unanswered. Nana Rose had a mobile phone, of course she did, but she wasn't answering that either. Daisy was still trying not to worry but had ended up leaving a series of increasingly frantic messages.

Daisy ran her eyes down the list of songs, suddenly realising the track that captured her current agitated mood was by Bill Haley and his Comets. With a trembling finger she pressed the button for 'Shake, Rattle and Roll'.

Just a few streets away, Rose knew she was late, although she couldn't remember what for. She'd dressed in a hurry and was aware her appearance was attracting attention.

The customers in the butcher's shop craned their necks as they watched a frail-looking old dear as she lurched across the high street, literally stopping traffic.

'She's going to catch her death dressed like that,' said the butcher.

They all continued to stare past the black puddings and legs of lamb hanging in the window, increasingly concerned at the spectacle of the woman who was wearing a floaty, floral, sleeveless nightie tucked into a lumpy knee-length skirt. On her feet she wore a pair of pink fluffy slippers, totally unsuitable for the wet and windy Welsh weather.

'Oh, the poor dear,' said one of the women waiting for chops. Putting down her shopping basket, the woman headed out to the street to try and help, but Rose just waved her away. She was a woman on a mission and no one could stop her.

The customers clucked and tutted as Rose headed down towards the bus station. Rose was getting anxious; there was somewhere she had to be, something she had to do, but she couldn't for the life of her remember what it was. A burst of music broke into her jumbled thoughts. That was it. Now she remembered. The secret. She must tell them her secret and she must do it quickly, before she forgot all over again.

A couple of builders hung over scaffolding to gawp at the half-dressed old lady singing along to their radio. Her quivering voice joined in with Elvis Presley's throbbing vocal as he sang the opening lines from 'Heartbreak Hotel'.

'It's a yes from me,' one of them hollered. 'You're through to the next round.'

'You made that your own. You're like an elderly Kylie Minogue,' joined in his mate.

'ERR-ERRRRRR! NEXT!'

The impromptu judging panel dissolved into hoots and snorts of laughter.

Rose let the audience applause wash over her and waited for Scotty Moore to play the guitar break; as the notes rang out, she grabbed the mic stand and let her left leg tremble and jerk. She curled her lip as she sang and swung the mic stand from side to side giving the audience the sexually charged performance they expected from a rock 'n' roll idol in their prime. Closing her eyes, she went for the big, emotional finish as she stuttered her way through the sentiments about people being so lonely they could die. She rocked her hips, went up on her toes and punched the air in time with the final note. The crowd went wild.

The builders stood, silent and awkward. One of them jumped down from his ladder and gently prised the broom from the old lady's hands.

Rose was fed up of busybodies. Why couldn't they just let her alone? Politely but firmly, she went on her way, saying, 'No thank you very much,' to the pushy shopkeepers trying to tempt her into their shops and the charity muggers who wanted her to donate to one-legged donkeys or confused clowns or whatever nonsense they were about.

Suddenly, she realised she was smack bang in front of the Roxy cinema. The big wide stone steps were an inviting semi-circle, drawing you up towards the box office in the foyer. She could escape here for a couple of hours, get away from all these nosy parkers. Yes, she'd treat herself to an afternoon matinee. That would be nice.

She hadn't heard of any of the movies advertised on the posters on the big glass doors, but she went in anyway. She remembered coming here just last week to see Elvis's new motion picture *King Creole*. She'd been on the arm of dishy Dennis Perkins and he'd insisted on sitting on the back row. She recalled only too well how irritating it had been to have to keep swatting his wandering hands away while she was trying to concentrate on Presley's performance. It was only when ten-foot-high Elvis looked down from the screen, heavy-lidded with his hair flopping over his eyes, and sang about looking for trouble, that dirty Dennis had given up groping and stuck his hand back in his bag of pear drops. Thank goodness.

The girl at the Roxy box office was not very helpful. It didn't matter how many times Rose asked for a ticket to the afternoon show, the girl just gawped at her. The cinema manager finally appeared but he was about as useful as a Mexican wave on the radio. Rose spoke slowly and clearly as if she was talking to five-year-olds.

'One... ticket... for... the... matinee... please.'

Nothing. The gormless pair just looked at her and then each other. She tried to explain that she didn't mind what film was showing, even a Western would do. Her feet were hurting now and she really could do with a sit down.

The manager gently led Rose over to a nearby sofa. There were plenty to choose from; the Roxy cinema building had been converted into a large furniture store years ago. He offered to get her a cup of tea.

'Now that's what I call customer service,' said Rose.

By the time the furniture store manager returned with plastic cup of sugary tea, the Special Offer Sofa where he had deposited Rose was empty. He hissed at Chloe, the girl on the customer services desk, 'I said keep an eye on her, where is she?'

The girl barely moved her eyes from her computer screen.

'I dunno, she just left,' said Chloe. 'I'm only on work experience y'know.'

Rose had remembered she needed to be somewhere. She still wasn't quite sure where that was, but she knew with absolute certainty that it wasn't where she currently was and that it was, in fact, somewhere… else.

Back at Blue Moon Vintage, Daisy had been rattled enough to eventually give in and call her mother. Lilian was now on high alert and berating her daughter for not letting her know sooner that Rose was missing. Lilian had made a worrying discovery when she'd driven round to Rose's house before heading to the shop.

'The front door was wide open, her handbag was left plonked on the kitchen table,' Lilian announced on arrival. 'I'm going to have to call the police.'

Lilian was now attempting to pace back and forth, but there wasn't really enough room in the cluttered vintage clothes shop. She stuck her head between a couple of mannequins and peered again through the bay window just like Daisy had been doing all morning. Daisy watched as her agitated mother knocked the display dummy right over. The figure crashed backwards, toppling the whole carefully staged scene she'd spent ages creating. The expressionless dummy fell on her back with one leg cocked in the air. It wasn't an attractive look. Worse still, the second dummy fell forward at an angle that plunged her headfirst between the other's open legs. Instead of a tempting tableau of sparkly evening gowns accessorised with feathers and fans, the window of Blue Moon Vintage now resembled a slightly pornographic massacre in a hen house.

'Just wait a little bit longer,' said Daisy as she attempted to wrestle the figures into less compromising positions. Daisy was desperately fighting against her usual impulsive nature in this situation – anything to avoid admitting that there could be something seriously wrong with Nana Rose.

Lilian's head snapped back in Daisy's direction. She looked like she was about to explode. 'Wait? How much longer?

Daisy tried to hold her nerve while her mother glared at her. She knew what she was thinking: that she wasn't taking Nana Rose's deterioration seriously enough, that she didn't *care* enough. It wasn't true. Just because she made light of things occasionally – like the time Nana Rose mistook a bag of quinoa for brown sugar and made a cup of tea you could stand your spoon up in – it didn't mean she wasn't worried.

As Daisy chewed on a fingernail, she thought about the colourful stories Nana Rose always loved to tell customers. It was a sales technique that worked brilliantly. She'd describe how a patterned silk dress would have been perfect for an afternoon tea dance at the old Gaiety Ballroom or how she'd worn a flared petticoat skirt *just like this one* to jive to Bill Haley and the Comets at lunchtime rock 'n' roll sessions when she was a girl. Customers loved it.

When Nana Rose had told a pair of twenty-somethings that the bags they were looking at had been on the arms of girls in the audience of Lonnie Donegan and Eddie Cochran concerts in the Fifties, they'd snapped them up. Daisy doubted the young shoppers had any idea who either of those people actually were, but it didn't seem to matter. Her grandmother's enthusiasm for rock 'n' roll music and all the memorabilia and fashion that went with it was infectious.

When Daisy was growing up, there'd been no posters of grungy pop stars on her bedroom walls. No sounds of wailing introspection drifted from her record player. She'd rejected songs with suicidal lyrics and lip-synching singers backed by a thumping machine drum beat. No, thanks to Nana Rose, what she loved was a slap back bass, a guitar riff that sounded like a ringing bell and lyrics about feeling alive and falling in love. The music she and Rose both loved took you to a particular place in time, where you sipped soda pop at an all-night diner lit with neon lights, danced in the arms of a guy in a leather jacket to music on the juke box and then drove home in an open-top Cadillac so you could see the night sky full of stars. As Rose loved to tell Daisy, time and again, back in the day she'd done all of those things, it always made Daisy so jealous; *that* was the life she wanted to live!

Daisy bit her lip now as she thought about how Nana Rose had recently started to tell the same stories over and over. While Daisy had once admired her Nana's ability to weave a tale as a sales tactic, she now worried Rose was losing the ability to know the difference between the past and the present, from memories and reality. There had been a rather alarming incident when Rose practically fought a customer over a polka dot blouse she'd insisted she wanted to wear for a date with someone called Dennis Perkins. A chiffon sleeve had got torn as they both pulled at it and Daisy had to offer the girl a large discount on another top.

Lilian stood facing Daisy with her arms crossed over her bony body. 'She's been working so hard, it's too much for her at her age.'

'I don't force her to come in; she loves it, you know that.' Daisy was immediately defensive. The shop had been a bone of contention between them from the moment Daisy announced the idea. Lilian was forthright in her view that Daisy should stick to online sales and forget about opening an actual high-street shop.

'Blue Moon is about right,' Lilian had said witheringly when Daisy had tried to explain her plans. 'It'll be once in a *blue moon* you make a sale around here. How much call for second-hand tat do you think there is in a small Welsh town like Llandovery?'

Lilian simply refused to share her own mother and daughter's enthusiasm for second-hand stuff and was equally rude in her appraisal of the music they both loved. Chuck Berry, Little Richard, even Elvis himself – they all left her completely cold. Lilian might be well into her fifties in

11

age, but she was certainly not into the Fifties era of music. Daisy simply could not understand how her mother remained unmoved. How could she not feel something when to Daisy it was like a punch to the guts? Jackie Wilson singing 'Reet Petite' would always make her spirits soar and the sound of Jerry Lee Lewis hammering out 'Great Balls of Fire' on the piano had her tapping and clapping, moving and grooving, rockin' and…

Daisy looked over to the juke box in the corner but decided there was no tune that would fit this particular moment.

A muffled budgie suddenly started to whistle from inside Lilian's handbag. She sprang towards it and plucked out her phone trilling its annoying ringtone. Even more annoyingly, the caller was Sanctimonious Sandra from the insurance company where Lilian worked, asking how much longer 'this was going to take'.

'Snotty cow!' Lilian shoved the phone back into her bag and then took it back out and stared at it, then looked at Daisy.

'I'm going to call the police.'

A flash of fluorescent yellow made them both gasp as the shop door was opened just then by a female police officer wearing a hi-vis vest.

'Does this belong to you?' she asked as she led a dishevelled Nana Rose into the shop.

The policewoman appeared weary and only stopped long enough to confirm that Rose *did* belong to Lilian and Daisy before she disappeared back to more serious police matters. Her powers of deduction had been severely tested as Rose had refused to volunteer any information when she'd been spotted stealing someone's coffee from a table outside Costa. It was only when the old woman insisted on repeatedly singing the song 'Blue Moon' that the enterprising officer remembered the name of the shop around the corner and reached a logical conclusion. Promotion to CID was surely just a matter of time.

Once the policewoman had gone, Rose stood smiling sweetly at her daughter and granddaughter as if butter wouldn't melt. Lilian chose that moment to ask the least important question.

'Why were you stealing someone's coffee? You don't even like coffee?'

Rose shrugged. 'Yes, as the saying goes, I'm a cup of tea in a world of skinny lattes.'

Lilian goggled at the lucidity of the old lady's response and simply turned and headed to carry out the one activity guaranteed to bring a semblance of normality to any given situation. She put the kettle on.

Daisy guided Rose into the changing cubicle, sat her on a high-backed chair and looked for something more suitable for her to wear.

'Here, Nana, try this.'

She handed her a pale-blue twinset in soft cashmere and Rose stroked the fluffy fabric with her cold hands.

'Oooo, lovely.'

'What were you up to, Nana? You know you really can't wander around the town like this. You're not properly dressed or anything?'

Daisy tried to keep her tone light, but her voice caught

13

in her throat as she watched Rose pluck at the pearl buttons on the cardigan. Seeing her nana like this was excruciating, there was no denying something was very, very wrong. Rose was looking at her with such a strange expression on her face, as though she was trying really hard to remember something. The old lady opened her mouth to speak but then closed it again and shook her head as though whatever it was had disappeared from her mind, again.

Daisy's attention was suddenly caught by the sight of what looked like a massive wound on Rose's bare upper arm.

'Oh, Nana, what have you done?'

Rose followed Daisy's gaze and then bizarrely started to chuckle. She looked up with a fresh light in her eyes as though she now knew exactly what she wanted to say. She put a finger to her lips.

'Shhhh,' she said, her eyes darting towards the back room where Lilian was still making tea. 'Promise me you won't tell your mother?'

Daisy made no such promise but Rose carried on anyway.

'I've kept this a secret for years. I don't know how I've done it but once you keep a secret for so long…'

She tailed off as she turned her body and stuck out her arm so that Daisy could get a better look. There on the freckled skin at the top of Nana Rose's wrinkled skinny arm was the last thing Daisy expected to see, a rather faded but still-beautiful tattoo of a blood-red rose.

Daisy stood in open-mouthed shock as she stared at the tattoo on her grandmother's arm. She barely noticed Lilian pull back the velvet curtain of the changing cubicle and take in the scene with one cursory glance.

'Oh for heaven's sake, cover that up!'

Daisy whipped her head towards her mother, 'You *knew* about this? You knew she had a… tattoo?'

'Of course I knew, but I made her promise not to show it to you in case it gave you any more silly ideas.' Lilian put down the mug of tea and deftly pulled the blue cardigan sleeve over her mother's skinny shoulder. Her careful actions were in marked contrast to the coldness in her tone.

Nana Rose reached out and patted Lilian's hand. 'There's something you *don't* know though, my girl.'

Lilian remained brusque, but the concern in her voice for her mother was beginning to break through. 'I expect there are *many* things I don't know, but let's see about getting you home, shall we? I think we ought to call the doctor.'

'NO!'

Lilian and Daisy were taken aback as Rose raised her voice, her whole body now clenched and taut.

'I have to tell you… before… too late.'

'What is it, Nana? You've not had your belly button pierced as well, have you?'

If in doubt, make a joke. It was Daisy's default setting, but Lilian shot her a look that said, 'Not now'. Rose took no notice of Daisy's lame attempt at comedy anyway.

'It's… your father…'

Now it was Lilian's turn to look confused.

'My… what?'

Daisy could not imagine where this was going. Her mother didn't have a father, she didn't have a grandfather.

15

Rose had been a single mother in the Sixties and no one had ever wanted to talk very much about all that.

'His name...' Rose left a dramatic pause that Lilian found completely maddening.

'You have never told me my father's name... never once in my whole life...'

Daisy flapped her hand towards her agitated mother. 'Let her finish.'

Rose looked steadily at them both; she suddenly seemed composed.

'His name...' She took a steadying breath in and out before continuing. '... was Elvis Presley.'

Chapter Two

Three Weeks Later

Daisy was standing in line at the airline check-in. She looked inside her bag, again. Passport – check, boarding pass – check, ticket for Graceland Experience trip – check. In a few hours she would be in Memphis, Tennessee. That fact made her think her whole life could be summed up in just one emoji: the one where the top of the head explodes into smoking pieces... Mind blown!

Perhaps this was what grief did to you? How would she know? She'd made it to her mid-twenties with losing anyone close before.

But Nana Rose wasn't just anyone.

Rose died the day after telling Daisy and her mother they were related to Elvis Presley. It was the last coherent thing she'd ever said. Imagine that.

The doctor said she'd suffered a series of strokes. Daisy had almost giggled inappropriately at the news; a stroke – it sounded almost pleasant, like a caress or a pat or even a tickle, but the effects were devastating.

The two of them had always been so close, much closer than any of her friends had been to their grandmothers, but then Rose never seemed like anyone else's grandma. Other people's nanas read traditional bedtime stories to their grandchildren, *Little Red Riding Hood* or *Goldilocks and the Three Bears*, but Rose had entertained toddler Daisy with stories about a man called Elvis, a place called Memphis and the birth of rock 'n' roll. Daisy's favourite story was a classic, but it had now taken on an even greater significance.

It was a hot summer day in Memphis, Tennessee… Rose always began as she told the familiar story. Daisy would snuggle in close, ready to hear about how the handsome man with the funny-sounding name had tried so hard to impress the boss, Mr Sam Phillips, sitting in the control booth of a tiny recording studio.

But no matter how hard poor Elvis tried, Mr Phillips just shook his head. Nothing Elvis sang sounded quite right.

Even when Daisy knew how the story ended, her little tummy would lurch with fear that Elvis Presley would never find a way to showcase his talent, leave his job as a truck driver behind and become the biggest, brightest star the world had ever seen.

No Elvis, no rock 'n' roll… it was as simple as that, according to Nana Rose. Every time she heard the story Daisy marvelled at the quirk of fate that led Elvis, along with bandmates Scotty Moore and Bill Black, to suddenly launch into a rocking version of 'That's All Right' in their lunchbreak and invent a whole new sound.

They were just three guys messing around, having fun – Nana Rose always relished telling the climax of the story – *but Mr Phillips knew at once this was the sound he had been looking for. He opened the door into the studio and said, 'I don't know what you guys are doing, but just keep doing it!'*

Nana Rose always made a big deal of how Elvis's huge success was the result of an accident.

'That's life for you, Daisy,' she would say, *'you never know what it has in store and where it might lead you...so just be ready to take your chances when they appear.'*

Daisy had loved the fact that Nana Rose made it sound like life was full of exciting possibilities and endless opportunities. Of course as she grew older Daisy realised that you couldn't always put a positive spin on anything and everything that might happen. She was certainly struggling to do it now.

There seemed to be some sort of hold-up at the airline desk. A shiny-faced woman in a blue pill box hat was refusing to check someone in. Daisy cast her eye around the busy airport and wondered how much longer it would take her mother to find 'a decent cup of tea'. All the way here, Lilian had fretted about how they were going to survive in a country that preferred coffee to proper British tea. Perhaps she was attempting to drink as much as possible before boarding to try and get her fix.

That was Lilian all over. She'd much rather talk for half an hour on the merits of tea versus coffee than tackle the rather pressing topic of whether they were descended from the King of Rock 'n' Roll. Daisy had tried to talk to her about it.

19

The day after Rose's funeral, Lilian had caught Daisy in a rather embarrassing situation. She'd opened up Blue Moon Vintage and lugged out a box of Rose's vintage records that she'd squirrelled away in the stock room.

With the juke box set to shuffle, Daisy flicked through the album covers until she found the one she was particularly looking for. It had a full-colour image of Elvis Presley's face. As she stared at the image, the shop was suddenly filled with hiccupping guitar chords full of reverb and echo, and a bass baritone mocked her dilemma by asking if there was indeed a bigger fool.

Taking the album cover over to the long mirror outside the changing cubicle, she had held the LP up next to her face. She'd studied Elvis in the picture: the dark swept-up hairstyle, the one, slightly raised eyebrow, the curled lip. She'd flicked her eyes back and forth between her face and Elvis's, tried to raise her eyebrow and curl her lip.

At exactly that moment her mother's voice had cut through the Jordanaires' backing *wah wahs*—

'Well, that just about sums it up!'

Shocked and embarrassed, Daisy had whirled around. 'Oh god, you'll give *me* a stroke next, creeping up on people like that.'

Lilian had turned down the volume control on the juke box, muting the strains of 'A Fool Such As I'.

Daisy had been hoping they would be able to have a proper conversation about the outrageous claim Nana Rose had made about the identity of Lilian's father. The realities of her sudden death and then all the arrangements that had needed to be made for her funeral had meant they'd not yet found the right moment. Daisy had been hoping it had now arrived.

She'd been able to think of little else other than the amazing claim and whether it could be true? She knew all about a trip Rose had made to Memphis in the Sixties when she was a teenager, before Lilian had been born. They'd talked about it so many times Daisy almost felt she had been there herself. Rose had shared so many memories of her time in Tennessee, although it now appeared she had left out one or two rather crucial details.

Launching into a potted history of Elvis Presley, whether her mother wanted to hear it or not, Daisy had tried to explain to Lilian why Rose's claim might not simply be the delusions of an addled mind. There were a lot of reasons to argue that it actually fitted the known and accepted facts quite well. Lilian had been born in the spring of 1961 – Sgt Presley had been demobbed from the army in April the year before. He'd arrived back in Memphis after his two-year stint in Germany and immediately headed for Graceland. That summer coincided with teenage Rose's visit there to see her friend Jennifer.

'Elvis *was* in Memphis when Nana was over there...' Daisy had insisted as Lilian regarded her daughter coolly, saying nothing. 'Yes, yes I know he'd already met Priscilla in Germany, but it was another *two years* before she came over to live at Graceland with him and he didn't marry her until 1967... seven years later. Everyone knows he had lots of girlfriends... lots...'

Lilian had stared at her daughter like she'd just sprouted a second head, words clearly failing her. Daisy had stared back at her mother's piercing blue eyes, the question nagging at her – were those eyes the same blue as Presley's? For Daisy, the feeling that she may, in some way, be truly connected to Elvis Presley was just too tantalising a prospect to dismiss out of hand.

For Lilian, the notion that Elvis Presley was her father was simply ridiculous. Her mother had suffered a stroke, a massive bleed on the brain. Was it any wonder that she was claiming something so far-fetched and bizarre? Rose was an Elvis fan, always had been, and Lilian had decided that's what this 'nonsense' must all be about. Her mother's obsession with rock 'n' roll music had finally morphed into utter madness. The passion for vintage Americana that her mother and daughter shared had always irritated her. But this? To get to this point in her life without knowing who she really was, who her father was… and then, just before she died her mother ups and decides to make the big announcement. It would be funny if it wasn't so heart-breaking. Rose belonged to a generation that held up the queen as a model of how to behave – *never complain, never explain*. How many times had Lilian heard her mother parrot that phrase? Too many times, she decided. She should have asked more questions when she had the chance, it was too damn late now.

As Daisy inched forward in the check-in queue, she remembered the conversation with her mother in the shop the day she got caught comparing her profile to Elvis's. It had not gone the way she had hoped. She'd tried to make Lilian open her mind just a teeny tiny bit to the possibility that Rose may have been telling the truth. Modern life had never seemed to really suit Daisy. She'd always felt out of place, even out of time. Could this, she reasoned, perhaps be the reason why?

Lilian hadn't been prepared to listen to any of those arguments. Instead she'd cut Daisy off by slamming her hand down onto the counter with some force. There on the glass-topped display, with an array of second-hand jewellery glittering beneath, were two golden envelopes emblazoned with the words 'Graceland Experience'. Daisy couldn't have been more surprised if her mother had launched into a word-perfect rendition of 'Hound Dog'.

It turned out that Rose had left a note.

It wasn't a note that explained anything clearly; as Lilian observed, 'That would have been far too simple!' Instead, she'd scrawled a message in her loopy handwriting on the back of an Elvis postcard. The picture showed him bare-chested with a floral garland around his neck and playing a ukulele. The flip side said: 'Time for the truth. You'll find it at Graceland.'

At some point in the weeks before her death, when her mental faculties were in severe decline, Rose had booked two tickets on an all-inclusive trip to Memphis. She'd made plans to send her daughter and granddaughter on a mission to solve the mystery of their past, but hadn't chosen to fill in any of the blanks herself. Perhaps it was because by then she couldn't even remember the details herself, or was it because she just didn't want to face the truth? What had really been going on inside Nana Rose's mind was now anyone's guess.

Up in the cafe-bar overlooking the departures hall,

Lilian was watching Daisy in the check-in queue. Several airline staff in matching sky-blue uniforms had clustered around 'Shiny Face', the over-made-up woman on the check-in desk. Lilian wondered if she was in fact a malfunctioning robot. No real woman had eyebrows like that, surely? Whatever was happening, there appeared to be time for one more top-up so she poured herself another tepid cup of tea from the tiny metal pot.

Lilian was thinking about how she was always made to feel like the odd one out.

She had pretended to stop caring years ago about who her real father was. She dealt with reality, not fantasy. Her mum had been a single mum in the Sixties. That meant neither of them had had it easy. Lilian knew what she needed to know. Her mother had scrimped and saved and worked several jobs to get them by. She actually admired her for it. It would have been easier to give her baby up for adoption like so many other young women were forced to do. It hadn't been a choice without consequences though. The other girls at Lilian's school had been unspeakably cruel; she had shouldered the shame for years, the looks, the comments, the girls who refused to be friends with the sulky, pouting child she became. They had demanded to know why she didn't know who her dad was on an almost daily basis but Rose discouraged questions on the subject, so Lilian learned not to ask. Not to care. If a man wasn't capable of stepping up to his responsibilities then she didn't want anything to do with him anyway. She reasoned he simply wasn't worth the tears or the time. As for going looking for him... Never!

Give a man like that the chance to reject her all over again? She should coco!

She'd built up her protective armour over the years, and part of that was insisting on being called 'Lilian' instead of 'Lily'. She felt it suited her much better. Trouble was, Rose and Daisy appeared to view her resistance to being called 'Lily' as a way of setting herself apart, of not wanting to be in their flowery 'gang'. It was nothing of the sort.

Daisy wasn't even called Daisy, not really. Lilian had named her 'Danielle' when she was born but Rose had dropped so many heavy hints about wanting to continue the 'floral tradition', she'd caved in and given her Daisy as a middle name: Danielle Daisy Featherstone.

Nana Rose had immediately taken to amusing the baby at every opportunity by endlessly singing some wildly inappropriate song about a 'gal' called Daisy and the damn name had stuck. Rose had found it hilarious to jive about with the baby on her hip, singing 'Wop Bop A Bamboo Loopy Doop' or whatever the words were. Daisy's first word was – you guessed it – 'Day-zeee' delivered with a big dribbly grin.

Ahh look, she likes it! Rose would say as the baby clapped and gurgled. *She's a baby*, Lilian had fumed. *She likes sticking her fingers into plug sockets and pushing carrots up her nose too, but you don't have to encourage it.*

In Lilian's opinion, Rose had always been 'quirky', not like any of her friend's mums. A blue spotty scarf tied around her head. A long green velvet dress worn open as a coat. A black leather biker jacket! Skinny jeans! That bloody tattoo!!

Lilian had made Rose promise to keep *that* from Daisy at least. The girl had started dressing oddly as soon as she could. One minute she was in pretty smocked dresses and T-bar sandals, the next it was ripped band t-shirts and rockabilly petticoats. The last thing Lilian wanted was for Daisy to think getting some random image branded on her skin for all eternity was a cool thing to do.

She finished her tea and glanced down at Daisy again; she wasn't difficult to spot in her baggy red tartan trousers and leopard-print beret, and she'd barely moved forward at all. Lilian sighed and picked up her cross-body bag and matching navy jacket. It was now or never.

By the time she'd reached Daisy, the queue was starting to move.

'What was the hold up?' she asked as Daisy inched her wheelie case forward a little.

'Some guy got all aggressive over his man bag. God knows what he's got in there but he got all shouty about it. Told them he knew the airline policy better than they did. There was a right to-do but they let him through in the end.'

Lilian nodded in response, but she wasn't really listening. She looked around them in the line and spotted a few people with golden Graceland Experience tags just like theirs tied to their luggage.

'I bet you can't wait to get there, can you?' Lilian said.

Daisy looked at her mother in surprise. She never thought Lilian would understand what a trip like this would mean to her. She thought her mum viewed her yearning for the swagger and excitement of America as a phase she'd grow out of. But Daisy knew it went deeper than that. She could feel it. How could she be inspired by narrow, rainy Welsh streets filled with narrow-minded, gloomy people? Where was the thrill in being pawed by spotty youths, whose idea of a 'hot date' was a trip to the pub followed by a bag of chips? If you were lucky! What was the point of tottering the streets with a load of pissed-up girlfriends who drank Prosecco like it was the answer to their mundane lives and had never even heard of Johnny Cash? She'd walked that line too many times and she didn't care if she never walked it again.

Nana Rose had filled her mind with so many stories about Memphis and the American South – romantic images of drive-in movies and ice cream parlours and pink Cadillac cars, where gentlemen with proper Southern manners called you darlin' and took you dancing. Daisy longed to taste her first mint julep as she sat on a porch swing and watched a much more interesting world go by.

She'd dreamed of making this trip for years, and now here she was, about to experience everything her heart had ever yearned for. Not only that but Nana Rose's confession set her on a mission to explore the possibility that the birthplace of rock 'n' roll had such a hold on her not just on a whim, but because it was in her blood.

Daisy closed her eyes and pictured highways and sky-scrapers so different from the terraced houses and suburban streets she was used to. She imagined herself on the deck of a paddle steamer boat as it ploughed its way down the mighty Mississippi River.

She opened her eyes and saw her mother was looking nervous. This trip didn't have the same tempting connotations for Lilian. Her mother was comfortable in her own familiar surroundings and now she was being asked to fly halfway around the world to try and find out who her father was. Daisy wanted to reassure her mum she understood this was difficult. She took hold of Lilian's hands and faced her full on.

'Whatever the truth is, we'll find out together, Mum, it'll be okay.'

Lilian looked at her daughter and winced as though someone was twisting a knife tin her chest.

'I can't do it, Daisy.'

Daisy knew this was a big ask; they'd lost Rose so suddenly, and without any time to process what that meant they were heading across the Atlantic Ocean on what might well turn out to be 'mission impossible'. She gripped Lilian's hands more firmly and tried again to convince her mum to keep focusing on the importance of what they needed to do.

'Nana bought the tickets, she wanted us to go.' Daisy's grief came in waves of nausea, but she just kept swallowing it down. Focusing on completing the task Nana Rose had set for them was the only way she was getting through this.

'She wanted *you* to go.' Lilian removed her hands from Daisy's grasp and instead gripped the handle of her case until her knuckles went white. 'You were always the one she talked to about the place. You'll be better doing this on your own, I'll just get in the way... I'm better staying here and sorting out all Nana's stuff.'

For once Daisy had nothing to say. Surely her mum wasn't about to...

Lilian pulled her in for a quick hug and whispered into her hair, 'It's okay, you go.'

Daisy stood rooted to the spot as her mother turned and walked quickly away. There was no time to argue, Lilian didn't even turn around to wave goodbye. One minute they had been holding hands – Daisy had thought they were in fact connecting in a way they very rarely did – then just moments later her mum was gone.

Was she supposed to follow? Run after her and plead with her to come back? Daisy knew that would be pointless.

She could still feel the sensation of her mother's whispered words close to her ear. What had she said? 'It's okay, you go...'

Daisy made up her mind. Nana Rose *wanted* her to go, her mum had *told* her to go, she *needed* to go... If she had to make this trip alone then so be it, she *would* go!

Chapter Three

Squashed into a middle seat on the plane Daisy found herself between two fellow travellers on the Graceland Experience trip. Next to the window was a friendly Welsh barmaid called Anita who'd won a competition to get her ticket and clearly couldn't be more thrilled. On her other side was a slightly snappy woman called Priya whose manner was as frosty as the recycled icy wind blasting from the air con nozzle above them.

All Daisy really wanted to do was close her eyes and try and recalibrate her own mood. Her see-sawing emotions had left her feeling worn out. First had been the thrill of the possibility that she was descended from rock royalty, then came the shattering blow of Nana Rose's death. The discovery of the tickets to send her and her mother on a quest to discover the truth had been daunting but exciting, but Lilian had now bottled the trip and left Daisy to face whatever was in store all alone. Consequently, Daisy was reeling and experiencing major turbulence while they were still taxiing on the runway; all she wanted to do now was close her eyes and sleep. Anita, however, had other ideas.

It only took Daisy a couple of minutes after take-off to realise that this middle-aged barmaid from The Mumbles loved Wales, Elvis and talking, although not necessarily in that order.

First, Anita attempted to regale both Daisy and Priya with all the details from the radio phone-in competition she'd won. Priya had rather rudely stuck in some earphones and after jabbing impatiently at the screen in the seatback in front of her, had pointedly directed all her attention to some wildlife documentary. That left Daisy as the only audience to hear all about it.

'It was a late-night show on the local station, you know... the one that Aled Jones sometimes presents?'

Daisy didn't know it but smiled and nodded as though she did.

'They started off by asking what Elvis's middle name was... I suppose that sorts out the real fans straight away, doesn't it?'

Anita left the question hanging in the air between them and Daisy figured she was using it as a test to see if Daisy qualified as a true Elvis fan herself.

'Well, of course, his full name is Elvis Aaron Presley,' answered Daisy. 'Although there is some controversy as to whether the "Aaron" is spelt with one or two "A"s.'

Anita beamed at her and vigorously nodded her blonde head, her ample bosom quivering like blancmange inside her tight pale-blue t-shirt. She reminded Daisy of someone, but she couldn't quite place who it was.

Anita ran through a few of the other questions, like having to name the town where Elvis was born.

'My mind went blank on that one,' Anita confessed. 'I knew he was born in Mississippi and not Tennessee, but I just couldn't recall the actual place. Luckily they gave me three choices... Jackson, Tupelo or Biloxi.'

It was Daisy's turn to nod vigorously now as they both said, 'Tupelo!' and then laughed at each other's competitive streak.

'Oh but then... you wouldn't credit it!' Anita's sing-song Welsh accent became high and shrill with her remembered indignation. 'I was in competition with another caller, Nigel, did I tell you that?

Daisy shook her head. She wished she'd heard this show when it was broadcast, it sounded very entertaining.

'Well, Nigel was a right smart arse, let me tell you. I knew from the moment Aled asked him if he was ready before the first question. "I'm ready, ready, ready to rock 'n' roll, Aled," that's what he said!'

Daisy pulled a face to show that she agreed with Anita's appraisal of Nigel as 'a right knob'.

'And then,' Anita added, 'one of Nigel's questions was to name Elvis's Memphis mansion!'

Daisy and Anita looked at each other, both with eyebrows raised as high as they could go, as if to say: *who doesn't know the answer to that?*

'He didn't get *that* wrong, surely?' Daisy couldn't believe there was anyone in the world who didn't know the name of the famous white colonial-style mansion.

'They even gave him three choices,' said Anita. 'Aled asked him, was it Neverland, Heartland or Graceland?'

Anita left a dramatic pause just long enough for Daisy to ask, 'What did he say?'

Anita shook her head slowly as if to show she still couldn't quite believe what she was about to say. 'He said… "it's Gracelands, Aled, Gracelands!"'

Daisy gasped in horror at the schoolboy error Nigel had made. Only the most ignorant music fan would make the mistake of adding an extra 's' to the Graceland name. Elvis lived at Graceland – it should NEVER be referred to as Gracelands.

'They didn't accept that answer though, did they?' Daisy imagined for a moment a smug fool like Nigel as her travelling partner in the seat next to her instead of Anita. How dreadful.

'Yes – they did!' Anita's big green eyes were on stalks.

The competition sounded like it had been neck and neck, right up until when Aled asked a question about the Sun Studio musicians dubbed the 'Million Dollar Quartet'. Daisy knew the black and white photograph of the famous music heroes well. Taken in 1956, Elvis was sat at the piano, Jerry Lee Lewis was nearest the camera and Johnny Cash was furthest away, against the wall.

'They asked you to name the guy in the middle… the one with the guitar?' Daisy was racking her own brain now, who was it? Jackie Wilson? Roy Orbison? She didn't want to blurt out the wrong name and embarrass herself now.

Anita smiled and looked like the cat who'd got the

cream. 'That's right, the guy with the guitar, and I knew the answer… It was Carl Perkins!'

Of course! Daisy almost slapped her own forehead. Carl Perkins, 'Mr Blue Suede Shoes' himself.

They both broke into an impromptu rendition of the song Carl Perkins had written that Presley made so famous.

That was it!

As Anita sang along to the rockabilly tune, Daisy suddenly realised who it was that Anita reminded her of… Dolly Parton!

When Daisy complimented her voice, Anita enthusiastically confirmed that, yes, she *was* a singer actually. She sang regularly at the Red Dragon pub where she worked. She started talking about all the country music she loved but then her face clouded over.

'Trouble is, see, they don't want my sort of music no more in the Red Dragon. They're looking for fresh blood, pardon the pun. That's why I was listening to the radio that late on the night I won the competition, I couldn't sleep. The landlord had told me that day he was axing my singing spots so they could hold a "Trachlyn's Got Talent" weekly event instead.'

Anita suddenly looked utterly miserable. It was like the light inside her had been switched off.

Daisy imagined what 'Trachlyn's Got Talent' would be like. They were hardly likely to uncover the new One Direction amongst the lads who worked at the local bottle factory or beheaded chickens at the abattoir. In her opinion, the noise she heard most when she watched the latest search-for-a-star singing reality TV shows was the sound of scraping on the bottom of a barrel. Running some lame copy-cat version in the Red Dragon instead of having a singer like Anita was a terrible idea.

She wanted to tell Anita not to give up – there would be other pubs and clubs who would snap her up, she was sure – but before she could say a word they were distracted by a commotion involving Priya.

The man sat across the aisle was leaning over towards Priya and they were in the middle of the most almighty row. At first Daisy couldn't make head nor tail of what was happening, but it quickly became clear that this wasn't some random air rage incident. Priya and this man knew each other, and they were clearly having a 'domestic'. He was shouting something about wanting to 'surprise' her by turning up at the last minute at the airport and coming along on the trip. She was clearly furious about him going through her emails to get the details and did not seem thrilled in the slightest at what appeared to be his big romantic gesture.

'I can't believe you hacked my laptop,' fumed Priya.

The man almost seemed to scoff at her fury.

'Yeah, you really need to get a better password, do you know how many people use their birthday?'

Priya was gripping the arm rests as though they were flying through the eye of a storm. She turned towards Anita and Daisy, who made no attempt to hide the fact they were hanging on the couple's every word.

'In FOUR years,' hissed Priya in Anita and Daisy's direction, 'in FOUR bloody years, Sid has never remembered my birthday!'

The women turned three pairs of indignant eyes on hapless Sid. He decided to take the worst possible course of action open to a man facing an already suspicious sisterhood; he began to mock Priya.

'I never even knew this one was much of an Elvis fan,' he said, jerking his head towards Priya as she ground her teeth. He gave an exaggerated roll of his eyes for comic effect and added, 'I'd have had her down as more of an Abba fan, to be honest. Do you remember that skin-tight white jumpsuit you wore to that fancy-dress party, trying to look like Agnetha-what's-her-face?'

He threw back his head and gave an explosive little laugh. 'Ha! Maybe you weren't trying to be one of Abba, maybe you were dressed up like the King after all and I never realised. Is that what it was, Priya?'

Clearly humiliated, Priya tried to ignore Sid and turned again to Daisy and Anita.

'I'm meeting up with a… a friend in Memphis,' she said with a nervous smile. Daisy thought how much prettier Priya looked when she wasn't scowling.

'That's female logic for you,' interrupted Sid, once again apparently unaware that he was talking to three women.

'She says meeting in Memphis is a halfway point for both of them and so this trip is actually *saving* money!' He shook his head in disbelief and looked as though he expected them all to agree… with him!

'What I meant,' said Priya with another apologetic smile towards Lilian and Daisy, 'what I meant was it was cheaper to do this than for me to fly all the way to Australia. That's where my friend lives now.'

Sid began to figure out that Daisy and Anita were not about to side with him in this dispute any time soon. He made a stab at what he thought was being reasonable.

'Look, Priya, I get it… I get it, you haven't seen this mate of yours in years, but I'm doing you a favour if you think about it.'

Priya cocked her head to one side as she tried to work out what Sid was prattling on about.

'How d'you know you're even gonna get on with each other? Eh? I bet you haven't even thought about that, have you? When I rang the hotel they were totally cool about moving your mate Valerie into a single room so we can have the double. You'll be able to spend all day together, doing all that Elvis-y stuff and then…

Priya was a tiny woman dressed in a bright-pink velour jumpsuit that looked like it would fit a twelve-year-old. Daisy wasn't prepared for the volume Priya reached when she drew herself up in her seat and screeched, 'YOU'VE DONE WHAT?'

It all kicked off a bit after that. A couple of cabin crew quickly materialised and tried to plead with Mr and Mrs Siddiqui to get back into their seats and stop screaming abuse at each other as they stood toe to toe in the aisle. Sid wasn't a very intimidating figure, in fact he was quite weedy, but he was a good head and shoulders taller than Priya and it was a very confined space.

One of the air hostesses diplomatically suggested Sid move to another seat at the rear of the plane for the rest of the flight and things calmed down as Priya sat back down. Anita leaned across Daisy and patted Priya on the arm.

'Men, huh?' was what she said to show sisterly solidarity. Daisy was still wondering why Sid had thought surprising Priya by suddenly joining her on this trip had been a good idea.

'It's complicated,' said Priya, taking a sip of her bottled water.

With Sid well out of earshot, she revealed that she thought their relationship was well and truly on its last legs. Sid turning up at the airport had thrown her completely.

'I really needed to get away for a bit... You can see what he's like, he thinks he knows everything. I can't think straight when I'm with him anymore, I just needed some space.'

Daisy wriggled in the cramped confines of her seat and nodded in sympathy. Anita and Priya's romantic experiences were reinforcing her theory that having a boyfriend wasn't all it was cracked up to be. She also decided she might as well give up on her fantasy of snoozing all the way to America.

For the next half hour, the women shared stories from their chequered love lives. Anita confessed to having been married 'a million years ago' but was now clearly disappointed in her long-time single status. Her encounters with men with names like 'Bryn the Post', 'Ivor the Driver' and 'Satellite Ron' were cautionary tales about feckless men who didn't deserve her. The names of the characters in her stories made the small Welsh town she came from sound like something from a children's cartoon, although the content would never pass the censor. (Daisy was also compelled to ask for clarification on 'Satellite Ron' who was apparently named after years spent rigging up dodgy satellite TV dishes and, disappointingly, nothing to do with space travel.)

Daisy resisted recounting her relationship history, such as it was, for as long as possible but the pincer movement of Anita and Priya on either side was impossible to resist. She wasn't sure either of the women would be able to relate to her stance on dating. Anita was old enough to be her mother, although about as far removed from Lilian as it was possible to get. Priya had clearly been stagnating in a long-term relationship for a while and was desperately looking for some way out.

Daisy tried to explain that she didn't want – didn't *need* – a man to complete her life. She doubted either of them would have experienced the fast-paced world of dating apps where one quick swipe resulted in a hook-up but often, before the first date was over, you were swiping again to see if someone better was out there. The endless possibilities and unwillingness to commit resulted in fleeting relationships. She'd decided she was pretty comfortable with that. It wasn't like she had any examples of lasting long-term love around her that she wanted to emulate. Nana Rose had never married. Single mothers in the Sixties were not considered a catch and although she had several 'gentlemen friends' later in her life, she refused all talk of marriage. Her own mother had been married briefly to Daisy's father but that hadn't worked out. Daisy saw him occasionally, but he wasn't what you'd call 'reliable' or 'hands on'. The result was three generations of women in her family who had all ended up stubbornly keeping Nana Rose's maiden name of 'Featherstone'.

Daisy thought the archaic tradition of having to change your name to that of your husband was ridiculous anyway... offensive even. She liked to think that 'Featherstone' was in fact the perfect name for them all; they were three women who appeared to have been blown this way and that by the events in their lives, but remained strong and solid as rock. You didn't *need* a permanent man, they were proof of that.

Daisy also wasn't about to discuss her clearly more casual approach to sex with two women she'd only just met. Maybe they would be shocked to hear she had sometimes had sex with guys she didn't consider to be her 'boyfriend'. To her mind, older people thought sex was much more important than it actually was. It was meant to be fun, it didn't have to mean that much; they were the ones with the hang-ups, not her. Maybe if she ever met someone who shared her interests, who was on the same wave-length, maybe then it would be different, but men like that had so far proved impossible to find.

She thought back to what she'd thought had been a promising relationship with Hugh the fitness instructor, although if she was to follow Anita's example of re-naming her back-catalogue Daisy supposed 'Hugh the Hunk' or 'Huge Hugh' would sum him up best. He worked as a personal trainer and 'life coach' at the local gym, although that wasn't where they had met... Good grief, no! They'd met in a local bar one night when she was about to make her escape from a raucous hen night. He'd rescued her and given her not only a great excuse for ducking out early, but also a rather unexpected new work-out regime. Daisy had never been a gym-bunny so appreciated the 'exercise', but for all his muscly athleticism the one muscle of Hugh's that never got much of a work-out was his brain. He was sweet enough, handy to have around for changing lightbulbs even, but he'd never had much of a lightbulb moment himself. Any musical, literary or historical references would land with a deafening thud in conversations with Hugh. As Nana Rose had observed all too accurately, *The lights are on, bless him, but there's no one much at home, is there?*

Daisy and Hugh had seen each other for a little while, until the day he wondered out loud why she was always in 'fancy dress'. Stung by the accusation, Daisy couldn't be bothered to explain her fashion choices and that was the end of 'Huge Hugh'. He was probably still wondering why, but it turns out size *isn't* everything.

As she recounted the edited 'Hugh the Hunk' highlights, Anita and Priya tutted in sympathy.

'You need to find someone who can be your *soulmate*, someone who really *gets* you,' said Anita.

Daisy thought Anita sounded incredibly naive for someone with her track history.

'Whatever you do, don't just… settle,' added Priya, clearly intimating that's what she felt she herself had done with Sid.

The progression of the drinks trolley down the aisle towards them was a welcome distraction and saved Daisy from further interrogation. The conversation with Anita and Priya was merely confirming her long-held belief that *no* man was better than the *wrong* man. Meanwhile the cabin crew were inching closer with their sing-song refrain: 'Any drinks or snacks, any drinks or snacks?' Daisy stifled a giggle as she thought it sounded more like they were offering 'any drinks or sex?' She needed to stop thinking about clunky, hunky Hugh!

Priya spotted Sid's discarded jacket on the seat he'd vacated and quickly grabbed it, rifling through his pockets.

'Drinks are on, Sid, I think, hey girls?' Priya said with a wink towards them as she continued to rummage.

Daisy put her feminist principles quickly to one side. Oh well, so much for sisters doing it for themselves, she thought.

Unfortunately it wasn't Sid's wallet that Priya pulled from his pocket, but his mobile phone. She narrowed her eyes as she peered at it and seemed to make a snap decision.

'Let's see if you use *your* birthday as your password,' she muttered as she tapped a code into the keypad.

Daisy had a nagging feeling that this was not going to go well. What was Priya looking for?

The answer was surprisingly easy to find. A few taps and swipes here and there, and suddenly some rather damning messages from someone calling herself 'Lizzy Lizard Tongue' were right under their noses. Priya held out the phone towards them to show them the latest one: *'I'm still hot for you Tiger Man! Ggggrrrrrrrr, Lizzy Lizard Tongue xxx'*

Anita and Daisy looked at the screen and then at each other. The woman had actually growled! Wow.

'I knew it!' Priya seemed almost elated by the discovery of Sid's unfaithfulness. 'He tried to make out I was going crazy... the bastard!'

Anita honed in on the contradiction staring them all in the face.

'But if he's having an affair with this Lizzy,' she said, 'why has he insisted on coming along on this trip with you?'

Priya had now settled back in her seat and was doing a mean Mona Lisa impression, all mysterious with an enigmatic smile. 'Hmmm, that's a very good question,' she said, with no hint of having the answer.

Daisy decided she had enough of a mystery on her hands without becoming embroiled in another, so she left Anita to question Priya further on Sid's possible ulterior motives. Reaching into her bag under the seat in front, Daisy pulled out a notebook and started sifting through the reams of research she had compiled about Elvis, Graceland and Memphis over the past few weeks. As excited as she was to get to the destination of her dreams, she was on an important mission and she needed to work out where on earth she was going to start to try and solve it.

Chapter Four

On the other side of the world, an impossibly handsome man was packing a suitcase. The long line of his nose and full lips gave him the look of a Greek god statue that had sprung to life.

His dark hair was swept up and back but a tantalising strand persisted on flopping down over his heavy-lidded eyes.

On the bed in front of him lay an open suitcase. With long, delicate fingers he folded the white costume and laid it carefully within the case. He took care to tuck the stray tassels into the centre.

The room was lit only by a single shaft of light shining through a gap in the heavy curtains. As he moved slowly and carefully, the light sparkled off the dazzling jewels set in a ring on his little finger.

Feeling apprehensive for the journey that lay ahead, he picked up a second ring from the nightstand next to the king-size bed; this one was black and gold with a silver lightning bolt emblazoned at its centre. This ring would surely bring him luck, it always did. After all, the symbol had been created to make the wearer believe that if you put your mind to it, you could achieve anything. Slotting it into a red velvet ring box, he tucked it in between the layers of rainbow-coloured silks at the bottom of his case.

Finally he opened the nightstand drawer; from between the pages of a Bible he withdrew a stiff paper envelope with golden lettering.

He dropped the ticket wallet emblazoned with the words 'Graceland Experience' onto the folded clothes and closed the case.

Still squashed into the middle seat between Anita and Priya, on a plane headed for Memphis, Daisy had finally dozed off. Her mind was full of pictures of what she imagined they were now flying over. The mighty Mississippi River forging its path though the corn and cotton fields, flowing past one-storey homesteads each with a rickety porch, on its way down to New Orleans. Way on down below, she pictured blues bars and rib shacks, guitar players and cheerleaders, Cadillacs, Chevrolets and people eating bagels and pretzels and eggs over easy – Americana in all its glory. She was almost there.

Waking with a start, Daisy discovered that Priya and Anita had finished a second bottle of champagne. Daisy had been nervous when Priya had ordered the first one.

'I don't touch the stuff normally, but drinking alcohol on a flight doesn't count, does it?' Priya had said, convincing herself as much as anyone. 'It's like being in international waters or something, isn't it?'

Priya's logic had not prevented her from getting completely and utterly pissed.

She was now waving her arms around like a windmill and talking so loudly she was drawing harsh looks from fellow travellers several rows away. She was directing her attention to a passenger towards the front of the plane.

'Look, look!' screeched Priya pointing madly towards the man. 'Iss tha' guy who caused all t' trouble at check-in, dij'ya see that? Woss e' doin' now?'

Daisy peered over the heads of the passengers immediately in front to watch the man, who had manoeuvred himself from his seat and was tugging at the overhead locker.

''E's gettin' tha bloody man bag out, again, look at 'im,' slurred Priya 'Tha's about fourth time 'e's done that! Woss 'e up to? D'ya fink I should tell someone?'

Daisy shook her head and tried to calm Priya down. 'And say what? That a man wants something out of his own bag? What do you think they're going to do, arrest him for being in possession of a dangerous paperback?'

Anita giggled and gave a little burp. 'Whoops, pardon... They might do if it's a Jeffrey Archer.'

Daisy realised her travelling companions were both as drunk as each other, but handling it in very different ways.

Clambering over Priya, Daisy decided to head for the toilet, telling her companions she was going to take a closer look at the man Priya was insisting was acting 'shusspicioussly'.

Daisy remembered the commotion at the airport check-in had started when one of the airline staff had tried to loop a cabin baggage tag around the man in question's leather satchel. He'd jumped a mile and got a bit aggressive. A manager had been called and there'd been quite an argument, something about 'airline policy'. They'd let him through so he must have checked out okay and, anyway, he didn't look like a terrorist or anything. Although now she came to think about it, as she edged her way down the aisle towards him, what was a terrorist meant to look like? He was scruffily dressed with a shifty manner but she didn't like to jump to conclusions.

As Daisy approached the bearded man in seat 15C, she saw he had that blasted leather satchel of his tucked onto his lap where he was cradling it like it was a baby. Okay, that was a bit odd. She then noticed he was poring over paperwork spread all over his tray table. She paused just behind his headrest and took a closer look; he was studying plans and diagrams of a large house in extensive grounds... Graceland! The man was examining maps of Elvis Presley's mansion and the surrounding land. What could that mean?

Daisy being Daisy, couldn't stop herself from sticking her nose right in.

'Oooo, that looks interesting,' she said, peering over the man's shoulder. 'I take it you are on the Graceland Experience trip too?'

The poor man almost jumped out of his skin as she spoke and instinctively started stuffing the maps and drawings back into his bag.

'I... Yes... yes, that's right... I suppose I am,' the man

stuttered, and the part of his face that wasn't covered with beard flushed crimson.

'Sorry, I don't mean to be rude, I'm Daisy…'

Daisy stuck out her hand but it hovered in mid-air as the man struggled to force the reams of paper back into the satchel. Eventually, he managed to disentangle himself from the folds of paper and clasped Daisy's outstretched hand, he was a little bit sweaty.

'Sean… Sean Price, I'm just doing a bit of… research, I'm fascinated by the… architecture, you know.'

Daisy hadn't really ever given much thought to the design specifications of colonial-style, antebellum houses like Graceland; she was much more interested in its famous occupant but, fair enough, she thought to herself, each to their own.

Sean seemed shy but Daisy managed to find out that he was also travelling on his own; she was reassured to discover she wasn't the only lone traveller on the trip. Sean gave a nervous smile in reply when she offered to seek him out when they got to the motel.

Unfortunately, when she relayed the information she'd managed to extract from shy Sean to Priya and Anita, they weren't as willing to accept his explanations. Daisy put it down to the amount of alcohol they had both consumed but conspiracy theories were flying left, right and centre as soon as she told them about the detailed maps and drawings Sean had of Graceland.

'He's clearly up to something!' said Anita.

'Obviously he's planning to rob the place,' offered Priya. 'Do you know how much Elvis and Graceland memorabilia is worth? I thought he looked shifty as soon as I saw him at the airport!'

Daisy didn't think it was obvious at all that Sean was up to no good. He seemed like a rather mild-mannered sort, a bit timid if anything; it had taken quite a bit of effort on Daisy's part to get him chatting at all. The only thing Daisy thought fishy was the pungent stink of the aeroplane toilet she had visited before making her way back to her seat. The weird smell still lingered in her nostrils, she hoped it wasn't also clinging to her clothes.

Anita and Priya continued to speculate on the dastardly deeds that Sean Price might be planning and Daisy left them to it, thinking they would soon burn themselves out of theories if she just ignored them.

It was perfectly possible that's exactly what would have happened. But unfortunately, it didn't. Sid chose this particular moment in the journey to escape from his exile at the rear of the plane and create an opportunity to have a 'quiet' word with Priya before they landed. This quickly escalated into both of them exchanging a series of very loud, somewhat offensive words with each other and cabin staff were forced to intervene again.

Just at the point when it looked highly likely that both Priya and Sid would be reported to the authorities for disruptive behaviour and probably banned from flying this particular airline ever again, Priya made her move.

'It sh'not usss you should be worryin' 'bout,' she hissed at the startled stewardess. 'There's someone on this plane plannin' a real crime!'

Before Daisy knew what was happening, Mr Siddiqui

had been escorted back to his seat and Priya was giving a colourful account of her suspicions about Sean Price in seat 15C to the concerned-looking air hostess. Daisy put her head in her hands and hoped that the stewardess was just humouring Priya and putting all of her wild accusations down to pissed-up paranoia.

When they all disembarked from the plane around twenty minutes later, it became quickly apparent that Priya's accusations had been relayed to airport security.

A pot-bellied, middle-aged man in uniform was waiting at the end of the concertina tunnel that connected the aeroplane to the airport. Daisy watched in horror as the security officer pounced on an unsuspecting Sean Price and gruffly accosted him.

She should have stayed out of it, that would have been the sensible thing to do, but once again, Daisy couldn't help herself. She felt guilty about Sean being dragged into Mr and Mrs Siddiqui's *domestic* and felt compelled to defend him. Sean shot her a look of surprised gratitude while Anita and Priya sobered up fast and were shamed into back-tracking over their wild claims. Daisy left them all attempting to explain themselves and made a hasty exit in the direction of Baggage Reclaim.

The air felt warm and moist when Daisy finally stepped out of Arrivals and headed for the cab rank. She had a note in her hand with the name of her destination on it: the Day's

Inn Motel on Elvis Presley Boulevard. She felt tired and grubby and couldn't wait to get there; however, finding a taxi was not going to be that easy.

As she neared the passenger pickup point, all she could see was the most enormous white stretch limousine parked across the entire area reserved for airport taxis. If there had been an orderly queue it was now an unruly mob, people were shouting and falling over each other's cases as they paced back and forth. The sound of honking car horns drew Daisy's attention to a backlog of cabs pulled up behind the limo. Some of the cabbies were leaning out of their windows yelling abuse in the direction of a short, stocky guy with a handlebar moustache, wearing a grey chauffeur's peaked cap. He was standing beside his sparkling white limousine and he didn't look like he intended to move anywhere.

Daisy sized up the situation instantly and felt irritation wash over her. This was the last thing she needed – all she wanted to do was take a shower, have a hot drink and flop into bed.

The yelled insults and curses that were being thrown in every direction flew right over Daisy's head as she marched towards the white limousine, pulling her case behind her.

'Excuse me?' she said primly, in the direction of the stocky chauffeur to no effect whatsoever. She took a deep breath and tried again, ramping up both the volume and the primness. 'HELLO, EXCUSE ME…SIR? Yes, yes you. Excuse me but would you please be so good as to move along, please? I don't think you are allowed to park here.'

The chauffeur turned his head but pulled a face as

though he hadn't understood a word she had said. Behind her, there were a few guffaws and someone started doing a mocking impression of her accent. 'Oi, lah-di-dah! Maree Poppins 'ere says mooove along, my good fellow!'

Daisy's face glowed red and she turned to give whoever it was a piece of her mind, but instead came face to chest with a strapping police officer in a short-sleeved navy-blue uniform and mirrored shades.

'Thank you, ma'am, but I'll handle this. Please step back.' He hitched up his belt as he spoke and a pair of metal handcuffs clinked together on his hip.

Stung and embarrassed, Daisy stood her ground, refusing to be intimidated, 'I was only trying to help and don't call me *ma'am*... I'm not the bloody queen!'

The officer looked down at her over the top of his sunglasses and Daisy caught sight of herself in their reflection. With birds' nest hair escaping every which way from beneath her leopard-print beret and two red hot spots flushing her cheeks, she looked like a deranged clown. In contrast, his hair was cut in what her mother would call a 'short back and sides' buzz cut over his ears and at the back of his neck, but longer and thicker on top; a few strands stood up on end at the front, but he still managed to look neat as a pin.

She pulled the damn beret off her head as the police officer slowly removed his shades. The joker in the crowd behind him was finding this side-show most amusing and now entertained the crowd with further impressions of what she presumed was supposed to be her voice. 'Well hel-looo, Your Majesty, how doo you doo?'

The officer snapped his head once in the wag's direction and the stand-up routine ended immediately.

The cop turned his attention back to Daisy and she noticed his eyes were an incredible shade of blue. She also noticed they seemed to be taking in every little detail about her. It made her feel even more aware of her dishevelled state and she tugged her denim jacket a little tighter around herself, concerned about the ancient Rolling Stones t-shirt she was wearing. It suddenly seemed disrespectful to have a bright-red tongue sticking out at an officer of the law.

'Pardon me, I meant no offence, Miss…?' The officer waited expectantly for her to supply the missing details.

'Daisy… Daisy Featherstone,' Daisy stuttered in reply.

'Well, thank you kindly, Miss *Featherr-stowne*,' the cop drawled her name as he replaced his sunglasses, hiding his piercing blue eyes. 'Officer Joe Cody, at your service'.

He moved away then, gesticulating to the impatient cabbies still sounding their hooters, telling them to pipe down and speaking in low tones to the chauffeur. Daisy couldn't hear what he said, but, in moments, the white limousine had pulled away and order was resumed in the taxi rank.

Daisy took her place in the queue for a cab and watched the comedian with the bad accent jump into the next available taxi; they were coming thick and fast now. She was just reaching out a hand to open the rear door of a car that had pulled to a stop for her when she was shunted from behind by a skinny woman, her spiky heels almost as sharp as her elbows.

'OW!' Daisy cried out in both pain and outrage – the

woman was attempting to steal the taxi right from under her nose.

In a flash, the blue-eyed cool cop materialised and managed to put himself and his broad shoulders between the tall taxi-stealer and the car. He opened the door with a flourish and said, 'I believe this is for you, Dayzee-Dayzee,' and indicated with a jerk of his sandy-haired head that Daisy should jump straight in. As she did so, he tucked her case in behind her, saying, 'You gotta watch these New Yorkers! You have a good day now, y'hear!' Then he was gone.

The impossibly handsome man had landed at Memphis International Airport while Daisy had been attempting to get a cab. His handsome features had cut no ice with the security officer on duty and his chances of gaining entry into the US were looking increasingly unlikely.

The border control guard looked again at the paperwork of the passenger stood on the other side of the bullet-proof glass and then back at the man's familiar face, the curled lip and quiff of dark hair. The guard sighed and picked up the phone. This wouldn't do, this wouldn't do at all.

As Daisy's cab pulled away from the kerb, she caught another glimpse of the police officer standing next to an enormous motorbike. His work here done, he swung a muscled leg over his machine. American cops were a very different breed to British bobbies, she thought. So distracted was she by the sexy sight of the cool cop, she failed to notice the white limousine circling back towards the airport pick-up point. The limo chauffeur was still banking on his VIP passenger appearing very soon; there was no way he could know the handsome man had just failed security clearance and was now 'unavoidably detained'.

Chapter Five

D aisy's relief to finally be on Tennessee soil and heading towards her motel made her feel giddy. She tried to play it cool, but her obvious delight for the sights from the taxi window was all the encouragement Daryl the driver needed.

'This your first trip to Memphis, honey?' he drawled over his shoulder without expecting much of a reply.

Daisy simply nodded, eyes on stalks as Daryl swung his cab back and forth through the outskirts of town, reeling off the places she should make sure she visited: Beale Street, the Peabody Hotel, the Martin Luther King Memorial, Jerry Lee Lewis's bright-pink honky-tonk cafe, the Rock 'n' Soul and Stax museums.

She didn't even comment on being called 'honey' – it would be politically incorrect back home, but somehow, here, it just felt kind and welcoming. Lord, she'd better watch herself, she thought, or she'd be chewin' tobaccy and skinnin' squirrel within the week!

Daryl eventually came up for air. 'You come to see Elvis too, honey?'

Daisy opened her mouth but didn't know what to say. She stuttered, but Daryl had seen it all before, 'There's a lot more to Memphis than just Elvis, y'know, but if you're lookin' for him, you'll find him here alright.'

By the time the cab swung into the drop-off zone outside her motel, Daisy was beginning to feel thoroughly overwhelmed. America was weirdly familiar while being totally alien at the same time. The entire place felt as though it had been set to 'enlarge' on a photocopier. The roads were wider, and the signs and billboards they passed advertising car lots, gas stations and diners were enormous. If Daryl the cab driver was anything to go by, the local personalities were bigger than she was used to too. It wasn't surprising that Americans thought of Britain as 'quaint' and the natives 'reserved'. Daisy wondered if it was the sheer scale of the country they lived in that allowed the average American personality to swell up in size. They had the space, they might as well fill it, with loud voices, louder clothes and a full on, can-do, 'have a nice day' attitude. She liked it.

Daisy stood at the door to the motel and watched Daryl head back towards the freeway with his arm raised in salute from the window of his cab. In her pocket was his business card and he'd said she could call him anytime to take her wherever she wanted to go. She'd decided on the plane where she was going to start, as the first step on her hunt to find out more about Nana Rose's time in Memphis. For now, she needed to check in and find her room; she was exhausted.

The motel reception area was decorated with an array of Elvis pictures and memorabilia. Daisy paused to stare at a garish plaster statue holding a guitar high up on his chest. She studied the face contorted in a sneer and marvelled at how Presley was so recognisable that something that looked as unlike him as this could still never be confused for anyone else. Strike a bent knee pose, hold a guitar, tremble a lip – you too can be Elvis!

Daisy joined the queue at the desk as two receptionists were attempting to deal with a sudden influx of guests. She was next in line to be greeted by a smiley guy named George. There was no sign of Anita or Sean Price anywhere; she hoped poor Sean hadn't been held back at the airport for too long. Priya and Sid, however, had beaten her to the motel; Daryl must've taken her on the 'scenic route'. Mr and Mrs Siddiqui were attempting to check in and were being dealt with by a less smiley young man wearing the name badge 'Carlton', but it was not going well.

Priya had clearly sobered up and was radiating an annoyed air, but Daisy could tell it wasn't directed at the motel staff.

Sid stood with his multi-coloured rucksack at his feet and was using a patronising 'I'm going to speak slowly because we're in a foreign country' voice.

'I sorted all this out over the phone a couple of days ago. Priya and I are going to take the double room and her friend Val is going to take the single. Is she here yet?'

Carlton the desk clerk looked at Sid uncomprehendingly and slowly shook his head, 'Is who here?'

Daisy watched as Sid clenched his hands into fists while behind him she could have sworn Priya was smirking. She'd clearly decided not to confront Sid as yet with the evidence of his liaisons with 'Lizzy Lizard Tongue'. Daisy couldn't think for the life of her what she was waiting for, but then other people's relationships were always a mystery to her. Perhaps this was how they got their kicks? She decided it wasn't worth speculating.

Sid trusted himself to just one more word, spoken slowly and clearly. 'Val-er-ie.'

Carlton looked desperately at his computer screen for answers, but he wasn't even sure of the question.

Priya tapped her foot in irritation and decided to speak, 'Look, why don't we just leave things as they are, you're making a right cock-up of everything now.' This was directed at Sid, and not at the confused Carlton, much to his relief.

Sid rounded on her; he'd clearly not come all this way to be shunted into a single broom closet.

'I'm not "leaving it", the bird on the phone said it would all be sorted, no problem.'

Priya snapped her mouth shut and grimaced.

Daisy had now reached the friendly smile of desk clerk George. Just as Carlton turned to his co-worker for help, George was addressing Daisy: 'I'm so sorry, miss, I can't seem to find your booking.'

Daisy felt her stomach flip and had an overwhelming

urge to burst into tears. This wasn't the way it was supposed to be at all, why was everything going wrong?

George kept his wavering smile fixed on Daisy, but hissed at Carlton from the side of his mouth, 'Where's Miss Loretta got to? She'll have to fix all this... Don't you worry there now, miss, we'll have this all straightened out for you in two shakes of a racoon's tail.'

Daisy smiled back bravely; that sounded promising – slightly bizarre, but promising.

Sid, however, was not so easily mollified. 'What sort of a place is this?' His voice was rising steadily. 'We'll not be having one of your famous "nice days" unless this is all sorted out pretty damn quick, racoon or no ruddy racoon.'

George was now tapping so fast on his keyboard Daisy was surprised there were no sparks. He stared at the screen while speaking to her. 'You did say Featherstone, miss? You see, we did have a *Lilian* Featherstone but we were told she'd cancelled. Now that we've moved these other folks around, I don't have any other free rooms.'

Oh lord, what had her mother gone and done? Why couldn't she just leave things alone instead of calling up and confusing everything? Typical!

George gave Carlton's customers a look which he hoped conveyed they were the ones who were at fault. 'Unless of course...' Daisy looked at him hopefully as he carried on. 'Unless there are any other single members of your party you want to share with, of course. Our beds are super-large?'

What? Daisy thought about having to share her room with Sean Price. They couldn't ask her to do that? Could they? She was definitely going to cry, any minute now, she could feel it. Her throat was so tight she could only squeak, 'Do you really have no other rooms at all?'

The door behind George and Carlton opened and Miss Loretta materialised and gave a cursory glance over their shoulders at the winking computer screens. She seemed to instantly assess the situation, placing her hands on her ample hips as she spoke in a leisurely drawl. 'What in the world is the hold up here?'

Without waiting for anyone to reply, she leaned across Carlton and tapped twice on his keyboard with her long green lacquered nails. 'I adjusted this reservation personally. A double room, wasn't it, folks?' Flashing a killer smile at Priya and Sid – and a look that could kill at poor Carlton – she turned to the rows of keys on the wall behind her and handed them a room key with an oversized wooden heart fob attached. 'There you go, sir, ma'am, now you have a nice evening, won't y'all.' Priya pressed her lips tightly together in a hard line but said nothing. The Siddiquis turned away from the check-in desk and headed towards the glass doors leading to the motel's rooms.

Daisy held her breath; would Miss Loretta save her too?

Miss Loretta moved closer to the desk and brought her voice down to a conspiratorial whisper. 'Now, miss, I've just taken a call to say one of your Graceland Experience party has been delayed... indefinitely. They had booked one of our superior rooms so it seems today is your lucky day. We'll upgrade you to that room for the time being and say no more about this unfortunate little mix-up. Will that be alright?' Miss Loretta was practically purring and Daisy could have kissed her.

Moments later, George was falling over himself to show her to her room, lugging her case up the metal stairs leading to the walkway running the length of the outdoor motel. He pointed across to the guitar-shaped swimming pool and informed her that every movie Elvis had ever made was available to view 24/7 as he threw open the door to her 'superior' accommodation.

Daisy decided the room was mighty fine – she decided it was also alarming how quickly she was picking up the lingo! She wasn't yet quite so familiar with the currency however, and she fumbled with her purse trying to find the appropriate denomination with which to tip George.

He pushed open the door to the en suite bathroom, showed her the TV remotes, pointed out the in-room microwave and refrigerator and opened the cupboard that housed the coffee machine. *Yes, this will do*, thought Daisy, *this will do nicely*.

She eventually produced a suitable tip for George; she knew it was good manners to always tip, it said so in her well-thumbed travel guide. He put her bag down on the huge bed as he thanked her profusely, then softly closed the door as he left.

No sooner had she let out a sigh of relief than she heard the sound of raised voices. She went straight to the window that looked out onto the covered walkway outside her room and tweaked back the net curtain. She was on the upper level of the two tiers of rooms and was looking down over the amazing guitar-shaped swimming pool. The light was fading now but the blue pool was lit with spotlights; Daisy thought it looked magical.

She pulled her notebook from her bag and carefully placed Daryl's card inside, marking the page where she'd written the words 'Walnut Grove House'. Suddenly, loud voices caught her attention again.

She figured the argument was in the room right next door and realised with horror that Priya and Sid were just a thin wall away. Of course!

She cracked the window ajar and Sid's voice sailed in on the still evening air.

'You just have to put your foot down with these sorts of people. It's a good job I'm here or you'd have got yourself into a right mess.'

Daisy couldn't work out what Priya said in reply but the shrill pitch of her voice accompanied by the sound of doors or drawers slamming shut as she spoke revealed she wasn't taking the lecture particularly well.

He clearly agreed: 'A bloody fine trip this is going to be with you in this mood.'

This time, Priya's words were all too easy to hear, 'WELL NO ONE ASKED YOU TO DAMN WELL COME!'

This was followed by a huge slam and Daisy just had time to jump back from the open window as Priya stormed past. Thank goodness she had been in too much of a head-down stomp to spot Daisy lurking at the net curtains... Awkward.

A wave of tiredness suddenly washed over Daisy as she stood there in the fading light of her first Memphis evening.

She was here, in the United States of America, at last.

Not only in America but in the very heartland of the place that took the southern blues of the Mississippi Delta and gave it to the world re-born as rock 'n' roll.

For years she had listened to Nana Rose sing the praises of the Southern States, the people, the food and, most importantly, the music.

Daisy had always thought it was wonderful her nana had been a brave and adventurous soul who had travelled to America when she was only a teenage girl. Now she was planning to follow in her footsteps. Other people's grandmothers taught them how to knit or bake a perfect Victoria sponge, but hers had shared her love of music and Fifties fashions and Daisy had discovered a whole new world of vintage memorabilia as a result. She'd even turned it into her job and opened Blue Moon Vintage.

In all those conversations, in all that time, could Rose really have been keeping a secret love hidden from not only Daisy but the whole world?

Her jumbled thoughts and emotions exhausted her even more than the four-thousand-mile journey she'd completed today.

In minutes, she'd shed her travelling clothes and climbed between the sheets of the bed. She never even noticed the framed photo of the King of Rock 'n' Roll on the wall above her, watching over her as she drifted into sleep.

Chapter Six

L ilian let herself into her mother's empty house with the spare set of keys she always kept in her purse. She picked up the slew of letters from the mat and placed them on the table in the hall. The number of jobs that still needed to be tackled weighed on her like a cloak of iron.

The stillness of the house was unsettling. There was always some sort of background noise at Rose's. Usually it would be Rose singing along (badly) to the golden oldies radio station she always had playing in the kitchen, or she'd have one of her many records playing on the cabinet record player in the lounge-diner.

Rose had lived in this 1930s semi for years. It was the same as millions of others, with decent-sized rooms, high ceilings, a wide bay window at the front and patio doors leading to a garden at the back.

What made the house unique, of course, was Rose. Now she was gone. All that was left were the choices she'd made over the years to make this house a reflection of her personality. Lilian had never held much store in things, random possessions, but now she stood in her mother's home and was surprisingly grateful for the touches of Rose she could see and feel all around her.

Lilian's house, a boxy modern detached on a nearby housing estate, was very different in decor to her mother's. Lilian favoured neutral colours, minimal accessories and monochrome artwork. She believed muted equalled tasteful and restful. Rose's home, by contrast, was an explosion of colour, cushions and chaos. Nothing matched and Rose had been completely comfortable flinging a Mexican-print throw over a chintzy armchair, or hanging a psychedelic pop art picture next to a Monet print of dreamy waterlilies.

Lilian went through to the lounge, her eyes resting on the Art Deco-style display cabinet in the corner. It housed Rose's collection of frosted-glass ornaments and random teacups and saucers in a variety of floral patterns. Who knew if any of them were genuine antiques with any real value? It had never seemed to matter to Rose. Lilian wondered what on earth she was going to do with all this *stuff*. Daisy would probably want to keep most of it.

On top of the cabinet stood a fringed leopard-print lamp and a large statuette of a Spanish dancer, her ruffled red and purple porcelain skirts flouncing out as if she was caught in mid-flamenco flourish. Lilian couldn't help but smile ruefully at the sight of the Spanish lady; something about the determined set of the dancer's jaw and the way her hand was firmly placed on her thrusting hip reminded her so much of her mother. Rose... gone. It was almost impossible to accept.

Lilian thought about the last evening she had spent with her mother at the hospital – how she had held a straw to her lips so she could sip Lucozade to ease her dry throat.

Rose had muttered and mumbled but Lilian couldn't make out the words she was trying to say. Daisy had suggested they should play some of Nana's favourite songs to soothe her, and Lilian had bristled at the idea at the time. But later, after Daisy had gone back to her tiny flat above the shop, Lilian had thought it was worth a try. Anything to try and make things a little better, maybe the music Rose loved could reach her.

Lilian remembered a storm had been raging outside, and the songs battled with the thunder and lightning to be heard. Lilian held her mother's hand but Rose hadn't appeared to respond. No miraculous recovery occurred. But unknown to Lilian, Elvis Presley's voice had stirred memories in Rose she had almost forgotten, the images swirling deep inside her confused mind…

A large white house, one… no, two white stone lions on guard, the delicate silhouette of a man and guitar in twisted metal, cars as big as houses cruising wide city streets. A beaten up Oldsmobile with a peeling blue and white paint job appeared, heading towards her. It looked as though it was hovering in mid-air, the shimmering heat from the road disguising where its wheels met the ground.

Snatches of music drifted around, a pulsating beat, a twangy guitar chord or two, a drum roll that signalled the end of a song but then it simply started over again. Rose tried but couldn't remember the name of the tune.

Rose was aware of a light touch on her hand and stepped from the sidewalk into a diner. The music grew louder now as she watched a man with slicked-back hair drop a dime into the juke box in the corner. Cool air brushed her hot cheeks as she walked across the chequered tile floor. An ice cream soda was set down in front of her by a familiar-looking waitress and she placed the straw to her lips and sucked the ice-cold fizzy liquid hungrily down her dry throat.

The faces around her were a blur and Rose couldn't focus on any of them long enough to tell who they were or even if they were people she knew.

She realised she was the one moving, spinning around on the spot as she twirled to the music still playing from the juke box.

It was evening now, although it was still warm. The sun was low in the sky outside the diner and it and cast long, lingering shadows from the tall buildings across the street.

Rose stopped dancing and found herself breathless. The light of a glowing neon sign above the cafe door caught her eye as it was reflected in the huge windscreen of a car parked outside.

Suddenly, she found herself on the street looking down at the back-to-front letters shining across the car. She turned and looked directly up at the bold sign and could read the word 'Arcade'.

A thunderous noise behind her caused her to leap away from the edge of the sidewalk.

In seconds she was engulfed in the noise itself as she held tight to the leather-clad body in front of her, she hoped the vibrations masked how hard her heart hammered in her chest as she pressed herself closer. The motorbike roared beneath her, speeding its way through the dark streets of Memphis.

When Lilian had leaned over to kiss her mother goodnight on that last night, she could have sworn there had been a small smile on Rose's lips.

Now Lilian wandered from room to room in her mother's empty house as though in a daze. So many memories assaulted her senses as she looked around; it was almost too much to bear but then again it was preferable to the image of frail Rose lying in her hospital bed that night. She didn't want that to be her lasting memory of her vibrant, colourful mother.

In Rose's bedroom she sat down heavily on the padded stool in front of the dressing table. The three-sided mirror reflected a trio of Lilians, like a strained-looking version of the Andrews Sisters. She tore her eyes away from her own reflections and focused instead on the array of objects on display: a heavy silver hair brush and comb, a red and gold enamel compact, antique glass perfume bottles in various colours, a carved wooden music box. She reached out to touch the things as though she was a little girl scared of being caught in the act. She lifted a fluffy pink powder puff out of its white ceramic pot and a small cloud of talc escaped and settled like dust on the glass-topped table. The phrase 'ashes to ashes' flitted across Lilian's mind and she wished with all her might for just one more chance to talk to Rose. Why had she never told her who her father was? Why had they both spent a lifetime pretending it didn't matter?

Lilian wondered if she would have been able to cope if her mother had decided to tell her. Had Rose left it until it was too late because she thought Lilian didn't want to know? Or because she thought she wouldn't be able to accept it? Faced with the chance to go with Daisy to Memphis, where, according to Rose's scrawled note they might be able to 'find the truth', what had she done? Turned and run away. She was a coward and she knew it but if there was something out there to find, she also knew Daisy was the right person for the job. Daisy would have much more chance of success without Lilian slowing her down and holding her back. Daisy threw herself into situations and took risks, she didn't need her careful, cautious mother holding her back.

Lilian looked into the mirror and looked herself straight in the eye. She had to admit she *wanted* Daisy to succeed. That was the real reason she'd decided not to go with her to Memphis. Rose's confession that Elvis Presley was Lilian's father might be outlandish and incredible, but Lilian needed to know for sure who her father really was. It was time.

She lifted the heavy silver hairbrush and felt the solid weight in her hand. Without thinking, she raised the brush and began to stroke it through her hair. The sensation took her back through the years to when her mother used to gently brush her hair each night, one hundred strokes to make it shine. Lilian closed her eyes and imagined her mother standing right behind her, urging her to go on.

Chapter Seven

O n her very first morning in Memphis, Daisy had snuck out of the Day's Inn Motel on Elvis Presley Boulevard as soon as it was light. Daryl's taxi had been waiting at the drop-off point just outside the glass foyer and she felt like a special agent, sneaking around on her secret mission.

Unfortunately the mission was not a success. Clutching a piece of paper with the last-known address of where Nana Rose had stayed when she visited Memphis as a young girl, Daisy had been excited to begin her quest. But, she realised now, it was never going to be that easy. Daisy knew Rose had stayed with her old school friend Jennifer who had come from England to live in a grand home on its own estate with her elder sister Jean, a GI bride who had married into a very wealthy family. But the house in the Germantown suburb where Rose had spent the summer of 1960 was long gone. Swathes of new residential homes had since been built over the land where Walnut Grove House had once stood.

Daryl had driven all around the area trying to find the right place, before they'd both had to admit that the search was pointless.

Daisy hadn't been planning to march right up to the front door of the house. It was too early in the day for house calls and she hadn't yet worked out what she would say to whoever might still live there, but she'd been hoping to do a decent recce and then work out the next step from there.

She returned to the motel in sombre spirits and with very little appetite for breakfast, or so she thought, but that was before the smell of crispy bacon and coffee and the sight of fluffy fresh pancakes greeted her in the busy breakfast room.

Daisy piled her plate. She suddenly felt ravenous, but she stuck to the food she could recognise and avoided the bowl of stuff that looked suspiciously like frogspawn; even she wasn't *that* adventurous.

Anita waved her over to an empty chair at her table and Daisy was grateful to see a friendly face. Priya and Sid were sitting close by, systematically chewing and flicking their eyes around the room, anything to avoid actual eye contact with each other.

She was relieved to see Sean Price sitting quietly on his own, tucking into a plate of scrambled eggs. He gave a smile of recognition when she caught his eye and Daisy smiled and nodded back. She hoped Priya had done the decent thing and given him a sincere apology.

A smartly dressed young man in a white short-sleeved

shirt and navy chinos was on his feet talking over the clinking cutlery. The name badge fixed to his shirt pocket said 'Todd' and he was obviously their designated tour guide for the trip.

Daisy had arrived as Todd was telling them all how much he loved Memphis.

'This place,' he said in his soft mid-western accent, 'is all about the music, the rock 'n' roll memories …and meat.'

Daisy almost choked as Anita's eyebrows shot skywards at the innuendo, but Todd was already explaining that he meant 'they sure know how to cook meat in Memphis'.

Todd carried on extoling the virtues of plates of barbeque ribs smothered in smoky sauce, juicy hamburgers with a side of pickle or, his particular favourite, fried chicken with waffles and syrup served with black-eyed peas from somewhere called Miss Polly's Soul City Cafe on Beale Street.

'Do you think Todd is a vegetarian?' whispered Anita with mock sincerity, sending Daisy into yet another coughing fit to cover her giggles.

He caught their attention when he revealed they would all be heading to a hidden speakeasy bar and restaurant above BB King's nightclub in downtown Memphis for their very own taste of Memphis later in the week.

'It's a real cool place hidden away down a little alley,' said Todd. He went on to say the menu included fried green tomatoes, jumbo shrimp with grits, and pork chops and greens. If they had any room left after all that, the speciality dessert of the house was pecan pie flavoured with local honey and Tennessee whiskey. Daisy thought it sounded fabulous, but Todd had a warning to the Brits about their pronunciation.

'For you Brits, y'all just need to remember, it's pea-CAUN for pie, a pea-CAN is what you piss in.'

'I got it, pea-caun, yes, sir!' said Anita with a grin and a wink at Daisy.

'You're picking up the accent already, you're going to fit right in here, aren't you?' said Daisy in reply; she was beginning to realise Anita was going to be a great travelling companion.

Anita leaned over to her new young friend and whispered, 'Well, I've always felt more Tennessee than Treorchy… if you know what I mean?'

Daisy just nodded. She thought she understood completely.

As they were served free refills of coffee, they listened to Todd describe what was on the agenda for the first day of their trip. Today they would start their adventure with a two-hour bus journey to Tupelo, Mississippi, to see the modest wooden shack where Elvis was born. The small town was apparently a real contrast to Memphis and they would spend a couple of hours there. Todd told them that downtown Tupelo hadn't changed all that much since Gladys Presley bought eleven-year-old Elvis his first guitar from the hardware store on Main Street. They'd swing by Tupelo Hardware Company Inc., and hear all about it.

As Daisy polished off the last of her breakfast, she made a mental note to try a different selection from the enormous buffet each and every morning. She wanted to try *everything*, even that yucky stuff she'd thought looked like frogspawn but Anita had told her were actually the famous Southern 'grits'. Some of the other hotel guests already seemed to be competing for some sort of breakfast Olympics judging by how much they had piled on their plates and how many times they went back to reload! Daisy decided to use some restraint, for a change. Much as she loved shopping for new outfits, she didn't want to have to completely restock her wardrobe by doubling in size during this trip.

She quickly dashed back to her room to grab her bag and denim jacket before heading to the allocated meeting point for the bus trip to Tupelo. She'd resolved to put the disappointment of this morning behind her. She already had other ideas forming on how to move her search forward. For now she wanted to concentrate on experiencing as much as possible and learning everything she could about Elvis and his life.

As she made her way back through reception, her heart suddenly flipped as she caught sight of a flash of blue shirt and a glint of metal belt buckle from the corner of her eye. The traffic cop from the airport cab rank was poring over the motel register with Miss Loretta.

What did he want? Was he looking for her?

Her quickening pulse slowed as the cop at the desk turned and gave her a nod of his head. 'Morning, miss, have a nice day now, y'hear?'

It wasn't him. This guy was far too skinny with sharp features that made him look a bit like a ferret. It wasn't cool cop at all. She chided herself for even beginning to imagine the blue-eyed officer would be looking for her. Why would he? Anyway, she needed to crack on with this trip, enjoy everything on offer and find out if there could be any truth at all in Nana Rose's claim about their family heritage. There wouldn't be time for anything else.

She hurried across the motel forecourt; the bus was due to leave and Todd had warned there would be no waiting for stragglers. She took her seat on the bus next to a chattering Anita. Priya and Sid were also sat side by side but still looking in opposite directions. The only one missing from Todd's list was Sean Price.

The organised trips weren't compulsory, but most travellers believed in getting value for money so it was rare for a no-show. Where was Sean? No one on the bus had any idea where he might be although Daisy suddenly wondered to herself if the sight of a police uniform in the motel lobby had something to do with his sudden disappearance.

Then George from the front desk stuck his head through the open bus door.

'Mr Todd, sir, I just saw Mr Price leave the motel, he looked to be goin' for a walk, I reckon.'

Todd was very strict about timings; he'd been very clear about the call time for the trip to Tupelo. If this Sean guy had wandered off, there was no way he could wait for him. Deciding it was a good example to the rest of the group as to why they should stick to the schedule, Todd thanked George and gave instructions to Howard the driver to 'hit the road'.

As the bus pulled away and headed down Elvis Presley Boulevard, Todd asked Howard to slow down a little and pointed out the group's first glimpse of Graceland on the other side of the highway.

Daisy leaned forward to look over Anita and out of the moving window. A large white house was just visible through the trees. She caught a fleeting glimpse as they drove by and then there was only the grass paddock to see beyond the surprisingly low stone wall.

Nobody on the moving bus noticed Sean Price, with his back to the highway. Clutching his ever-present leather satchel, he'd positioned himself to the left of the open gates with their famous decorations of guitar players and music notes. He was peering through a small arched section of white railing up towards the house on the hill where Elvis Presley had lived and died.

Daisy settled back in her seat and thought about how good it felt to be heading for the place where everything began: Elvis's life and his music. This was where the story started and she couldn't help but wonder, did her own story have its roots in Tupelo too?

Chapter Eight

Lilian wasn't sure how much time she'd wasted wandering aimlessly from room to room in her mother's strangely silent house. It felt completely different to any time she had ever been there before. Even the air was different. It was like Rose's death had sucked the very life out of the place.

Lilian gave herself a little shake and a bit of a talking to. There was far too much to do for her to spend time wallowing in nostalgia and self-pity. She decided to prioritise and resolved to clear out the fridge first. No use letting things fester and stink up the place.

The kitchen in her mother's house was never what Lilian considered 'tidy'. A bunch of daffodils were wilting in a gaudy orange vase on the stripped pine table. The sorry display was surrounded by the everyday debris of Rose's life. Newspapers, magazines, an unwritten birthday card... Who had that been intended for? A couple of bills... Were they paid or unpaid? Half a packet of mints and an empty spectacles case lay close to Rose's abandoned handbag. The brown leather bag was a sturdy design with a gold clasp at the top and a robust curved handle that stuck straight up in the air. Lilian had always thought it looked like something the queen would carry.

Before she realised what she was doing, Lilian found she had flicked on the little radio that sat on the pine dresser beneath the disorganised shelves of mismatched crockery.

She worked for a while with a backing track of the kind of music she knew Rose and Daisy would love. She found it strangely comforting. She would have said she never took any notice of these sorts of songs, but then how did she recognise track after track on this oldies station? Rose always had the dial set to this frequency. Lilian decided the jaunty delivery of Marty Wilde as he sang about being a teenager in love was certainly preferable to stony silence.

Lilian shocked herself by knowing the words to songs by Eddie Cochran and Bobby Darin too. How had that happened? By osmosis? Even when the DJ announced a track by an artist she wasn't sure about like Connie Francis or Johnny Burnett, she was certainly familiar with the songs. How did she recognise 'Lipstick on your Collar' or 'Only Sixteen' from just the opening bars?

The systematic cleaning and clearing work she carried out was having a definite therapeutic effect. Lilian felt better for doing something methodical and useful; it suited her nature. She and Rose had always been so different, why was that? It was bad enough to never know who your father was, but she'd always struggled to find a connection to her mother too. As she worked, the nagging questions that often bothered her flitted through Lilian's mind. Did she resent her mother for not giving her a traditional family set-up? Probably. Had she always wished Rose had been more like the other sensibly dressed mothers? Definitely. The thought of bringing a friend home from school to find Rose jitterbugging around the kitchen with a colourful tea towel knotted on top of her head had filled a young Lilian with horror. That's not how the other mothers behaved.

Lilian herself had made a determined effort to be just like those other, *sensible* mothers when she had a child. She never dressed wildly, acted crazy or embarrassed anyone by dancing in the aisle at the supermarket when a song she liked came through the store speakers. Did Daisy appreciate any of this, though? Oh no, not a bit. Despite all Lilian's best efforts to be the mother she thought she should be, she and Daisy had never seen eye to eye.

Lilian had always felt Rose was mainly to blame for that too. She'd always encouraged Daisy's fanciful ways. The two of them would spend hours with their heads together, giggling about goodness knows what, shutting Lilian out completely. *Don't tell Mum… Don't tell your mother…* They were both as bad as each other.

The more she'd tried to create order in all their lives, the more things seemed to spiral out of control. When Daisy was just a baby, Brendan had left her. He said he felt Lilian didn't need him. He'd asked her several times to marry him after Daisy was born but she could never bring herself to accept and say yes. That didn't mean she didn't need him. It didn't mean that all. She never told him that though. When he said he was leaving, she'd simply let him go.

Lilian sat at the pine kitchen table. The kitchen around her was spotless, spick and span as though Mary Poppins herself had cast a spell that made it so. Perhaps she had, Lilian barely remembered doing any of it herself.

She found herself thinking about Rose's tattoo. As her mother lay sleeping the day after making her ludicrous 'Elvis was your father' announcement, Lilian had lifted up the sleeve of Rose's nightgown and looked at the image for a long time. It had struck her that it must have looked amazing when it was first done. Lilian totally disapproved of tattoos but this one was a beauty, despite how old and crinkled it had become. The red rose in full bloom, its open petals soft and velvety. Tufts of green leaves poked from beneath the bloom with clever dark shading making it look like the whole flower hovered over Rose's skin. Lilian had eventually covered it up and continued to look at her mother as though she had never seen her before either.

She was jolted out of the memory by a voice on the radio, Elvis's voice. He was singing the song she remembered her mother always used to sing as a lullaby when she was a little girl. She hadn't heard her mother sing the words for a very long time. As she realised she would never have the chance to hear her sing them again, her tears began to fall.

As the sentimental ballad 'Loving You' played on, Lilian let herself imagine... Could this really be her father singing to her right now and was Daisy going to be able to find out the truth once and for all?

Chapter Nine

There was precious little to see at the tiny wooden house where Elvis had been born.

The white wooden homestead stood on a raised platform surrounded by manicured box hedges. Clean and pristine, it dazzled in the sunshine.

A large sign nearby proclaimed that the shack had been built by Elvis's father Vernon, though it was highly unlikely he'd also been responsible for the Health and Safety-approved steps and handrail that led up to the property.

Inside there were just the two rooms. One bedroom with a metal-framed double bed and a living space dominated by a kitchen table covered in a green and white gingham cloth. A large black iron cooking stove rested against the bare brick of one wall.

A guide told the group the stove was the very one the Presleys used to cook their meals and huddle around for warmth. Daisy tried to imagine how cold the little shack would have been on the January night in 1935 when Gladys gave birth in the bedroom to Elvis Aaron and his stillborn twin, Jesse Garon. The thought of a mother having to endure such hardship and heartache made her feel desperately sad for Gladys Presley. She'd known the historical facts about the family's poor background and how Elvis's twin had died during their birth, but now, standing in the very place where it happened, Daisy was imagining it all much more clearly. Her heart broke a little for the suffering poor Gladys had endured.

The decor in the house was a surprising mix of swirly patterned rugs and ditsy-flowered wallpaper. The guide assured them everything they saw resembled the 1930s style the Presleys would have chosen. The table was laid with white crockery and glassware, no doubt to make you feel as though the family had just stepped out for a pre-supper walk. The modern electric fan next to the sideboard rather shattered that illusion, thought Daisy, although she understood the need for it in the often muggy Mississippi heat.

She was about to complete the shuffle through the rooms when her eye was caught by a plain brown hat hanging amongst the sprigs of green leaves and pink petals of the bedroom wallpaper. She recognised that hat. Sure enough, just along the wall, over the matching dark brown fireplace was the famous sepia photograph of the young Presley family, with serious faces all looking slightly to the left of the camera. There was Gladys, hair pulled back, a man's heavy leather belt pulling her flowered dress in at the waist. Standing between his seated parents, toddler Elvis wore a hat to match his daddy, tilted at an angle, all the better to see clearly his chubby cheeks and pouty lips. Vernon wore a working shirt, the collar open at the neck, his wife's hand resting on his shoulder. His brown trilby hat was pushed back on his head, and a small lock of hair had escaped and curled down over his forehead, a rockabilly touch before the look had even been invented.

The guide confirmed that, yes, this was Vernon's very own brown trilby hat, hanging here, aged and worn with the very same matching brown fabric band around the base of the crown.

Daisy gazed at the hat for as long as she dared. For the first time she found herself in the presence of something personal that truly connected her to Elvis and his own parents. She was surprised by how much it moved her. To have tangible evidence of the lives of Vernon, Gladys and baby Elvis within touching distance made Daisy feel for the first time that anything was possible. These were real people, just like her. Not just characters from a book or a movie, or even a voice on a record. These people had lived and loved. They felt the same emotions as anyone else, they got themselves in and out of trouble, and had good times and bad. Somehow this all made Daisy feel the possibility of a direct link between the Presleys and her own family was not such a ridiculous notion after all. Relationships developed and babies were born every minute. Biology worked the same way whether your name was Presley or Featherstone.

Eventually the impatience of the people behind her meant that Daisy had to move on from where she stood, transfixed by Vernon's old brown trilby hat. She pulled out her phone and took a quick picture. She wanted to remember it in every detail. It was a hat, it was just a hat, but at the same time it felt like so much more.

A little while later, the group left the birthplace site and completed the obligatory visit to the downtown Tupelo hardware store. A friendly shopkeeper had happily recounted the well-worn legend of Gladys buying her son a guitar 'right here in this very store' instead of the more expensive bicycle the poor young boy had coveted.

Emerging into the afternoon sunshine on Main Street, Daisy and Anita looked up and down the shop fronts and across to Reeds Department Store.

Todd was corralling his group, attempting to ensure everyone knew how much time they had left in Tupelo. 'Okay, people, so you've seen where Gladys bought Elvis his very first guitar way back in 1946. There are a few stores around that were here even way back then, though the kinda motorcars hereabouts would have been a little different, I reckon. We're gonna be heading back to Memphis in a little while but you've got about twenty minutes for a look around and to take any pictures of the hardware store before y'all are due back on the bus.'

Anita squinted up and down the street. 'I'm not sure there's that much more to see here, it's a bit of a one-horse town.'

Daisy smiled at Anita's cowgirl turn of phrase. 'D'you fancy checking out those shops across the street? You never know what you might find in a place like this?' Daisy's instinct for hunting down a fashionable treasure or vintage discovery was always bubbling just below the surface.

'You go ahead.' Anita rolled her shoulders and stretched her aching back. 'I'm tuckered out. I think that jet lag is finally catching up with me. I'm gonna ask Howard to let me wait on the bus for '*y'all*.'

Daisy thought a nap on the way home to Memphis sounded like a fine idea – but there was always time for a little shopping adventure... always! She waved Anita on her way. 'Okay, honey. See ya later, alligator.'

With a wink, Anita set off for the bus parked around the corner. 'In a while, crocodile.'

West Main Street Tupelo was wide but the traffic was not particularly heavy. Daisy waited for the lights to change and dashed across the road while the cars were at a stop.

The green-and-white striped awnings outside Reeds Department Store declared it had first opened its doors in 1905. She glanced in through the glass entrance and saw a black-and-white chequered floor and a sweeping staircase curving up from the foyer to the next level. She hesitated, then stepped back from the door and decided to window shop along the street instead of getting lost inside the large store.

The window displays under the shade of the awnings were disappointingly uninspiring and she was about to turn back and retrace her steps when her attention was suddenly caught by a pair of boots in a tiny shoe shop. Not just any pair of boots, but the most beautiful pair of cowboy boots she had ever seen. Burnished brown leather with a small stack heel and a slightly upturned toe, the boots were traditional in shape, but starting at the ankle and winding its way up the outside of each boot was a beautifully designed red and green climbing rose motif.

Daisy looked longingly at the boots in the centre of the window display. They were unlike any others she had ever seen.

Well, hello, and where have you been all my life?

She glanced over her shoulder and saw Todd still standing outside the hardware store pointing out something down the street to a couple in matching tourist uniforms, all bulging pockets, bum-bags and baseball caps. Satisfied she had time for a closer look, Daisy ducked into the shop.

In a matter of moments, the boots were on her feet and Daisy was parading up and down on the pale-pink carpet for a shop assistant whose badge declared her name was *Trixie*.

'Well, don't they look like they were just made for your little ole feet?' Trixie's southern belle lilt suited her naturally sunny disposition.

Daisy looked at Trixie's fresh young face, with her wide blue eyes and shiny straight blonde hair. She looked exactly like the sort of girl the phrase 'butter wouldn't melt' was invented for. This wasn't just a sales pitch though, she was sure of it. Trixie meant every word; honesty just plain shone from the girl.

Daisy gave her a twirl. 'I can't believe they fit.'

'They're the only ones we have like that in stock. I've been waitin' to see who would come along to try them. It's like they were waitin' here, just for you.'

Something about Trixie's comment chimed with the way the boots made Daisy feel. It *did* feel as though she was destined to have them. The unusual rose pattern embossed into the leather would be a fitting tribute to her music-loving nana. She imagined Nana Rose clapping with delight at the sight of Daisy dressed like a Nashville native – she had no doubt she would thoroughly approve. To think, if she'd headed back to the bus with Anita she would never have even seen them.

Daisy wriggled her toes inside the leather. 'They are lovely.'

'Every gal needs a good pair of cowboy boots.' Trixie nodded wisely.

Daisy wondered if this was strictly true. Cowboy boots weren't exactly de rigueur back home.

'Hmmm, I wonder if I'd actually get enough wear out of them?' She was toying with Trixie, of course she was going to buy them; they certainly made a statement and not one that would fit in well with life in Llandovery.

Trixie looked at Daisy as if she'd lost her actual mind. 'Why, a pair of boots like that will take you just about anywhere you need to go! If I were you, I'd wear them right outta the store.'

Daisy instantly put her reservations to one side. She'd spent most of her life feeling like she didn't fit in back in Llandovery, she wasn't about to make the same mistake here. The boots made her look like a local and made her feel like she belonged. It was an unusual feeling and Daisy decided she liked it very much.

She paused for only a beat before declaring, 'Sold! Can you wrap my sandals?'

Daisy stepped back out onto West Main Street still admiring the boots, *her boots*, firmly in place where her strappy flat sandals had been just a few moments before. Trixie was right, they really *did* suit her. Her legs looked more tanned against the brown leather and they gave her short summer dress a more edgy look than the girly sandals she now carried in a brown paper bag under her arm.

Dragging her eyes away from her feet, she looked up and down the street. Maybe she should look for a hat next? A Western-style cowboy hat would certainly complete her transformation from a Welsh valleys girl to a Southern belle.

Tupelo seemed more deserted than it had been when she entered the shoe store. She couldn't see any of the rest of her group looking in the shop windows and Todd had disappeared from outside Tupleo Hardware Company Inc. A lone station wagon passed by on the opposite side of the road as she registered how quiet Tupelo had become.

As she started to retrace her steps back towards the main entrance to Reeds she suddenly heard a grinding noise. The bus! Parked around the corner from the hardware store, just up from the junction of West Main Street and Front, the bus, her bus, was reversing out of the parking lot and driver Howard was noisily crunching the gears.

Daisy's stomach lurched as the bus kicked up a cloud of sandy dust as Howard revved the engine, pushed into first gear and pulled away in the direction of Memphis. She broke into a run, the heels of her new boots clip-clopping along the sidewalk, and began to shout, 'Hey! NO! Hey, STOP! What about ME?'

Her words were drowned by the noise of the labouring motor and Daisy watched in despair as the bus picked up speed away from her, leaving her standing at the crossroads gazing helplessly as it disappeared into the distance.

Alone on the street, she had only a moment to register her shock before another booming engine noise drowned out the sound of the escaping bus.

An enormous black motorcycle pulled up alongside her, the roar of the engine sank to a low growl and the uniformed cop in mirrored shades sat astride it tipped his peaked hat and spoke over the thrum of the machine. 'Can I help you, miss?'

'The bus, my bus... I was... buying boots...' Daisy stuttered and stumbled to try and explain her predicament.

The motorcycle cop lowered his sunglasses as he ran his eyes down Daisy and took in the boots and just about everything else about her situation. He was incredibly relaxed. 'Those boots sure are mighty fine.'

Daisy felt the cop was sort of missing the point but then did a double-take.

'You!'

Officer Joe Cody gave a relaxed nod of his head and answered in a leisurely drawl, 'Lucky for you I was passing through these parts.'

Daisy was relieved to see an almost-familiar face but wasn't quite sure how it was going to help. The way the officer was looking at her made her feel he found her most amusing. Did he think she was someone who always needed to be rescued? How annoying! She was also aware her new boots made her look like a dizzy dolly instead of a genuine damsel in distress, damn them.

She realised the police officer was waiting for some sort of explanation as to why she was standing in the street, shouting after buses. You couldn't blame him for already thinking she was some sort of basket case, this wouldn't really be helping her cause.

'The bus… my bus has gone without me. I have to get back to Memphis, what am I going to do?' She didn't want to also confess that she'd used all of her carefully measured out daily allocation of dollars on the rose-patterned boots now on her feet.

The good-looking cop pushed his cap up on his forehead and… wait a minute, did he just wink at her? 'I think we can handle the situation. Hop on.'

Daisy looked blankly at him. 'Hop on?'

With a flick of his tongue, he moved his chewing gum from one side of his mouth to the other as he casually put his sunglasses back on; he really was one cool dude. 'You ever ridden on one of these before?'

Daisy looked at the throbbing beast of a machine… and then at the bike! Dear lord, she needed to pull herself together, the thought of getting up close and personal with Officer Cody was making her legs go to jelly inside her new boots.

She managed to breathe one word: 'Never.'

Officer Cody was cool as a cucumber despite the Mississippi heat. Daisy was convinced the temperature was increasing by the minute. But *cool cop* simply thrust out a hand as he spoke, 'Well, sweetheart, you haven't lived until you do.'

Daisy realised neither of them were wearing a helmet as she grabbed his hand but instantly decided it would be a helluva way to go.

Swinging one cowboy boot over the bike, she hitched herself onto the padded leather seat towards his blue-shirted back.

The officer spoke in a delicious drawl over his shoulder as he revved the engine. 'Hold tight now, honey.' She didn't need to be told twice.

The bike thundered between her legs as they sprang from the kerbside and swung off West Main Street and onto Front. The bus was long gone and the wind whipped her hair back from her face and tore at her dress as they sped along the highway. The thought of ending the journey naked apart from her boots flashed across her mind – *because of the wind*, she told herself. It therefore seemed only sensible to tuck herself as tight as possible into Officer Cody, wrap her arms around his body and hold on for dear life. Daisy just had to hope he wouldn't feel her thudding heart as it hammered out a frantic beat in her chest.

. . .

Several miles ahead, Anita was sound asleep with her head resting against the window of the bus as it rolled steadily on its way.

Oblivious to the motorcycle cop hot on their tail, the occupants of the bus idly looked out across the open land either side of the highway at the occasional homesteads dotted randomly amongst the patchy grasslands.

Sid remarked to Priya that despite the common use of the phrase 'backyard' in America no one around here actually appeared to have such a thing as a front or back garden. Instead, the one-storey ranch-style homes were plonked in what appeared a haphazard manner, some close to the road, some way back, with no white picket fence or even so much as a hedge to signify where one property ended and the neighbour's began.

Priya listened to Sid's seventeenth pointless observation of the day and thought this trip really wasn't turning out the way she had expected.

Driver Howard suddenly spotted a flash of light in his rear-view mirror. He looked again as the low sun picked out a gleam of chrome on something way back on the road. There it was again – this time the flash came from his wing mirror. Whatever it was had speeded up and was gaining on him fast. He checked his speed dial. He was just under the speed limit, the fool behind must be in one hell of a rush.

Moments ticked by but then the white light that occasionally flashed at the edge of his line of vision suddenly turned to blue. Howard's stomach lurched, as did everyone's on the bus as his foot instinctively hit the brakes hard.

Todd scrambled to stop his clipboard from launching itself from his lap. 'What's going on?'

He regularly worked with Howard for weeks on end, he was usually one of the smoothest and safest drivers in the company.

'We got a cop on our tail.'

Todd looked back down the bus and through the rear window. 'We're getting pulled over?'

Everyone on the bus was now craning to see what was going on. The motorcycle cop had his blue light flashing and waved an arm to indicate the bus should pull up at the side of the road.

Howard slowed right down as the cop swung alongside the bus. It was Priya who clocked that the cop wasn't alone. 'That's Daisy, on the bike, LOOK!'

Anita woke with a start at the sound of Daisy's name and in the same instant spotted a flap of yellow sundress and a bare leg wearing a cowboy boot as it sped past the bus window.

She turned in confusion to Daisy's seat beside her. Empty.

By now, everyone on the bus was pulling themselves out of their seats and shouting and pointing at the police officer and his female passenger. The bus ground to a halt and the cop brought the bike to rest at an angle just ahead of them on the road.

Daisy felt the eyes of everyone on the bus on her as she attempted a graceful dismount from the bike. Still clutching the brown paper bag containing her sandals, she stood in front of her rescuer as he slowly took off the mirrored sunglasses and revealed a pair of piercing blue eyes. 'Well, there you go, little lady.'

Daisy was desperately trying to calm herself down following the exhilaration of the high-speed chase and the feeling of being pressed up against the broad shoulders of Officer Cody.

Standing on the Tupelo to Memphis highway, with a handsome guy asking if she was okay, Daisy realised that it *did* feel like she'd been rescued by her very own knight in shining armour. Far from offending her feminist principles, she also realised she was finding the whole experience incredibly sexy.

Howard pressed the button to open the door on the bus and the clamour amongst the passengers died down instantly as they all strained to hear what was being said between Daisy and the officer, who still straddled his motorcycle.

The cop was talking intently as Daisy listened, nodding occasionally, then he reached into his top pocket for a notebook and began to write something down. He tore off a page and handed it to her.

'He's giving her a ticket!' Sid's announcement was met with a murmur of agreement from many on the bus.

Anita snorted in scorn, then answered proudly, 'Don't be daft! He's giving her his number.'

A gasp came from several female members of the group then as Daisy raised her eyes from the note in her hand, leaned forward and planted a little kiss on the cop's cheek.

Gallant to the end, the officer tipped his peaked hat as Daisy turned towards the bus. His face cracked then into a delighted smile behind Daisy's back as she climbed the three steps up into the bus and was greeted with whoops and cheers.

Daisy held her head high and tried not to grin as she negotiated her way through all the cat calls and down the centre aisle to her seat, but her cheeks were flame red.

She eventually flopped into the seat next to Anita, whose eyes burned into her with a questioning stare.

'What?' Daisy couldn't quite bring herself to look at Anita's face as she affected a casual air.

Anita said nothing but her neat eyebrows shot upwards, asking their own question.

Daisy maintained as innocent a demeanour as she could muster as she tucked the slip of paper into the denim jacket she'd left under the seat. 'His name's Joe Cody... but because of his eyes...people call him "Blue".'

A satisfied smirk spread across Anita's face. 'Well of course they do!'

Daisy kept all her rather more lustful thoughts about Blue tucked away as neatly as the note he'd given her with his number. She'd let him take down her particulars, so to speak and given him her contact details, so he now knew her mobile number and which motel she was staying in. Like a real gentleman, he'd politely asked if he could see her again; she'd readily agreed and rewarded him with a quick kiss to thank him for the rescue. She wasn't sure, but he actually seemed to blush as her lips met the smooth skin of his cheek.

As Daisy replayed the kiss again in her mind, Howard swung the bus back onto the road and began to pick up speed. The bus passed Officer Cody, still astride his gleaming motorbike, and Daisy turned for a last glimpse. Blue gave a small salute before turning tail and heading back to Tupelo.

Chapter Ten

The impossibly handsome man paced the small room like a caged tiger. What was taking so long? Why didn't they realise who he was?

He clenched his long fingers into a fist and then stretched them out; they looked strangely bare. Why had they taken all his rings? What did they want with his jewelled belt? Would he ever get them back? This stuff was worth a small fortune. They would be going through his luggage now, emptying his suitcase and mocking his white tasselled jumpsuits and silk-lined capes. He could imagine the taunts – who did this guy think he was? Some kind of superhero?

He chopped at the air with his bare hands and threw out a few karate kicks to try and burn off some of the frustration building up inside himself.

He might have known the paperwork would not be in order; the number of forms that had to be filled out nowadays, you'd think he was attempting to have an audience with the President of the United States himself.

The guy on the desk had been a complete jobsworth, acted like he'd never seen anything like it before. What a fool.

He sank onto the bench opposite the locked door and ran his hands through his hair. He'd always hated travelling; it made him uneasy to be anywhere strange and unfamiliar. This place was certainly those things. This wasn't exactly a hero's welcome, no sir.

He started to drum his fingers on his knees. It began as a nervous tic, but the rhythm morphed into a steady beat and his feet took up the cue and started tapping along. When he realised his percussion fitted one of his favourite songs, he abruptly halted the drumming beat and sang the first line. The backbeat started again as he accompanied himself like a one-man band: he sang about an exhausting journey, travelling over mountains and through valleys, desperately trying to reach a destination that always felt too far away. The song was about a man trying his hardest to get somewhere, to someone. He sang the lyrics and meant every word. Would he ever reach his intended destination?

Chapter Eleven

As the Graceland Experience bus rolled its way through Mississippi, Todd, the tour guide, took up the hand mic to give his passengers a potted history of the trip the Presley family had made along the very same highway almost seventy years before.

'It was sometime in the fall of '48 and Elvis was just thirteen years old when his Papa Vernon and Mama Gladys loaded up their 1939 green Plymouth sedan with the few belongings they had and set off for what they hoped was a better life in the big city of Memphis, Tennessee.'

Daisy settled back in her seat and gazed out of the window as the bus sped through the flat landscape. She was intrigued by the thought that she was literally following in Elvis's footsteps on this journey across the Southern States. She imagined the Presleys' rusty old car with a couple of battered suitcases strapped to the roof. She listened as Todd explained that, despite their hopes, life for the little family was even harder in Memphis to begin with; they lived in a succession of small boarding houses, sharing just a couple of tiny rooms. Daisy wondered what would have become of the Presleys if they hadn't gambled on the big move to Memphis. Would Elvis still have discovered the rhythm and blues music that he turned into rock 'n' roll if he'd stayed in Tupelo?

She was learning from Todd's narration that it was unlikely the family had very high expectations on that trip. Tennessee appeared to be a marginally more tolerant place than Mississippi back then, but segregation was still as rigid. The Presleys were white, but as far as Southern society circles were concerned they were little more than poor white trash, thanks to Vernon's recent short spell in prison. By all accounts, it was less a case of setting off in search of a promising new future as they headed north to Memphis, and more a case of attempting an escape from their troubled past.

Daisy wondered if wanting to leave difficult situations behind and start afresh was a family trait she might share?

As the landscape whizzed by, she spotted yet another ramshackle homestead set back from the highway. A high-backed wooden chair lay on its side on the peeling porch as though it had been upturned suddenly. A scruffy brown dog tied with a length of string to a stake in the ground was barking towards the house. She leaned forward, intrigued as to what might have happened, or be happening there, but in an instant the image was gone.

Anita turned towards her. 'It makes you wonder, doesn't it?'

'Hmm?' Daisy's eyes were still fixed on the ever-changing scenery before her eyes.

'How much of what we can see now looks the same as it did to Elvis when he made this trip with his ma and pa?'

Daisy looked at Anita in surprise – they were thinking almost exactly the same thing! Then she looked around at the others on the bus listening to Todd talk about Elvis's schooldays at Humes High and felt foolish, realising that everybody else was re-living Elvis's life in their mind's eye too. If she was hoping that alone made her in some way special and connected to Elvis then she needed to think again; that's why everyone was on this trip, to delve into the backstory of Elvis's life and see the world through his eyes for a while.

It made Daisy feel embarrassed that she was secretly entertaining hopes that she and Elvis Presley were closely connected. Based on the thinnest evidence, Daisy was attempting to establish a link between herself and the King but she suddenly didn't feel very special at all. She pulled a face and shrugged like a moody teenager.

Anita was mystified by Daisy's change in demeanour; where was the friendly, funny girl who had been practically fizzing with excitement after her encounter with the handsome motorcycle cop?

'What's up, love? You bored of being with us oldies already?'

Daisy was instantly mortified. She didn't want to appear rude. 'No, not at all… of course not.'

Anita was smiling. 'It's okay, chick. I can see why you'd rather be with your hunky Officer Blue Eyes.'

Daisy opened her mouth to protest, but saw straight away that Anita was teasing her. She laughed and pushed her hands through her hair, which was still tangled from the high-speed motorbike chase.

'What brings a young girl like you on a trip like this anyway?' Anita had been waiting for the right moment to ask. 'You're the youngest person on this trip by a country mile.'

Daisy looked down at the rose-patterned cowboy boots on her feet and felt the familiar ache in her heart. 'It's all thanks to my Nana Rose.'

Anita waited while Daisy decided just how much to confide in her new friend.

'She always said we would make this trip together one day, but... well... she died just a few weeks ago. I'm sort of making this trip... in her memory.'

Daisy risked a sideways look at Anita. It wasn't a total lie but she didn't feel able to tell the whole truth. Not even to Anita. Telling someone she had only just met that she was trying to find out if Elvis Presley was her grandad was too much of a risk. What if they thought she was crazy? Or alerted the authorities? She wasn't actually sure which one of those options was worse. She decided to stick to the 'honouring her nana's memory' story, it was safer for now.

'Oh, love, I am sorry.' Anita took Daisy's hand in hers and gave it a reassuring pat. 'And now she'll never be able to come. What a shame.'

Daisy shook her head vigorously. 'Oh, she has been here! It was a long time ago but she was here. She was younger than I am now actually, she was only just eighteen.'

Anita was slightly taken aback. 'So that would be when? In the Sixties?'

'That's right, it was 1960.' Daisy nodded.

Anita looked quizzically at Daisy. 'And I thought you were an odd traveller, but that's a very unusual trip for a young girl to make back then, isn't it?'

Daisy thought proudly of her nana. She might not have revealed all her secrets before she died, but Daisy knew this story well enough; she'd heard her tell it so many times. She might not feel ready to confide in her new friend completely, but she spent the next hour explaining to a captivated Anita how a young woman in her late teens made the journey to Tennessee in 1960 for a trip that changed her life.

Summer 1960 – Memphis

Rose Featherstone spent the summer of 1960 in Memphis thanks to a girl called Jenny Jenkins. The two had been best friends in primary school back in Wales and as they became teenagers the fact that Jenny's elder sister Jean had moved to America as a GI bride had a huge impact on both their lives.

For Rose it meant an early introduction to rock 'n' roll and Elvis Presley, when Jean would send her little sister magazines and records with all the latest pictures and sounds from the US charts. Together the girls would pore over the pictures and listen to the songs on Rose's Dansette player.

The parcels from Jeannie, as she now called herself, introduced the best friends to a whole new world. They spent hours drooling over pictures of cars so long they would stretch the length of three terraced houses should one have attempted to park outside. Jenny's mum exclaimed in shock at the sight of magazine advertisements featuring smiling women in pastel-coloured dresses and frilly white aprons posing next to gleaming refrigerators the size of telephone boxes. Mrs Jenkins had a side pantry where she kept butter and her daily delivery of milk. What on earth would an American housewife keep in that huge refrigerator is what she wanted to know... a spare husband? Rose knew Mrs Jenkins' own husband had disappeared not long after Jenny was born, so she reasoned she may well have been in the market for a convenient spare. She certainly never had a good word to say about the one who had deserted her. Apparently, he'd said he was 'popping out' but then never came back – no note, no explanation or as Mrs Jenkins was fond of saying, 'not so much as a doodle on a doily'.

Then one day a package arrived from Jeannie and it happened; they heard Elvis Presley for the very first time. The record was 'Heartbreak Hotel' and the girls thought the Dansette player was faulty at first as Elvis's trembling voice hiccupped its way through the song, the jarring chords punctuating his voice at random intervals.

So they played it again... and again.

Jeannie had enclosed cuttings from the local paper in Memphis about this new young singer, Elvis Presley, although they also called him 'The Hillbilly Cat' and 'The Memphis Flash' in the reports Jeannie had torn out. There was a single black and white photograph of him alongside the news report. His eyes were heavy-lidded and looked completely black, and his lips were full and pouting. The girls knew they'd never heard or seen anything like him ever before in their lives.

And so it went on. Jenny and Rose waited with growing excitement and expectation for the parcels Jeannie would send over, keeping them up to date with the latest news. They were able to follow Presley themselves too, making sure they were first in line when his debut movie, Love Me Tender, *came to their local cinema a few months later. There he was at last, moving, talking, singing and ten feet tall to boot! They couldn't help but fall helplessly and hopelessly in love.*

But the following year everything changed. Mrs Jenkins was taken ill and sadly died. Before Jenny and Rose knew what was happening, it was the day of the funeral and Jeannie arrived from America, announcing she would be taking Jenny back to America with her to live in Memphis.

The girls had spent years fantasising about America, watching movies every Saturday morning at the Roxy Picture House starring Fred Astaire and Ginger Rogers, Judy Garland and Mickey Rooney. America seemed like a dream world to them.

The pictures they'd seen of the house Jeannie lived in with her husband Frank looked like something straight out of Gone with the Wind, *but even so, Rose and Jenny begged and pleaded for Jenny to be allowed to stay in Wales. Of course it did no good, Jeannie's mind was made up and the girls were forced to say goodbye, never knowing if they would ever see each other again.*

Over the next few years they wrote to each other regularly, Rose from her small back bedroom with a view of factory roofs, Jenny from Walnut Grove House, a colonial-style mansion in the suburbs of Memphis sitting in acres of open land. They never gave up hope of Rose being able to come over for a visit.

By the time Rose turned eighteen she had saved up a little bit of money from her job in the typing pool. That and a heartfelt phone call from Jeannie promising to look after Rose convinced her parents to finally agree to let Jeannie and Frank buy an aeroplane ticket for Rose to visit them and Jenny in Tennessee.

The flight to America was long and there were hours to wait at a stop-over in New York before Rose boarded a second flight to Memphis. Everything about being in America completely amazed eighteen-year-old Rose. She thought things couldn't be any more alien if she had flown to the Moon.

At first, even Jenny, who now preferred to be known as Jennifer, seemed strange to her. Jennifer (sometimes she even liked to use both her first names and go by Jennifer-Jane which Rose thought was quite the mouthful) spoke with a southern twang to her natural Welsh lilt now. Even more incredibly, she picked Rose up from the airport in an open-topped car that she drove – on the wrong side of the road – all the way back to Walnut Grove House.

Rose was lost for words at her first glimpse of the house. As they swung through the estate gates and Jennifer steered the car up the winding driveway, Rose remembered Mrs Jenkins' tiny, two-up, two-down terrace and understood properly, for the first time, why Jeannie had insisted on bringing her little sister over to live with her.

Jennifer-Jane and Jeannie had grown more than a little alike in the two years they had spent living together in Tennessee. Jennifer was taller and slimmer than Rose remembered. Her long blonde hair was much shorter and the curls and waves behaved themselves much better now.

Big sister Jeannie was now the mother of boisterous six-year-old twin boys, Bobby Ray and Beau Barley, but she was nothing like the harassed mothers Rose saw back home. Those women were instantly transformed from maidens to matrons as soon as they became mothers. Rose had seen them, pushing heavy prams up steep Welsh hills, their overcoats wrapped over large bosoms, headscarves knotted tightly under chins as they set their faces into the wind.

In contrast, Jeannie showed off her still-tiny waist in tailored dresses in bright colours. Her sunshine-yellow hair was always perfectly in place and she exuded the laidback air of an adopted southern belle.

As Jennifer gave an impromptu tour of the large plantation home, Rose was also taken aback with her ease in referring to rooms such as 'the library' and 'the drawing room' as though every home had one. Even more shocking to Rose was Jennifer's blithe acceptance of the presence of servants. Black servants!

'Well, of course we need help,' was Jennifer-Jane's breezy response when Rose questioned their necessity. 'It's fine work, they're grateful for it and we treat Louella and Jude just like family.'

In her whistle-stop tour of the house Rose wasn't shown the staff living quarters although she eventually found for herself a small attic room where Louella and Tilly Mae the housemaid slept. Many other members of the staff lived on site, including Louella's husband Caesar, who worked in the grounds, and Matilda the cook. Their homes were wooden cabins away from the main house. The shabby collection of huts was hidden from view by a row of black walnut trees.

Rose asked Jennifer how many servants Walnut Grove House actually had. Jennifer began to count them off on her fingers but after half a dozen lost interest and waved her hand dismissively. 'Oh, there's not that many, I can't say I've ever really counted and, anyway, they all look the same to me.'

Rose winced a little at Jennifer's offhand tone, but until she had arrived in Tennessee her only contact with black people had been a couple of bus drivers who drove the No. 141 bus back home. She decided the domestic arrangements at Walnut Grove House were not her business and dropped the subject. The girls had a whole summer ahead of them to enjoy and get re-acquainted and Rose didn't intend to start off on the wrong foot or waste a minute of it.

They spent their time 'hanging out' as Jennifer called it, on the shaded porch of the house during the warmth of the day, sipping homemade lemonade and chatting.

As the sun went down, Jennifer often drove the streets of Memphis in the convertible Chevrolet that Frank let her borrow sometimes, pointing out landmarks and places of interest. They ate hamburgers in a downtown diner with leather-seated booths and a brightly coloured juke box, and they watched paddle steamers ploughing their way down the Mississippi. They even took tea with Jeannie and some of her friends one afternoon at the genteel Peabody Hotel. To Rose's astonishment a parade of ducks appeared from the 'elevator' and proceeded down a red carpet across the fancy lobby of the hotel to take a bath in the indoor fountain. Jennifer assured her this curious tradition occurred every day at the same time to entertain the hotel guests and had done for many years and Rose was not hallucinating.

On their way home from the Peabody tea party Jennifer pulled her car over outside a rundown building on Union Avenue. Next door was a large record store called Poplar Tunes. The girls spent a good while sifting through the stacks of vinyl records and listening to music in the booths.

It was only on the way back to the car that Jennifer pointed to the deserted corner building and revealed to Rose that this had once been the home of Sun Studio where Elvis, Jerry Lee Lewis, Carl Perkins and so many others had made their records. Jenny told Rose that Mr Sam Phillips had now opened a new, bigger studio down on Madison.

Rose peered through the dirty windows into what had been the front office and imagined Elvis standing inside chatting with the woman at the desk who took the studio bookings.

Jennifer broke the spell. 'He's back, you know.'

'Back?' Rose jumped away from the window. 'Who's back?'

Jenny grinned at her startled friend, 'Elvis! He's been in Germany on national service but it was all over the news on TV a few weeks back. He's come home to Memphis, they baked him a welcome home cake and everything, although I expect he's gone off to Hollywood already to make a new movie.' She paused for dramatic effect, then asked, 'Do you wanna go and see where he lives?'

Rose had no idea what to expect as Jennifer drove the car out of Memphis on Highway 51 South. Her tummy bubbled with excitement at the thought of seeing where Elvis Presley lived. Perhaps he would be there after all and they would catch a glimpse of him! Jennifer, in contrast, was pretty blasé about the situation. She'd lived in Memphis so long she had got used to knowing that Elvis lived there. Anyway, as she pointed out as she drove, he'd been away in the army for two long years and she'd recently discovered Bobby Vee and someone called Fabian who seemed to have replaced Elvis in her fickle affections.

They appeared to be heading towards open countryside; the landscape opened up either side of the highway and the buildings became scarce at the sides of the road. When Jennifer slowed the *car and swung off onto a grass verge. Rose couldn't tell at first where she was meant to look. Then Jennifer pointed across the wide road towards the opposite side, where cars were speeding past back towards the city.*

In the fading evening light, Rose saw a low dry stone wall running all along a strip of grass which was all that separated it from the road. Her eyes tracked the wall back towards the direction of Memphis and she gasped as she suddenly spotted dark red swirls of metal, almost invisible against the dusty brown driveway. The wrought-iron gates embellished with matching curved figures, each holding a guitar and separated by scattered metal music notes, were firmly closed.

She stared at the gates; this then was the entrance to Graceland, the home of Elvis himself.

It wasn't until Jennifer nudged her and pointed slightly to the right of the gates that she saw a house half hidden by tall trees way back from the road. The house was large, although not enormous, and stood proudly on a small hill. Peering hard, at first all Rose could make out were four white columns in the centre of the building with a pointed white gable roof above. She then saw windows either side of the portico, two up and two down. Was one of these Elvis's bedroom? There seemed to be more buildings just one storey high either side of the house but Rose couldn't really see properly with all the trees in front.

'D' you wanna get a closer look?'

Jennifer didn't even wait for Rose to reply, but flicked on the indicator and swung the car back onto the highway when there was a break in the traffic. Further down, she found a place to turn the car right around and headed back towards Memphis. This time the house would be on their right and they would be a lot closer.

Pulling up on the grass verge just down from the music gates, Jennifer turned the engine off and pulled the lever to open her door.

'You coming?' She jumped out of the car and Rose followed quickly behind.

They both stood at the stone wall which looked a lot like crazy paving. Its jagged top was just too high for them to see over, but then Rose noticed that here and there were scrawled messages and doodles on the smooth front of the pinky-brown slabs of rock.

'Fans write to Elvis and even leave him their telephone numbers here,' Jennifer told Rose. 'Do you want to leave yours?'

Rose shook her head, embarrassed at the thought, but then had a change of heart. She reached through the open window of the car and delved into her handbag. Taking a red lipstick from the inside pocket, Rose found a flat part of a pale stone and inked a small picture of a red rose. She stood back and looked at the colourful addition to the mosaic of artwork. Perhaps Elvis would notice it as he drove by.

The girls made their way towards the closed gates and found they had a good view of the house where the brick wall either side of the driveway dipped into a low arc. They stood for a while looking up at the mansion, hoping for any signs of movement. Rose moved in front of the Graceland gates and traced the outline of one of the music notes with her hand and curled her fingers through the mesh.

A door in a small brick cabin just inside the gate suddenly opened. Rose jumped back; someone was coming.

• • •

Somewhere along Elvis Presley Boulevard, Daisy was woken from her nap as Todd's amplified voice on the hand mic announced they would soon be back at the motel. '... and as you can see, Graceland is quite something to see, even at night.'

Everyone on the bus turned to look at the sight of the illuminated mansion as they drove alongside, its white pillars picked out in spotlights. Even the famous music gates, now tastefully painted in white and forest green, were backlit to show off the strumming figures and music notes as though they were dancing shadows.

Daisy looked back towards the closed gates as the bus sped past, picturing her grandmother standing in that exact spot. If only she knew what had happened next.

Chapter Twelve

The night before Rose died, Lilian had kissed her mother goodnight and left a CD softly playing her favourite music to keep her company in her hospital room.

A little while after Lilian had gone, a nurse had come to check on Rose; she'd smoothed the covers on her bed and gently picked up the old lady's hand. Her pulse was regular and she was breathing evenly in her sleep.

The portable CD player the patient's family had brought in fell silent as the last track on the disc ended. The nurse watched as the old lady murmured and shifted restlessly in the bed. The music seemed to be soothing her. Before she left, the nurse pressed Play on the CD player and re-started the music. A few guitar notes and a rich voice filled the room asking questions about how lonesome Rose felt tonight just as the nurse left her bedside. As the music washed over her, Rose's memories began flooding back.

• • •

'Hey, what you doin' there, sweetheart?'

Startled, she jumped back from the gates, tripped over her own feet and landed flat on her back.

The sun was low now and the man who bent over her was surrounded by a bright halo of light from the dipping sun. His movements were slow and he pushed back the quiff of hair that had fallen in front of his eyes as he bent to help her, but still she couldn't see his face clearly.

Rose tried to say the man's name, but the words wouldn't come. Lying alone in her hospital room, the memories so long held at bay flooded her confused unconscious mind and her heart was full of pain.

She was pressed tightly against him. She couldn't get any closer. If she could have climbed inside him, she would have done. Her head buried into his jacket, her eyes shut tight, the hammering of his heartbeat against her cheek.

The world fell away, suddenly and completely. They were falling, falling, air rushing up and past them, the sounds of the funfair all around them whipped away on the wind so it was just the two of them swooping and soaring. She never looked down, only felt the highs and the lows as her stomach flipped and he held her even tighter.

Rose's fingers gripped the bedcovers and she held on as if for dear life. She felt propelled towards somewhere she wasn't sure she wanted to go. For so long she'd refused to remember, it hurt too much, made her feel too lonely. Why had he come back again?

His voice was whispering in her ear. 'You're so pretty... my sweet Rose.'

She could feel the warmth of his words on her neck and yet those same words sent shivers down her spine. Her body was trembling as she sensed him standing so close, and closing her eyes, she breathed in the very scent of him.

Rose was restless again. The song was nearly over, the spoken lyrics echoed around the room, inside her mind, which was it?

Rose decided she had sympathy with the words she could hear... *Yes, that's right*, she thought, *if he won't come back, they should just bring the curtain down.*

A little while later, the nurse returned to check on her patient.

'Oh my dear.' She placed Rose's cold hand back inside the warm covers and touched the old lady's cheek. It was wet with tears.

Chapter Thirteen

The itinerary for the Graceland Experience trip gave everyone a day at their leisure in Memphis in between the visit to Tupelo and the much-anticipated tour of Graceland. Most of the party seemed mad keen to visit an out-of-town shopping mall, but Daisy was not planning to join them.

She told Anita and Priya she preferred to rummage in second-hand stores and old-fashioned markets. It wasn't hard to convince them that an ultra-modern, pile 'em high, sell 'em cheap shopping centre held no appeal for her. But as much as she did love treasure hunting in new 'old' places, that sort of shopping was not part of Daisy's plan today.

Daisy had a lead. The search for Walnut Grove House might have hit a dead end, but Daisy knew she had to keep exploring different avenues. Just being here, boots on the ground in Memphis, Daisy felt as though the threads of Elvis and Nana Rose's lives lay around her in all directions.

If she could pick up just one loose end and follow it, who knew what may unravel in front of her?

She'd been busy chatting to all of the motel staff, making conversations that led to whether they knew of anyone still around who had known Elvis back in the day? There had to be someone, surely? Maybe what they remembered would lead to something else? She was aware there would be many locals who would claim a connection to Presley. She'd heard that in Liverpool you couldn't walk a couple of steps without bumping into someone who claimed to have been to school with a Beatle, or danced their lunchtimes away in the Cavern. The underground club where the Beatles had been discovered had been tiny, if everyone who said they'd been there actually had been, it would have had to have been the size of Wembley Stadium... at least! Daisy therefore presumed it would be even worse in Memphis with Elvis, but she had to at least try.

Luckily, one particular name had kept cropping up again and again: an old radio DJ called 'Jumpin'' Judd Crocket. He'd had a show on a Memphis radio station back in the day and although he hadn't been the first to play Elvis's music, like WHBQ's Dewey Phillips, or been part of the Memphis Mafia like DJ George Klein, Jumpin' Judd claimed he'd been around the King enough to know some tales of his own.

As he was now well into his eighties, Daisy was doubtful Judd Crocket would be doing much *jumpin'* these days. More likely she'd find him *'rockin'* in a chair in some home for old-timers and bewildered former disc jockeys. So she was pleasantly surprised when she stepped into the dimly lit downtown bar where she'd been told Judd Crocket could be found most days. Sat alone at a corner table was a sprightly-looking elderly gentleman with a neat white moustache, wearing a red baseball cap. Instead of mumbling incoherently into his beer, Judd was chatting animatedly with the barman.

Daisy asked if she could buy him a drink and was rewarded with a big, welcoming, toothless smile. Her hands shook a little as she deposited the beer glass in front of Judd, she was excited to think she was about to talk to someone who had actually known Elvis Presley.

Jumpin' Judd certainly hadn't lost his patter. He was delighted to entertain Daisy with story after story of his many encounters with Elvis; unfortunately Daisy wasn't inclined to believe them all. It wasn't that Judd was lying, as such, but over time his tales had acquired a top spin that meant the truth had been left far behind. A wink here and there from the barman as he wiped down tables reinforced Daisy's impression that Judd spent his days at The Rum Boogie Cafe just so he could be found by eager Elvis-hunters hungry for a titbit or two from his favourite table. He'd re-invented himself as a tourist attraction.

'Y'see this beauty here on ma finger?' Judd stuck out a gnarled hand so Daisy could get a closer look. A gold sovereign ring was on his little pinky. 'Elvis took this off his own hand and gave it to me, he said, "Judd, ma friend, you gotta take this ring, man, I want you to have it, shows what good buddies we are." Yeah, that's what he said alright.'

Daisy peered at Judd's left hand as he nodded his baseball hat for emphasis. The ring appeared far too yellow and shiny to be a genuine Elvis artefact. In fact, Daisy was pretty sure you could buy trinkets just like this one in any of the souvenir shops up and down Beale Street. She was beginning to doubt that Jumpin' Judd had any information at all that could help her. The thought was slightly depressing, but Judd was such good company she didn't have the heart to cut him off in mid flow.

She passed a very pleasant hour with Judd, bought him a couple of beers, but then decided to politely make her excuses and move on. She hadn't been able to find out anything about whether Nana Rose could possibly have dated Elvis Presley. She wasn't sure what she had been hoping for – maybe that Judd would bang his sovereign-ringed hand onto the table at the mention of Rose Featherstone and say, *Rose Featherstone! Of course, she was the one who got away. They made such a handsome couple, Elvis used to talk about her all the time!*

Judd had just cackled at the mention of Elvis and girlfriends. He'd offered the revelation that, 'Elvis liked 'em dark and purty, for sure,' but anyone who'd ever seen a photo of his wife Priscilla could figure that out. Trouble was, as Judd confirmed, Elvis also famously liked blondes and red-heads too... Anita Wood, Ursula Andress, Juliet Prowse, Ann-Margret, Linda Thompson, Ginger Alden... The list was endless.

The one thing Judd did confirm was that Elvis had relationships with a huge number of women and had many more girlfriends than those everyone knew about. Of course it didn't necessarily mean that Rose was one of them, but it also didn't mean that she wasn't!

Daisy thanked Judd for his time and stepped outside into the bright sunshine. She pulled her mobile phone from her bag. Maybe she should give her mother a call and see how she was getting on? She'd only called Lilian once since she'd got here, just to let her know she'd arrived safely, although she had been sending pictures regularly.

There were several missed calls on the phone. Not from Lilian but from Officer Joe Cody – Blue! Her tummy flip-flopped and she almost dropped the phone from her fumbling fingers. Finally, he'd called. It had been less than twenty-four hours since their Tupelo encounter but it felt like longer. She'd been desperately hoping he would call and now he had and she'd had no service and missed it. Typical!

The sharp disappointment of missing a call from Blue immediately distracted Daisy from the continuing difficulty of her ongoing Memphis mission and she had to admit to herself just how keen she was to see him again.

She finally got through to voicemail and held her breath as she listened to see if he really had left a message. Perhaps she'd missed her chance; after all, he was a good-looking, hunky cop with oodles of Southern charm who had offered to show her the local sights, how many chances like that came along? What if he'd changed his mind when she didn't answer, thinking she was playing hard to get?

When his voice came through it was like warm honey dripping into her ear, but a lot less sticky. In his easy-going drawl he told her he'd like to offer some 'Southern hospitality' if she had time… If she had time? Of course she had time, although she was now kicking herself at how much time she'd spent listening to Jumpin' Judd Crockett's tall stories.

As quickly as her flustered fingers would let her, she messaged back and found Blue was already in town, quite close by and wanted to meet up now. Now? She hadn't missed her chance after all, thank goodness, but there wasn't time to play it coy. She quickly messaged back to say she was on her way. She reasoned it was probably a good thing that she didn't have much time to think about meeting up with Blue. Was this an actual date? She was feeling uncharacteristically nervous about seeing him again, but she didn't have time to figure out why.

As she headed up Beale Street and towards Peabody Place, she quickly re-touched her lips with a red lipstick from her bag. She was wearing her vintage Levi jeans, but she'd rolled them up at the ankle and teamed them with a halter-neck red top to keep herself cool in the Memphis heat. At least her lips now matched the scarlet-red polish on her toenails, visible in her trusty flat sandals. It made her feel a bit more 'pulled together' although she did inwardly chastise herself for caring so much. It was her nana's past love life she was meant to be concentrating on after all, not her own, but she was pretty sure Nana Rose would understand. In fact, she thought, Nana Rose would understand all this better than anyone!

The sight of Blue leaning against a shop window up ahead drove any lingering worries about her seemingly impossible mission from her mind in an instant. He looked so cool. You didn't see guys quite like this in Llandovery. He was wearing jeans too, a pair in faded blue with a plain white t-shirt casually untucked, his sunglasses looked like Ray-Bans. Classic. Like a modern-day James Dean.

'Hey you.' He came forward as she approached and they greeted each other a little shyly. He asked what she'd been up to, but she didn't want to confess about meeting with Jumpin' Judd Crocket or indeed anything about what she was trying to achieve while she was in Memphis. He thought she was simply a tourist on the rock 'n' roll trail and that's exactly what she wanted him to believe. She reasoned that an officer of the law might take a dim view of someone trying to establish a connection to Memphis's most famous son; he might even think she was some sort of crazed gold digger. She simply said she'd just been sightseeing and that she hadn't wanted to go with the others on a trip to an out-of-town mall. That much at least was true.

Blue nodded as though he understood completely. 'D'you know about this shop?' he asked, indicating the clothing store they were standing right in front of. Daisy suddenly noticed the golden swirly lettering painted on the window *Lansky Bros*.

'Oh wow! Where Elvis used to shop?' She knew all about the store that proclaimed itself 'Clothier to the King'. This had been where Elvis had bought jazzy shirts and peg pants with pink stripes down the side even before he was famous.

They spent a fun half hour inside. It was a great ice-breaker as Daisy pulled out shirts and jackets on the rails that had clearly been inspired by designs Elvis had famously worn in his private life and on film. There was

127

even a blue knitted sweater with a turned-up collar like the one he'd worn in *Jailhouse Rock*.

She spotted a yellowing receipt from 1957 in a frame on the wall and stood on tiptoe to see, fascinated. It was clearly made out to Elvis Presley although the eight items listed were not so easy to read. The total came to $103.12. Daisy thought you wouldn't be able to buy much in the store today for that price. She'd loved a black Western-style shirt with lustrous turquoise embroidery on the shoulders and across the back – but she'd put it straight back when she looked at the tag. Following in the shopping footsteps of the King came at a pretty hefty price nowadays.

When she said as much to Blue, he led her over to a display of t-shirts. These were much more in her price range and she couldn't resist a grey marl one with a silver 'TCB' emblem embossed on the front – Elvis's personal 'Taking Care of Business' motif. They left the store with Daisy delighted to be swinging a Lansky Bros bag from her arm.

'You hungry?'

Daisy remembered her rumbling tummy when Blue asked the question and nodded her head vigorously.

'Wow, that's hungry!' Blue laughed, teasing her. She didn't usually like to be teased by men, but this didn't feel mean in any way. 'You wanna go eat at Elvis's favourite diner?'

Daisy grinned and nodded again. She was so hungry she would have agreed to eat anywhere, but Blue was clearly determined to show off his local knowledge. She didn't even know Elvis had a favourite diner. They walked a couple of blocks with Daisy trying hard to match Blue's long strides. He seemed to ease up the pace when he sensed he was walking too fast. Daisy figured he must be pretty hungry too.

The Arcade Restaurant was set on a corner and fulfilled every American diner cliché with its neon signs, leather-seated booths and menu of burgers, shakes and Southern specialities. There was even a row of red stools running the length of the bar, with Cocoa-Cola signs and notices that read *Home Made Hot Biscuits* propped on the high shelves behind. It was like stepping back in time. Daisy was sure Nana Rose had told her about visiting a place just like this when she here. On their way in she'd spotted a sign outside announcing it was Memphis's oldest restaurant and if it had been a favourite haunt for Elvis, she was sure Rose would have checked it out. The thought that she was once again following so closely in her grandmother's footsteps gave Daisy a warm glow.

They slid into a booth and Blue handed her a menu. It was huge. Daisy ran her eyes down the dishes and felt like she'd been fully transported into a Fifties movie. This was, quite possibly, the closest thing to heaven on earth she could ever imagine.

She spotted a peanut butter 'n' banana sandwich, with extra bacon – clearly an homage to the King but not one she felt comfortable ordering. Blue went for something called 'The Rainmaker' which was a classic turkey club sandwich. Daisy thought that sounded good but finally decided on the Arcade cheeseburger. It seemed silly not to.

As they sipped their cokes and chatted about this and that, Daisy was amazed at how easy Blue was to be around;

he kept up a steady back and forth asking about her life in Wales and giving snippets of insight into his work as a Shelby County cop. He pointed out how fortuitous it was that he'd been in Tupelo on an errand when their paths had unexpectedly crossed after her boot-buying escapade. He explained that Mississippi was well off his regular patch, so Blue put their chance reunion down to sheer dumb luck.

When the waitress suddenly appeared with their orders, Daisy realised it may have been a mistake to order the cheeseburger after all. It was almost as large as her head! How on earth was she going to eat this and still maintain any sort of dignity? She decided the best thing to do was to forget about that and relish the entire, messy, delicious experience. It was a good metaphor for life really, when she thought about it.

Blue didn't seem phased in the slightest at the sight of her occasionally disappearing behind her enormous burger, which had to be held with both hands, re-emerging periodically to pop another fry into her mouth. She gave the Arcade burger experience her best shot and very nearly ate the lot.

'Dessert?' Blue was teasing her again and she felt comfortable enough to flap a napkin at him in response. It caught him on his upper arm, where the bulge of a tanned bicep emerged from the white cotton sleeve of his t-shirt.

'Assaulting a police officer is a very serious offence, young lady.' Blue wiped his mouth with his own napkin and lowered his voice to a husky whisper. Daisy felt a real jolt of attraction. Was this what had happened to Nana Rose; had she been swept off her feet by a guy with twinkling blue eyes and a Southern drawl? Daisy could certainly see the appeal.

Thoughts of Nana Rose made her pensive and quiet. She was so desperate to tell her about all the sights and experiences of Memphis, and Rose would have loved so much to hear all about it. It was so hard for Daisy to accept that she was gone.

They split the bill and stepped out of the air-conditioned diner into the humid late afternoon air.

'So...' Blue looked up and down the street as though he was trying to figure out what happened next – where to go, what to say.

Daisy felt an unfamiliar wave of insecurity wash over her. She'd thought they'd been getting on really well and she didn't want to go back to the motel alone... not yet. She'd promised Anita and Priya she would head down to Beale Street with them tonight to sample the music bars and nightlife, but that was still hours away. Now she was worried. Was Blue going to suggest heading somewhere else or was he looking for a way to finish this date and leave?

'So... I really need... I gotta walk my dog.'

Daisy looked up at Blue with her mouth open and a bemused look on her face. Was that a euphemism for something?

Blue gave a little snort of laughter at her expression. 'Huh, I gotta dog – Snoopy, he's a big, daft thing and I don't like to leave him alone for too long, he gets lonesome.'

Daisy was still processing this information, but felt a small pang of jealousy for a creature Blue obviously adored.

'Oh... right, okay.' She tried hard not to sound disappointed that she was being dismissed... for a dog.

'Unless...' Blue seemed to be studying her face, trying to gauge her mood.

Daisy tried to give Blue a level stare back, which was tricky as he was a good head and shoulders taller. Whatever happened, she would not give him the satisfaction of knowing she was bothered, she knew better than to give any man – no matter how attractive – that sort of power over her. She'd never done it before and she wasn't about to start now.

'You could come up to the house and meet him if you want? It's not that far, my motorcycle is parked up round the corner. I gotta be at work by eight-thirty so it'd just be a quick visit, if you'd like?'

Blue got all of the words out in a bit of a rush, as though he was worried she might misconstrue his motives unless he laid everything out as quickly as possible.

Daisy felt he gave her too much credit. Perhaps he thought young Welsh ladies were not the sort to agree to accompany strange American men back to their home. He'd clearly not met many young Welsh ladies! Daisy was a grown up. If she wanted to ride on the back of a hunky cop's bike back to what might be a dilapidated shack in the woods for all she knew... well hell, there was only one way to find out. She was pinning all her instincts on this guy being someone she could trust.

This time they both donned motorcycle helmets before climbing on board the bike, Blue produced a spare one from under the seat and they were soon heading north out of the city.

Crushed against Blue's back once again, Daisy relished the sensation; he felt so good. His body was strong and athletic and there was a fresh, citrus smell clinging to him as tightly as she was. She also did a quick cross-check that she hadn't taken complete leave of her senses. Was this too reckless, even for her? She quickly dismissed the notion and decided that she wanted to experience Tennessee through the eyes of a local and when an opportunity like this arose, how could she possibly resist? No one could blame her. Although, if she ended up bound and gagged in a basement for the next fifteen years, no one would actually know! She told herself not to be so ridiculous.

They passed a sign announcing they were entering an area called Millington. It was residential with houses set here and there either side of the wide, empty road. Not big, posh houses, they were mainly one-storey traditional ranch-style homes, some neatly painted and others more down at heel. Daisy was itching to see where Blue called home. She hadn't even asked if he lived alone? He surely wouldn't be bringing her back if he lived with his mother? She was also fairly confident that an invite like this must also rule out the risk he might actually be married. Good to establish.

After a little while, they swung off the road and up a short track towards a brick-built house. At least it wasn't a tumbledown wooden hut with a tin roof. Phew! Daisy tried to look over Blue's shoulder to see better, but a large willow tree in the front yard was blocking her view. As they came around the tree, Blue slowed the bike down to a stop and they both jumped off. She took in her first glimpse of the house as she removed her helmet and handed it over.

The house wasn't large but it had a certain charm. It was stone-built in a style that looked like crazy paving. Two grey stone pillars held a triangular portico over the wooden front door, two windows faced the front, one on either side, and she was thrilled to see a covered porch ran right across the front of the house surrounded by wooden railings. Now she looked closer she saw a small dormer window in the slate roof – perhaps there was also an upstairs floor?

Blue saw her taking it all in and grinned. 'It's only humble, but it's home.' The sound of a barking dog interrupted him and he laughed and yelled, 'Alright, alright… I'm comin', Snoop, hold on… I brought someone special to meet ya.'

Daisy followed him up the steps and spotted a white wooden swing seat hanging on chains from the rafters at one end of the porch. She was thrilled by it. It was more *Seven Brides for Seven Brothers* than *Gone With The Wind*, but she decided she liked it; it was adorable.

Inside, the front door opened straight into one large room with an old brown leather sofa that looked well-worn but comfortable. Plump cushions and an Aztec-patterned rug in fiery tones of red and orange gave the room a cosy feel. There was even an enormous stone inglenook hearth. Daisy had a sudden vision of cosying up with Blue in front of a roaring fire. Blue, however, was moving straight through the room headed for a back door straight ahead. Moving to catch him up, Daisy noticed a wooden staircase – there *was* an upstairs. A compact kitchen was on her right through a small archway. She presumed the door on her left, behind the staircase, was the bathroom.

Blue unlocked the screen door to the rear of the house and they stepped out onto another decked wooden platform. The barking dog was louder now but Daisy still hadn't seen him. She focused first on the amazing view. The land ahead was flat with patchy grass all around, but then a hill rose up towards the horizon and there was forest as far as she could see.

'Good, huh?' Blue looked as pleased as if he had personally planted every tree. 'Some of the guys at work live in apartments right in the city. Handy for work 'n' stuff, I s'pose, but I don't think I could breathe in one. You know what I mean?'

He headed down the steps in front of her and Daisy suddenly saw a large pen a little way from the house. Inside was an enormous Great Dane that was literally losing its mind.

'Okay, okay... I'm here, Snoop...give me a second, darn it.'

Blue unlocked a gate in the high-sided wire mesh cage and released the animal, which launched itself straight at his chest.

If meeting Snoopy was a test, Daisy hoped to pass with flying colours. She put up with the sniffing and licking as the dog investigated her thoroughly. She joined in with running back and forth, in and out of the trees at the edge of the woodland, playing hide and seek with the goofy Great Dane, and loved every minute. There was no boundary fence between Blue's house and the next property or the woodland so Daisy could see why the pen was necessary to keep Snoopy safe. It was enormous, but clearly a dog this big had to get more exercise than even his large enclosure allowed.

They finally collapsed, exhausted, onto the front porch, Daisy on the swing seat, Blue on a wooden bench in front of the window with Snoopy lolling at his feet. They swigged from two bottles of beer Blue had brought from the fridge and Daisy took in the view across the quiet road to the couple of houses she could see opposite. It seemed like a nice neighbourhood. Sitting here with Blue, she felt more content than she could ever remember. The awkward first dates with guys back home had never made her feel like this: relaxed and peaceful, like she was finally able to be herself. She could get used to this, she thought. Rainy Wales and her struggling shop were half a world away and she wasn't sorry about that at all.

Just then Blue reached back through the open window and produced an old acoustic guitar.

'You play guitar?' Daisy was delighted – could this get any better?

Blue took the pick stuck into the strings at the neck and plucked a few notes to see if it was in tune.

'Only a little,' he said, his eyes on his fingers as they shaped a chord. 'Do you sing?'

Daisy laughed at the question, 'A little,' she said. 'I don't suppose you know that everyone from Wales thinks they can sing... a little.'

Blue had never heard of such a claim but they spent a while happily attempting half remembered duets of country classics. Daisy knew some of the words to 'Jolene' and Blue figured out some of the chords to 'Green Green Grass of Home'. Neither of them could complete a tune until Daisy asked if he could play 'Blue Moon'. That was one song they both knew and they made a fairly decent job of getting all the way through it, and in Daisy's opinion it didn't sound half bad.

Blue propped the guitar up against the bench he was sitting on. Snoopy had slept through their entire performance.

'So Blue Moon is the name of your store?' Blue was chuckling as he spoke, at Snoopy's lack of reaction. He wanted to know all about Llandovery then and she told him about her shop and how much she loved selling vintage treasures to her customers. She didn't mention there weren't as many customers as she would like, that the bills were piling up and that she'd never felt like she belonged in Llandovery.

'And is there... do you have a boyfriend back home in *Clandovey*?'

Daisy couldn't help but smile at his mispronunciation of the Welsh town. She shook her head. 'No... there's no one, right now.' Her mind flicked back across the last couple of 'dates' she'd had. Back home you had one trip to Nando's and a guy expected several extracts from the *Karma Sutra*. She thought back to Blue's unexpected appearance in Tupelo, like a hero in a movie, how he'd swooped in to rescue her and they'd literally stopped traffic. Today he'd patiently indulged her tourist curiosity and shown her some Memphis sights, he'd even sat and listened as she talked with her mouth full of cheeseburger. He'd now practically serenaded her on his own front porch. Daisy couldn't help but wonder what Blue would be expecting in return.

These were the thoughts skittering across her mind as Blue suddenly put down his beer and got to his feet. 'Sorry but I gotta head back into town soon, some of us have work to do, y'know.'

Daisy blushed almost as red as her halter-neck top at how much she had dared to presume, dared to hope. 'Oh right, yes of course, are you... will you be able to drop me back downtown?'

She stood up too quickly from the swing seat and it unsteadied her, propelling her forwards towards Blue. He reached out a hand and caught her arm, his touch ice-cold from the chilled beer he'd just been holding, and she gave a little gasp.

Blue placed his other hand gently on her other arm and looked down into her upturned face. He spoke softly. 'Well... there is a bus that that goes right into town, the stop is just down the street.'

'Wha...' Daisy started then saw Blue's mouth twitch. He was teasing her... again. She put her hands onto his chest to give him a shove. 'Oh... you...'

Blue barely flinched as she pushed at him. He stood solid and kept his hands on her upper arms. 'Hey, I'm sorry, as if I'd ever leave you stranded?' Daisy looked up into Blue's face as his voice became a murmur. 'I mean we can't have that now, can we?' He kissed her then with lips that were warm and tasted of Budweiser. The words of Rhett

Butler to Scarlett O'Hara flashed across her mind: *You should be kissed, and kissed often and by someone who knows how*. Blue certainly knew how. This was what you called a kiss! The palms of her hands were pressed between the two of them into his chest as he held her firmly by the shoulders; she couldn't move but he didn't press his advantage. Instead he released his grip gently, running his hands down her bare arms as he stepped back, a thoughtful look on his face.

'Daisy, I'd really like to see you again... while you're here.'

She wanted that too, and she wanted to be kissed like that again and again. Blue's kiss didn't compare with any other in her experience. Not too sloppy, nor too tight-lipped, it was soft, sincere and... just right.

As she stood there comparing past kisses like a love-sick Goldilocks, she pushed to the back of her mind the knowledge that this relationship was destined to be fleeting. She was only passing through and therefore it could never be anything more than a holiday romance.

Blue was waiting for an answer, his eyes still on her and his warm touch just inches away. How could a girl apply any sort of logic in such a situation?

She'd worry about the consequences later. For now Daisy moved her body closer to his and murmured, 'Oh yes... yes, me too' and then kissed him right back.

Chapter Fourteen

Daisy had assured her mother that she didn't need to worry about Blue Moon Vintage while she was away. They had planned to take the trip together, after all, and Daisy insisted she could manage any online interest from her mobile. Daisy had said there was little chance of anything needing to be done in the shop. Lilian, however, was not one to leave things to chance.

She'd opened up the shop after finishing work, picking up the post from the mat and checking everything was safe and secure. Some of the mail looked worryingly official and urgent so she tucked them into her bag; she'd decide what to do about those later. Lilian thought it would be just like Daisy to let problems pile up without dealing with them properly. She'd offered to help with the accounts several times but Daisy had resisted all her attempts to get involved. It was so frustrating to be pushed away constantly, why didn't Daisy understand she only wanted to help?

She looked around the shop, unsure what else she could do. The rails of second-hand clothes held no appeal, but she found herself standing at the juke box looking down at the list of songs, her finger hovering over a couple of Elvis tracks... Should she? Dare she? But just then her mobile phone sounded an alert and she reached into her bag to see if it was another message from Daisy.

The picture on the screen was of her daughter in a yellow sundress standing outside a small wooden house. Someone had obviously taken the snap. She hoped that meant Daisy had made at least one friend. The caption read *The house in Tupelo where Elvis was born*. Lilian looked more closely, staring past her daughter with her arms flung wide and studying the small wooden building itself, Elvis Presley's birthplace. Was this tiny house, thousands of miles away, anything to do with her at all? Could her own father have been born here? Really, was it possible? Had someone with her blood lived here, played here, eaten chicken and cornbread at the table, sat out on the front porch on hot Mississippi nights? The whole idea seemed so alien, the world of poor Tupelo folk so far removed from Lilian's ordered and ordinary life, that she might as well have tried to imagine being connected to life on a whole other planet.

Lilian sank onto the pink velvet boudoir chair at the side of the changing cubicle. If links to a heritage in the Deep South of America were hard to accept, then she couldn't even begin to entertain the notion that she could be anything to do with the phenomenon that was Elvis Presley. It was like the whole thing was a bad joke at her expense. While Rose had remained religiously devoted to her beloved rock 'n' roll music over the years, Lilian had deliberately and consistently listened to anything else. She'd always viewed Rose's obsession with vintage Americana – which was inclusive of not only the music but the fashion too – as a highly inappropriate interest. When Daisy first showed signs of sharing the peculiar passion, Lilian had at first despaired and then made a concerted effort to ignore. Resistance was futile and anything she said or did to attempt to dissuade either of them was more than likely to simply encourage them more.

If only she'd asked Rose more questions when she'd had the chance. Why hadn't she button-holed her mother and made her tell her more about her father? It seemed obvious now but somehow, in all the years, those times had never really been there. Lilian's natural inclination to keep calm and carry on had not served her well in this respect, she realised now. If she'd badgered and pleaded, made a fuss or thrown a tantrum, surely then Rose would have had to tell her something?

She'd often wondered if extreme personality traits swung back and forth from generation to generation as each offspring rebelled against the parent. That seemed to be how it worked in this family. Rose's wild tendencies were counter-balanced by Lilian's own more conservative, cautious nature but then Daisy in turn rejected everything sensible and yearned for excitement and risk-taking. It left Lilian feeling like *Ab Fab*'s Saffy with both her mother and daughter playing over-the-top Edina.

The fact that she worked in insurance had long struck Lilian as comically ironic – yet another example of her attempt to create order within the chaos of life. Insurance was a funny old business really. Every day she dealt with people attempting to dodge the consequences of whatever the world threw at them by taking out an insurance policy to cover it. If only she'd been able to insure against her mother going off her rocker and announcing she'd got herself knocked up by a dead rocker! Yeah, it wasn't very likely you'd be able to take out any sort of policy to cover that particular scenario!

Lilian gave herself a shake and decided to take herself home. There was a quiche in the fridge and a new drama starting on ITV at 9pm – that was tonight sorted.

She took one more glance at the picture of Daisy posing in front of the clapboard Mississippi homestead. It was funny how much at home she looked there. Lilian couldn't imagine feeling the same way. Let Daisy try and trace a link if she wanted, it was best to let her get it out of her system. The more she thought about it, the more Lilian doubted there would be anything to find. That way of thinking made her feel much calmer. The trail must have gone cold by now so then Daisy could come home and they could put all this nonsense out of their heads and things could settle back down into a new normality. That's all Lilian really wanted.

Chapter Fifteen

Daisy linked arms with Anita on one side and Priya on the other as the trio made their way down the centre of Beale Street at night. The place was jumping. Daisy thought she had never really experienced the meaning behind that phrase until this very moment.

Blue had brought her back into the city on the back of his bike a little earlier and had dropped her off by the FedEx building around the corner. They'd shared another lingering kiss before he zoomed away, leaving her standing on the sidewalk feeling strangely alone, similar to the way he'd found her in Tupelo just the day before.

The sun was dipping low now and the bright lights of the city were starting to sparkle. Luckily, she'd had a silky red and white kimono jacket in her bag which she'd flung over her skimpy top and secured with its black wide sash belt for the motorbike ride back into town. She even had a pair of red fold-up ballet pumps with her that she'd switched for her sandals. She liked to have alternatives to hand, just in case. She'd noticed an admiring glance from Blue when she produced the jacket and shoes and put them on. Daisy had always known the right outfit brought confidence but it was so refreshing for it to be appreciated, it made her feel ten feet tall. A quick touch-up to her lipstick once Blue had gone and she was ready to join her new friends and see what Beale Street nightlife had to offer.

Scores of people thronged the street. No traffic was allowed, only pedestrian revellers cruised Beale hungry for sights, sounds and maybe some southern fried chicken to round it all off. One bar they passed had an old bluesman perched on a tiny stage in the window. He played a mournful harmonica tune as he twanged the strings of his ancient guitar. There were just a couple of drinkers sat watching him in the gloomy interior; Daisy and co were in no hurry to join them.

Further along the street, a young girl had gathered more of an audience in a sparkly cocktail bar with her sweet-voiced country singing. Daisy looked questioningly at Anita, but Anita shook her blonde head and pulled them further up the road. She seemed to know what she was looking for, despite never having been here before.

Priya was a little subdued and passively allowed herself to be pulled along in the wake of Anita as though she was a dinghy attached to a galleon in full sail. Daisy was happy just to soak up the atmosphere, a fizz of new excitement inside her every time she thought about Blue, although all this walking was working up quite a thirst.

Suddenly Anita turned towards the entrance to a tiny club. It looked like a greasy spoon cafe, but the nondescript street-level frontage was topped with a gaudy marquee. Surrounded by flashing multi-coloured lights, the black lettering in the centre of the dazzling white background proclaimed: WELCOME – LIVE MUSIC 7 DAYS A WEEK.

Anita must have the ears of a bat, thought Daisy, as it wasn't until she was inside the doorway she heard the familiar riff of 'Blue Suede Shoes' being played by a rocking trio positioned on a small stage at the far end of the long narrow room. The singer held his guitar high up on his chest as he sang into a retro-style mic on a stand, next to him a tubby guy played slap back bass and bringing up the rear was a skinny fella on drums. Anita waved her arm towards an empty table nearby and grinned as if she'd discovered the Holy Grail.

Within minutes, a waitress came to take their order. Anita scanned the cocktail menu with the seasoned eye of a professional bar worker and ordered them all a drink called a 'Naughty Apparition'. Resistance was futile but one sip of the concoction of tequila garnished with mint, a squeeze of lemon and a dash of honey all served over ice and Daisy was sold. Priya had hesitated for a moment but then guzzled hers with no argument either.

'Did Sid want to come with us tonight?' Anita got straight to the point as Priya sucked greedily at the straw in her 'Naughty Apparition' and immediately put her in the spotlight. Like Daisy, she couldn't work out why Priya had not yet revealed to Sid that she knew all about his affair with Lizzy Lizard Tongue.

'Probably,' Priya replied. 'That's why I didn't invite him!'

She slammed her already empty glass onto the table and signalled the waitress for a refill. Daisy tried to move the conversation along,

'I asked that Sean fella if he wanted to come out with us tonight too, but he clearly wasn't interested. What is up with all the guys on this trip?'

Priya fixed Daisy with a hard stare and said firmly, 'Well for a start… they're men!'

Anita and Daisy shot each other a look that said, *'Best not to open this can of worms!'* Priya was obviously not ready to unburden herself about any more of her marital problems. She probably thought she'd told them too much already.

Instead, Anita took the opportunity to question Daisy further about her own love life.

'Last guy I dated back home,' Daisy told her, carefully avoiding the subject of Memphis police officers as she wanted to keep her feelings about Blue to herself for now, 'was the guy who fixes the computer in the shop.'

Before she could expand further on why there could never be any big romance with gormless Gareth, Priya spluttered in horror, 'A techie? That doesn't seem your style!'

Anita nodded wisely. 'You can do so much better than that!'

Daisy felt Gareth wasn't getting a particularly fair hearing, but had to agree the two of them weren't exactly on the same wave-length. To say he wasn't into music was an understatement. They'd once got into a serious bout of talking at cross purposes concerning Chubby Checker,

Chuck Berry and Roy Chubby Brown. She shuddered at the memory. Mind you, he could speak fluent Klingon, so that was a good reason to, you know, *NEVER SEE HIM AGAIN!* She stifled a giggle – poor geeky Gareth.

The waitress had spotted more empty glasses on their table and was back at Anita's elbow. 'What can I get for ya gals?'

'Some decent fellas!' Anita stated boldly, with her empty glass raised to toast the declaration.

Laughing now, the three them chinked their glasses in agreement as waitress Peggy smacked her chewing gum between her teeth. She'd been a waitress a long time and seen the scene before her eyes more times than she cared to remember. Women out on the town, fed up with their menfolk at home and secretly hoping for a Southern gent to come and sweep them off their feet. She was still waiting for her Rhett Butler too, but didn't think it likely he was gonna wander by anytime soon.

'I can't guarantee that, gals, but stick around an' there'll be lots more great music for y'all. Good music's better than any fella anyhow… Same again?'

'Amen to that.' Anita grinned. 'Bloody men! Who needs 'em?'

Daisy felt now definitely wasn't the time to rhapsodise about her afternoon with Blue, especially as Anita was showing all the signs of alcohol-induced melancholy.

'I thought the last bloke I dated was different,' Anita slurred. 'He was a rep from the brewery, shiny suit but nice eyes, you know the sort. Anyway, we went out a few times but then he started moaning about me singing at my regular gig at the Red Dragon, you see. Well, he got his knickers in a twist about me doing a couple of spots a week, thought I should just stick to working behind the bar. Cheeky sod! I told him, "Look 'ere, boyo, who are you to tell me when and where I can or can't sing?"'

Anita stirred the straw in her drink and then suddenly looked up at Daisy and Priya as a fresh thought hit her. 'Oh god! I bet Trachlyn's Got Talent was all *his* idea!'

Daisy pulled what she hoped was a sympathetic face as she realised Anita was probably right in assuming the creep from the brewery *had* sabotaged her prized singing spots. He obviously couldn't handle Anita getting that sort of attention.

'What is it with men who want to control everything you do, but carry on doing anything they damn well please?' Priya's rhetorical response summed up the mood on the table perfectly.

Anita concurred, repeating herself for emphasis, 'Bloody men! Who needs 'em?'

Daisy excused herself and made her way to the 'restroom' – she vowed never to call public toilets 'ladies loos' ever again, 'restroom' was so much cooler. The rockabilly trio on stage were storming through 'Baby Let's Play House', the singer stuttering the word '*B-b-b-b-b-b-baby*' as she wove through the tables.

In the sanctuary of the restroom, she took a moment to go over in her mind events so far and think about the fact that tomorrow they were going to Graceland. Graceland! The thought of stepping inside Elvis Presley's home was thrilling, with or without any possible family connection.

Daisy Featherstone looked at herself in the mirror. She was proud of her name but the need to know more about where she really came from was now burning inside her. She reasoned it must be the same for her mother too, surely even more so. Was that why she hadn't come, because it was all too much? Lilian had never been given any clues to her father's identity. All through her life she had deliberately never asked and so Rose never told. No wonder Lilian had grown up with a formidable 'I don't need anyone' attitude, thought Daisy. Better to be hard as nails than soft as putty, less chance of getting hurt. Whatever feelings Lilian had about it all must be bottled up so tight it was a wonder her head hadn't exploded like a cork out of a bottle of shaken fizz.

Nana Rose's death had left such a huge hole in their family. But would finding the truth about her grandfather help to fill that hole? Daisy pondered the question; even if it was the King of Rock 'n' Roll himself, could it ever go any way to compensate for the loss of Rose? Was that what she was trying to do, distract herself from her grief?

Daisy bit her lip and gripped the sink with both hands as if to steady herself. She couldn't start to doubt her own motives now. She wasn't trying to *replace* Rose, that would be impossible, but she did want to understand her better. They'd always been so close and also so alike, but to really understand and remember Rose properly, Daisy had to try and find the missing piece of this puzzle. The answer to who her grandfather was would not only reveal so much more about Rose, it would also tell Daisy more about herself, she was sure of it.

The identity of Lilian's father, her own grandfather, had suddenly taken on an importance it had never had before. Could Elvis, *the* Elvis Presley, really have anything to do with it all? It seemed incredible, but he was human just like everyone else. Wasn't he?

Daisy remembered a quote she'd seen somewhere where Elvis had said: 'I put my pants on one leg at a time'. She knew he meant he was just like any other guy. He had friends, met girls, dated even, could he really have crossed paths with Rose when she was just a girl? Could one thing have led to another? It seemed... impossible... and yet... Rose was so adamant. Her confused state surely hadn't turned her into an outright liar. She'd looked both Lilian and Daisy in the eyes and told them in no uncertain terms that they were related to Elvis Presley. Something in that claim resonated with Daisy. It connected with something deep inside her. Somehow, in some way, it had a ring of truth.

But then why would Rose have kept something like that to herself all these years? It wasn't too hard for Daisy to figure out the answer to that one – for the same reason that she hadn't breathed a word about all this to Blue or even Anita and Priya and had no intention of doing so either. Not yet. They'd think she was looney tunes. Or worse, some sort of fame-hungry wannabe who wanted nothing more than to be interviewed about her outrageous claims on *Good Morning America* while staking even more outrageous claims to the Presley fortune.

No, even if she discovered that Elvis Presley *was* her biological grandfather, Daisy couldn't imagine facing his only daughter Lisa-Marie in court and fighting her for any inheritance. She shuddered at the very thought of the trouble that would cause. She'd be disbelieved and hated by every Elvis fan in the entire world, and there were millions of them; they could make the entire Featherstone family's life a misery. She wanted the truth to bring some sort of comfort, not a lifetime of notoriety.

Tequila had certainly brought some clarity to her thinking. Who'd have guessed it would have that effect? A couple of 'Naughty Apparitions' and she'd started to get her muddled mind in some order.

Back at the table Anita and Priya presumed the opposite and welcomed her back with indulgent smiles, believing the cocktails had knocked her for six and she'd probably spent the last twenty minutes throwing up.

The rockabilly trio had finished their set and were packing up their instruments ready to head off to their next gig in another bar across town. Anita was holding forth on how life was something to be *lived* and opportunities were to be *grabbed*.

Priya was a receptive audience. 'That's bloody right. Life stuck in a rut is no bloody life at all.'

Daisy was about to whole-heartedly agree – hadn't she grabbed the opportunity to come on this trip when it unexpectedly presented itself? With Rose gone, the ties that bound her to her hometown felt loose and insubstantial and she'd relished the chance to escape to a place where she felt so inspired and alive. But before she could speak, she was cut short by waitress Peggy's voice announcing from the mic on the stage, 'Guys and gals, please give a red-hot Blues City Cafe welcome to MR CHANCE BAILEY.'

A good-looking, grey-haired man of around sixty stepped up onto the stage. With a matching silver beard, wearing a two-tone western jacket over blue jeans and with beaten-up cowboy boots on his feet, he was a dead ringer for Kenny Rogers.

Priya thought differently. 'Oooo, he looks just like that Howard Keel – you know, the one who was married to Miss Ellie in Dallas!'

Anita said nothing, possibly because if she opened her mouth her tongue might just hang right out of it.

Chance leaned into the mic and a low rumble of a voice rolled across the space between the stage and their little table. 'Evenin', folks, I hope y'all are in the mood for some good ole tunes tonight. Here's one of my most fav-ou-rites.'

He struck a chord on his guitar and sang the opening line from 'Chantilly Lace', a pure Fifties confection of politically incorrect ponytails and pretty faces and girls who wiggled and giggled. One look at Anita, and Daisy could tell that she loved it! By the time he got to the bit that revealed what it was that he particularly liked, he seemed to have sensed Anita's laser stare cutting right across the room and was singing straight at her.

Daisy couldn't be sure how it actually happened, but within the next half hour Anita was no longer sat with them at their table but instead was up on stage, next to Mr Chance Bailey, looking for all the world as if it was where she belonged. She whispered in his ear, he gave her a devilish grin and there they were, singing the Johnny and June Carter Cash classic duet 'Jackson' as though they'd performed together a hundred times.

Their fever did indeed seem hotter than a 'pepper sprout'… whatever that was? They had the attention of everyone in the room and it didn't look to Daisy as though there was much likelihood of *this* fire going out any time soon.

A good while later, after a wide and varied selection of songs, Anita and Chance completed their impromptu performance, accepted the appreciative applause, exchanged contact details along with some lingering looks and finally headed their separate ways.

Back at the motel, as the three women made their way down the walkway towards their rooms, Priya felt she couldn't let Anita completely off the hook,

'So what happened to your "Bloody men, who needs 'em" mantra?'

'I never said that!' Anita snapped, her memory clearly as short as her temper.

Priya and Daisy snorted with laughter.

'Yes you did! That's exactly what you said.'

Anita pulled a comical face and smirked then, but had no answer for Priya.

Daisy decided Anita deserved a pull on the other leg before they all turned in. 'So, you gonna take a chance on *Chance*, then, Anita?'

But Anita was more than a match for her and mocked her right back. 'Huh, says the girl besotted with a guy named *Blue*!'

Was it that obvious? Daisy felt herself blush to the roots of her dark hair and felt that gave her away more than anything she might have said.

Priya had well cheered up since earlier in the evening and was practically hooting as she said, 'Chance and Blue, those names, I mean, you couldn't make it up!'

'Well, your fella is called *Sid!*' said Anita in response, 'so I don't know what you're laughing at.'

Priya sobered up quick but had a sudden determined air about her; 'Huh! Well, we'll see about *that*!'

She fumbled with her key as they reached her door, finally finding the lock. The door swung open into the darkened room; Sid must already be in bed. Priya lurched forwards and kicked the door shut behind her without so much as a backwards glance.

Anita and Daisy gawped, then guffawed.

'I don't know who I feel more sorry for right now,' said Anita as they stumbled further down the walkway. 'Priya or Sid?'

'I know what you mean,' said Daisy, scrabbling in her bag for her room key. Where was it? She couldn't have lost it with that enormous wooden heart fob attached to it. She began to quietly sing the Abba tune 'Take a Chance', steadily ramping up the volume as she got to the repetitive chorus.

She made a dive for her room before Anita could swat her, still singing as she entered the room and closed the door. Anita loomed up at the window onto the walkway and mocked her, calling, 'OK, Moody Blue, two can play at that game!' Then launched into a tuneful burst of Elvis's Seventies hit song.

Touché, thought Daisy, laughing as she closed the curtains. Clearly, she wasn't as good at keeping secrets as she thought, she needed to work on that!

Chapter Sixteen

Daisy had fallen quickly into a deep sleep, the tequila no doubt helping enormously.

Snug in the large double bed, she was watched over by a picture of Nana Rose she'd propped against the bedside lamp and a portrait of young Elvis that hung on the wall over by the coffee machine; American hotel rooms rarely, if ever, contained a kettle.

The picture of Rose was one of her favourites; she'd prised it from its frame to bring with her on this trip. She remembered so well the day it was taken. Rose and Lilian had come down to Cardiff for the day to visit her student digs. Lilian had spent a lot of time tutting and picking up discarded clothing and empty coffee cups while Nana Rose had flung her arms around Daisy and pushed a tin of homemade Welsh cakes into her hands the moment she arrived. Eventually they'd taken her out for a much-needed meal and Daisy always remembered trying to eat her bodyweight in lasagne to make up for the meagre rations she usually lived on as a penniless fashion student.

She also remembered Lilian's rather low opinion of the thrift-shop look she had been wearing that day. While Rose had ooohed and aahhed over the high-waisted loose trousers, worn with striped blue braces and a yellow beret, the second-hand men's lace-up brogue shoes that completed Daisy's outfit had been the final straw for her mother.

'You could be wearing a dead man's shoes,' she'd said, appalled at the thought.

She was even more appalled when Daisy strutted down the street as Rose shouted, 'Coming through, dead man walking' to confused passers-by.

Rose had brought a camera along and they'd taken a few photos to commemorate the visit before the two older women left for the train journey back home. Daisy had taken one of her mum and Nana sitting on a wall outside the station. It was early evening and the sun was shining straight at them, a typical amateur photographer blunder. Lilian's squint had made her pull a terrible face so Daisy cut her out of the picture she eventually framed, but Rose had held her hand up to shield the glare and was smiling broadly and blindly towards the camera. The golden glow captured in the picture gave Rose a radiance that made Daisy think her nana looked the way she must have done as a young girl. In fact, as she'd packed the picture in her suitcase ahead of her trip to Memphis, it had occurred to Daisy that a young Rose would have looked a lot like a teenager called Priscilla Beaulieu.

• • •

Loud banging on the door of the motel room woke Daisy with a start. Bleary and confused, she opened the door expecting to see Anita or more likely Priya, fresh from some new fall-out with Sid. Instead, there were two stocky men standing shoulder to shoulder in matching uniforms of suit and tie and dark sunglasses.

Daisy looked down at her patterned pyjamas and back at the men. Her first thought at being woken in the middle of the night by two strangers who looked like something straight out of *Men in Black* was *not* that she could be in imminent danger, but that *they* might be horrified by her choice of Mickey Mouse nightwear.

The slightly taller of the two men spoke first. He didn't mention the Mickey Mouse pyjamas. 'You need to come with us now, miss.'

Daisy was struggling to process what was happening. 'What? Now?' She didn't even think to add to more obvious question, '*Why?*'

The shorter man spoke from behind his shades, the smile that was twitching his mouth taking the edge off his stern appearance. 'The boss wants to see you.'

Daisy felt there was no alternative but to follow the men's instructions. She threw a leather jacket over the ridiculous pyjamas and pushed her feet into a pair of red ballet pumps lying on the floor where she had kicked them off earlier.

She was soon sitting on the back seat of a black limousine as it sped down Elvis Presley Boulevard. The street was dark and deserted and Daisy wondered how the men could see the road while wearing shades.

She finally worked up the courage to ask a question. 'So your boss… He's…' She let the question hang in the air for just a moment and the shorter, more smiley guy answered immediately,

'You know very well who "the boss" is, honey.' His tone was friendly, teasing even.

Daisy decided that two could play that game. 'But isn't Graceland in the opposite direction?'

The taller man who was at the wheel simply stated, 'We ain't goin' t' Graceland.'

Before she could ask anything further, the second guy added, 'Yeah, 'E has rented Libertyland tonight. He just loves havin' the whole amusement park to himself, don't he, Joe?'

Joe's tone now became more relaxed and jovial too. 'Too right, Charlie, bet you won't take three times round on the Zippin Pippin tonight without barfin' up your burger.'

Charlie clapped his hands together and wagged a finger in Joe's face. 'You got yourself a bet!'

They chuckled amiably together and Daisy felt the world lurch beneath her as though she was already on a roller coaster as the car swung off the highway.

Joe spoke over his shoulder as the street lights flashed an eerie yellow light across the car at regular intervals. 'We know why you're here, young 'un.'

What did that mean? What did they know? Why *was* she here?

Before there was time to find answers to any of her

questions, the car drove through a darkened archway and pulled to a stop. Charlie jumped from the car and opened the backseat door. Peering out, Daisy could see the looming shadows of enormous fairground rides against the night sky. There were a few people milling about by a couple of wooden stalls.

Charlie reached towards her and took her hand, gently guiding her out of the car as he spoke softly. 'You're gonna get all the answers you're looking for, sweetheart.'

She allowed herself to be led forward just a few steps then the sky in front of her suddenly burst into a dazzling spectacle of multi-coloured lights. A whining musical tune whirred into life to accompany the sight of a slow-moving Ferris wheel rotating slowly into action. Daisy gazed in astonishment at the empty coloured carriages swinging one after the other as they worked their way up and over and down towards her as the wheel turned a cycle – red, blue, yellow then red again. Joe and Charlie remained standing silently just behind her, but now they each gave her a little shove forward.

'C'mon now, don't be shy.'

'Let him get a good ole look at you.'

Stunned by the vision in front of her, Daisy registered a solitary figure in one of the blue carriages making its way up to the top of the wheel.

She knew who that was.

She breathed his name. 'Elvis?'

Sixty feet in the air, there was no way the figure in the carriage could have heard her, but he shouted down over the drone of the music, 'Daisy? Is that you, baby?'

This couldn't be happening.

The swinging blue cart crowned at the top of the wheel and Daisy lost sight of the figure completely. Rooted to the spot, she kept her eyes fixed on the cart as it lowered itself towards her. The front of the carriage cage was open, a metal gate the only safety barrier. The first part of the man that came into vision were his black heeled boots, then the wheel rotated further, lowering the cart some more. Legs in tight black trousers, bejewelled hands resting on the knees, now appeared. A silk scarf in scarlet red was hanging from the man's neck; it was bright against his black shirt in the glow of the fairy lights that adorned the Ferris wheel. It was him. He was unmistakeable. He spoke again, his voice rich and familiar,

'I've been dying to see you, baby... Baby?'

Slowly, Daisy moved her transfixed gaze towards the man's face...

Her eyes snapped open.

The room was pitch black, just a shaft of moonlight from between the curtains at the window pierced the gloom.

She started to exhale in relief, but the shuddering breath caught in her throat as she spotted him. There, in the darkness, at the end of her bed stood a man looking down at her. He spoke, 'Baby?'

Daisy lunged for the bedside lamp and light filled the room.

Elvis Presley, resplendent in a dazzling white jumpsuit complete with jewelled cape, stood there, large as life.

Daisy screamed.

Elvis screamed.

Daisy pressed herself back against the headboard and clutched wildly at the bedcovers as Elvis staggered back in shock. He raised his hands in front of him and spoke again. 'I so sorry... please forgive...'

His voice was thick with an accent Daisy couldn't place.

The motel room door burst open with a bang and Anita and Priya tumbled into the room. Priya was wielding a shoe while Anita, brandishing a large can of hairspray, roared, 'WHAT THE HELL IS GOING ON IN HERE?'

Priya took in the sight of terrified Daisy at the head of the bed, then followed her stare to the white-caped figure. 'Daisy... are you alright? VAL!'

Elvis held his outstretched arms towards Priya and spoke in a voice thick with emotion. 'Priya, my baby!'

Priya ran straight into his arms and as he buried his face into her hair, he lovingly murmured, 'Kroshka.'

Daisy and Anita remained frozen as their terror turned to utter shock. Anita was the first to find her voice. 'Priya? You know him?'

They both continued to watch in amazement as Priya snuggled herself further into the arms of her caped object of obvious desire. Unseen at the open doorway, a bleary-eyed Sid surveyed the scene.

'Well, it certainly looks like it!' His voice dripped in sarcasm and Anita and Daisy stared at him as he stood there in striped boxer shorts and a rather inappropriate Mr Tickle t-shirt.

Still clinging to Elvis, Priya didn't seem the slightest bit bothered to be discovered *in flagrante*. In fact, she was positively beaming. Proudly, she began formal introductions,

'Well, we've never actually met in person before.' She continued to gaze up in adoration at the man who held her tightly. 'But this is Val... Valentin.'

Val shook his head a little as he looked at Priya in wonder. 'They tell me at reception... this your room.' Tearing his eyes from Priya, he looked at Daisy with apologetic puppy dog eyes. 'I so sorry.'

What *was* that accent?

Anita spoke for the room; 'Does anyone have a Scooby Doo what is going on?'

Sid's sarcasm turned venomous. 'I think I've got a fair idea!'

Priya ignored him and added proudly, as though it explained everything, 'Val is Russia's *leading* Elvis impersonator.'

Anita felt this last piece of information only really added to the confusion. 'Well, of course he is!' Irony was clearly wasted on this crowd, but she continued with eyebrows raised. 'Does he dress like that all the time?'

Valentin had the grace to try and explain. 'I wanted nice surprise for my Kroshka.'

That didn't really help too much so Sid took it upon himself to throw a little more light on the situation.

'This whole trip was a set-up so she could meet up with this... this... *gigolo*. She let me think "Val" was Valerie – a woman, a girlfriend she used to go to school with who'd emigrated to Australia!'

Priya didn't even bother to look in Sid's direction, she simply whispered up at Val while stroking his luxuriant sideburns. 'Come on, Val, let's get out of here.' Leading him past Anita, she gave a rueful shrug and giggled. 'For some women it's firemen.'

Sid spread his weedy legs and puffed out his chest, spreading Mr Tickle's arms to their fullest extent in an attempt to bar the door. 'Priya, what the hell do you think you are doing?'

Priya kept a tight grip on Val's hand as she drew level with Sid and spoke directly to him for the first time since this bizarre incident had begun. Her words shrank Sid instantly and left their exit path clear,

'What's it to you? *Tiger Man!*'

Chapter Seventeen

D aisy lay for quite a while listening to the continued commotion on the walkway outside her motel room. She was wide awake now. The sudden appearance of a Russian Elvis impersonator at the end of your bed will have that effect, not surprisingly.

As the arguments eventually quietened down, her thoughts drifted back to her dream encounter with the real Elvis; at least, it had seemed so real. It had felt as though she was about to make some sort of breakthrough, like she was on the brink of discovering something important.

She tossed and turned in the bed, trying to settle her restless mind and body. Was she any closer to finding out the truth? There certainly was something about the atmosphere of this place that got under your skin. Memphis did indeed feel like her spiritual home but she needed more than just that feeling to prove a solid genetic connection to the birthplace of rock 'n' roll.

She turned over again and the photograph of Rose, her

face glowing in a Cardiff sunset, caught her eye. Daisy sat up and reached for the picture.

The Rose she had known had been full of love, life and fun, but that was clearly not the full story. Being a young unmarried mother must have been extraordinarily difficult, but Rose was from a generation who knew how to keep things private. They didn't share their tears and troubles with the wider world, posting personal information on social media and searching for sympathy via Facebook or Twitter. It was always worth remembering, thought Daisy to herself, that the lives that went before were just as full of drama and heartbreak, love and loss, as those today. Romance and passion were not recent inventions and if Nana Rose had fallen for someone in the same way as she was falling for Blue, it wasn't hard to imagine exactly how she must have felt.

She looked intently at Nana Rose's smiling face; if only she could delve into the memories that were stored behind those twinkling eyes, and discover more about what had really happened.

Memphis, Summer 1960

Rose had come to, flat on her back in front of the Graceland music gates, and for a moment could not remember where she was. Whether it was the Tennessee heat, a lack of food or the thought of being so close to Elvis Presley's home, she couldn't be sure, but for the first and only time in her life she had fainted.

Squinting up at the man who loomed over her, she was flustered and embarrassed but he spoke in a kindly drawl and gently helped her to her feet. Once she got to look at him properly, she went weak at the knees all over again.

Rose's chance encounter at the gates of Graceland quickly led to an unexpected whirlwind romance. The man was handsome with an easy charm and a devilish sense of humour that Rose found impossible to resist. He was instantly besotted with this tiny dark-haired girl who he quickly realised had far more sass and spirit than the fainting spell that brought them together might suggest.

Rose begged Jennifer-Jane to help her continue this dangerous liaison. They were both terrified that she'd be sent straight back home to Wales if Jennifer's big sister Jeannie and her husband Frank found out. Jeannie's acceptance into genteel Tennessee society had not been easy and she lived in fear of something causing the polite invitations to ladies' luncheons and gala balls to suddenly terminate. This situation would be exactly the sort of thing that could sully the family reputation.

At first it was easy enough for the girls to cover their tracks. Jennifer was already courting an approved admirer from a respectable family in Shelby County. Wade Benson Junior was an eligible bachelor with enough money and prospects to keep Jennifer-Jane Jenkins in the style to which she had become accustomed. Luckily, he was so devoted to his Jen-Jen he was more than happy to help keep their secret. The fact that he also got to spend time alone with his girl as a result was a happy state of affairs for him too. Maybe a few dates without a chaperone would allow him to get past 'first base'.

Preoccupied with balancing the needs of whirlwind twins Bobby Ray and Beau Barley while also keeping up appearances with her new clique of friends, big sister Jeannie believed Rose was *a convenient chaperone for Wade and her little sister on dates to coffee bars and movie nights. In truth, the girls would say they were meeting Wade and friends away from the house and then return together after spending passionate nights in the arms of their lovers.*

As time went on, the girls grew braver with the risks they were willing to take.

Rose quickly discovered she couldn't always guarantee she would be able to make it to an agreed rendezvous point so that the girls could arrive back at Walnut Grove House together and at an acceptable time. That's when Jennifer introduced her to the estate's secret tunnel.

Hidden in the basement of the outbuilding where Jen had her office was a door that led to a subterranean passageway. Jennifer explained that at the time of the Civil War, there was a network of such tunnels in the area connecting Southern estates such as Walnut Grove to what became known as 'The Underground Railroad'. It was a term used to describe the escape routes used by black slaves on their dangerous journey to freedom. 'Underground' referred to the secret nature of the operation while 'Railroad' described the links between various safe havens – known as 'stations' – that slaves attempted to navigate with the help of those sympathetic to their cause.

'You see, not all of the passageways and routes were literally underground, but we are lucky to have one that really is,' said Jennifer as she opened the thick wooden door and showed Rose the entrance to the tunnel for the first time. 'The people who helped the slaves at each point were known as "conductors". I think it's so wonderful that someone here at Walnut Grove House risked their own life to help others in such an incredible way.'

Jennifer's time spent learning about the running of the estate on which she lived had yielded unexpected rewards. Rose realised that the history of slavery, segregation and the ongoing difficulties between black and white Americans was complicated and constantly evolving.

At first she was nervous about the idea of plunging into the unknown darkness of the tunnel. 'Where does it go?' she asked. They chose one sunny afternoon to explore it together, that way it didn't seem quite so intimidating and scary a prospect.

Jennifer showed her a ledge just inside the door where oil-burning lanterns were kept. She advised that the lanterns should never be removed from the tunnel, simply left at one end or the other each time they were used so there would always be one available.

The tunnel sloped downwards quite steeply at first then levelled out. Jennifer and Rose had to bend their heads slightly in places, but in others it was tall enough for them to stand up straight. It was well built with wooden struts evenly spaced and the ground beneath their feet had long since been worn smooth. Long stretches seemed straight, with the light from their lanterns illuminating a good way ahead; other times a kink in the direction of the tunnel made it twist and turn slightly, although there were no sharp corners.

The passage was several hundred feet long, enough to take them off the Walnut Grove estate land completely and after a brisk ten-to-fifteen-minute walk, they arrived at a similar wooden door to the one they had left behind in the office building basement. The door opened inwards and Rose stepped out into cool semi-darkness despite the heat of the day. She found it was set into the side of an archway beneath a road bridge. The mossy ground indicated it *may once have been a waterway but the riverbed had long since dried out.*

The Walnut Grove secret tunnel was the key to Rose being able to conduct her clandestine romance with less chance of detection. Jennifer could come home alone if necessary, making out the two of them were returning together and Rose would follow later, using the tunnel as her way to slip back to the house. Other times she would retire to bed having said goodnight to all, then slip away via the tunnel while everyone was asleep. A car, or more often a motorbike, would be waiting at the archway to whisk her away when she emerged. The risks were high but, to Rose, the rewards were worth it.

Flying through the Memphis nights on the back of a motorbike, holding on tight to the leather-jacketed figure in front of her, she thought she would have crawled over broken glass if she had to. This was Rose's first experience of true love and she was prepared to risk everything for it.

Chapter Eighteen

D aisy clanked her plate piled high with pancakes onto the table and stifled a yawn as she took her seat opposite Anita in the motel breakfast room. Maybe a sugar rush would wake her up.

Anita regarded her from beneath freshly lacquered lashes. 'Morning, my love, you recovered from your encounter with Elvis last night?'

'What?' Daisy spluttered her hot coffee before realising Anita was talking about the sudden appearance of Valentin.

Laughing, Anita carried on, 'Mind you, I think it was just as much of a shock for Priya as it was for you! She's a dark horse.'

Daisy shook her head slowly; last night had certainly been eventful, what with one thing and another.

'Yeah right,' she said between mouthfuls of pancake, 'Priya was mocking *us* about Chance and Blue and all the time she's waiting for a Russian Elvis impersonator to show up and whisk her away.'

Anita leaned towards Daisy for added emphasis. 'Russia's *leading* Elvis impersonator, don't you know!'

Daisy almost choked on her pancake.

'It's not really that funny, though, is it?' Anita added with more concern. 'Not for poor Sid at any rate.'

'Hmmm...' Daisy wasn't at all sure that describing him as 'poor Sid' was particularly accurate. Once Anita, Sid, Priya and Valentin – the improbable Russian Elvis impersonator – had left her motel room in the early hours of the morning, she had been hoping to finally get some restful sleep. Unfortunately an unholy row had erupted on the landing outside her room as Sid refused to go quietly.

It turned out that he'd suspected Priya was up to something, which is why he had insisted on joining her on the trip to Memphis at the last minute. What he hadn't realised was that she was also on to *him*.

'It certainly shook him up when Priya revealed that she knew all about Lizzy Lizard Tongue.' Daisy lowered her voice as they exchanged the juicier bits of gossip.

Anita's green eyes were wide. 'I don't know how she kept it to herself all this time?'

'Mmm, I know.' Daisy chased a couple of blueberries around her plate, 'Well, from what I could tell, once Priya mentioned the lovely Lizzy, Sid pretty much did one. I don't reckon we'll be seeing him again.'

Anita wondered aloud if Valentin would be joining them for the rest of the trip now, in the ousted Sid's place.

'I suppose so,' mused Daisy, adding mischievously, 'do you think he's packed enough jumpsuits?'

The two of them giggled like naughty schoolgirls,

'Oh my goodness.' Anita dabbed at her eyes with a paper napkin. 'He can't dress like that all of the time surely?'

It turned out that Valentin had indeed packed clothes other than sparkly cat-suits for his long-awaited assignation with Priya. Following his detention at United States Immigration, Val had been heartily relieved to be reunited with his luggage. The paperwork issue had finally been resolved and Val had been able to explain that his extensive Elvis wardrobe was not evidence that he would be working illegally as an entertainer during his stay in the country, just that his beloved 'Kroshka' was partial to a jaunty jumpsuit and he didn't intend to disappoint her.

The loved-up couple arrived in the breakfast room with their arms entwined around each other's waists and proceeded to feed each other strawberries in a slightly nauseating public display of affection.

Valentin was wearing jeans and a short-sleeved pale-blue polo shirt, although Daisy noted that the collar was flipped up, Elvis-style.

Averting her eyes, Anita explained to Daisy that 'Kroshka' was a Russian term of endearment. They had a bit of disagreement over that, with Daisy asserting that she thought 'Babooshka' was the phrase most used by Russians whispering sweet nothings.

'Babooshka actually means grandmother,' Anita stated with smug satisfaction. Her trivia knowledge could be impressive and wide-ranging, the result of years of eavesdropping on weekly pub quizzes from behind the Red Dragon bar. Working in a pub could be 'quite an education', apparently.

Daisy was on her third cup of coffee and starting to feel real excitement for the Graceland trip scheduled for later that morning when a rumbling voice behind her declaring, 'Heyyyy baby, that's-a-what-ah-like!' announced the surprise arrival of Chance Bailey.

Well, Daisy was caught by surprise, but despite the hot-pink blush that flushed Anita's cheeks, Daisy suspected that this was something Anita and Chance had cooked up between them. In fact, Todd had already added Chance's name to the list on his clipboard and it was all settled that he would be accompanying them for the tour of the mansion. Surprise, sur-bloomin'-prise.

'It's incredible, isn't it?' Anita chattered while stirring her coffee vigorously. 'He's lived in Memphis all his life and yet he's never, ever been to Graceland.'

Daisy fluttered her eyelashes back at Anita. 'Fancy that!'

Before Anita had time to respond, Sean suddenly appeared at their table, jacket on, leather satchel in hand,

'Is it time to go yet? Are you two ready? I've been waiting in reception for ages.' Sean was in an eager mood like they'd never seen before.

'Hold your horses there, Seany, you're keen this morning... for once!' Anita introduced Chance to Sean, who shifted anxiously from foot to foot as if he was pawing the ground ready for a race.

Daisy was keen to see Graceland herself, but Sean's mood of impatient urgency felt a tiny bit out of place.

A little while later, they were all boarding the mini-bus for the short drive to Graceland. Priya and Val were still canoodling while Anita, of course, had to sit next to Chance. She pulled an anguished face as she realised Daisy was to be paired with Sean, but Daisy didn't really mind. She might find out what his story was; she was still intrigued by him. She tried to strike up a conversation, but only got a couple of mumbled responses. She decided not to let it bother her, she didn't want anything to spoil today.

Daisy had dressed especially carefully for today's excursion, in a vintage black dress with a bold red rose pattern. As soon as the dress had come into the shop she'd pounced on it, never expecting she'd eventually wear it to visit the home of Elvis Presley. She'd teamed it with her red ballet flats. Compared to the rest of the group, she looked wildly over-dressed, but Daisy didn't care about that. This was a big day and the dress was also her way of silently honouring Nana Rose.

As they drove towards Graceland, Todd explained that once at the house they could take their time walking through all the rooms and out into the grounds and outbuildings that housed the trophy room and Elvis's racketball court. The final part of the tour included the memorial garden where Elvis was laid to rest in a grave next to those of his mother and father, Gladys and Vernon, and his grandmother Minnie-Mae. Headsets had been handed out to everyone and they would be able to listen to a commentary on what they were about to see at their own pace. That suited Daisy perfectly. She intended to take her time and soak up as much information and atmosphere as she could, once she got inside the Presley home. She much preferred the idea of experiencing Graceland on her own and not having to make conversation with anyone else as she immersed herself in Elvis's world.

Standing inside the entrance hall of Graceland, Daisy looked towards the dining room on her left. The voice on her headset told her that Elvis always sat at the head of the table facing the spot she was stood in right now. The table was laid with white crockery and silver serving platters, pretty fancy considering they were being told Elvis's favourite meal was humble meatloaf served with mashed potatoes. To her right was the living room with a long, low white sofa, ornate stained-glass windows were either side of the entrance to the music room with a white baby grand piano just visible beyond. A pair of colourful peacocks decorated the glass panels, the deep blue of their plumage matching the swag curtains and glass ornaments carefully placed on the mirrored coffee table. It was a glamorous room, no doubt about it.

Daisy lingered as she listened to the commentary, her eyes flickering from place to place around the amazing space she found herself in. She'd seen pictures of the inside of this famous house many times, but she was really standing there, inside Elvis Presley's home.

She thought about other historic places you could visit, like palaces or stately homes, but couldn't think of a single one that was quite like Graceland. The narrator told her that Graceland was the second most-visited house in America, second only to the White House. But this wasn't an official residence or somewhere that had been lived in by a succession of notorious occupants over history, this was a home.

It struck Daisy quite hard that despite all the fancy touches, this was a house that you could really imagine people living in. It wasn't overly large and was surprisingly homely. As soon as you stepped through the door, you felt you were in a welcoming space. She wasn't sure what she had expected, but she hadn't really expected that.

She moved down the hall and peered into a bedroom that had once been used by Elvis's parents and later his grandmother. The commentary explained that Elvis had always called his grandma Minnie-Mae by the nickname 'Dodger' and something about that detail gave Daisy even more sense that Elvis had surrounded himself here with family and kinfolk just like a good ole Southern boy would do. He hadn't moved away, denied his roots or kept his extended family at arm's length, no matter how famous or rich he became. Instead he'd brought them with him to this mansion on a hill, letting his mother keep chickens out back while he parked a pink Cadillac she couldn't even drive out front. It told you a lot about what was important to Elvis.

Daisy had lingered so long looking between just the first couple of rooms that everyone else had now wandered through to the next part of the tour. She pulled her headphones off and heard the bus bringing the next wave of tourists pull up on the driveway outside. For now she was alone, but only for a few more minutes. She turned her gaze towards the staircase that led to Graceland's upper floor. A velvet rope between the bannisters declared the upstairs bedrooms out of bounds and not part of the tour. Daisy knew that access to this area had been restricted ever since Elvis had died back in 1977. She understood why. His body had been found in the bathroom right above where she was currently standing and it would indeed be disrespectful to his memory to have ghoulish visitors jostling to take pictures of the place where the life of the King of Rock 'n' Roll had ended. She knew the unusual double doors to Elvis's bedroom were made of black padded leather. It was said that behind them everything had been left exactly how it had been when he died. How amazing would it be to just try and get a glimpse of those doors? She pressed herself against the wall at the bottom of the stairs and looked up to where blue curtains with a gold trim hung across the wall at the top. She craned her neck trying to see around where the stairs curved to the right in front of them. The angle was just too much. Daisy put one foot at on the bottom step and levered herself up... If she could just see a little bit further.

The front door behind her opened suddenly as new visitors filed in and she quickly jumped back down. Just then, one of the tour guides stepped out from the dining room and gave her a harsh look. Daisy wasn't sure what she had seen, but tried giving her a nervous smile. The stern female guide did not smile back.

Daisy was about to make her escape through the dining room and into the kitchen when she got another surprise.

As she looked back towards the front door at the new wave of people swarming towards her, the stained-glass panels around the doorway caught her eye. They were in the same style as the peacock ones in the living room, but these featured a distinctive black, red and green rose pattern. She recognised that design. Her hands were shaking as she pulled out her camera and took a picture of the glass panel above the door, a reversed letter 'P' for Presley in the centre surrounded by several decorative climbing red roses. What could this mean? Was it simply a coincidence or was this some sort of clue? The rose pattern looked remarkably like the tattoo design Nana Rose had worn on her shoulder. Did this mean there *was* a connection between Rose and Elvis Presley?

Daisy passed through the kitchen, mind still reeling, and only the sight of the Jungle Room that greeted her beyond snapped her back to present reality. Just as she thought she had the measure of the tasteful Graceland reception rooms, and frankly rather ordinary, if somewhat dated, kitchen, the complete madness of the Jungle Room made her question everything she thought she was beginning to understand about Elvis.

Here was rock 'n' roll excess in all its glory. Oversized, ornately carved wooden furniture sat on green deep-pile carpet that crept, like moss, up the walls and even across the low ceiling. What hadn't been claimed by the carpeting was covered in wood panelling that gave the room a treehouse feel. White china monkey statuettes peeped from behind artificial ferns and one entire wall was a stone waterfall. It was bizarre.

She made her way carefully down a steep staircase, also carpeted in green shag pile on all sides and descended into the basement recreation rooms. The first, decorated in acid yellow and navy blue, had Elvis's famous triple TV wall with his signature lightning bolt motif emblazoned nearby. Across the way, a huge pool table sat in the centre of a room draped entirely in patterned fabric. It was like peering into the tented lair of a sultan.

Daisy emerged into hot sunshine as she followed the herd out of the main part of the house. She was more confused than ever about why she was here. Elvis Presley was one of the biggest stars the world had ever known. Like him or loathe him, whether you preferred the Beatles or Sinatra or, heaven help you, Bob Dylan… that was up to you. What couldn't be denied was that Elvis was an icon, a legend, with a lifestyle to match. How on earth could Daisy and Lilian and Rose ever be connected to any of that?

Shading her eyes against the sun, she spotted Anita and Chance coming out of a one-storey building at the end of a paved pathway a little way ahead. Anita 'coo-eed' across the lawn towards her and Daisy answered with a small wave of the hand.

She stood looking around the open space behind the house, her eyes following white picket fencing along the edge of a paddock. She saw a man, on his own, leaning on the rails watching the grazing horses. It was Sean, she was sure of it. Yes, he even had his ever-present satchel slung over one shoulder – what did he carry in there?

Sean had been mad keen to get to Graceland this morning, but it didn't look like it was Elvis's home that was holding his interest right now; what a strange guy he was.

Anita and Chance came over and Daisy found they had already seen the house, the flat-roofed building that housed the racketball court and all of the gold discs, costumes and personal artefacts that were displayed in the long narrow Trophy Room. They were now heading over to the meditation garden.

'Good lord, girl, what took you so long in there? You're meant to be jus' visitin' you know, not movin' in,' Chance was teasing Daisy, and she turned bright red as he looked down on her from his six-foot-two frame.

Anita looked at Daisy with concern. 'Are you okay, love, are you feeling a bit hot?'

Daisy reassured her she was fine, but Anita carried on fretting.

'Are you sure? There was a woman just now who had a bit of a turn, didn't she, Chance? She got all upset when they were telling us about Elvis playing the piano and singing "Unchained Melody" on the very night before he died. She just burst into tears, poor love.'

Daisy felt embarrassed that there were people here, right now, who truly felt they had a real connection to Elvis. He had touched so many lives and people genuinely loved him. Unlike her, those people probably weren't snooping about looking for evidence that they were related to him though. Mind you, she kept having to suppress a nagging suspicion that one of her fellow travellers was up to something dodgy. Daisy was starting to think that Sean was indeed acting like someone who was only there to case the joint. Was he after trying to rob the place? Daisy realised Anita and Chance were looking at her with concern as she stood pondering Sean's odd behaviour.

'What's in that building over there?' She pointed to the door she'd seen Chance and Anita come out of at the far end of the car port.

'Oh, that's the office,' answered Anita. 'There's not much to see but it's where they used to deal with all of his fan mail. How many thousand letters did they say he got a week, Chance?'

Chance rubbed his beard as he thought. 'Oh, honey I'm sure I jus' can't quite remember *exactly* how many, but it had to be brought in by the sack load ever' single day I think they said.'

Daisy told Chance and Anita she'd catch up with them later and made her way over to the nondescript building that was dubbed 'the office'. She knew she'd seen the inside of this building before.

The large one-room office hardly looked like the kind of place where the business of a rock 'n' roll icon was conducted. The headset explained that this office, with its cheap-looking furniture and dingy-patterned carpet, had nothing to do with Elvis's notorious manager Colonel Tom Parker. The folk who worked in this pre-fab outbuilding mainly handled Elvis's correspondence from fans and it had also served as a base for his father Vernon, who had the unenviable task of trying to keep track of his generous son's personal expenses.

Daisy wondered, if she were allowed to examine the

contents of these filing cabinets would she find something, like a bill or receipt that linked Rose Featherstone to Elvis Presley? Might she be within touching distance from yet another clue that hovered just out of reach?

She actually recognised the room from the newsreel footage she had seen of Elvis's homecoming after he returned to Memphis from his army stint in Germany in 1960. The year Nana Rose had been here in Memphis.

A VT of the interview Elvis conducted with the press was running on a loop on a screen set up in a corner of the room.

Daisy watched the familiar images of Elvis in the grounds of Graceland, picking at the icing of a welcome home cake then walking into the office and taking his seat at his father's desk, a phalanx of microphones positioned in front of his face. Her eyes flicked between the film and the actual chair where he had been sitting for the press conference.

Elvis looked lean and fit. Even in the black and white footage you could tell that his hair, shorn at the sides but styled into a floppy quiff at the front, had not yet been dyed black but was a more natural shade of brown.

He also looked a little lost.

Daisy knew this film captured the first time he had returned to Memphis since losing his mother Gladys. She had died right at the start of his two-year stint in the army and coming back to Graceland without her was clearly making this homecoming a bittersweet experience.

Elvis was deferential and polite to the questions about the plans for his career, but the mood shifted when a reporter boldly asked about his love life. Elvis uhmmed and ahhed a while before eventually conceding that there was indeed a 'little girl' he was seeing over in Germany. He was talking, of course, about Priscilla, but he claimed 'there was no big romance'. There was sympathetic laughter from the group of male newsmen when he shook his head and said, 'I gotta be careful when I answer a question like that.'

Daisy knew from her research into everything she could get her hands on about Elvis that there were a couple of reasons he was being particularly coy. Firstly, Priscilla was indeed a 'little girl' when he met her – she was only fourteen years old. However smitten he might have been, he was no fool – it was two years before he saw her again, sending for her to come over for a visit to his home in Los Angeles once she had turned sixteen. The other reason he shifted so uncomfortably in his chair as he was questioned was that throughout all of his time in Germany, right up until he was reunited with Priscilla and for a good while afterwards, he actually had a steady girlfriend right here in Memphis, local blonde bombshell and TV star Anita Wood.

Daisy watched the newsreel as it looped around a second time, Elvis was so charming and good-looking, it was no wonder women adored him and also no wonder he was notoriously unfaithful throughout his life. Could Rose have been just another one of his conquests? Was she just one of many pretty girls Elvis drew into his inner circle for a short, intense time, putting them on a pedestal, making them feel like they were the only woman in his world, before moving onto another, leaving a trail of broken hearts behind? Was that why Rose never told anyone about him, because getting over something like that would have been the hardest thing and she thought no one would ever be able to understand what the experience had been like?

Daisy completed the rest of the tour with her mind pondering these questions and many, many more.

She saw Sean Price again as she made her way to the meditation garden; he was walking back from the main driveway. Perhaps he'd been taking some photos of the front of the house? She was going to ask, but he pretended not to see her and scurried away.

Irritated, Daisy put all thoughts about Sean and his rudeness out of her mind and joined the line of people quietly waiting to pay their last respects to Elvis. The four graves of Elvis, his mother, father and grandmother were laid in a semi-circle and she was surprised to also see a small plaque nearby embossed with the name of Elvis's stillborn twin brother Jesse Garon.

Slowly, the line edged around the low wrought-iron rail that prevented anyone from stepping too close to the graves. All at once she was there, right in front of the tombstone bearing the name Elvis Aaron Presley. A rather macabre thought struck her; this was the closest she was ever going to get to Elvis. She shivered involuntarily in the warmth of the afternoon sunshine. All around the grave were trinkets, flowers and teddy bears left by fans. It had never occurred to her to bring anything. She saw a single red rose lying slightly forlornly on the grass between the graves. Perhaps the wind had blown it there, although the air was warm and still. She quickly bent down and scooped it up, dropping it lightly onto the grave where it landed on the gold lightning bolt TCB emblem. Daisy knew the letters stood for the Memphis Mafia's motto *'Takin Care of Business in a Flash'* and she felt *she* had taken care of as much business as she could herself today. She'd paid her respects, it was time to leave.

She found the rest of her party over at the gift shop mall on the opposite side of Elvis Presley Boulevard. Most had managed to take in the Elvis car museum and a tour of his private jet, the Lisa-Marie, in the time she had spent loitering in the main house and grounds. Perhaps she'd come back another day to see all that, but today she had no appetite for tacky souvenirs.

There was a hold-up before the mini-bus could set back off when they realised Sean was nowhere to be seen, but then someone said he'd told them he'd wanted to walk back to the motel and they were able to leave after all.

Back in her room, Daisy lay down on the bed fully clothed feeling utterly exhausted. The broken night's sleep was catching up with her and she felt emotionally drained. No sooner had she closed her eyes than she fell fast asleep.

Chapter Nineteen

Loud banging on the door of her motel room woke Daisy with a start. Oh dear Lord, the Memphis Mafia were back!

The room was in complete darkness, how long had she been asleep? She was still wearing her black and red rose vintage dress. The digital clock said 23:47, it was almost midnight. With a hammering heart, she approached the door.

'Who is it?' Her voice was shaky and squeaky, even to her own ears she sounded about ten years old. She had to get a grip.

'It's only me, honey… Blue.'

Daisy's stomach flipped all over again as she tentatively opened the door to find Officer Joe Cody standing there in all his uniformed glory. She goggled at the sight of him there on the threshold of her room. Damn, did he get better-looking every time she saw him?

Unable to form a sentence and unwilling to trust her voice with too many words, Daisy finally settled for simply breathing. 'Hi.'

Blue grinned and replied, 'Fancy a run out to Graceland?'

Daisy presumed he was making some sort of joke; he knew she'd spent the day at the mansion and it was practically midnight after all. She gave a little laugh and said, 'Been there, done that, although I didn't actually buy the t-shirt.'

Blue raised one arm onto the door frame and leaned towards her; she caught the fresh, citrusy aroma she was starting to adore as he said, 'Well, the gift shops are closed now so I can't help with that, but I can offer a backstage after-hours tour of the house.'

Daisy stared at him for what felt like a full minute. The sight and sound and smell of him was too overwhelming for a girl who'd woken suddenly. She felt fuggy-headed and confused. Blue stayed where he was, letting the weight of his words sink in, and finally she came to her senses.

'I'll get my jacket.'

Once more riding pillion on Blue's police motorbike, Daisy wondered if this was simply another dream. A late-night visit to Elvis's home was just the opportunity she'd been desperate for. Away from all the other tourists, would she be able to explore a bit more, find something, anything, that could help solve this puzzle Nana Rose had left behind? She couldn't imagine what it was but there was something to be discovered at Graceland that proved Daisy was linked directly to Elvis Presley, she was sure of it, she could just sense it.

Within a few short minutes, they were swinging around and heading straight up to the tightly closed Graceland music gates. Blue pulled the bike up and killed the engine. Daisy looked towards the house and saw it was beautifully illuminated, the four white columns gleaming against the stonework, giving it an ethereal glow.

She had no idea what Blue was now expecting to happen, but before she could question him, a door in the small brick building just inside the gates opened and an elderly man came out. He walked slowly towards them then stopped and peered at them through the wrought iron. He was an old-timer for sure, his wavy white hair wispy on top but turning into sideburns that joined together in a snowy beard on his chin. He was wearing blue jeans and a check shirt open over a faded Sun Studio t-shirt that had, a bit like its owner, clearly seen better days.

His face cracked into a sudden smile as he drawled, 'Howdy there, Blue, you keepin' well?'

'Rockin' and rollin', Wes, you know how it is.'

They exchanged pleasantries for a couple of minutes before Wes eventually turned his attention to Daisy.

'Well, hello there, little lady.'

Daisy had lost the power of speech all over again. What was it about these guys with their cowboy accents that took her breath away? Instead she offered a shy smile in response.

Wes nodded his head at Blue and asked, 'You guys coming in?'

Coming in? Daisy wanted to pinch herself to make sure this was really happening. But Blue just calmly said, 'Yeah, if that's okay?'

'Sure is,' said Wes as though it was the most natural thing in the world. 'It's just me on duty for the night now. You know the way, meet you in the carport.' With that, he simply turned on his heel and began slowly walking up the curved driveway towards the mansion.

Blue kicked the bike back into life and the next minute they had turned off Elvis Presley Boulevard and were heading down a side road. In just a little while and a couple of turns later, they were approaching a large white gate which began to slowly open as they drove towards it. Once inside the electronic gates, Blue headed for a large building that Daisy realised must be the back of the Graceland mansion itself. He drove the bike into a large carport where a couple of trucks and golf buggies were parked, and dismounted, indicating for her to do the same.

Blue took Daisy by the hand and led her towards the house, telling her over his shoulder, 'If he wanted to avoid the fans at the music gates this is the way Elvis would often come and go.'

As he spoke, a screen door just ahead of them started to rattle and then swung open, Wes popped his head out from inside and held the door open for them to enter. As she went to set foot over the threshold, Daisy finally found her voice, blurting out, 'Are you sure this is okay?'

Blue gave her a little shove to push her inside. 'Daisy, chill out, I'm a cop... and he's a Presley!'

Daisy looked blankly from Blue to Wes. 'He's a... a what?'

Wes chuckled, rubbed his hand on the behind of his jeans and then stuck it out towards her. 'Wesley Presley at your service, ma'am, pleased to make your acquaintance.'

Daisy shook his hand in a daze repeating stupidly, *'Wesley Presley?'*

'No one's ever been able to figure just how me an' the big E are kin but there's a whole lotta kissin' cousins in these parts I could blame. As for the name, well, we put that down to my mama and her crazy sense o' humour, but how about you just call me Wes.'

Still chuckling to himself, Wes led them across a short hallway that Daisy did not recognise from her tour of the house earlier in the day, and all at once they were in the kitchen.

She hadn't taken too much notice of this room when she came through earlier that day. She'd been too preoccupied with thinking about the rose motif she had seen on the windows around the front door. Now she tried to soak in every little detail. It had a real Seventies vibe, with all the wood panelling around the walls and patterned carpet in muddy tones of brown and green. Colourful Tiffany-style lamps hung from the ceiling, bringing an extra touch of kitsch to the kitchen; with their decorations of apples and pears they looked like upside-down fruit bowls.

Wes was banging around the place, opening and shutting cupboards and setting out mugs on the Formica worktop. 'You folks wanna cup o' coffee?' He didn't wait for an answer from either of them. 'I'm on duty all night so I know I could do with one.'

Blue was leaning against the breakfast bar, looking as though hanging out in Elvis's kitchen at midnight was just a regular everyday occurrence.

Daisy answered, 'That would be lovely, thank you.'

Wes eyed her as he generously spooned the instant coffee, 'Well ain't you the sweetest little thang, I'm just a sucker for that accent. I've always loved the way you folks talk, say sumthin' else…'

Daisy blushed from her toes to her hairline. 'Mr Presley… Wes, I just can't believe I'm here, thank you very much.' She sounded more prim and proper than she had ever done before. She took the steaming mug from him as he turned and opened the fridge, looking for cream for the coffee.

'Ah bless you, Blue knows he's welcome to come by and keep me company any time and any friend of Blue's is a friend of mine.' Wes paused and looked between his two visitors for a moment before adding, 'He's never bought any other little girl here to meet me before though.'

Daisy shot a look at Blue, but he didn't meet her eyes. Wes carried on as he poured cream into their coffee and offered them sugar. 'This kitchen's always kept stocked with essential vitals, there'll be a few cookies around too I shouldn't wonder. We still look on this place as home, y'see, I reckon that's why it never feels like a museum no matter how many folk come walking through those doors.'

Blue nodded his head. 'You know there were still

members of Elvis's family living here when Graceland was first opened to the public. Tell her about Aunt Delta, Wes.'

Wes gave a long whistle and rubbed his beard before telling Daisy a couple of stories about Elvis's Aunt Delta. He told how she was living at Graceland when Elvis died and was still there when it opened as a tourist attraction in 1982. She lived in the room just across from the kitchen for more than ten years after Graceland was opened to the public. Even though her bedroom and the kitchen were out of bounds of the tour during that time, Wes chuckled as he told how visitors would sometimes encounter a bad-tempered Aunt Delta on her way to cook up bacon while still wearing her nightgown. Legend had it that she even pulled a rifle on a couple of the unluckiest ones.

'Yeah.' Wes was smiling at the memories, 'Aunt Delta sure was a piece of work.'

Daisy noticed Blue was looking at a couple of small monitors on the worktop near where he was standing, the black and white flickering pictures showing CCTV footage of the house and grounds from the outside. So, she thought, that's how Wes was keeping watch while he was inside with them.

Blue suddenly pulled out one of the drawers in the breakfast bar and beckoned her over. 'Hey Daisy, come and look at this.'

It was dark inside the drawer and as she peered in she wasn't sure what she was supposed to be looking at. Blue pulled out his flashlight and shone it into the empty space. There was something written there, in childish handwriting.

The words 'Lisa's home' and 'Graceland' were clearly inscribed into the woodwork.

'This is where she'd sit to do her homework,' said Wes. '*When* she did her homework. Elvis let Lisa-Marie do pretty much whatever she wanted when she was here, but as she so rightly says just there, it *was* her home, it still is.'

Daisy saw a phonebook sitting in the back of the drawer. Wes followed her look and pulled it out,

'1993,' he said, reading the year it was printed off the front. 'The year Aunt Delta went to meet her maker.' Tucking it safely back in the drawer, Wes suddenly seemed to remember something else. 'There's a few neat things hidden around these parts that average visitors don't get to see. Come look at this…'

He headed through the kitchen and into the dining room beyond. Daisy followed but as she did, so she spotted a carpeted staircase tucked into an alcove. Blue clocked her doing a double-take as she looked at it and told her this stairway was the secret way Elvis used so he could come and go from his bedroom to the kitchen without using the grand staircase opposite the front door.

Wes was standing on the other side of the dining table when she caught up with him. He pulled out the chair at the head of the table, Elvis's chair. 'Take a seat, little lady,' he said.

Daisy's eyes were on stalks but she quickly sat down in the chair before Wes changed his mind.

'Here's a little thing no one ever gets to see when they come through here on the tour.' Taking her hand, Wes guided it beneath the table and told her to feel around on the underneath. Sure enough Daisy discovered a couple of wires, leading to a large button. She ducked her head beneath the table and saw what looked like a doorbell fixed to the underside of the table.

'That's so Elvis could call for more meatloaf whenever he felt like it.' Wes was chuckling and Blue looked thrilled at the special treatment Daisy was receiving.

They made their way back into the kitchen and started chatting some more as they finished their coffees. The two guys were easy with each other, joking back and forth and talking about people and places they both knew.

'Blue here was just a young rookie when we first met, what will it be now? Almost ten years back, I reckon?' Wes cocked his head to one side and shook it in surprise at the length of the time gone by.

Blue nodded slowly as he thought back to the call he'd attended at the Presley mansion one April night all those years ago. Someone had driven a vehicle into the Graceland music gates and caused a fair bit of damage. Whether it was a crazed fan or just a random drunk, no one ever knew as the driver was long gone by the time Blue and his partner arrived on the scene.

Laughing, Blue said, 'The first thing outta Wes's mouth that night was "you best check Jerry Lee has an alibi".'

Daisy look puzzled but Wes explained, 'Jerry Lee Lewis got himself arrested years before, when Elvis was still alive. He drove up to the gates wavin' a gun about and demandin' to see Elvis. Bearin' in mind his nickname is "The Killer", we called the cops that night too!'

It turned out it wasn't Jerry Lee who tried to drive

straight through the gates on the night Blue and Wes met though. Lewis was safely down at The Vapors nightclub playing honky-tonk piano and drinking his favourite bourbon whiskey.

With a deep chuckle, Blue added, 'I had to check it out; from all you hear it's the kinda thing you could still believe he would do!'

'He sure is one crazy sonofa…' Wes shot a look at Daisy and pulled himself up short. 'It was the only time the gates were missing from the driveway since Elvis himself had them put there in 1958,' he added. 'They were gone for two days while they were being repaired.'

Remembering more stories from his time as Graceland gatekeeper, Wes also told them about the night a young Bruce Springsteen jumped over the wall and came to knock on the front door to see if his hero was at home.

'Elvis was away in Lake Tahoe so we just walked Mr Springsteen right back down the driveway and put him back out onto the street. He was only a hot-headed young 'un,' Wes said, 'he didn't mean no harm.'

'That's one of the things that struck me about Wes first time I laid eyes on him,' said Blue, looking over affectionately at the old man. 'He was just so laidback and happy in his work. I never met anyone so well suited to their job. He just loves being the gatekeeper to Elvis's world and I can't think of a better guy to be on hand to welcome fans and visitors from all over the world. They deserve a proper Memphis welcome and that's exactly what they get from Wes.'

Wes looked a little humbled by Blue's speech but

muttered something about it being an honour and not just a regular job.

'I've been so busy, I miss being able to come by all the time like I used to,' Blue said.

'I miss you too, son,' said Wes.

Blue put his empty coffee mug on the Formica surface. 'I'll find more time to swing by Wes, I promise.'

Wes's face lit up as he took in this news. 'Well, I reckon I could put up with that if you insist on it.'

They were both grinning like idiots now and Daisy marvelled at how much they each seemed to get from this friendship. It reminded her of the relationship she'd had with Nana Rose; the years between them had fallen away so easily when they were together.

Wes and Blue now took to teasing each other about how little they missed each other while simultaneously plotting fishing trips and hanging out at their regular haunts. They carried on catching up on this and that as Daisy stood hugging her coffee mug, drinking in everything that was happening as well as the strong coffee.

All at once a movement on one of the CCTV monitors caught her eye. Wes and Blue were laughing about something or other and didn't notice, but Daisy took a step closer and looked more keenly at the pictures. Yes, there it was again, a movement in the corner. Daisy wasn't sure what part of the grounds she was looking at, but there was definitely someone there. The figure moved and suddenly darted across the frame. The picture changed to show another angle but she was positive what she had just seen.

Someone was inside the gates of Graceland. Even so, she didn't want to jump to conclusions,

'Uhmm, did you say you were the only one on duty here tonight?'

Wes was smiling as he said, 'That's right, honey, jus' me on my lonesome, though it's mighty fine to have your company tonight.'

Daisy pointed to the monitor. 'I'm sure I've just seen someone on the screen.'

Immediately, Wes's easy manner was gone and he and Blue tore round the breakfast bar and stared at the screens. At first nothing, but then…

'There… there's a guy down by the meditation garden.'

Wes pulled out a walkie-talkie from his back pocket, but Blue's hand was on his arm.

'Be quicker to handle this ourselves, Wes, I can radio for back-up if we need it.'

With that, and a quick instruction to Daisy to 'stay put', they were gone. Daisy stared for a good while at the monitors but couldn't see anything happening. She hoped to goodness she hadn't imagined it, although – perhaps it would be better if she had.

It was a very weird feeling standing alone in Elvis's kitchen in what must now be the early hours of the morning. She edged around the breakfast bar and peered towards the dining room at the front of the house. What was going on out there?

The secret stairway caught her eye and before she knew it, she found her feet had taken her to the entrance of the alcove. There were a couple of steps then the staircase turned and… what was she doing? She was standing at the turn of the stairwell looking up at the stairs covered in the brown and green patterned carpet that led up to a door at the top on the right. Her hand found itself on the wooden handrail that ran right up and as soon as she touched it everything seemed to happen so fast… up the stairs, through the door, across the landing that could be seen from the main entrance, a right turn, up a few more steps and then there was another door, white but strangely decorated with three panels of red carpet facing her. She knew this was wrong, she shouldn't be doing this, it was impossible she had come this far, but… she *had* come this far, she couldn't stop now. She opened the door, her eyes adjusted to the darkness on the landing and she saw where she was. The black padded leather doors were there on her left. This was it, the entrance to Elvis's bedroom, his inner sanctum, where no one had ever been allowed to set foot since the day he died. Well, no one apart from very close friends and his family. Was *she* his family? Could that justify what she was about to do?

She stood with her trembling fingers on the handle of the black leather padded door. Her heart was hammering so loud it was all she could hear as she strained her ears for signs that Wes and Blue were back and she was about to be discovered. Surely this door would be locked, or if not then as soon as it opened alarms would sound and she would summon the wrath of Elvis himself as she breached this final frontier. She knew it was wrong, but she couldn't stop now.

She took a breath as deep as her tight lungs would allow

her and turned the handle. The fact that it opened, and swung outwards, didn't surprise her. This all felt like it was meant to be. There was no time to hesitate so she stepped inside, only to find she was in a small lobby. To her left it opened out into a room that she knew to be Elvis's private office, to her right two more brown wooden doors.

In a flash she had opened one of those doors and there she was, standing inside Elvis's bedroom.

Chapter Twenty

In a nightclub down on Beale Street, Anita was attempting to reapply her lipstick as she leaned towards the mirror in the ladies' loo. She'd had a fair few cocktails, all that dancing had worked up a thirst. She steadied herself on the basin and paused, lipstick in hand, to give herself a chance to focus on the image looking back at her.

Her hair was a little mussed up, but the blonde tendrils hanging around her face were flattering. She didn't look like she'd been dragged through a hedge backwards or anything.

Her face was flushed; she wouldn't need to reapply any blusher. Her trademark black mascara was still firmly in place, no panda eyes or unsightly smudges making their way across her face.

She looked good, she was in fine shape. The pretty blue blouse she was wearing was open at the neck, giving just a hint of cleavage and it skimmed over her hips, covering her ample bottom but revealing her shapely blue-denimed thighs. She pursed her lips and applied a smudge of pink to her lips. The rock 'n' roll band on stage were starting a new song, she could hear the opening bars of 'Lawdy Miss Clawdy' if she wasn't mistaken.

Anita dropped the lipstick back into her bag and swung the chain strap onto her shoulder. She was about to turn and leave but something made her look back at her reflection for just a moment more. Was she kidding herself? Was she behaving like a foolish young girl? Was she crazy to think that she might have come to America, to Memphis itself and found someone to love, someone who could treat her right and give her a chance of happiness? A voice in her head was saying, '*If something seems too good to be true – it probably is.*'

Anita looked at herself again.

The black mascara was too heavy. She hadn't changed her make-up style for years, the look was dated and ageing.

The blonde hair was home-dyed and not quite the honey-blonde colour she wanted. Too bright, too brassy, it looked what it was: cheap.

The fabric of her blue blouse gaped between a couple of the buttons straining across her bust; she really should lay off those morning pancakes.

The green eyes she had just been looking into, shining and full of hope and dreams of the future, now looked glassy and tired.

Suddenly she knew she couldn't go back into the club where Priya was waiting for her, she just couldn't face it. Their 'girls' night out' had seemed like a good idea when Chance announced he had a gig down in Shreeveport,

Louisiana he couldn't get out of and Val decided he needed to catch up on some sleep. Daisy had been a no-show which was a shame. But now Anita wasn't in the mood for dancing and the fruity cocktails were making her feel queasy. It dawned on her that a young girl like Daisy simply would not want to spend all her time with oldies. She didn't blame her.

Anita looked around the small room for a means of escape. The thought of squeezing herself through the tiny high window should have made her laugh but instead she just wanted to cry. She decided the only sensible option for now was to lock herself in one of the toilet cubicles.

It wasn't often that Anita gave in to melancholy. She hadn't led a charmed life, far from it in fact, but she'd learned how to put on her game face. She'd done it when her marriage had ended, when her parents had died within weeks of each other, when one feckless man after another had broken her heart, even when the little baby boy she'd carried inside her for just a few short months failed to make it into her arms for just one brief cuddle. They hadn't told her it was a boy, they hadn't really said very much at all, she just knew.

It had taken a while to put on a game face after that. She'd carried on, of course she had, doing what everyone told her to do, taking one day at a time. As if there was any other choice? She'd put one foot in front of the other, carried on breathing in and breathing out. It wasn't enough for some people. It hadn't been enough for Alun. He had been struggling, she had known that, it was his baby too, but she'd had nothing left over for him. When he finally left, she'd understood why. That's why she hadn't put up a fight, because she understood, that and she simply didn't have the energy.

A little while after losing the baby, she started collecting feathers. They were everywhere, tiny little pure white feathers. On the seat of the bus, in the aisle of the supermarket, they could appear anywhere from the depths of her handbag to inside an empty beer glass. Sometimes she saved them and sometimes she didn't, but she always thought they were tiny tokens from the angels. It gave her a little comfort when the world felt far too harsh and real.

She could do with a sign now. Where were the flippin' angels when she needed them? Sat on the lid of the toilet seat, she rummaged in her bag for a tissue and gave her nose a determined blow. Someone had once told her that you only needed to ask the angels for what you wanted in life and they would help you get it. She'd always wanted to come to the American South, then, just when she was at her lowest, along came a late-night radio quiz and she'd won herself a ticket. She gave the impression she'd pretty much given up on men, all that *bloody men, who needs 'em* talk the other night – Anita Griffiths had kissed her share of frogs and didn't want to admit, even to herself, that she needed anyone, let alone a *man*. But if she was honest, having a man like Chance Bailey walk into her life was the answer to more prayers than she could count. Were the angels really helping to fulfil her wish list... and if so, why couldn't she appreciate it?

Trouble was, as she sat in the cubicle, rather worse for wear after a skinful of 'Naughty Apparitions', she was tormented by the thought that everything *was* simply far too good to be true. Chance Bailey was far too good to be true. If she carried on with this holiday romance, for that was surely what it was, the only possible outcome was that she would get her heart broken. It was alright for someone like Daisy, she thought to herself. A young girl like that, with her whole life ahead of her, of course she would be attractive and desirable and she should make the very most of that. She and Blue made a gorgeous couple, they could throw caution to the wind and just enjoy themselves. Anita believed that when you got older, the stakes were higher and the knockbacks were harder to take. Daisy had time to have her heart broken and bounce back several times, but for Anita time was precious and she couldn't afford to waste it.

Chance couldn't really be interested in her, an ageing barmaid from South Wales; there was no future for them. They may both be from 'the south' but they were two very different places. He toured the music clubs of the Southern States and lived almost permanently out of suitcases in hotels and motels across Mississippi, Tennessee and Louisiana. She had a life in Swansea. Well, sort of a life, an apology for a life! Pulling pints in a village pub and auditioning for parts in the local am dram society that she didn't even have a hope of getting.

The memory of Moira's raised hand halting her audition in the village hall and her condescending manner as Anita had attempted to land a starring part in the next Trachlyn Town Players' production loomed large – the humiliation!

Tears welled again and she pressed the soggy tissue

against her mouth to stop the sob building up inside her from escaping from her lips. Blinking furiously, she tried to stop the tears from falling. The scrawled graffiti on the toilet door swam in front of her eyes. Then she saw it. Just one word written in bright-red ink inside a neatly drawn heart... DAVID. She had never told a living soul that was the name she'd planned to call her baby boy. It was the name she always called him by when she thought of him. There was no memorial to him anywhere in the world, no plaque or gravestone, not even a tiny one like she'd seen at Graceland for Jesse Garon, Elvis's stillborn twin brother, but the name was forever etched onto her aching heart. She'd never even told Alun she wanted to call the baby David. They'd never had that conversation. Her wide eyes were suddenly dry, the sickly sensation in the pit of her stomach instantly replaced by a warm glow spreading through her like she was enveloped in a giant hug. It was a sign. It must be. Just the sight of that name gave her hope things might all work out. She was following the path she was meant to be on, all at once that's how it felt. David and the angels were telling her so. She didn't care if it did sound like complete nonsense. It made sense to her. Despite never taking a breath in this world, David was her son; he was part of her. She may never have held him in her arms, but she held him in her heart and she felt him stir within her, urging her on.

She wished Daisy had come with them tonight, of course she wasn't avoiding them because they were a bit older – Daisy wasn't like that. The girl was what Anita would call 'an old soul', someone wise beyond her years who could connect with people of all ages and appreciated and understood things outside her own youthful experience. Anita already felt a strong affection for her and looked forward to growing their friendship – she just knew they could be good for each other. Daisy needed support right now, she was clearly suffering after losing her grandmother, and Anita intended to be there for her. But there was something else going on with Daisy too, Anita was sure of it. She hadn't quite worked it out but Daisy was preoccupied and worried about something she was keeping to herself. Anita just wanted to help her with whatever it was.

She was reapplying her lipstick, yet again, when Priya came in to find her. 'How much war paint d'you need?' she demanded to know as she burst through the door, a half-drunk cocktail in her hand. 'You've left me sat out there on my own for half a bloody hour. What you playin' at?'

Anita steadied herself on the basin and turned to face her new friend. 'Priya, are we making holy fools of ourselves... me with Chance, and you... you with Valentin?'

If Anita felt *she* was ridiculous hooking up with a country and western singer, what did that make Priya and her Russian Elvis impersonator?

Priya sized up the situation as quickly as she downed 'Naughty Apparitions'. She'd taken to this drinking lark like a duck to water. 'Lishten to me, girl.' She was only slightly slurring her words. 'There's a whole load of shitheads out there who might as well have "Vampire" stamped on their passports as their occupation.'

Anita waited, perhaps Priya would start to make sense in a little while.

Priya read the confusion on her face correctly. 'Vampires, blood-sucking, life-draining vampires!'

Still Anita waited.

'Men who drip poison into the hearts of women, a harsh word here, a shrug of indifference there, making us feel worthless and useless, draining the very life spirit from our souls... Vampires, the lot of 'em.'

Anita understood. Drunk or not, Priya actually made a lot of sense.

'I'm telling you, girl.' Priya turned to face the mirror and addressed Anita's reflection. 'When you find yourself a... a non-vampire, a man who feeds your soul instead of one who sucks your lifeblood, don't question it, just hold on tight and see where the ride takes you.'

Anita nodded back at the reflected Priya. 'A non-vampire,' she said softly, 'I wonder what you call the opposite of a vampire?'

Priya fluffed up her hair with her fingers and shrugged. 'Umm, not sure... An angel, I suppose.'

Back in the bar they'd lost the table they'd had down in front of the band, but they hopped onto a couple of stools at the bar instead. Priya ordered them more drinks, though Anita went with a virgin cocktail for this round; she decided pacing herself was a good idea.

In bursts of conversation as the band played on, Priya filled Anita in on how she came to hook up with Valentin

Vasiliev. Who'd have thought an online bingo chatroom was where you'd find a Russian Elvis impersonator lurking!

Priya was vague on how they'd first struck up conversation and Google Translate had both helped and hindered their dialogue. In fact, autocorrect had almost scuppered the whole thing on more than one occasion. Chatting about Priya wanting to re-decorate her home took a horrifying turn when Val received the news that Priya wanted to 'defecate' in her kitchen. Anita was shocked, not only by the image, but also by how trivial and mundane a virtual romance could be. A kitchen make-over... could they really not think of anything more interesting to chat about?

She'd only just stopped wiping her eyes when hysteria took over again as Priya followed the kitchen redecoration bombshell with the story of when she believed Val was cooking up *placenta* and chicken for his supper when he'd actually intended to write 'polenta'.

'Even a man who feasted on after-birth seemed preferable to Sid, mind you, the way he was carrying on.' Priya rolled her eyes as she filled Anita in on the numerous times Sid had batted away her suspicions that he was having an affair so convincingly she'd thought she was losing her mind. She'd ended up so confused she'd thought the only way forward was to get right away from Sid and deal with it from afar. 'It seems cowardly, I know, but I just couldn't think straight anymore when I was with him. I knew things weren't right, all the signs were there, but every time I tried to talk to him he'd just turn it back on me.

I'd started to believe he was right, that I really was going crazy.'

As Priya described how Sid had surprised her at the airport, suddenly producing a ticket and announcing he was coming along too. Even Anita was bemused by his behaviour.

'So he must have wanted to save the relationship then?' she said. 'He'd dumped the other woman and decided he wanted to be with you after all?'

'You'd think so, wouldn't you,' Priya deadpanned as a reply. 'I didn't know what was going on. I think I was in shock. I'd been planning all along to call him as soon as I reached Memphis and tell him I wanted a divorce. He could have argued till he was blue in the face that he was innocent of all charges, but I knew I'd be able to handle it better from here. I needed to be somewhere where he couldn't get to me or undermine me. That was the plan anyway.'

Anita asked gently, 'And Val?'

'I never intended to have an affair behind Sid's back. It wasn't about what might happen with Val, I was going to end it with Sid anyway.'

Priya faced Anita, anxious her new friend would understand that she hadn't intended to behave badly. 'Even as we boarded the plane, part of me was thinking I must have imagined Sid was cheating on me, that he was right, I was just a paranoid idiot... then I found that message from Lizzy Lizard Tongue on his phone and I knew my betrayal was nothing compared to his.'

Anita and Priya spent the next half hour swapping tales of complicated families, bonkers boyfriends and disastrous dates. By the time they got round to discussing Chance and Val, both were happily cheerleading for each other.

'A Russian Elvis impersonator, I mean, they can't be that common – even in Russia!' stated Anita in all seriousness. 'Bring him to Britain to perform, that'll be his IUD.'

Priya snorted so hard drink came out of her nose. 'I think you mean USP – an IUD is a form of contraception.'

'Oh, ha! I need autocorrect on my gob,' giggled Anita. 'Yes, that's it, USP – unique selling point, that's what I meant.'

Priya mulled over the sense behind Anita's garbled idea. She had lots of downtime sitting on reception at the car showroom where she worked. The job really wasn't all that demanding. All the time she spent playing Candy Crush so she looked busy could be used to be a part-time showbiz manager. She could organise bookings, build Val a website, raise his profile on social media. It was a whole new world, but she was hard-working and a quick learner.

'Would he get a visa, though?' Anita's question threatened to burst the big fat bubble Priya was floating in, but she pushed that worry away with a shrug and turned the attention back to Anita.

'What about you? You went a storm the other night in that club. How about you and Chance teaming up to tour the pubs and clubs back home? We could offer both acts as a double bill!'

But Anita shook her head. 'There's precious little call for our kind of music back home,' she said with just a slight trace of bitterness.

As the faces of supercilious Moira and perspiring pub

landlord Emlyn loomed in her mind, Anita straightened her shoulders and made an instant decision. 'No, if we're going to make a go of things anywhere then I reckon I'll have to move here.' As soon as she heard her own words out loud, Anita knew what she was saying made complete sense. Time was ticking, 'chances' like this were not to be missed, if you'd pardon the pun!

Priya raised her glass to toast the determined gleam in Anita's eye, but anything she was about to say was swept away by a startling turn of events. Keith, the stocky, balding bartender, seized a pair of drumsticks from the optics right above where Priya and Anita were perched on bar stools. One moment he was pouring drinks and mopping his sweaty brow with a bar towel, the next he was using the bar, the pumps, glasses, bottles and ice buckets all around him as an improvised drum kit as he energetically and expertly played along to the band's version of 'Summertime Blues'. Priya and Anita whooped and cheered with the rest of the bar, as the little guy with a look of Danny DeVito showcased his party piece and gave a drumming masterclass right under their noses.

Anita drained her glass and joined in with Keith, clapping along. *Yes, sir*, she thought, *you wouldn't see anything like this at Emlyn's makeshift Trachlyn's Got Talent at the Red Dragon.* This was where she belonged. She couldn't wait to tell Daisy she wanted to make Memphis her new home, she had a feeling Daisy would completely understand.

Chapter Twenty-One

I t was dark in Elvis's bedroom. Daisy wished she had Blue's flashlight as she didn't want to risk looking for a light switch. The first thing that came into focus was the enormous bed. It was in the centre of the room and was absolutely the biggest bed that she had ever seen. She was rooted to the spot; she didn't dare move an inch. There was enough light for her to start to make out the room a little clearer. It was a clear moonlit night outside but in here the windows were covered in dark-coloured drapes that hung right to the floor. A shaft of light was coming from over on her right where there was an opening that must lead to the bathroom. Perhaps there was a window letting in the moonlight but knowing that was where had Elvis died, Daisy had no desire to take a closer look in there.

She swept her eyes quickly over the room; she knew she didn't have long.

In the far corner was a low, round chair completely covered in pale fur, and above it hung a gold Moroccan-style lamp. A large old-fashioned TV set in a dark wood console stood facing the bed. Sitting on top, poised like it was about to pounce, was a huge ceramic tiger.

The tiger wasn't the only statue in the room; to her left, just inside the door, was one of Jesus Christ. The figure was large and stood facing into the room, his hands stretching forwards from beneath his robes.

Now she was here, inside this most secret of places, Daisy's mind was reeling. How was this even possible? Why had the door been unlocked? Could a cleaner have made a mistake? The room certainly didn't look dusty or cob-webbed, it must be regularly cleaned to keep everything so clean and well preserved.

As she stood there, she wondered to herself what she had been hoping to discover – Elvis himself sat watching his favourite comedy shows, feasting on burgers? No, of course not! What then – a picture of Rose on his bedside table? Even more ludicrous! A sense of a connection then, perhaps... Something that would confirm there was a link between her and this man, this rock star, this world-famous icon?

She noticed a couple of phones by the side of the bed, one on the table and one fixed to the wall; even in the darkness Daisy could tell they were bright red. A framed photo of Elvis's parents, Vernon and Gladys, stood on the bedside table along with a small book and lots of other objects that were too difficult to make out in the half light.

Daisy looked again at the bed; a pair of pale-blue pyjamas were folded neatly and placed carefully on top of the gold-coloured covers. The sight of them made her eyes suddenly fill with tears.

Elvis wasn't just an idol, he was a man. He was part of a family. He had a daughter he had dearly loved. He'd been loved too, not just by his fans but by people who knew him and shared his life.

The sense of Elvis as a real person flooded through Daisy as she stood in the room where he had spent so much time hidden away from the pressures and expectations of the world. How isolated and alone he must have felt at times. Everyone wanting more and more from him until there was nothing left to give; this was the room where he had retreated to escape from it all, the place where he could be alone and just be himself.

An overwhelming feeling of sadness and loss rose inside her and escaped as a stifled sob from her lips. Elvis wasn't just a voice on a record or a picture on a screen, he had been a real person made of flesh and blood – whether or not, it was blood they shared. In that moment, standing there in the place where Elvis was able to be his most private self, Daisy felt grief for a grandfather she had never known and also for the loss of this charismatic, incredibly talented, famous man. Her own loss and the loss of Elvis Presley to the world were somehow all mixed up together; she wasn't sure where one ended and one began. Her senses heightened, she caught a spicy, woody aroma in the air and knew at once it was Elvis's cologne.

She instantly felt compelled to leave. She shouldn't be here. Taking a last look as she stepped backwards, she carefully closed the door and retraced her steps on shaking legs. At the top of the secret stairway she heard the screen door beyond the Jungle Room bang loudly and almost flew down the stairs to arrive breathless and damp with sweat back in the kitchen.

There was quite a commotion coming from the Jungle Room and Daisy moved quickly away from the staircase, praying her guilt wasn't written all over her face. She couldn't tell how many people were now in the building, but heard Wes, sounding out of breath and panting with effort, say, 'Cuff him, Blue, and call for back-up, I can't handle too much of this at my age.'

In contrast, Blue sounded fully in control. 'Take it easy, Wes, we got this.'

Daisy walked nervously towards the voices and was shocked to see it was just three of them; even more amazing was that the struggling man they held between them was someone she knew.

'SEAN!'

Blue and Wes both looked at her in surprise,

'You know this guy?' Blue was quizzical, but Wes's eyes narrowed with suspicion.

'Yes, he's… he's on my trip, he's staying at my motel.'

Daisy was looking straight at Sean, but his bearded head was down staring at the green shag pile carpet.'

Wes spoke slowly, not releasing his grip on Sean's arm. 'We caught him just before he got to the meditation garden. Elvis was brought here to rest to stop grave robbers like you.'

'I'm not—' Sean and Daisy spoke together. 'He's not… he's not a grave robber. He can't be!'

As suspicious as Daisy had been about what Sean Price was up to, she couldn't believe it was something so horrific.

Wes looked between Daisy's stricken face and Sean's mortified expression.

'What's in the bag, son?'

At the softening of Wes's tone, Sean finally was able to raise his head. He swallowed a couple of times and then said, 'It's my dad.'

The mood changed once Sean spoke and with a little more coaxing, they all discovered that this daring break-in was in fact a bungled attempt to scatter the ashes of Sean's father, Teddy Price.

Sean explained that he'd made a solemn promise to his dying father that he'd bring his ashes to Graceland and scatter them here, a place he'd always wanted to visit. 'I knew it wouldn't be easy,' Sean said. 'I didn't really think about that when I made the promise, though.' He explained he'd tried simply emptying the scatter tube he kept in his satchel a little here and there during the Graceland tour they'd done earlier in the day, but the sheer volume of people had rendered this plan impossible.

'Every time I even thought about it someone would come along, or I'd see people watching me as if they thought I was up to something.'

Daisy felt yet another guilty prickle at the back of her neck, but said nothing.

Sean was now sat on the large furry throne that dominated the jungle room while Daisy and Blue sat facing him on the long matching sofa. Coming in from the kitchen, Wes carried a tray decorated with pictures of Hawaii and bearing four fresh mugs of coffee. He placed it carefully on the low footstool between them.

'Well, you *were* up to something, son,' he said as he took his seat next to Daisy and Blue.

Sean looked up from his coffee mug and saw Wes had an amused expression on his face.

'I'm so sorry for all the trouble, I don't know what came over me. Lynette said right from the start that this was a ridiculous idea.'

'Is Lynette your wife?' asked Blue.

'Is that why she didn't come with you to Memphis?' questioned Daisy.

Sean revealed his wife Lynette was pregnant and too far gone to travel. 'And there's Harry to think about, he's only seven, I'm not sure he really understands that his grandad is gone for good.' Sean's eyes were wet with tears and he blinked rapidly to stop them falling.

'Tell us about your dad, son, I take it he was a big Elvis fan?'

Sean looked gratefully at Wes, he couldn't work out why this man was being so pleasant and friendly after finding him trespassing. They certainly did things differently around here. He was also most confused about what the young woman from the motel was doing here at Graceland in the middle of the night, but the night's turn of events were unfolding so peculiarly it simply slotted in with all the other strangeness.

'I never really understood my dad's fascination for rock 'n' roll music and Elvis.' Sean seemed to only register what he was saying once he'd said the words out loud. He pulled up short and looked at Wes, Daisy and Blue as his face turned red. 'Oh god, I mean... that sounds a terrible thing to say considering where I am! It's just... well... the whole Teddy boy thing Dad had going on, long after he should have grown out of it all really. The clothes, the hair... I mean, I just never got it. I suppose I found it all a bit embarrassing.'

Daisy thought about Rose and her passion for vintage clothes and Fifties music and how Lilian had always mocked her for it. How sad that both Sean and her mum were so embarrassed by something their parents loved so much. She thought about how much of Rose, the passionate, quirky, funny woman she'd always been, had started to fade towards the end. Her illness had robbed her of so much of what she loved, all the things that made her 'Rose', as her memories faded away one by one until the only thing she seemed to have left was her music.

'I bet your dad was quite a character, wasn't he?' she said quietly. It was a shame she hadn't bothered to try and find out more about Sean. She'd been so preoccupied with her own quest but might have been able to help Sean with his if she'd known what he was trying to do.

They all listened then as Sean talked about the way his father had always dreamed of coming to Graceland and visiting Memphis. Teddy Price had longed to walk the streets where the music he loved had been made and stand on the spot in Sun Studio where Elvis had sung 'That's Alright Mama' and started a musical earthquake that continued to rock the world to this very day. Sean shocked himself as he recalled all the stories his father had told him over the years; he'd absorbed more than he had ever realised about Elvis and Graceland and Memphis.

'He would have given anything to be able to come here, walk down Beale Street, see Graceland with his very own eyes.' Sean paused and gazed around the room himself. He was *inside* Elvis Presley's home, if only his dad could see him now. His voice cracked as he said, 'When he was in the hospital, he knew he hadn't got long left and he asked me... asked me if I would take him to Graceland.'

Daisy was blinking her own wet eyes furiously now and held her breath as Sean carried on.

'I thought he was delirious. I mean, you know, he couldn't even get to the bathroom by himself by that stage.' Sean took a gulp of coffee before he was able to carry on. 'But of course that wasn't what he meant.'

Daisy let the tears drip down her face; she also understood what Sean's dad had meant.

'I went and got some brochures and we kind of played a game, planning a trip for the two of us that we knew we'd never make... not while he was alive anyway. At the end, when he couldn't even see the pictures anymore, I'd read out the itinerary of the various trips and I'd see him smile. I'd tell him about all the things we would see and do, and I made a promise, I *promised* him I'd bring him to Graceland.'

'And you have, boy, I think your ole pa is right here with us.' Wes was leaning forward with his hands on his knees, watching as Sean bowed his head and nodded gratefully.

'You know, this is a very special place, son.' Wes spoke slowly as if to be sure Sean could understand every word of his Southern drawl. 'You can feel it for yoursel' right enough now you're here, I'll wager. There's a good many folks who feel a mighty powerful pull to this place, folks from all over. I've spent many a time wondrin' about all that, why they come here and why they still wanna come here after all these years.'

Daisy's eyes never left Wes's face as the old man nodded wisely at Sean; she was transfixed, keen to know the answer to that very question herself.

Wes's old blue eyes shone brightly, a youthful contrast to his weathered, leathery skin. 'Well, I reckon it's down to music... music, memories and jus' a little bit of ole magic.'

They all sat for a while, letting the memories and the magic swirl about them as Graceland itself seemed to beat with the rhythm of a heartbeat. They were each lost in their own thoughts, the spirits and memories of loved ones hovering near: Teddy... Rose... Elvis.

Blue spoke for the first time in a while. 'What was your dad's name, son?'

Sean looked up in slight surprise. Hadn't he already told them that? He saw the three sympathetic faces looking at him expectantly and answered, 'It was Ed, Edward – but of course everyone always called him Teddy.'

Blue turned to Wes with grin and said, 'Is there something we can do for Teddy?'

Wes narrowed his eyes and nodded slowly. 'I reckon.'

Sean and Daisy looked from one to the other in confusion, but Wes only added, 'But we better get you lot outta here right now, the sun's comin' up and I sure don't wanna lose my job.'

Daisy jumped up and picked up the tray of mugs,

making her way towards the kitchen. Behind her, Sean and Blue straightened the furniture and replaced the guitar and teddy bear in their usual positions on the chair that Sean had been sitting on. Suddenly Daisy found the entrance to the kitchen was blocked. Wes stood in the space between the two rooms, one arm across the doorway. He looked down at her with a kindly twinkle but his words froze the blood in her veins.

'So you got Graceland all to yourself for a while back there, little lady.' He was almost whispering the words, his face close to hers. 'Y'all didn't get up to anything ya shouldn't now, I hope?'

Daisy's eyes were wide and her mouth opened and closed a few times before she heard herself say, 'O... o... of course not.'

Wes dropped his arm and watched her pass by into the kitchen, a small smile never leaving his face. She attempted to put the tray onto the work surface near the sink but misjudged the space and knocked into an upright blender that stood next to the microwave. The tall Perspex jug teetered and was about to fall but in an instant Wes was at her side and reached out to steady it. He took the tray from her shaking hands and called over his shoulder to Blue, 'This young 'un needs some rest I reckon, y'all ready to go?'

As they all made their way back through the den to the screen door out back, Daisy saw the sky was tinged with orange as the sun began to break over the horizon. She turned towards where Blue's motorcycle was parked under the carport.

'That'll attract too much attention at this time of day.'

Wes steered her away from the carport and towards a barn over by the paddock. Blue whispered to her that it was best they weren't all seen leaving at dawn and that anyhow there wasn't room for Sean on the motorbike too. So how, wondered Daisy, were they going to leave Graceland?

Wes led them into the stable barn and turned to face them. Was he seriously expecting them to saddle up and ride *horses* back to the motel? Surely that would attract even *more* attention, and no one had so much as asked her if she was able to even ride a horse.

Daisy stared in amazement as Wes began kicking at the straw on the floor. Suddenly, he uncovered a large brass ring and stopped kicking and began to roll up his sleeves.

'Lend an ole fella a hand there, will you, Blue?'

The two of them stood either side of the brass ring, grabbed hold with both hands and heaved it upwards. The floor began to shift; with a creak, a large wooden square raised itself out of the floor and settled back on its hinges, revealing a couple of worn stone steps descending downwards into the dark. A secret tunnel!

'This'll take you over yonder beyond the highway,' said Wes, wiping his hands down on his jeans. 'You'll come out in a little cabin hidden in the trees behind the parking lot. Lord knows, we've had to save that little piece o' land so many times with all the things they have springin' up over there all the time, but somehow, thank the Lord, it's still there.'

Daisy looked at Sean and saw he had a curious smile playing on his lips and was shaking his head as though he'd always suspected a tunnel like this existed at Graceland.

Blue flicked on his torchlight and shone it down into the passageway, 'Okay then, everyone ready?' He didn't wait for either Sean or Daisy to reply but began to make his way down the stone stairway. Sean nodded and followed on without a word of protest, but Daisy hesitated.

Wes took her hand and held it tight. 'It's okay, honey, I got you.'

She stepped into the hole left by the trapdoor and found her footing on the first smooth stone step. Leaning towards her, Wes kept tight hold of her hand as she stepped down again and again. She paused to look back up at him as Blue flicked the light of his torch towards her. Suddenly she saw something, there on Wes's bare outstretched arm. A black and red rose tattoo, an exact match to the one on Nana Rose's arm. She gasped in shock but in that instant Blue's arm was around her waist and Wes released his grip on her hand. The trap door closed above her head and Wes was gone.

Chapter Twenty-Two

L ilian drove her Skoda onto Rose's drive, ready to face yet another day at the coal face of clearing and sorting that was the instant result of the death of a parent.

She was still sat inside the car, hands gripping the steering wheel, when Rose's neighbour rapped lightly on the window, asking, 'Lily love, are you alright?'

Jolted out of her trance-like state, Lilian quickly undid her seatbelt and grabbed her handbag off the passenger seat. 'Yes, yes, I'm fine, Wendy, thank you.'

'It's just you've been sat there for fifteen minutes, you know, do you want to come and have a cuppa at mine before you go in?'

Lilian knew she really needed to crack on, but she nodded with relief and let Wendy guide her across the driveway and past the flowerbeds into her own neat semi.

She passed a pleasant half hour or so at Wendy's, it was nice to let Rose's next door neighbour chatter on about Rose, she could almost pretend her mum was just next door, fixing herself some lunch while jigging along to the radio. She drank her tea and ate a couple of custard creams, just agreeing here and there while Wendy talked about what a wonderful woman Rose had been. Lilian was just about to leave when Wendy suddenly said something that got her full attention.

'Sorry, what was that, Wendy?'

'Oh well, it's just that your mum was getting more and more confused over the last few weeks, maybe even months now I come to think of it.' Wendy's face beneath her neat silvery pixie cut hair-do was full of concern.

'Yes, but you said something about her mentioning a man? Someone you hadn't heard her talk about before?' Lilian tried not to show irritation as Wendy picked up the empty mugs and headed for the sink. *Concentrate, Wendy... Please concentrate.*

'Well yes, but it was probably something and nothing, I don't know why I mentioned it really.' Wendy spoke with her back to Lilian so didn't see the younger woman roll her eyes in frustration.

But you did mention it, Wendy, Lilian wanted to scream. *Now say it again while I am listening properly.*

Wendy rinsed the mugs and began to dry her hands on a tea towel decorated with a red Welsh dragon. When she eventually caught sight of the expression on Lilian's face, her words all came out in a bit of a rush. 'She said something about a man called... Wesley... "Oh, my Wesley loves this or that song", she'd say or "You've never seen anyone eat as many burgers as my Wesley... I don't know where he puts them all!" She started to just drop him into conversation as though she'd been with him that very day...' Wendy tailed off as she saw the look on Lilian's face change from one of interest to total exasperation.

'Pah... You do know how big a fan of Elvis *Presley* Mum was, don't you, Wendy?' Lilian couldn't help a sarcastic tone creeping into her voice. 'Presley... Wesley... Do you see what might have been happening there?'

Wendy looked shamefaced, but pressed on a little further regardless. 'I know she loved Elvis, of course, but this sounded like she was talking about a man she knew, someone she knew very well...'

Lilian was desperate to bring this exchange to a close. The last thing she wanted was for Wendy to find out Rose's last confused claim was that she'd had an illicit liaison with Elvis Presley and therefore the King of Rock 'n' Roll's daughter – Lilian herself – was standing right there in her kitchen! Was there no escape from Elvis bloody Presley? He seemed to get everywhere!

Lilian left Wendy regretting she'd said anything and let herself into Rose's hallway. She stood for a while, wondering where to begin today. She thought it was probably best to wait for Daisy to help go through her mother's bulging wardrobes upstairs, she'd have more idea about what to do with all that stuff. She slipped off her shoes, headed into the through-lounge and cast her eye over the colourful cushions and eclectic ornaments adorning every surface... Where to start today?

Her eye was drawn to a particular piece of furniture in

the dining room close to the patio doors that lead to the garden. It was a low wooden gramophone unit; the record deck itself could be found by lifting the lid in the centre of the retro piece of furniture and there were built-in speakers either side. Lilian knew that it had been Rose's pride and joy. Lilian padded across the room in her stockinged feet, gently raised the lid and settled it back on its hinges to see what record had been left on the turntable. She wasn't surprised in the least by what she found – here he was again!

The circular golden label on the record proclaimed it to be a 'Sun Record Company' recording with its distinctive rays of sunlight logo above a crowing cockerel. The outer edge of the label was decorated with music notes and 'Memphis, Tennessee' was stamped for good measure right at the bottom. Lilian peered closer to read the name of the track 'That's All Right' was printed above the name 'Elvis Presley'. Before she was able to stop herself, her fingers had flicked the switch to turn the player on, moved the arm across and carefully placed the needle onto the record.

The strumming guitar that signalled the start of the song sounded like a train hurtling down a railway track, Elvis's young voice soared high over the guitar licks and the slapping bass was so full of reverb and echo it sounded like he was hollering the song from the bottom of a well.

She stood and listened for a few moments – was she just trying to torture herself, she wondered? Just as she went to move the arm off the spinning disc, something else caught her eye.

Some papers were sticking out from between the

cupboard doors underneath the record player, stopping them from closing properly. She opened the doors a little to push them back inside, but a whole cascade of paperwork tumbled out and over her toes.

Giving a little groan, Lilian knelt on the carpet and started to scoop up the mess. There were yellowing old newspapers, cut-out scraps of articles and pictures and several large scrapbooks with bulging dog-eared pages. She wasn't interested in poring through whatever collection this was but the front page of one of the brittle newspapers caught her eye. **KING ELVIS IS DEAD** said the bold headline in thick black lettering taking up almost all the page. Alongside was an unfortunate photograph of Presley, looking horribly bloated and dishevelled. The newspaper pulled no punches, tagging the picture **HE WAS 42 AND ALONE** as if the tragedy of the event needed to be hammered home to readers even more.

Goodness, there really was no escape, she thought to herself. She sat back on her heels as she flicked through the piles of memorabilia; she never knew her mother had all this stuff, although she couldn't say she was all that surprised. There were lots of newspapers, all from the same date – August 16th 1977, the day Elvis Presley had died. Lilian actually remembered it very well.

It had been the school summer holidays, of course, but as a prefect Lilian had volunteered to go into school and help prep for the new term while the place was quiet. She remembered the atmosphere that morning was unusual, she'd had the feeling a summer storm was brewing.

The school had been open but there was no one else

around and so she'd taken advantage of the situation. She'd braved the deserted staffroom and made herself a coffee, sure that no one would mind. She was a prefect after all. She'd then headed to a first-year classroom to start taking down the end-of-term wall displays of erupting volcanoes. She'd worked steadily for an hour or so on her own when a curious noise began to bother her. It sounded like voices, or was it music playing? No, there it came again, the sound of someone talking, although she couldn't make out what they were saying. There was something else, too, an occasional sound she couldn't quite place that kept occurring between the music and the voices.

She'd climbed down from the desk she was standing on. Perhaps some kids had got inside the building and were messing about? She'd thought it best to check it out.

Lilian had made her way down the corridor from her classroom and towards the direction of the gymnasium. The noise had grown louder as she got further down the hall. Someone was definitely playing music…were a group of kids having an illicit party down there? The strange noise suddenly happened again. Was someone being sick? Oh dear lord, she hoped she wasn't about to discover some of the wilder pupils having sex!

She'd stopped outside the door to the caretaker's room. Someone was definitely in there. The music was loud and clear, and she could hear every word as Elvis Presley sang 'Love Me Tender'. She'd listened harder. There it was again, It sounded like a wounded animal yelping from behind the door. Had someone trapped a dog inside the room for a sick joke?

She'd opened the door carefully, scared that whatever was trapped inside might come hurtling out as soon it saw an escape route, but it wasn't an injured animal that was making the noise. A blue transistor radio had been perched high on a shelf in the tiny room, not much bigger than a broom closet, Elvis's voice, cracked with emotion, sang out of it. Ged the school caretaker was hunched in the corner, his middle-aged face tearstained and his eyes bloodshot. Ged was known for being a joker. He always had a smile and a cheery wave while he whistled his way around school, whether he was sweeping leaves on the drive or setting out chairs for a concert. Now he was sat there sobbing like a baby as a voice cut in over the end of the song to declare, *Elvis Presley is dead. Long live the king.*

Lilian sat and thought about Ged as she gathered together the newspapers from the day Elvis died into a loose pile. The poor caretaker had been as devastated by the death of his music hero as he would have been if one of his own family had died. She would never forget the sound of his heartbroken sobs. She also remembered that once she got home that day, her own mother was also tearstained and devastated by the news of the death of her favourite singer. Lilian had thought it quite peculiar at the time. Now she supposed everyone remembered where they were when they heard the news that Elvis Presley had died. It was one of those defining moments of a generation, like when JFK was shot, or when the news broke about Princess Diana's car crash. Now, though she was faced with the outrageous possibility that the day she was remembering, August 16th 1977, was in fact the day her own father had died. Was *that* why Rose had never told her? Was Rose waiting for Lilian to turn eighteen but when Elvis suddenly died she decided it was best never to say anything at all?

As she attempted to stuff the pile of papers back into the gramophone cabinet, she spotted a discoloured scrapbook. She gently opened it to see what had been pasted onto its pages. This time she discovered pictures of young Elvis, lithe and wiry, his legs spread wide, an arm flung above his head. Close-ups of his face in the black and white pictures showed dark shadows under his hooded eyes, his lip curled back and his hair unkempt and wild. Rose must have been collecting this stuff for years. As she began to tidy a few loose cuttings back into place in the scrapbook, a single photograph suddenly fluttered out from where it had been tucked inside the back cover.

Lilian picked it up, expecting to see another fan magazine picture of Presley or a publicity still from one of his early movies. Instead, she realised she was holding a small photograph of a young couple. The girl was wearing a pale outfit of a pretty blouse tucked into a full skirt. The young man next to her was much taller and wore jeans and an unbuttoned shirt. He had his arm draped over the girl's shoulders and they were both leaning in the doorway of a place called 'Arcade Restaurant'. Lilian peered closer at the photograph. It wasn't very clear. The couple were small in the centre of the picture and she could see part of a motorbike parked by the kerb on the edge of the shot.

The girl had her dark hair up in a ponytail and was looking directly at the camera, while her boyfriend – she presumed they were boyfriend and girlfriend – was looking down at her in the crook of his arm. Was this a young Rose? It had to be. Lilian was actually quite shocked by how much the photograph reminded her of Daisy. Rose didn't look much older than a teenager herself in this picture and who was the man?

She sat for an age with the mysterious photograph in her hand. Why had she never seen this picture before? If it was important enough for Rose to have kept for all these years, why wasn't it in a frame on display for all the world to see? There were already so many unanswered questions, this was now yet another to add to the list.

Chapter Twenty-Three

Memphis, Summer 1960

R ose pushed a stray lock of hair from her eyes and went back to chewing nervously on a fingernail. Why had she agreed to meet him here?

She was on a quiet street in downtown Memphis that she had never been on before. There were only a few storefronts dotted amongst the warehouses and rundown office buildings. There really wasn't much to see: a shoe repair shop and a dingy jeweller's, an alleyway full of bits of broken-down vehicles.

She shaded her eyes against the bright early afternoon sunshine and looked up and down the street again. There wasn't so much as a milk bar or a coffee shop to wait inside. She shifted her weight as she leaned against the fire hydrant and tried to look cool while she fanned herself because she was too hot.

Her flared pink skirt and white cotton shirt had looked sweet and fresh when she'd got ready that morning, but now she feared she looked like a melting ice cream sundae with her ponytail in disarray as the temperature rose.

Suddenly, she heard a shout and her heart leaped as she wished she'd let Jennifer come along with her after all instead of letting her and Wade drop her off by the Chisca Hotel. What was she doing, hanging around street corners by herself – it was exactly the sort of thing her parents had expressly told her not to do before she came to America.

She saw a movement in the shady doorway of a shop on the opposite side of the street, but the sun was in her eyes and the figure just a shadow. All at once, Wes was across the road and standing right in front of her with a lopsided smile across his face.

'Here she is, my pretty little Rose.'

Rose landed a playful punch on his arm, 'I was beginning to think I was in the wrong place.'

Wes's face contorted in pain. 'Hey, steady on little one, I'm sorta tender right about there.'

Rose thought he was mocking her size but Wes was pulling up the sleeve of his blue cotton shirt. He wore it open exposing his white vest underneath and the cuffs were loose too. He yanked the material up to his elbow and revealed… a vivid black and red tattoo of a rose on his forearm.

'Whaddaya think?'

Rose looked from the inky flower on Wes's arm to his laughing face, her mouth open in shock.

'Sure is a beauty, ain't it?' He looked from the rose into her face and added, 'Jus' like you.'

His lips were on hers in a gentle kiss before she could find her voice; she jumped back from him so suddenly she almost lost her balance. 'Is that a real tattoo? I can't believe you've done that.'

Wes reached out and held her shoulders to steady her and looked a little insulted at her reaction, 'Well I'd been fixin' to get me some sorta tattoo for a while but I could never make my mind up what to get. Then I got to thinkin' how I said I'd never forget you, Rose, and well, it jus' seemed the right thing to do.' He dropped his hands from her shoulders and shoved them into the pockets of his jeans.

'Oh, Wes, I'll never forget you.' Rose put her hands on his chest and leaned up to kiss his cheek.

All at once Wes's lopsided smile was back. 'Well, there's only one sure way to prove that, honey.' He jerked his head towards the store across the street that Rose now realised was a tattoo parlour.

Her eyes grew wide as she took in the peeling posters stuck on the inside of the window but then she noticed the intricate white lettering on the faded black store sign above it proclaiming, 'Rebels and Angels Tattoo Parlour'. She gently peeled Wes's shirt sleeve away from his arm and looked again at the fresh rose's leaves and petals on his still sore skin. She'd never seen anything quite like it ever before in her whole life.

'Okay then,' Rose said with a casual shrug of her shoulders. 'You're on.' And she stepped towards the kerb to cross over to the shop.

'Hey there.' Wes grabbed for her arm and pulled her back, 'I was only foolin' with ya, Rose.'

Rose turned to look him in the eye and replied evenly, 'Well, I don't just fool around, mister, I thought you knew that about me already.' She let him absorb the words then gave him a knowing wink and headed across to the store.

Giving a low whistle and a shake of his amazed head, Wes followed.

.   .   .

For several days Rose couldn't make up her mind whether or not to show Jennifer the fresh rose tattoo on her upper arm. She almost did on several occasions, but the thought of Jennifer-Jane reacting with horror or looking at her as though she was foolish stopped her every time. She and Wes weren't crazy, they knew their relationship was destined to be short, but they were in love. It was real and they had done something that cemented their love and made sure they always remembered the time they had together. Trying to explain that to someone else just wouldn't sound right, Rose thought. It would be too easy to dismiss what they had done as reckless, but as far as Rose was concerned it was anything but that.

As the summer wore on, Rose and Wes spent as much time together as they could, but they couldn't hide from the inevitable conclusion; the time for Rose to return home was drawing nearer and they would have to say goodbye.

Rose fantasised about returning to Wales and one day leaving the typing pool office at lunchtime to find Wes standing on the rainy pavement with a bunch of flowers waiting for her, but in reality, she had difficulty picturing Wes fitting into a small Welsh town. Similarly, she wondered what life would be like if she begged him to marry her and they set up home in a little house on the outskirts of Memphis, but their worlds were too different, something would always materialise to tear the dream to pieces. Wes wasn't in full-time work and she had a job and family waiting for her at home. Trying to match their two lives together just seemed too impossible to contemplate.

Rose fell in love with Wes because he was kind and loving and fun to be with, but she had to admit that the fact he was a Presley certainly made the whole affair incredibly exciting. He spoke now and then about Elvis, although she tried not to bombard him with too many questions. At one point he even offered to take her up to Graceland to meet Elvis, but the opportunity never actually occurred and Rose felt Wes wasn't all that keen on the idea anyway. The more time she spent with him, the less interested she was in his famous relative and she wouldn't want Wes to think she was only going out with him to get close to Elvis. She had fallen in love with her very own Presley and that turned out to be more than enough for Rose.

Before she knew what was happening, Rose was packing her case to go home while Jennifer sat on the end of her bed, her big eyes watching her friend as she folded every dress and rolled each sock.

'You can come and visit again soon, anytime you like.'

Jennifer's words were a little unconvincing, not that it mattered, they both knew a repeat visit was unlikely in the foreseeable future.

'If Wade and I should ever get around to actually setting a date, you'll simply have to come over for the wedding,' she added.

Rose smiled and nodded. 'Of course I will.' But the reality of saving enough money to afford such a trip didn't make this plan a certainty in her mind. Still less certain was the chance of her employers allowing her to make more extended trips abroad; she'd pretty much used up her holiday allocation for the next few years on this trip alone.

Jennifer looked pained as she watched Rose move around the room, retrieving her hairbrush from the dresser and a stray shoe from under the bed. Something between them had shifted over the course of Rose's stay, both of them felt it. They'd felt like strangers at the start of the visit, it had taken a little time for them to remember each other properly and feel as close as sisters once more – but it had happened, so why now was there was a distance between them again? There was a point when they came together as tightly as they had ever been, but it didn't last and they gradually withdrew from each other once more, leaving them separated as though they were already on opposite sides of the Atlantic Ocean.

Rose felt awkward as she pushed her few meagre possessions into her small case, knowing when she next unpacked the items it would be in the cold back bedroom of her terraced house back home. She'd become far too comfortable far too quickly with having servants cook and clean for her. Come to think, she hadn't even made her own bed for the last few weeks, she'd better snap out of that routine sharpish or her mother would have something to say about it.

Rose was also less than excited for Jennifer-Jane's hopes of becoming Mrs Wade Benson. It surprised her how their personalities had become almost transposed since she and Jennifer were at primary school. Then, she was the more feminine, delicate one and Jenny was more of a scruffy-haired tomboy, always ready to arm wrestle any boy in the class into submission. Now Jennifer was poised and ladylike and, just like her sister Jeannie, more concerned about fitting in with polite Southern society. Having the 'right' connections meant everything, apparently.

Rose felt no real envy for the lifestyle that Jennifer aspired to have with Wade, a nice enough young man with a future mapped out in his father's burgeoning haulage firm. 'We can get any parcel, anywhere, from Alabama to Alaska,' Wade was fond of boasting to anyone who would listen. In fact, it was the single most interesting thing Rose remembered ever hearing him say, which said it all really. No, a lifetime of listening to Wade Benson Junior pontificate on all matters postal was nothing to feel jealous about.

In contrast, her relationship with Wes had been full of exciting discoveries, thrilling adventure, fun and passion. She rode on the back of his motorbike with the wind in her hair and they played records on the juke box down at Arcade Restaurant while he introduced her to Southern delicacies like fried green tomatoes and jambalaya. When the Cajun-spiced stew made her cough, he passed her a glass and they both had tears streaming from their eyes when she gagged and gasped at her first taste of Tennessee whiskey. Best of all, he took her dancing. Once she'd felt his arms around her and they'd moved together to the rhythm of the music, it was clear to Rose that not only was she willing to lose her virginity to Wes, she was more than ready.

In the end they only ever went the whole way once. They'd ridden out to a secluded spot overlooking the Mississippi river and Wes had unfurled a blanket that was tied to the back of his motorcycle. The evening was warm and clear and Rose knew that only the stars looked down on them that night, and they weren't judgemental at all.

Afterwards, they were both unusually quiet. Wes eventually whispered words of love into her hair and they clung to each other, realising that what they had done had only made it more difficult now for her to leave, as she must. Wes never rode out that way with her again, and Rose thought she understood why.

Rose never confided in Jennifer about how intimate she and Wes had been. It wasn't really something that cropped up in conversation – how would that even go? Rose knew Jennifer-Jane believed the old adage 'keep your hand on your ha'penny' and thought that was good currency, even in this part of the world where it was all dollars, nickels and cents.

Rose had learned many things about this particular corner of the States on her visit and one of the most surprising had been that while America seemed advanced and modern in so many ways, scratch the surface and its people were just as reserved and circumspect as the British, more so on occasions. It was as though they contrived to create etiquette rules and patterns of behaviour just to distance themselves from their Wild West heritage. It was all 'No, sir' and 'Yes, ma'am' at every turn, which was just lovely, of course, but Rose also felt that any indiscretion would be judged harshly here. So she never confided in Jennifer about what happened the night Wes brought out the blanket, she just couldn't. It was also why she simply couldn't bring herself to show Jennifer her tattoo. Rose could just imagine the very sight of it would have sent her friend into a full-on Scarlett O'Hara-style meltdown, complete with calls for smelling salts and the need to be fanned by a passing maid. No, it was best she kept that little secret under wraps, what good would it do to upset the apple cart?

Her final goodbye to Jennifer was at Memphis Airport. Jeannie and Frank came along too as if to make sure they'd done their duty in returning her to her homeward transport safe and sound. If only they knew, thought Rose.

Something in Jennifer's demeanour made Rose think she strongly suspected some of what had gone on with Wes. Jennifer-Jane's transformation into adopted Southern belle had made her somewhat scornful of the kind of people she now thought the Presley family were. Elvis may have been the King of Rock 'n' Roll, but his background gave him very little status in her newly opened eyes and any elevation in status his fame had brought him certainly did not extend to Wes – some distant relation most likely on Elvis's jailbird father's side.

That's what it was, thought Rose, as a look passed across Jennifer's face as they embraced for the final time as her flight was called: relief! Her friend was relieved that she was leaving and sparing her the shame of a continued dalliance with someone as unsuitable as Wesley Presley. Rose was almost tempted to show her the tattoo after all – almost, but not quite.

The long, disjointed journey home passed in a fog of memories and misery for Rose as she relived each and every moment spent with Wes. She could almost feel the distance between them stretching as each plane ploughed its way through the air on each leg of the trip. The further she flew, the more her heart ached. She closed her eyes and saw visions of their two matching rose tattoos and felt enveloped in the bond they had created between them. It comforted her.

As soon as she stepped from the plane in London, all that comfort was ripped away in an instant. It was as though the aeroplane had been a sealed container which had preserved all her feelings and belief that she had done nothing wrong. The chilled air around her as she walked on tired legs towards Passport Control was contaminating those feelings. Suddenly, she felt reckless and foolish and very, very alone. What had she done?

She was fearful that friends and family would be able to instantly discern what had happened, what she had become, but those fears were not realised at all. Confusingly, it was almost *disappointing to find that they didn't see any obvious difference when they looked at her. She should have been reassured, but all Rose really wanted to do was to scream and shout. 'Can't you see that I've changed? I'm exotic, fearless and loved. I'm a woman now, I know about the world!' But she said none of these things.*

She hadn't really changed all that much though, had she? The girl who rode pillion on a speeding motorcycle through darkened downtown Memphis, who let herself be branded in a seedy backstreet tattoo parlour, who gave herself to a man she barely knew on a blanket on the ground, now seemed a totally different person in the cold British light of day. Rose wasn't even sure she'd recognise that girl if she was standing right in front of her. That girl was so very far away. Instead, Rose's resolute side took over. She knew it would do no good to pine for a life that wasn't hers and a land that would never be home, no matter how homesick she appeared to feel for it.

She smiled politely and answered truthfully that she'd had a wonderful time and, yes, America was an exciting and thrilling place, but she kept all other thoughts and observations completely to herself. If she just carried on carrying on, getting up, going to work, eating bland stews and mashed vegetables without revealing how much she yearned for a side order of black-eyed peas or biscuits and gravy, everything would gradually get back to normal. It had to.

It was a good plan, it might well have worked, but Rose's homesickness for Memphis was lingering and morphing into something that was making her genuinely ill. The smell of frying fish turned her stomach over, a cup of tea left an odd metallic taste in her mouth and she was tired, so, so tired, all of the time. Perhaps she'd caught a bug or a virus? Her mother put it down to 'overexerting herself' while her father warned that taking time off sick from work wasn't really an option after all the time she'd already spent 'gallivanting'.

She was two and a half months' gone before she accepted that neither gastroenteritis nor gallivanting were to blame for the way she was feeling. She was pregnant.

Telling her mother wasn't the hardest thing she had to face; walking back into the house once she knew her distraught mother had told her father the news was ten times worse. The atmosphere was icy from the moment she stepped into the front hall. The ticking clock on the wall tutted its disapproval as she removed her winter coat, which was already too tight to fasten over her growing stomach. In the end it wasn't rage or harsh words that made her bow her head in shame as she stood in the front room, (The front room! Only used for funerals, Christmas and dealing with your teenage daughter's unplanned pregnancy!) No, it wasn't angry shouting that caused Rose to stand with her eyes fixed on the swirly patterns on the rug, it was simply her father's silent disappointment. And to think she'd been so worried about revealing her tattoo, it seemed almost laughable now, but Rose thought it was unlikely anyone would see the funny side and continued to keep that indiscretion secret.

She reeled from the blow that the pregnancy had landed into her life, but refused to be knocked out. Once she'd made the decision to keep the baby, her parents kept their bitter disappointment about how her life was progressing to themselves in the main. The family motto should have been 'least said, soonest mended'. She hoped and prayed that once the baby arrived tenderness would prevail, and so it eventually transpired. In the meantime she considered herself fortunate that her family did not *throw her out, as many others would have done in the circumstances.*

There was a distinct lack of questions about the father of the child. Her mother and father immediately presumed that there was no chance of whoever was responsible surfacing to shoulder their responsibilities. In fact, Rose often wondered if the appearance at their door of an actual American would have tipped them over the edge completely. What would the neighbours say!?

She wrestled for weeks with the issue herself. What good would contacting Wesley do? Did she really expect him to drop everything and come to her side? Could she seriously consider moving to Memphis if he asked her to? Would he ask her to? Was it fair for her to keep the news about the baby, his baby, to herself? Questions whirled in her mind, making her tummy flip and lurch long after the morning sickness had subsided.

Eventually, she decided the correct thing to do was to write him a letter, she would explain everything as gently and clearly as she could. She was mindful it would be an enormous shock for him too, but she would stress that she didn't expect anything from him at all. She was planning to have the baby and her parents were willing to help her out a little while she worked part-time. There would be no blame or recriminations in the letter, she hadn't been forced to do anything she didn't want to do, but there would be no girlish hopes or fanciful dreams either.

It took at least half a dozen attempts before she had a finished version of the letter. She considered addressing the envelope to Mr Wesley Presley, c/o Graceland, Highway 51 South, Whitehaven, Memphis, Tennessee, USA, but then thought of all the thousands of letters sent by fans to that address from all over the world. The chances of it reaching Wes that way were slim; it would just get lost in the sea of mail that spilled from mail sacks delivered to the Graceland office each and every day.

Instead, Rose decided to send the letter via Jennifer-Jane. She had no choice, it was the only way to reach Wes. She realised she also had to confide in Jennifer, she needed to explain why it was so important she got the letter into Wes's hands; he was the father of her baby and he deserved to know. She kept the note to Jenny short and sweet, then slipped the sealed, heartfelt letter to Wes inside the envelope addressed to Walnut Grove House.

Then Rose waited anxiously for a reply.

Chapter Twenty-Four

By the time Daisy woke after her night-time trip to Graceland, she'd missed the bus for that morning's trip to the Civil Rights Museum down by the Lorraine Motel in town. Todd had stuck to his strict rule that there would be no waiting for no-shows; if you didn't show you didn't go, so Daisy wasn't surprised or bothered that they'd left without her. She needed some time to herself anyway. Anita had no doubt taken Chance along in her place and Priya and Valentin only had eyes for each other so no one would miss her too much.

She lay staring at the ceiling for the longest time, trying to process all that had happened last night.

She'd barely said a word to Blue or Sean as they'd made their way through the tunnel from Graceland and then back to the motel. Dawn was breaking as she'd crawled under the covers into bed and despite the thoughts whirring in her brain, she'd immediately fallen into a deep and dreamless sleep.

Her stomach growled now, telling her it must be nearly lunchtime already and she thought she might try and catch the others up later for afternoon tea at the Peabody Hotel.

She reached for her phone on the bedside table; there was a text from Anita asking if she was okay and a couple of missed calls from Blue, oh, and a voicemail. She pressed speaker and her mother's voice filled the room.

'Daisy, it's your mother here. I hope you are enjoying yourself? I presume so as we haven't heard from you in a couple of days. Just to let you know everything here is, well it's... fine. Anyway, that's all really. I expect you are off having fun somewhere... I hope so. Speak to you soon, love. Bye for now.'

Daisy realised she'd listened to the message while sat cross-legged on the bed with her eyes screwed up tight and her fingers pressed against her mouth, like a bad impression of two of the three wise monkeys. She released herself from her curled position and tried to relax. Her mother's voice was clipped as always, but here and there it had a softer edge to it. She'd ended 'speak to you soon, love' and when she'd added 'I hope so' about her having fun, it felt like there was genuine warmth to those words. That was nice to hear. Perhaps she was missing her? Wonders would never cease.

She fought the urge to call her mother straight back and spill out a whole load of stuff about Wes, the matching tattoo, the fact they may very well be related to Elvis Presley after all... but she couldn't, not yet. Instead, she picked up her phone and dialled another number.

• • •

A half hour later, Daisy systematically chewed and swallowed as she devoured a burger washed down with a banana milkshake; who knew that being at the centre of a deepening mystery could give a girl such a huge appetite?

She watched the parking lot as she sat at the table in the diner across from Graceland. The place was full of tourists filling up on traditional American junk food before or after their pilgrimage to Elvis's home. The food helped her feel a little better; yesterday had been an eventful day and she hadn't had nearly enough food or sleep.

Blue rode his motorcycle into the car park as she watched through the window and she gave him a wave when he looked over to see where she was. As he entered the restaurant, he winked at a waitress and pointed to the booth where Daisy was sitting. The woman in pink and white uniform nodded and was bringing over a mug and a steaming pot of fresh coffee before he had even sat down.

At first Blue took Daisy's quick-fire questions about Wesley Presley in his stride: How long had he known him? Had he always worked at Graceland? Was he married? Did he have any kids?

Blue grinned as he answered each in turn: *ages... for as long as I can remember... not that I know of... well, none he's admitting to!* Blue laughed out loud after the last remark, but saw Daisy take a sharp intake of breath.

'Hey, what's all this? You've not gone off me and set your sights on ole Wes now, have you? I mean he's a charmer 'n' all that, but...' Blue's teasing tailed off when he saw the look on Daisy's face as she shook her head from side to side. 'Daisy, what is it darlin'?'

It all tumbled out in no particular order and Blue attempted to follow the stream of information about her grandmother, matching rose tattoos, a visit to Memphis in 1960, what happens when someone has a series of strokes and then the punchline of Elvis being declared her grandad.

Blue sipped his coffee thoughtfully and showed his police training by asking a series of pertinent questions on the areas he thought were relevant. Had Nana Rose ever made such an outrageous claim before she showed signs of failing health? Did the dates of her visit to Memphis match up with her pregnancy? What did Daisy know about Rose's visit to Tennessee in the Sixties? What was the name of the family she'd stayed with?

In hopeful excitement, Daisy attempted to answer each and every question. She was more relieved than she could say that Blue appeared to be taking her seriously and not calling for emergency back-up or men in white coats. Perhaps with Blue's help she could finally get to the bottom of all this. She answered carefully: No, Rose's claim that Elvis was the father of her child was a complete bolt from the blue... Yes, Lilian had been born on April 1st 1961 a few months after Rose's visit to America (the indignity of being an April Fool only heaping misery on poor fatherless Lilian)... Rose's childhood friend was called Jenny or Jennifer and her family had lived in a place called Walnut Grove House.

Blue suggested they do some more work before demanding answers from an unsuspecting Wes. Daisy realised she agreed wholeheartedly. Rushing in too fast in this instance could be a risky strategy and do far more harm than good, even she realised that. Spotting the tattoo on Wes's arm raised almost as many questions as it answered, and she needed to be very careful about her next move. Having Blue beside her now made her feel so much calmer.

She watched as Blue made some calls, but his initial investigations drew a blank with Walnut Grove House, as she'd already discovered the mansion and grounds were long gone. However, Blue managed to locate records showing when the house had been owned by Mr Frank Reeves and his wife Jeannie, and that in turn led him to Jeannie's little sister Jennifer-Jane who had indeed ended up married to haulage entrepreneur Wade Benson Junior.

WB Haulage was now a large and successful company in Memphis and although Wade Benson Junior was long retired, Blue's detective work revealed the thriving business was run by his and Jennifer's nephew Beau Barley Reeves. Blue arranged an appointment for them at Mr Reeves' office that very afternoon. Blue seemed to have taken this latest development in Daisy's life in his police officer stride and Daisy was seriously impressed with his calm and methodical approach.

Mr Beau Barley Reeves was as polite and courteous as any well-brought-up Southern gentleman, but rather confused by the arrival of a Shelby County police officer and a young British woman in the middle of his working day. He was relieved to find the questions related to some sort of family history of the girl's grandmother and nothing to do with his business affairs.

He offered them coffee and tried his best to rack his brains for any information to help them, but claimed his knowledge of his Aunt Jennifer-Jane's affairs was limited.

'Ah regret to inform you that ma Aunt Jennifer passed over many years ago.' He looked sympathetically at Daisy as he delivered the news, aware that this would do nothing to help her in whatever quest she was on. 'Ah do recall she had a girlfriend from overseas called Rose who came to stay with us when ma brother Bobby Ray and me were young uns but we were too busy playin' cowboys an' injuns to pay her much mind at the time.' He smiled a little uncertainly at the police officer in front of him.

Daisy nodded. Nana Rose's friend Jenny was dead and Rose never knew anything about it. What could have happened over the years for them to cut off all contact?

Officer Cody pressed Beau a little more, asking if there was anything else he could remember about Rose, anything at all?

Beau sat with his elbows on the desk in front of him, resting his handsome face on his clasped hands as he racked his brains. Suddenly he raised his chiselled chin and said, 'The only thing that comes to mind is from around the time of ma Aunt Jennifer's wedding to ma Uncle Wade.'

Daisy leaned forward. 'But Nana Rose didn't come over for the wedding... did she?'

Beau Barley shook his head. 'No, ma'am, and that's what remember, there was a lot of fussin' about all that! Mama and Aunt Jennifer had a very big argument right before the wedding day.'

He bit his lip and let his eyes roam over the ceiling for a

while as he cast his mind back trying to recall any detail of the events. 'Mama had arranged everything for the wedding, she loved to have everything just so and she was expecting Jennifer's friend Rose to come over and take her place as one of the six bridesmaids. As recall there was a yellow chiffon dress and a matchin' wide-brimmed hat jus' waitin' here for her but then at the very last minute, Aunt Jennifer said Rose wasn't comin' after all. She said she didn't want her there and she wasn't invited. Mama was furious, 'specially as it meant there wouldn't be an even number of attendants at the wedding.'

Beau pulled a rueful face at the nit-picking detail but Daisy leaned forward, intrigued, 'Why would Jennifer *not* invite Rose to her wedding... and why wait until the last minute to tell her sister, who was paying for it all?'

Beau sat deep in thought while he dredged his memory for any more nuggets of information. A strange look suddenly passed across his face as his childhood memories met his adult understanding of the world.

'Ah do declare there was something said... about... a baby?'

Daisy gasped and repeated, 'A baby!' but Blue placed a steadying hand on her arm.

Beau was beginning to join up the dots now in a way he'd never had to before. 'Ah thought it awful strange they were arguing about a baby, but that's why Aunt Jennifer said Rose wasn't invited. Ah believe she only told Mama because she went on and on about it all, she could be very persistent when she put her mind to it. Aunt Jennifer said Rose had a baby and if she came there would be trouble and it would cause a… a scandal of some sort. She said she didn't want to hear Rose's name ever again.' He looked mortified as he filled in the last details.

Daisy sat in shock, but Blue nodded in response and then asked, 'What was the date of the wedding, do you know?'

'Well, let's see,' said Beau. 'Ah'm not sure about the exact date but ah recall talk of Jennifer being a June bride 'n' all that – Bobby Ray and I had jus' turned seven years old, so it was sometime in the June…of 1961.'

Blue and Daisy looked at each other and quickly did the sums in their heads. Lilian was born on April 1st, just three months before the wedding date.

'So Jennifer knew her friend Rose had a baby and didn't want to invite her to the wedding… She was ashamed of her!' Daisy looked at Blue as she spoke and a look of dawning understanding passed between them.

Beau Barley looked uncomfortable now. 'Ah imagine it was very diff'rent times back then and Mama and Papa liked to think of themselves as respectable folks. Did the baby have something to do with Rose's visit to us at Walnut Grove? Was the father from here in Memphis?'

'Of course he was!' Daisy felt indignant on Nana Rose's behalf. Who were these people to sit in judgement over her? She also couldn't help but wonder if that harsh judgement had caused events to unfold in a particular way?

Blue was much more diplomatic and shook Beau Barley warmly by the hand as they stood up to leave. 'That's exactly what we intend to look into next; you've been most helpful, thank you kindly for your time, Mr Reeves.'

. . .

Blue dropped Daisy downtown outside the Peabody Hotel so she could join the rest of the excursion party having late afternoon tea and he could get back to work. There was nothing she could do for now but slot back into the tourist trail the rest of her fellow travellers were following. The next step of her own personal journey would have to wait a little while longer.

She rushed across the lobby and into the ladies' restroom to tidy up before presenting herself in the elegant restaurant. Daisy was relieved she'd had the presence of mind to throw on a vintage tea dress that morning. She had teemed the knee-length blue and white polka dot frock with red converse sneakers which wasn't exactly ladylike, but it did give her a slightly rockabilly look that she thought would be acceptable. She decided to go the whole hog and fished a hairband out of her shoulder bag and twisted her unwashed hair up into a ponytail. After adding a finishing touch of red lipstick, she was ready.

The party of Graceland Experience tourists were mostly too busy helping themselves to sandwiches and cakes from the three-tiered stands on the tables in front of them to notice when she snuck into the room. The first person to spot her was Valentin, who gallantly rushed to find an extra chair so she could squeeze in next to him, Priya, Anita and Chance. Sean was also at the round table laid with a white tablecloth and floral bone china and was talking more animatedly than she had seen him on the whole trip so far.

'I mean, thirty years? To believe in something so

strongly that you could do that for thirty years?' He shook his head in disbelief and took a bite of his dainty sandwich.

Daisy accepted a teacup from Anita as she passed it to her and looked at her quizzically.

'While we all went round the Civil Rights Museum, Sean found a new friend,' said Anita with a sideways look at Sean.

Sean spluttered on his sandwich, 'C'mon, you have to admit, the woman has shown amazing fortitude, I mean... thirty years!'

'I'm not disputing that,' countered Anita, then she turned to Daisy and explained,

'There's this woman outside the museum who has been holding a vigil ever since...' She tailed off and Sean interjected, '1988!'

'Right, yes, 1988. Something about her being the last person evicted from the place before they turned it into a museum.'

'She thinks making the very place where Dr Martin Luther King was killed into a museum is glorifying his death rather than the work he did in his life,' said Sean earnestly. 'They spent millions developing the site, but the upshot was they closed the motel and cleared out all the poor black people, like her, who had nowhere else to go.'

Daisy buttered a scone as Sean held forth on the matter for the next twenty minutes. She was actually happy to have something else to think about.

Sean explained that Jacqueline Smith had worked as a desk clerk at the Lorraine Motel from the early Seventies and had also lived there until she was evicted.

'She was in room 303,' said Sean. 'Just a couple of doors down from where Dr King was shot when he came out onto the balcony from room 306.' Priya shuddered and reached for Val's hand as Sean carried on. 'She sits under an umbrella with everything she owns in the world beneath the table in front of her covered with a tarpaulin, day after day. Right behind her there's a red and white wreath on the balcony where Dr King fell when he was shot, but she deliberately sits with her back to it.'

'What is she hoping to achieve?' Sean had Daisy's complete attention now.

'As far as I could gather, she's making the point that turning the Lorraine Motel into a housing project for those on low income would have been a better legacy for Dr King.'

'Instead of making it into a shrine?' Daisy could follow the argument the woman seemed to be making.

'Well, it's a bit more than a shrine,' said Anita. 'The museum tells the story of the whole civil rights movement, for those who bother to actually go in.'

'Not everything she said made complete sense to me,' said Priya, 'She just kept going on about "gentrification and rejuvenating the community" and lots of other stuff I couldn't follow.'

'You had to be patient with her,' said Sean, reaching for his camera. 'I'm not sure how much sense any of us would make if we'd been protesting for as long as she has.'

Sean's words made Daisy think about Nana Rose and how keeping the name of the father of her baby a secret for so many years seemed to have caused her failing mind to play tricks on her. It was like the buried emotions corrupted over time, like a damaged computer file. When Rose finally decided to retrieve the information, it was all jumbled up and difficult to decipher. Her love for Elvis Presley and his music had intertwined with memories of her lost love Wesley. As an old lady she couldn't be sure where one ended and the other began. Daisy was also now wondering if the trauma of being rejected by both Wes and her friend Jennifer had added to Rose's suffering and subsequent confusion and her heart broke even more for her grandmother.

Sean flicked through the shots he'd taken that morning and held his camera out towards Daisy so she could see the photographs. She looked at an image of a remarkably glamorous, slim black woman. She wore dark glasses and had a black scarf draped over her head and tied at the neck. The red and white painted signs around her proclaimed things like 'Exploiting the Legacy' and 'Gentrification is an Abuse of Civil Liberties'. A smaller sign in black lettering read 'Stop Worshipping the Dead'.

What a strange place Memphis was turning out to be, thought Daisy, as she flicked through the pictures. Sean carried on talking about his conversation with the remarkable Ms Smith – the two most popular tourist attractions in the city were both memorials to dead men, Martin Luther King and Elvis Presley.

Daisy zoomed in on a photograph of the woman looking directly towards the camera; her arms were defensively folded and her mouth set in a hard line. Over her shoulder was a gaudy marquee sign emblazoned with the Lorraine

Motel name. Daisy shook her head in wonder as she realised that for this particular desk clerk dressed in black, Heartbreak Hotel was a very real place indeed.

As a waitress cleared their table a little while later, Daisy was grateful that Sean's sudden fascination with Memphis history had diverted any unwanted attention into what she had been up to in the last few hours. The last thing Blue had said to her as he dropped her off was, 'You know you'll have to speak to Wes soon.' It was much more of a statement than a question.

She'd bitten her lip and nodded her head, but words had eluded her. If she didn't know what to say to Blue, what on earth was she going to say to Mr Wesley Presley? All the clues were now pointing to Wes being her long-lost grandfather, the father her own mother had never known, Rose's lost love. This was a very big deal indeed. With all her heart, she was hoping that when she and Blue met up again later this evening he would help her come up with a plan for what to do next.

Chapter Twenty-Five

Daisy was surprised to find Blue driving a silver Ford truck when he came to pick her up that night, and not his motorcycle or even a squad car.

'Well, we can't roll into a drive-in movie with the blues and twos blazing now, can we, darlin'?' said Blue with a wink as he opened the passenger door so she could hop in.

A drive-in movie? Daisy beamed at Blue as he headed the car out onto the freeway. She was going to a drive-in movie, now that was just about as vintage Americana as it was possible to get. She was definitely going to enjoy this.

Blue had thought of everything; there was a cooler of soft drinks on the back seat, along with bags of popcorn and potato chips and a blanket in case the evening turned cold.

When they arrived at the outdoor cinema there were two films listed: one was a modern action sci-fi and the other was a showing of the black and white classic, *Casablanca*. Blue swung the car into the lane for the wartime romance while doing a passable Humphry Bogart impression: 'Here's lookin' at you, kid!'

Daisy knew she was no Ingrid Bergman, but answered with the famous last line of the movie: 'I think this is the beginning of a beautiful friendship.' Blue turned to look at her as she delivered the line and the meaning behind her words crackled like static electricity between them.

The truck was the perfect choice for movie watching as it had one long front seat where they could cuddle to gaze up at the screen. Blue tuned his car radio into the frequency for the soundtrack and the booming orchestral music of the opening titles surrounded them.

They watched the movie in silence for a little while, Daisy entranced by the experience of seeing the screen against a backdrop of a darkening evening sky. After a while, Blue turned the volume a little lower and began to talk. He'd been thinking about the recent turn of events all day.

Daisy expected him to question her about what she was going to do or say to Wes, but instead he started talking about Nana Rose. He'd given it a lot of thought, he said, and he was sure that whatever had happened between Rose and Wes had not been a sordid or meaningless affair.

'That's not the kind of guy Wes is, or was, I'm sure of it,' he said. 'And let's look at the evidence here – no one gets matching tattoos unless it's the real deal, they just don't.'

Daisy had to admit he made a convincing argument and she was surprised to feel something akin to relief wash over her as she realised the thought of Nana Rose being wanton and reckless in her youth had been bothering her quite a bit.

There was also the nagging sense of injustice she felt about Jennifer cutting Rose out of her life because she'd had a baby.

'What a cow!' Daisy didn't hold back in her opinion of the way she thought Jennifer-Jane Benson had behaved.

Blue nodded but kept his voice even. 'I'm not defending her, but Southern folks can be very traditional in their ways,' he said. 'To be an unmarried mother would've been a very big deal back then and Wes, well, to someone like Miss Jennifer-Jane he'd just be poor white trash from the wrong side of the tracks, I should reckon.'

Daisy was now indignant on poor Wesley's behalf. 'Do you think that's why Rose never told anyone about him? Do you think Jennifer swore her to secrecy in case it tarnished her precious family name? How could someone who is meant to be your friend do something like that?'

'We may never know what really happened between them,' said Blue thoughtfully, 'but I'm sure Rose and Wes were really in love. I know Wes well enough and you sure knew Rose. When you meet someone you truly connect with, I mean... you just know, don't you?' He shifted a little in his seat and flicked his eyes back to the movie on the screen as Daisy turned to look at him. She couldn't be sure in the darkness, but it looked like he was actually blushing.

Lost for words, she answered by nuzzling into his neck; damn, he smelled so good! The nuzzling led to kissing and the kissing led... well there's only so far anyone could get carried away in the front seat of a truck at a drive-in movie, although pulling the blanket from the backseat over themselves helped considerably.

Breathless and dishevelled, Daisy eventually emerged from under the blanket. 'Officer Cody, you're going to get us arrested!'

Blue ran a hand through his now unruly hair and admitted sheepishly, 'I suppose we oughta take care.'

They attempted to watch the rest of the film while wrapped in one another's arms, but Daisy could feel the beat of Blue's heart as she laid her head on his chest and the sensation made her aware of every nerve ending in her body. Her senses heightened, she could feel each and every individual hair on her head, a somewhat bizarre indication of deep desire, but Daisy was sure that's exactly what it was.

It struck her even more keenly how hard it must have been for Rose to leave Wes back in 1960. Did she know she was pregnant before she left? If she had, how could she ever have got on that plane back to Britain? If Wes had known she was carrying his baby, would he have been able to just watch her walk away? What if she didn't know? What if they had both tried to go back to their usual lives and then Rose had discovered she was pregnant – pregnant and alone back in Wales, so very far away? Did she try to tell him? How? Did she write him a letter? Surely he wouldn't have turned his back on her? This was a man who had tattooed an image of a rose on his arm – the same rose that matched the one Rose had kept hidden all these years. Surely those tattoos meant something binding and powerful? What was it that forced Rose and Wes apart and kept them from being together for all these years?

As if Blue was reading her cartwheeling mind, he kissed

the top of her tingling head and said softly, 'I can't bear the thought of you disappearing from my life.'

Daisy gazed up at him, appalled at the very thought of being torn away from Blue but knowing there was still so much to sort out before she could concentrate on her own feelings.

Daisy watched the screen as Rick walked off into the mist, away from Ilsa, to the strains of 'The Marseillaise'. Tears pricked behind Daisy's eyes as she watched the lovers say goodbye. The stirring music of the French national anthem signalled the end of the movie and as the words THE END filled the screen, Blue broke the uneasy mood. 'Hey, it's too early to call it a night, let's go dancing!'

'Dancing?' Daisy looked at him in amazement; this was a gear change she wasn't expecting.

'You don't wanna go back to the motel yet, do you?' Blue was already starting up the truck and reversing out of their parking spot as he asked, and Daisy realised he was right. Neither of them wanted this night to end.

When he pulled up outside a dilapidated shack on what looked like an out-of-town industrial estate just twenty minutes later, Daisy's enthusiasm faltered for a moment.

'Hey, don't worry, it looks a lot better from the inside.' Blue laughed, noticing the expression on her face.

The one-storey building had bars on the windows and the pre-fabricated dingy grey exterior was peeling badly, but there were plenty of cars and trucks parked in the lot in front, so Daisy put her faith in Blue and followed him in through the double doors. As soon as they stepped into the nondescript lobby, Daisy could hear the twangy guitar and jaunty fiddle of pure country music. As Blue pushed open the swing door to the club itself, she was amazed to see the room was wood panelled with red and white gingham tablecloths on circular tables dotted around a dance floor. There were Stetson hats, denim jeans and cowboy boots in every direction and the whole place was lit by glowing lamps and fairy lights bathing the place in a golden haze.

Blue grinned at the wide-eyed expression on her face and took her by the hand to lead her to a table on a raised area that looked like an old-fashioned front porch with a straw half roof. She settled herself at the table, pleased she was wearing a denim shirt knotted at the waist. She hitched her long flouncy white skirt up a little to better show off her rose-patterned cowboy boots; she was desperate to look like she belonged.

At the far end of the room, the band were on a small stage in front of a gold glitter curtain and Daisy was thrilled to see couples dancing together to the music – properly dancing, not just jigging on the spot or shuffling their feet self-consciously.

It was too noisy to talk much but Daisy was happy to sip from the bottle of beer that Blue had ordered from the waitress. His sign language skills were just one of his many talents. Another, she thought to herself, was knowing this was exactly what she needed. The homely atmosphere and jaunty music were so friendly and welcoming it was good for the soul.

After a while the fiddle player took hold of the

microphone and announced something called the 'Cotton-Eye Joe'. Instantly, the dancers on the floor rearranged themselves into formation while others left their tables and found their place amongst them. The music started up and Daisy watched in awe as the group moved back and forth as one in a perfectly executed line-dancing performance. It looked incredibly complicated to Daisy as the music changed and the dancers lined up in new positions. The choreography got increasingly confusing as the fiddle player called out instructions like 'applejack', 'camel walk' and 'travelling buttermilk'.

Daisy was so absorbed in watching the action on the dancefloor that she was taken by surprise when Blue stood up and offered to take her hand. She looked at him like he was crazy. 'I-I can't do that!'

He grinned, leaned down to her ear and said, 'I'm gonna teach you the "Sweetheart Shuffle". It's easy, just follow me.'

With that he took her down onto the floor and stood behind her with his hands on her shoulders while they watched the other dancers as the music changed. Daisy saw the couples sway from side to side on the spot while the man stood behind his partner, keeping their hands held at shoulder height they crossed their feet a couple of times one way, then the other, then the girl twirled under her partner's arm and then they swayed on the spot again for a count of four. The couples all moved around the floor in a big circle for this dance and Daisy thought that although it didn't look too difficult, she might be about to make an absolute fool of herself.

Either the fiddle player sensed her nerves, or Blue gave him a wink, and he took up the microphone again and began calling out each move as the dance progressed. One moment she was standing on the edge watching the action, the next Daisy and Blue were part of the formation, swaying, kicking, crossing their feet and twirling along with the rest of them. Feeling safe and loved and totally at home, Daisy danced while the band sang about honky-tonk bars and Cadillac cars and she thought to herself how much Nana Rose would have loved this.

Chapter Twenty-Six

Elvis and Wes

Graceland without Elvis had been a very strange place to be. Sgt Presley had been away for almost two years by March 1960, completing his military service in the United States army based in Germany.

Young Wesley Presley was grateful to his distant cousin for the casual work as a security guard at the Graceland gates. Fans still came by and there were staff and deliveries to check in and out regularly. Still, it just wasn't the same without the King in his castle.

As the date of Elvis's demob approached, a sense of excitement built not only amongst his fans, but also within the grounds of the Graceland estate where everyone was determined to make sure everything was just the way the boss liked it. Wes was even put to work washing and waxing Elvis's cars, including his 1954 pink Cadillac; by the time Wes finished, he could see his own face in the paintwork.

SUZAN HOLDER

Wes couldn't wait for Elvis to return, but he knew the homecoming would be bittersweet. After his career took off, Elvis bought Graceland for the woman he loved most in the world – his mother Gladys. But his 'Satnin' would not be there waiting for him at their Southern mansion. Just after Elvis started his basic training in 1958, Gladys had suddenly died, at the age of forty-six, after a bout of hepatitis, and her homely presence was still much missed by all who had known and loved her.

Wes understood that Elvis would therefore be anxious during his journey home, but what he didn't know was that the star had more than one trouble on his mind. After so long away, Elvis was nervous about whether his fans would still be loyal or if he even had a career to return to? Everyone had said that rock 'n' roll music would never last. What would he do if the kids had moved on to someone or something new?

The turbulence on Elvis's flight out of Germany also echoed the bumpy ride that was his love life. Just a few months before discharge he'd met an exceptionally pretty young girl with dark hair and blue eyes. Elvis had plenty of girlfriends, but still suffering with grief from the loss of his mother, Presley found particular comfort in the company of Priscilla Beaulieu. Now he was forced to leave her behind and he wasn't sure if they would ever see each other again.

It was late evening on March 3rd 1960 when Elvis Presley set foot on British soil for the first and only time in his entire life. The day before, he had waved goodbye to fourteen-year-old Priscilla at Frankfurt airport and boarded a plane to take him home to America, home to his fans, his career and Graceland.

Prestwick airport in Scotland was a re-fuelling stop and Elvis walked down the steps of the plane wearing full dress uniform.

Patient and polite, he stopped to talk to the small number of fans who'd gathered at the base after hearing rumours that Sgt Presley would be arriving. Those lucky enough to witness the moment reported he was the best-looking man they had ever seen.

Elvis breathed in the Scottish air and remarked, 'I kinda like the idea of Scotland. I'm gonna do a European tour and Scotland will certainly be on my list.'

Just two hours later, he re-boarded the plane, never to return.

His DC-7 aircraft landed next in New Jersey and Elvis still had several hours to travel by train for the final leg of his journey back to Memphis, Tennessee. His hometown police department provided a squad car to finally drive the exhausted star through the music gates of his mansion home, but there would be no chance for Elvis to relax.

Wes caught only a glimpse of his cousin as the convoy swept past on the driveway. Elvis looked thinner than he remembered, although Wes was relieved to see how much hair had grown back since the army had forced him to shave his head. The quiff was back.

Within hours the world's press descended on Graceland and Wes was kept busy checking credentials to make sure only accredited reporters were admitted. It all went off without a hitch. When he watched the newsreel footage later, he saw a tired and slightly bemused-looking Elvis conduct a good-natured press conference in the office building out back of the house, fielding questions while seated at his father's desk.

Once the reporters had gone, Elvis walked around the Graceland grounds taking everything in. He made his way across the lawn to say hi to his Uncle Vester, sat on a chair just outside the gate house.

SUZAN HOLDER

Vester greeted his brother's boy warmly. 'Good to have you home, son,' he said.

Elvis stood with his hands on his hips, surveying his empire. 'It sure is good to be home,' he answered before he suddenly spotted Wes lingering in the doorway of the brick cabin. 'Hey, man,' Elvis said, raising his hand in a mock salute. Wes grinned and saluted back, but he thought Elvis looked a little sad; maybe it would take a while longer before he settled back into his old, wild ways.

Despite his lingering grief, Elvis began to pick up the pieces of his former life. Local TV star Anita Wood had been his steady girl before he'd left for Germany and they'd written to each other throughout his time away. Just before clocking off for the night, Wes opened the gates as blonde Anita arrived at Graceland, no doubt eager to be back in Elvis's lonely arms. Wes couldn't help but feel jealous of his relative's easy access to beautiful girlfriends. Elvis had romanced his first leading lady Debra Pagett, after starring with her in the movie Love Me Tender *and Wes had been dumbstruck at the sight of Hollywood star Natalie Wood on the back of Elvis's motorbike when she'd come to visit him in Memphis. Wes wasn't hankering for a movie star girlfriend, but it would be neat to have a pretty girl on his arm – just a regular girl who was fun to be around would be fine.*

The very next day Elvis headed for Forest Hill Cemetery to see the stone angels he had commissioned to stand watch over his mother's grave. He carefully rearranged the fresh flowers that were there. While he'd been away he'd fixed it so a new bouquet would always arrive each and every week, like clockwork, from Burke's florist store.

Elvis had surrounded himself with friends and family while living off base in Bad Nauheim, Germany. His father Vernon and grandma Minnie-Mae Presley moved from Graceland to Germany, along with several chums from home like Red West, Lamar Fike and Cliff Greaves. He'd bonded with a couple of new guys too while serving his army time and Charlie Hodge and Joe Esposito now arrived at Graceland for the first time to take up their places in Elvis's unique entourage. They found Elvis was getting back into rock 'n' roll mode. There were recording sessions and TV appearances scheduled, songs had to be sorted through and film scripts were piling up to be read. In readiness for his return appearances, Elvis dyed his light-brown hair jet black, just like his idol Tony Curtis.

'The colour makes my eyes look a deeper blue on screen,' he told the guys.

Colonel Parker had been drip-feeding Elvis fans and the media titbits of news and previously recorded music to keep his boy's career ticking over while he was stationed in Europe. Both Elvis and his manager were terrified that the rock 'n' roll bubble would burst while he was off the scene and a new pretender would emerge to claim the King's crown. Colonel Parker used Elvis's call-up to the army as an opportunity to re-package this snarling, sneering long-haired sex machine as a more family-friendly, all-round entertainer. He had flat refused Elvis's pleas to be allowed to join the Special Forces in the hope that he could continue his singing career alongside lighter army duties. Parker convinced Elvis that any special treatment would be held against him in the long run.

'Show them you're just a regular Joe, do your duty and keep your nose clean, son,' said Parker from the side of his mouth while chewing on a cigar. Elvis, as usual, did as he was told.

Duty done, Elvis's triumphant return was completely stage-managed by Parker and both had been heartily relieved to see the number of folks who turned out to line the route of his train journey back to the Deep South.

The Colonel had been busy while Elvis was away. Now his star was home he too was put straight to work. First off, a recording session in Nashville with Scotty Moore, DJ Fontana and the Jordanaires. They worked through the night and recorded six tracks including the mournful 'Soldier Boy' and more successful 'Stuck on You' and 'A Mess of Blues'.

Elvis, his band and backing singers grabbed what sleep they could on the train ride from Nashville to Miami the very next day. They had a few days rehearsal before taping a Frank Sinatra TV special which Ol' Blue Eyes had rather reluctantly been convinced to call 'Welcome Home Elvis'. Sinatra appeared a little uncomfortable with his role of fatherly benefactor to the whip-thin young Presley. He made a remark about Elvis having lost his sideburns, but most of the jokes in the script were on him. Comedian Joey Bishop at one point teased his fellow Rat Pack compadre by saying he'd never heard women screaming at a male singer before! The studio audience joined in with the mockery by rather cruelly groaning when Sinatra offered to sing solo for them.

Despite being gussied up in a black dinner suit and matching bow tie, when Elvis sauntered onto the set, the screams were deafening. He performed the ballad 'Fame and Fortune' but really loosened up when performing 'Stuck on You'. He clicked his fingers, swayed his hips and when he hitched up an imaginary belt and looked directly down the camera lens, the swoons were audible.

The stand-out moment of the show was when the two singers

performed a duet, each singing the other's song. 'You do "Witchcraft",' Sinatra told Elvis, still attempting to keep the upper hand. 'I'll do one of the other ones.'

As the music started, Elvis copied Frank by shrugging his shoulders to the music. 'We work in the same way,' said Sinatra, 'only in different areas.' He sang a middle-of-the-road version of 'Love Me Tender' as, next to him, Presley jerked involuntarily as he sang and shook the quiff of his hair loose so it fell across his brow. He played with the timing, paused and stuttered the word 'W-witchcraft' then seamlessly blended his harmonies with Frank for the final phrase of 'Love Me Tender'.

'Man, that's pretty,' Sinatra was forced to admit. Elvis was back.

Returning home to Memphis, Elvis was kept busy juggling his complicated love life. There was rarely a moment when Elvis was more than a few feet away from a pretty girl, but he and Anita had a special bond. He wanted her by his side whenever he was at Graceland and splashed out on an expensive diamond necklace for her, but still he just couldn't shake off his feelings for the girl he'd met in Germany, Priscilla. He might go weeks or even months, but then he'd get the sudden urge to call her; he just liked hearing her sweet voice.

After weeks away in California filming GI Blues, his first movie since leaving the army, Priscilla got a call from Elvis. As usual he took no notice of the time difference and the phone rang in the early hours of the German morning. The voice she heard down the line sounded thoroughly dejected.

'I just finished looping the goddamn picture,' said Elvis, 'and I hate it. They have about twelve songs in it that aren't worth a cat's ass.'

Priscilla was a schoolgirl with no words of wisdom to offer, but Elvis liked that she listened patiently.

'I feel like a goddamn idiot breaking into song while I'm talking to some chick on a train,' moaned Elvis.

He decided to distract himself from worries about his movie career with a trip to Las Vegas. Accompanied by his faithful retinue of pals, they hit the casinos and showrooms of the famous strip. Elvis and his entourage toured the city in style. As two black limousines swept up to the front of the Riviera Hotel late one night, onlookers were amazed to see Elvis emerge surrounded by a coterie of guys wearing black mohair suits and dark sunglasses. Then and there they acquired the name – the Memphis Mafia.

They took in some shows and played a little blackjack and roulette, but Elvis had mixed feelings about Vegas. The 'sleep all day, party all night' system suited his preferred routine. Elvis was nocturnal and everyone around him had to reverse their attitudes to day and night to keep up with him, but Elvis never forgot that Vegas had also been the location of early humiliation.

In 1956, just as he was breaking through as a huge star coast to coast, Colonel Parker secured a two-week residency for Elvis at the New Frontier Hotel and Casino. It was a frontier too far at that stage of his career. Despite his hit records and the wild enthusiasm of his young fans at live appearances all over the South, the middle-aged, middle-class audience in the Vegas showroom were distinctly underwhelmed. One critic remarked that Elvis's appearance was like serving 'a jug of corn liquor at a champagne party'. Elvis never quite forgave Vegas for that.

· · ·

Back in Memphis, things were moving so fast in Elvis's life he wasn't sure which way to jump. While he was in Germany, he'd been fearful that 1960 would be the year his career stalled. Instead he had returned to a rapturous welcome from fans and the Sinatra TV special had aired in early May with record ratings. The Colonel had secured great recording and movie deals, but Elvis thought most of the songs and scripts were 'lame'. Anita, Priscilla and the guys all listened in turn to his moans and tried to reassure him that the next song or film would be better.

Even more galling to Elvis was his father's revelation that he intended to marry platinum-blonde mother of three Dee Stanley. Elvis was as appalled by this news as he was by Dee's annoying habit of referring to him as 'my little prince'. While Elvis enjoyed hanging out with the young Stanley boys – Billy, Ricky and David – he made a point of not attending Vernon and Dee's July wedding in Alabama. Instead he attempted to ignore the event entirely by going boating on McKellar Lake in Memphis. In public Elvis kept things civilised, telling the press, 'She seems pretty nice. I only had one mother and that's it. There'll never be another. As long as she understands that, we won't have any trouble.' Privately his torment was clear; once his father moved Dee into the room at Graceland that Vernon had once shared with Gladys, Elvis could not bear it. A short while later, he paid for a new house for them to live in, away from Graceland.

He spent the rest of his summer break trying not to think about Vernon and Dee, the botched mixing on his recording of 'It's Now or Never' and how much he missed Priscilla.

With time on his hands before shooting started in August on his next picture, Flaming Star, *he threw himself into a dizzying array of distractions. As well as boating on McKellar Lake, he* took up karate, played energetic games of touch football with the guys and rented out the best amusement spots in town. Elvis and his gang became regulars at Libertyland Fairground, the Memphian Movie Theatre and the Rainbow Rollerdrome, always turning up in the dead of night so they could have the run of each place away from prying eyes.

Elvis and the guys played hard. Whether they were going in for a tackle on the football pitch, or seeing how fast they could skate 'the whip' holding hands in a long line across the rink, Elvis threw himself into every activity with gusto. Trouble was, when it was time to get back to work, the guys still wanted to play. The other guests at the Beverley Wiltshire Hotel in LA complained so much about the antics of the Memphis Mafia during the filming of Flaming Star that Elvis was forced to move out of the hotel and rent a house in Bel Air instead.

Eventually, filming completed, they all returned to Graceland and resumed the round of non-stop activities, but one day in September Elvis woke up at lunchtime, bored. None of the entertainments on offer appealed to him that day; he decided instead to go shopping.

As he drove his shiny new Rolls Royce Silver Cloud back towards the Graceland music gates a few hours later, his mood was good. Especially when he remembered the look on the face of the car showroom cleaning lady when he'd suddenly presented her with the keys to her very own brand-new Cadillac. Hell yeah, that sure felt fine.

He slowed the car down as he turned into the driveway; the guys on the gates were good and always swung the wrought-iron railings open in time for him to pull in before the fans who gathered there had too much time to see if he was at the wheel or not. Today though, he decided to stop and sign some autographs and the guards hung back, keeping a watchful eye. He passed the time of day with a mother and her daughter and some shy youths who stuck out scraps of paper for him to sign. They told him they loved his records and a girl in horn-rimmed spectacles said how much she was looking forward to seeing GI Blues when it was released.

'I jus' can't wait to see what it was like for y'all in the army,' said the girl.

Elvis thought about the scenes when he was singing to Juliet Prowse on a rotating Ferris wheel and performing in a puppet theatre show. He grinned at the girl. 'Yeah, honey, it was jus' like that.'

As he waved goodbye to the fans, he spotted his cousin Wes loitering beside the gatehouse. The kid looked as miserable as a half-drowned polecat and he called over to him. 'Hey there, Wesley, why don't ya come up to the house for some of Alberta's cookies?'

Wes stopped kicking the gravel at his feet and smiled gratefully at Elvis. 'Sure, boss, I'll be right there.'

Sitting out on the back porch a little while later, Elvis and Wes ate cookies and drank milk like a pair of raggy-assed kids. Elvis snuck a sideways glance at Wesley as he demolished another cookie; his distant cousin had grown up some while he'd been away, for sure. He wouldn't be a teenager much longer.

'You doin' okay?' Elvis made it sound like he was simply shootin' the breeze.

Wes gulped down some milk before wiping his mouth and answering, 'Sure.'

Elvis nodded and looked out across the paddock at the grazing horses. He could wait, he had time… In fits and starts, Wes told Elvis a little of what was on his mind. Elvis listened, keeping his eyes on the horses in the distance. He'd figured it was girl trouble but Wes sure had it bad. Since Elvis had returned from Germany, Wes had fallen for a girl who lived halfway across the world. What were the chances? Elvis thought about Priscilla. He'd only met her a few months before he'd been discharged but the little girl had gotten right under his skin. He'd thought he could forget about her once he got home – he loved Anita after all – but there was something about that little Air Force brat that had gotten a real hold on him.

'I dunno what to tell you, man.' Elvis was having enough trouble thinking about his own love life.

Wes pulled a small photograph from his pocket. He didn't own a wallet so it was tucked inside a used envelope, but it had already become creased and worn at the edges. The picture was the only one he had of Rose. It had been taken by Jennifer's boyfriend Wade and showed the couple with their arms around each other standing outside the Arcade Restaurant.

Elvis looked at the picture in Wes's hand and gave a low whistle. 'She sure is a pretty little thing, Wes.' He took in Rose's petite frame and dark hair and thought yet again about Priscilla Beaulieu over in Germany, a little girl like that could bring a man to his knees. 'I reckon you just gotta give it some time,' Elvis said, trying hard to sound like he meant it. 'Some other girl will have you hooked before you know it.'

Wes studied Rose's face in the picture and thought about her funny sing-song accent. He squeezed his eyes tight shut and cleared his throat with a hoarse cough as he shoved the picture back into his pocket. 'Yeah, you're right, man. Women, hey? Can't live with 'em—'

'Can't live without 'em!' answered Elvis, slapping Wes on the back.

As he watched Wes amble his way back down to the gatehouse, Elvis's mood was melancholy once more. He decided to get his father to increase Wes's hours on gate-keeping duty. He was a good kid, it would be a shame if he got into mischief trying to get over some girl. Keeping him busy was all Elvis could think of to do – or perhaps if he bought him a Cadillac?

Elvis turned to go back inside. Maybe he should give Priscilla a call? Or he could get Joe to go fetch Anita and bring her up to the house. Maybe he'd just do both, he could call Priscilla while Anita was on her way... Anita or Priscilla, Priscilla or Anita? Elvis felt so lonesome it would take more than two women to tend his aching heart.

A few weeks later, sat in his private office next to his bedroom upstairs at Graceland, Elvis listened to the demo of his new single. He'd poured his internal anguish into the powerful ballad with heart-rending lyrics but Elvis wasn't happy. 'Are You Lonesome Tonight' had an unusual spoken section midway through and Elvis had been uneasy about whether he could do it justice. On the night he'd recorded it he'd put off working on the track until after 4am. When he eventually agreed to tackle the song, he'd asked producer Chet Atkins to throw everyone out of the studio and switch off all the lights. Only when he was alone, in complete darkness, was Elvis able to perform the song the way he wanted *to. But as he listened now to the record play out, it wasn't just the clipped last note that bothered him.*

He'd been perched on a stool in the centre of Nashville's Studio B singing into an overhead mic at the session. As he finished singing, and before the lights were switched back on, he'd moved to get off the stool and accidentally clunked his head on the microphone right in front of him. He reckoned the loud clunk had destroyed his best take but a canny engineer managed to snip most of the noise out and only someone paying extraordinarily close attention would ever pick up on the slight click sound Elvis's head butt had left. Chet Atkins thought Elvis's performance was so special he decided to sacrifice the final consonant of the song rather than make him re-take it. No, it wasn't that. Elvis shook his head in annoyance as he set the record to play again. The mix was all wrong. His voice was way out in front and the Jordanaires backing vocals were far too quiet. He picked up the phone to call the Colonel.

Elvis's song 'Are You Lonesome Tonight' echoed from the upstairs window and clear across the Graceland grounds. Down at the gate, Wes turned and listened to the words about straying memories, lost sweethearts and loneliness. His girl was long gone, he'd tried and failed to reach her and now he knew how lonesome a man could be. He'd lost his love and his broken heart ached for Rose.

Chapter Twenty-Seven

Daisy's mind was full of imagined scenes featuring a teenage Rose and a young and handsome Wesley Presley. She pictured them together, laughing, dancing, kissing. She pictured them apart, upset? Angry? Lonely?

If she was right and Wes was her grandfather, what could have happened between him and Rose that caused their love affair to fail so spectacularly? Had her grandmother dumped Wes before heading back home to Wales? Had Wes rejected a pregnant and vulnerable Rose? Had something occurred beyond either's control that caused the relationship to end?

Daisy was acutely aware it was a delicate subject. It was against all her usual instincts, but she was determined not to blow the situation now. She knew it would be wrong to rush headlong into confronting and questioning Wes. He seemed like a nice guy, but who knew how he would react to being accused of being Lilian's absent father?

She was also constrained by the schedule of the

Graceland Experience trip she was part of. Today they were booked on a tour of the famous Sun Recording Studio and, anyway, she could hardly just march up to the Graceland gates and demand to speak to Mr Presley on a 'personal matter'. Blue said he was working on setting something up so that Daisy could see Wes again. Until then she had to try and keep her fevered imagination under control and bide her time. She could do with more thinking time anyway.

The mini-bus dropped the sightseeing party off on the corner of Union Avenue and Marshall, and Daisy looked down towards the old recording studio where a huge prop guitar protruded from the corner of the triangular building and seemed to hover in mid-air above the entrance. She paused to take a couple of photos and looked around to ask someone to take a shot of her with the iconic SUN logo in the background, but everyone seemed wrapped up in themselves today. Anita and Chance were constantly whispering to each other and had taken to abruptly ending their conversations when anyone else came near. Priya and Val had spent the entire journey from the motel trading Welsh and Russian words and sayings – all of which were equally unintelligible to anyone else!

Daisy saw Sean lingering by the bus, looking awkward as always, and gave him a smile and a nod. She was relieved to see him gratefully smile back and he jumped at the chance to snap a couple of pictures of her before they made their way over to the studio building. Their late-night encounter at Graceland had usefully served as a bonding experience.

They all made their way through the gift shop full of t-shirts and memorabilia, and up the stairs to the small museum on the first floor.

Daisy was impatient to get to the one-room recording studio itself – the place where Elvis and Scotty Moore and Bill Black had accidentally begun a rock 'n' roll revolution. The setting for the story Nana Rose had told her so many times. She gave the assorted items on display in the glass cases lining the walls of the small upstairs room a cursory glance, but nothing much grabbed her attention. That was before Patrick, the tour guide, started his presentation, however. His enthusiasm and evangelical zeal for all things 'Sun' was infectious. He gave a brief rundown of the history of the tiny studio started in 1950 by Sam Phillips and his assistant Marion Keisker. The place Sam opened was known back then as the Memphis Recording Service and if it hadn't been for Marion the world might never have heard of Elvis Presley. Patrick told the story with an urgency that made everyone shudder with horror at the thought that Presley might have remained undiscovered if not for that tiny quirk of fate.

'Back in 1953 Elvis was working for Crown Electric, driving his truck back and forth on Union, day after day,' drawled Patrick, clearly a Memphis native. 'It took him a little while to get up the courage to come in and record a song, anyone here who might know what song he chose?'

Patrick looked at the assembled group and a couple of hands shot up.

'It was "My Happiness",' said a middle-aged woman from South Carolina. 'It was a present for his mother.'

Patrick grinned in response, 'Yeah, that's what folks say,

but I reckon that was just an excuse he gave Marian so he could book a slot in the studio and hear what he sounded like on a record.' Patrick nodded his head as he warmed to his theme. 'Well, Marian liked what she heard, made a note of Elvis's name and the fact he told her he didn't sound like nobody else he could name. Later on, she badgered Mr Sam Phillips about giving the young kid a try and eventually that's what happened.'

Patrick completed the well-worn tale of how Sam had put Elvis together with guitarist Scotty Moore and bass player Bill Black, but nothing got cooking until the guys messed around in a break in recording with a tune called 'That's All Right' which had originally been recorded by black blues singer Arthur 'Big Boy' Crudup.

'Mr Phillips knew at once the guys had come up with just what he was looking for,' said Patrick. 'You see Sam had already made what is now thought of as the very first rock 'n' roll record with 'Rocket 88' in 1951. That was by Jackie Brenston and his Delta Cats, but Sam reckoned if he could get a white guy to make the same sort of music as Jackie – then he could make a million dollars!'

Daisy could feel the excitement bubbling in her tummy as she listened, yet again, to the story of how rock 'n' roll music was born and couldn't believe she was right where it all started. She was itching to get down to the studio itself and stand in the spot where Elvis had sung into the Shure 55 microphone; apparently they still had the very one he used!

Just then some annoying Australian guy asked Patrick about the large mixing desk in the display case just behind where he was standing. Daisy rolled her eyes. Why were men so obsessed with twiddling techy knobs?

But Patrick's eyes gleamed as he leaned forward and said, 'Ah, well, this here is the very radio desk where DJ Dewey Phillips broadcast the first-ever interview with Elvis Presley to the world back in 1954. He played "That's All Right" over and over when he first got hold of it and sent word to Elvis's mama and daddy to get Elvis to come straight into the studio to talk to the listeners. They went and pulled him out of a movie theatre downtown and got him to go up and see Dewey live on air... and that's how everything started for Elvis.'

Patrick beckoned the group to lean in closer to him as he lowered his voice and said, 'This desk of Dewey's you see here lay forgotten and undisturbed in the basement of the Chisca Hotel for years. The place was abandoned and due to be demolished, but late one night a little while back, me and a friend of mine took a chance and went to see if there was anything left of the old WHBQ 'Red Hot and Blue' set-up. We couldn't believe it was all still there. Well, we had no choice! We decided to, how shall I say, "rescue" it and bring it here for folks like y'all to enjoy.' He winked and a smattering of appreciative applause broke out amongst the group but Patrick waved it away. 'Now,' he said, his voice a rallying cry once more, 'who's ready to enter the inner sanctum, the mother church, the very birthplace of rock 'n' roll?'

Patrick had whipped them up into an excitable frenzy and they all descended the stairs to the modest one-room studio, finally ready to fully appreciate all the music and magic that had emanated from the historic space.

Later, as she folded her brand new t-shirt on her lap and the bus drove back to the motel, Daisy was satisfied that her visit to Sun Recording Studio had been everything she had always hoped it would be.

It had been easy to imagine Elvis chatting nervously to Marion Keisker in the faithfully re-created dated front office and then later picture him fretting in the studio as he tried to impress Sam Phillips sitting in judgement behind the glass partition in the control booth. The whole place was soaked in the musical memories created over the years. It was as if the very walls had absorbed the incredible sounds and now the building thrummed with an energy all of its own.

Daisy had been sure she could feel vibrations in the air as she'd touched the original dingy wall tiles and carefully placed her finger on the scorched piano key where Jerry Lee Lewis had once stubbed out his cigarette.

Everyone on the trip had found something they particularly enjoyed in the tiny studio. Priya and Val had loved posing with Elvis's vintage mic, striking ridiculous poses as they pretended to sing while the other captured a photo.

Anita had squealed with excitement on seeing a large blown-up photograph of the Million Dollar Quartet hanging on the wall directly behind the very spot it where it had been taken. She'd blown a kiss to the guys in the picture – Elvis, Jerry Lee Lewis, Johnny Cash and Carl Perkins – and remembering the final question in her radio quiz, loudly declared, 'Thanks a million, guys! It's down to you lot that I'm actually here!'

Sean was over-awed with the drum kit left behind by U2 when they recorded their 'Rattle and Hum' album at Sun in more recent years. A man of few words as ever, he'd simply whispered 'Cool' as he ran a hand over a cymbal.

For Daisy, the ultimate moment had come when they'd all listened to an excerpt from the impromptu recording of Elvis chatting to the guys on December 4th 1956. Stories varied as to how the 'Million Dollar Quartet' occasion had occurred on that day – how it came about, who was actually in the room at any one time. But there, on tape, captured for all eternity was Elvis mucking around with a version of 'Don't Be Cruel' while Jerry Lee played a honky-tonk backing on piano and Carl Perkins strummed some energetic guitar fills. Best of all, Elvis's youthful southern drawl described seeing Jackie Wilson perform the number on stage and then Elvis had demonstrated how he modelled his own performance on what he'd seen and heard Jackie do.

Elvis's laidback hillbilly voice had rolled around the room like he'd just ambled in to shoot the breeze. 'When he done that "Don't Be Cruel", he was tryin' too hard.' Elvis had told the guys about Wilson. 'But he got better boy, phewee, man he sung that song… he was out there cuttin' it, man… I went back four nights straight.'

Daisy had hung on his every word, closing her eyes to listen really hard. His southern twang was so pronounced she could barely make out every word, but the sense of Elvis's presence had never been stronger to her than at this moment. It was like he was standing right by her shoulder and the sensation gave her goose bumps. The Presley bloodline that she was now sure connected them, made her feel as though Elvis was communicating directly with her.

As the mini-bus delivered them back to the motel, the thought of the task that lay ahead of her also made Daisy shiver. Blue had left a message – it was all arranged. She would get to see Wes in the morning and with any luck she would finally get some answers to her questions. Tomorrow was going to be a very big day.

Chapter Twenty-Eight

As dawn broke the next morning, the sun's weak rays dappled the lawn in front of the Graceland mansion. Shafts of yellow light found their way between the trees and a hazy mist rose and lingered low to the ground in the chilly morning air.

Memphis was barely awake, the streets were quiet and the working day had not yet begun. The servings of bacon, biscuits and gallons of hot coffee that kick-started the morning for most Memphians would not be consumed for a couple of hours yet.

In the stillness of the dawn a group of figures quietly made their way across the dewy paddock grass. Behind them the white colonial house stood glowing peacefully in the strengthening sunshine. Daisy's sandaled foot slipped on the wet grass and she grasped Anita's hand to stop herself from falling. The shoes were a mistake, she realised. Her toes were wet and cold as she gingerly followed where

Wes and Blue were leading them. She wished now she'd worn her new cowboy boots. Perhaps Trixie the salesgirl knew what she was talking about after all. Anita kept a tight hold of Daisy's hand, while on the other side she had her arm linked with Chance.

There were eight of them in the little group. Sean was following Wes and Blue, his satchel bouncing on his back as he strode behind them. Then came the linked trio of Daisy, Anita and Chance. Bringing up the rear were Priya and Valentin, the Russian dressed today in a striped blue and white 'Speedway' jacket he had bought from Lansky Brothers store on Beale Street the day before. It was just like the one Elvis wore in the movie and Daisy couldn't help being unnerved by the presence of this Presley lookalike in their midst as they attempted to carry out their secret mission.

Anita spoke in a low voice as they headed towards a small cluster of trees. 'No wonder you've been acting so oddly for the last couple of days, fancy you and Blue hatching a plan like this!'

Daisy pulled a face and shrugged a little. She didn't trust herself to answer.

'You could have clued me in, you know,' Anita carried on.

'I was sworn to secrecy,' said Daisy quietly.

'Well, I'm good with secrets,' said Anita, giving Chance an exaggerated wink as he shot her a sideways glance.

They all gathered in a semi-circle and looked at each other, a little uncertain as to what to do next. Blue took control as usual and turned to Sean. 'Okay, Sean, so we're all here to help carry out your pa's last wish of being laid to rest here at Graceland. D'you wanna say a few words?'

Sean stood cradling his satchel in his arms like a baby. 'Um, well, I dunno…' he stuttered. 'I hadn't really thought of anything…'

Valentin suddenly spoke up with a question in his heavy Russian accent. 'Would you like if I sing?'

Sean looked appalled at this idea, but before he could respond a mobile phone started to ring. The sound was coming from the bag he was holding. He grappled with the fastening and pulled a long cardboard tube covered in forget-me-nots from the bag and thrust it at Priya. 'Hold onto Dad for me, will you?' he said as he continued to rummage for the ringing phone. Priya, in turn, looked utterly horrified but had no choice, and held the scatter tube of Sean's dad's ashes at arm's length.

The volume of the ringing phone grew louder as Sean plucked it from the depths of his leather bag. 'It's Lynette!' he said. 'I gotta take this.'

They all looked on expectantly as they listened to the one-sided conversation.

'Hey, everything okay? WHAT!?'

Everyone's eyes were flicking back and forth to each other's faces as they were forced to eavesdrop on Sean's conversation with his pregnant wife back home. Finally, Sean spluttered. 'Her waters have broken… the baby is coming! Yes, I'm okay. Are you okay? No, no, of course you're not… I know, love, I'm sorry.'

Priya rolled her eyes at Daisy as if to say: *Men!*

Sean was listening intently to the phone clamped to his ear again. 'Yes, we're about to do it now, everyone's here… They all say hi!'

The group responded with a variety of muted greetings to the poor woman in labour thousands of miles away. *'Hiya'*, *'Hey there, Lynette'* and so forth. It seemed wildly inappropriate in the circumstances; the woman was about to give birth and could not have cared less about their good wishes. What she needed was industrial-strength painkillers and for her husband to not be on the other side of the Atlantic! Sean seemed to be a little oblivious of these facts.

'I'll get back as soon as I can, sweetie, I promise… Oh, Lynette, sugar, before you go, I've thought of a name for the baby. How do you like Wes? WES, yeah, it's a bit different, isn't it? Very American… Wesley… rhymes with Presley. I thought Dad would like that.'

Sean grimaced as Lynette replied and he held the phone away from his ear. He quickly switched the phone off as he addressed the group. 'She loves it… Either that or it was a really big contraction!'

No one was sure what to do next. Priya was still awkwardly holding Teddy Price's ashes in the forget-me-not scatter tube but Sean was simply looking shell-shocked by the news from Lynette. The phone call had given Daisy an idea. She pulled her own mobile phone from the back pocket of her jeans and swiped at the screen a few times. All at once, they heard a shuffle drum and a piano playing a fast intro and a song started – Elvis's 'Teddy Bear'. Was that alright, she wondered, or would they think she was being insensitive?

She looked nervously at Sean as the song carried on, but a delighted smile slowly spread across his face. Daisy held the phone up as Sean took the scatter tube from Priya's hands and moved a short way away from the group. Daisy was a little concerned that the song might be too jovial for the occasion but, in fact, the sweetness of the lyrics made it the perfect send-off for Teddy Price and lightened what might have been an uncomfortable mood. They all watched in respectful silence as Sean carefully scattered his father's remains around the roots of an old poplar tree. As he came back towards the group, he looked more relaxed than Daisy had ever seen him before.

'Thanks,' he said to Daisy, then looked around gratefully at the others. 'Thanks so much for coming, this is more than I, or my dad, could ever have hoped for.'

Wes's old eyes were as misty as the morning as he said in a voice thick with emotion, 'Sure, it's nothing, boy, Elvis himself would be glad to know we're still takin' care of his fans for him.'

Anita was blinking rapidly, hoping her mascara wouldn't run, as she reached into her shoulder bag and produced a small brown fluffy teddy bear. Around its neck was a red heart-shaped tag reading 'I love Elvis'. 'I got it from the gift shop yesterday,' she explained. 'It was the nicest one they had.'

Sean nodded and they all watched as Anita walked

towards the poplar tree and gently placed the bear on the ground. 'That's for you, Teddy,' she said.

Blue rubbed Sean's shoulder. 'You okay, buddy?'

Sean reached for Blue's hand and pumped it vigorously as he said, 'Thank you, thank you both so much.'

He moved on to shake Wes by the hand, but the old man pulled him in for a hug instead. 'Like I say, Elvis liked to take care of folks and that's all we're tryin' to do.' Wes released Sean from the bear hug. 'If I'm ever stuck for knowin' what's best, I often jus' think to mysel', what would Elvis do?'

They all made their way back across the lawn to the barn. The underground tunnel would be the best route for them to escape from the property before Graceland staff started arriving for work and asked any awkward questions.

Daisy hung back from the group a little and fell into step with Wes. 'That was a wonderful thing you did for Sean,' she said.

'Hell, I didn't do it to get no halo,' said Wes, rubbing the stubble on his chin. 'That "Teddy Bear" music of yours was a neat touch too.'

Daisy was bursting with questions but wasn't sure of the best way to start. '*Softly, softly catchy monkey*'. Another one of Nana Rose's sayings that had never made the slightest sense to her was now circling in her mind. 'How long did you say you've worked here at Graceland?' she asked; it seemed a good idea to start on solid ground.

'Man and boy.' Wes exhaled a snort of air. 'Elvis gave me

a job when no one else would give a skinny kid a chance. Kept me outta a whole heap o' trouble, I'll bet.'

As they neared the barn, Daisy managed to convince Wes that there was nothing she would like more than to see the inside of the security lodge down by the gates.

'There ain't all that much to see, I don't reckon,' said Wes. 'But I've spent so much time in that place I stopped takin' much notice years back.'

Blue simply nodded when they told him Daisy was hanging back with Wes for a while. He followed the others into the barn as they headed back to the motel for breakfast, turning to mouth 'good luck' just before they all disappeared from view.

Wes installed Daisy on a squashy old armchair in the corner of the one-roomed building down by the famous music gates, while he sat on a high-backed wooden chair by the open door. The tiny room was flooded with early morning light coming through two large windows on opposite sides of the cabin. On the other walls were two smaller round porthole windows, one facing up towards the house and the other towards Elvis Presley Boulevard. The rest of the space on the walls was covered in notes and Post-its, and there was an Elvis calendar hanging above an old green metal filing cabinet. On the desk was a bank of CCTV monitors just like the one she had seen in the kitchen up at the house.

'There's not a whole lot to see,' said Wes as he watched her looking around. He got up from the chair and moved over to a small coffee machine on top of a tiny fridge. 'Dunno about you but I'm hungry, let's see what we have.'

He opened up a small round tin and offered her a cookie. 'Still made to Alberta's famous chocolate chip recipe, take a couple, don't be shy.'

Daisy devoured the crumbly, melt-in-the-mouth cookies and sipped her coffee. The simple breakfast seemed to give her strength and she leaned forward and asked, 'Can I be cheeky? Will you show me that tattoo on your arm?'

Wes eyed her over the rim of his coffee mug and said, 'My tattoo?' His eyes darted over to the closed music gates as he began to roll up his shirtsleeve, saying, 'Why, I've had this pretty rose so long it's a wonder it ain't clear faded away.'

Daisy gazed at the familiar flower on the old man's arm. Just as she had thought when she first caught sight of it, the image was an exact match to the one Nana Rose wore near her shoulder. She needed to word her next question very carefully.

'When did you get that done, do you remember?'

Wes leaned back on the wooden chair and looked once more at the closed Graceland gates in front of him. 'Oh, I remember, honey, jus' like it were yesterday.'

Daisy held her breath and waited... and then Wes began to talk.

'I was younger than you are now, no more than a kid but I'd taken to helpin' out Uncle Vester here at Graceland. One day a young 'un had a bit of a turn right there, just outside those gates... Course that wasn't unusual, lots of folks suddenly come over all queer when they see Graceland for the first time, but this little girl... well, she was somethin' else.'

304

Daisy hardly dared to break the spell, but, in a voice barely louder than a whisper, she asked, 'Do you... do you remember her name?'

Wes continued to stare at the twin figures of twisted metal on the ornate gates. He let out a sigh and right at the end of the breath was his answer. 'Rose.'

Daisy's hands flew to her mouth to stop herself from crying out. She remained rooted to the spot, staring at the figure of the old man with his snowy white hair and stiff, straight back. This was her grandfather. She *was* a Presley.

Wes turned and looked at her, his blue eyes now bright and alert. He didn't say a word; he took in everything about her from the tip of her dark ponytailed hair to the scarlet polish on her toes. Eventually he spoke, gently asking, 'You got something to tell me, girl?'

Daisy was shocked. Did he already know? Could he have guessed? Before she could find a way to reply, Wes moved over to the desk and hit the button to open the gates; members of Graceland staff were arriving to start the day shift.

Wes called out 'How ya doing?' and 'Have a good day now, y'hear' to a few of the folks as they passed by on their way up to the house. The burst of normality bought them both a bit of time before they had to face each other again. When he settled back down in his chair, Wes didn't directly question Daisy again. Instead he said, 'First time I saw you I thought you seemed familiar. Rose was such a pretty girl but she had this cheeky side to her, you know? I get the feelin' the two of you are as alike as can be. Am I right?'

Daisy simply nodded, grateful that Wes seemed to be

trying to make this as easy as possible for her. She told him everything she knew. Rose Featherstone was her grandmother. She and her mum Lilian had never been told anything about who Lilian's father might have been. They knew Rose had been on a trip to Tennessee to visit a friend several months before she had her baby, but once she was born no one had ever encouraged questions and no answers were ever forthcoming.

'So what changed?'

Daisy looked into Wes's earnest face and her heart broke a little with what she had to tell him. As gently as she could she explained about Rose's memory problems and the strokes she had suffered. When she got to the part when Rose had claimed Elvis Presley was Lilian's father, a look of pain passed across Wes's face.

'So she doesn't remember me at all?'

Daisy flew to Wes's side. 'Oh no, I think she was very mixed up, that's all.'

Wes's head snapped up at that one word. 'Was?'

Daisy simply nodded as a tear ran down her face. There was nothing else to say. The two of them stood for a while, both lost in their memories of Rose, one remembering her as a vivacious young girl, while the other pictured her towards the end.

After a little while, Daisy remembered her mobile phone was still in the back pocket of her jeans. 'I have some photos of Rose, and my mum – your… your daughter… Lilian. D'you want to see?'

As Wes peered at the photos of Rose and Lilian on the small screen, tears began to slide down his weathered cheeks. Neither of them would ever be able to explain if they were sad or happy tears, if he was crying over the death of Rose or was moved by the sight of his daughter. The other question Daisy found impossible to answer was the one Wes quietly asked of her now: 'Why didn't she tell me?'

Chapter Twenty-Nine

After Daisy left Wes to go back to the motel, he sat keeping watch over the Graceland gates for a long time, thinking about what might have been. In particular, he recalled a day many years before when he'd taken a trip up to Walnut Grove House to pay a visit to Rose's friend, Miss Jennifer-Jane...

Memphis 1961

It was more than six months since Rose had left Memphis and returned home to Wales. In all that time Wes had come to realise that he only ever missed her more, never less.

What was it Elvis had said to him? 'Give it time...?' Well, time wasn't helping. In fact, Wes finally decided, letting Rose go had been the stupidest thing he had ever done... and he'd done some pretty stupid things.

The way he saw it, no other girl compared to his sweet Rose. He missed her sing-song voice, the funny things she would say and the way she could nestle into the crook of his arm. No one else fitted him quite the way Rose did and he'd come to believe that no one else ever would.

Elvis could have any girl he wanted, he only had to click his fingers – and yet when Anita wasn't around he often talked about a girl called Priscilla he'd met while he was over in Germany. Sure, didn't he even talk about bringing her over for a visit sometime? All the way from Germany! That wouldn't go down too well with Anita, but if that's what Elvis wanted, Wes was pretty sure he'd move heaven and earth to make it happen.

Wes didn't have Elvis's power and resources, but he was sure he missed his Rose just as much as Elvis hankered after this Priscilla. Trouble was, Wes didn't so much as have a postal address to write to. He couldn't quite remember why now, but both he and Rose had decided a clean break was best. He shook his head as he thought of it; he hadn't even gone to the airport to see her off. What fools they had been!

There was only one thing he could do, he would have to go and see Miss Jennifer-Jane and ask her for an address so he could write to Rose. He wasn't sure yet what he was going to say in the letter… Ask her to come back? Offer to move to Wales? If he thought about it too much he'd lose his nerve altogether, but he knew he wanted to tell Rose how much he loved her, how much he missed her. First things first, he needed to speak to Jennifer, perhaps she would know the best thing to do.

It was late morning when he arrived at the gates to the Walnut Grove estate. He could easily have driven through the open gates on his motorcycle, but decided against such a rowdy arrival. He hadn't been invited after all. He parked the bike behind the perimeter wall and made his way up the driveway on foot.

Tilly Mae the housemaid had been surprised to see him when she opened the door, but duly showed him into the morning room and went to fetch Miss Jennifer.

Wes paced around the room while he waited; he'd never been invited inside this house before. Everything in the room sparkled and glinted in the sunshine streaming in from the window. From the mirrors on the wall to the polished mahogany furniture to all the trinkets and treasures positioned on every surface, the effect was dazzling. He felt very shabby as a result and tugged the sleeves of his over-shirt down to his wrists, then realised how crumpled they looked and quickly rolled them back up to their usual place above his elbows again.

When Jennifer-Jane finally swept into the room, neat as a pin in an ice-blue twinset, a string of pearls around her slender throat, he thought at first it was her elder sister Jeannie, the two now looked so alike. Unfortunately, it wasn't only Jennifer's sweater that was an icy shade. Wes was soon aware that Jennifer was none too pleased to see him and help to reunite him and Rose was not going to be forthcoming.

Jennifer sat primly on the edge of a wing-backed armchair and regarded him with a cool stare as he hemmed and hawed his way through a mangled explanation as to why he and Rose had not exchanged details and why he had suddenly tipped up on her doorstep asking for help to reach her. When she finally spoke, the news was not good; she told him Rose had put their 'holiday romance' behind her and he must do the same.

'You must see that it would never have worked,' Jennifer said with a small smile that didn't reach her eyes. 'If Rose had wanted to continue this... relationship, she would have contacted you herself by now, through me I suppose, but she hasn't sent any

such letter. In fact, the only message I have for you from Rose is to tell you she has someone else in her life now. I'm sorry, but she said if ever you came asking, I should tell you to forget all about her.'

After that there was nothing else to say. Wes couldn't get out of the house fast enough and wished to God he hadn't left his motorcycle at the end of the long drive. It would have suited him much better to have roared away from Walnut Grove House in a cloud of dust and a shower of gravel.

Instead, Jennifer-Jane stood at the window and watched him make his sorry way on foot away from the house and out of her neatly ordered life. She'd done the right thing, for Rose as well as for herself, Jennifer was certain. She presumed the baby would have been adopted by now anyway. She'd cut off all contact with Rose as soon as she'd found out how reckless and foolish she had been. She simply had to distance herself from such a scandal. Wes felt her eyes on him as he walked away but never turned back.

While Wes waded through his memories, Daisy sat on the edge of her bed and realised she could barely remember how she had got back to her motel room.

She had experienced several surreal moments during her time in Memphis – stopping the traffic in Tupelo while on the back of a police motorbike, waking up to find a Russian Elvis at the end of her bed, stepping inside the cloistered bedroom of Elvis Presley himself, to name just a few. But discovering that Wesley Presley was her grandfather and that she was indeed distantly related to

Elvis – ELVIS! – pretty much knocked everything else out of the park.

She remembered that both she and Wes had cried when they realised the truth, they'd hugged and they'd also asked each other questions that neither one could answer. Then they'd both agreed she needed to talk to her mother and that they would see each other later.

After that, Daisy was rather blank. She thought Wes had suggested calling Blue to pick her up, but she must have insisted she could walk back. Lord knows how she had avoided being knocked over by the speeding cars on Elvis Presley Boulevard as she crossed over onto the opposite side of the freeway and then walked back along the side of the busy road until she reached the pull in for the Day's Inn Motel.

Now she sat dazed and amazed, wondering how on earth she was going to break the news to her mother. Her stomach lurched as she thought of Lilian… Finding out that she was related to the biggest American rock 'n' roll star of all time would be so shocking, Daisy could envisage her mother with electrified hair on end and smoke coming out of her ears. But it wasn't funny, this was serious. Daisy needed to handle this situation carefully for all their sakes. It wasn't her mother's fault she was in this position and Wes had been desperate to explain that he hadn't cruelly abandoned a pregnant Rose all those years ago either. He'd sworn he had no knowledge of the fact she was carrying his baby when she returned to Wales. In fact, he'd told Daisy he'd tried to reach her but Jennifer-Jane had put an end to that desire.

She'd left the old man staring out at the place where he and Rose had met so many years ago. Trying to come to terms with the fact he had missed out on fifty-odd years of having a daughter and the one person who could have explained why was dead.

Daisy was finding it hard not to feel angry with Rose. Why had she rejected the father of her baby and then kept him a secret? What possible purpose had been served by denying her mother the right to know who her father was? Why had she denied Wes the chance to know his own daughter? Just thinking about how life might have been so different for them all set Daisy's head spinning.

Rose's final confession had come practically on her deathbed. For all the years Daisy had known her, Rose had been obsessed with rock 'n' roll music and the Southern States of America. How could she love everything like that so much when all it must have done was remind her every day of Wesley Presley? It didn't make sense. Unless... Daisy's mind was working overtime trying to work it all out. It still felt like there was a vital piece of the puzzle missing... unless... Rose's deep love for the music and atmosphere that sprang from Memphis was *because* it reminded her of Wesley? Had she secretly held onto her love for him throughout her life? Was that why, when her mind became so confused, her combined her love for Elvis and Wes had morphed into one big obsession that led to her blurting out the outrageous claim that Elvis, not Wes, was the secret father of her baby?

Daisy didn't know, but she did know that if she waited any longer to make the call to her mother, she might just lose her nerve altogether. Taking a deep breath, Daisy picked up the phone.

Lilian was on her way back to the office after her lunchbreak when her mobile rang in her bag. She stopped outside the window of Griffiths and Wood Insurance while she fished the phone from the depths, 'Hello, Daisy...' Lilian stuck her finger in one ear as a lorry roared past on the street. She couldn't hear a word Daisy was saying. 'Just a minute, love, I'm right by the road, I'll have to go inside... hang on...'

Lilian's co-worker Sandra gave Lilian a withering look as she entered the front office with her phone clamped to her ear, clearly thinking all personal calls should have been taken within the allotted lunch break. There was a reason Lilian always called her Sanctimonious Sandra behind her back. Lilian did her best to ignore her, but it wasn't easy.

Sat on the bed in her motel room in Memphis, Daisy was wishing she'd eaten more than a chocolate chip cookie and drunk considerably more coffee before attempting this conversation. There was no easy way to do it, she discovered. Once she felt she had Lilian's attention, she simply blurted it out. 'I've found him, Mum, your dad... my grandad. He's here.'

'He's there?' Lilian had a sudden vision of Daisy with Elvis Presley hovering at her elbow.

'Well, he's not *here*, right now. He's not stood next to me or anything.' Why was she making such a mess of this? 'He's here in Memphis. I've met him, spoken to him, he's called Wesley... Wesley Presley.'

The news came as a triple shock to Lilian; she *did* have a

father and his name was the *same* as the man Wendy had mentioned the other day? And wait... what was that about him being called *Presley*? Stupidly, she couldn't think of one single sensible question to ask.

'Mum? Mum, are you there?' Daisy wondered for a second if her mum had passed out, but fainting wasn't really Lilian's style.

Lilian broke her silence with one short statement. 'Well that's that, then.'

Daisy was taken aback. It wasn't what she'd imagined was going to happen. Didn't her mum want to know more about Wesley? Find out what he was like? Start to make some plans for coming over to meet him? Daisy floundered for how best to continue the conversation. 'He's really nice, Mum,' she offered, 'Wes, I mean, actually I think he's one of the nicest people I've ever met.'

'Really?' Was that a note of sarcasm Daisy detected creeping into Lilian's tone? 'I hardly think a man who abdicates all responsibility for his child would win many awards for humanitarian of the year.' Yep, that was definitely sarcasm, Daisy was in no doubt now.

Sandra was watching Lilian through narrowed eyes. Something very strange was going on, she was sure. Lilian swung her chair around so she was practically facing the wall; she was damned if she was going to let Sanctimonious Sandra know what this was all about. The woman might as well be scoffing popcorn as the drama unfolded.

Lilian was attempting to process the information she was receiving. It wasn't easy. Meanwhile, Daisy seemed to gabbling away about this Wes and someone called Blue and how Lilian must drop everything right this minute and head over to meet them all, as if it was the most natural thing in the world. Well, none of it felt very natural to Lilian. In fact, she felt like an alien who had crash-landed on a strange new planet. As if to underline the point, Sanctimonious Sandra was blatantly staring at her now as though she had sprouted a second head.

'Daisy… DAISY… NO!' Lilian had to stem the stream of consciousness coming from her daughter on the other side of the Atlantic.

'No? What do you mean, no?' Daisy was confused, did her mother not believe what she was saying? Was she in complete denial that Wesley Presley could be her father?

'I mean, no, of course I'm not going to jump on a plane and head over to… *Memphis*.' Lilian pronounced the name of the city as though it was a dirty word.

'Oh… but—'

'No buts, Daisy, I'm not going to discuss it further. You've done what you wanted to do and solved this… this… little puzzle, but it really doesn't change a thing. Not for me. You need to come home, Daisy, there are far more important things to deal with than some feckless man who has never given two hoots about us.'

Lilian then managed to turn the conversation into a lecture on how Daisy needed to learn to run a successful business and how she had to 'get a grip' of the perilous finances of Blue Moon Vintage. Daisy cursed under her breath, realising her mum had been opening the post and snooping about in the shop. Damn!

Lilian then abruptly ended the call saying she couldn't

317

talk as she was at work. Daisy fired off text after text trying to explain that Wes had no idea Rose had been pregnant and he'd told her his attempts to get in touch had been blocked. Jennifer-Jane had told him Rose wanted nothing more to do with him, so how could it be all Wes's fault?

When Lilian finally answered the torrent of texts, her answer was brutal and unequivocal.

I'm not interested in this man's excuses and you shouldn't fall for them either. Your grandmother was young and foolish, I expect better of you, Daisy. You have a life and responsibilities here. Stop this nonsense and come home. Mum x

Daisy sat looking at the phone in her hand in complete shock. What had just happened? Lilian had always had the ability to throw cold water over any situation, but this...? The news that her own father had been found... that he was a living, breathing person she could meet and talk to... let alone the fact that he was a Presley... but Lilian just didn't seem to care.

It had never occurred to Daisy that her mother would reject Wes out of hand, without even trying to get to know him. It was as if all the pent-up feelings of abandonment that Lilian had felt all her life now had an outlet, all the hurt and pain could now be blamed on Wesley Presley. Finally Lilian had somewhere to direct her anger and Daisy's dream of bringing father and daughter together was over even before it had begun.

Daisy's stomach churned and her hands shook as she realised that everything she had done, everything that had happened to lead her to this moment now all appeared to be for nothing. She realised she had been harbouring a fantasy of extending her stay in Memphis, maybe even starting a new life here. She'd pictured her mum coming out and having an emotional meeting with Wes. She'd wanted to introduce Lilian to Anita and Priya too and of course Blue… Blue! Daisy's heart sank further still as she realised the full impact of her mother's reaction. What on earth had she been thinking? How the hell had she thought she and Lilian would be able to reconcile their regular lives in Llandovery with the lives of Graceland guard Wesley Presley and Shelby County Police Officer Joe 'Blue' Cody?

Had she really believed she could move here, set up a vintage clothing business in downtown Memphis, get to know her grandfather and have her mum fly back and forth for visits now and then? She'd been dreaming and now it was time to wake up. Her mum had a point; she had responsibilities back home and she really needed to get on top of things at Blue Moon Vintage. A failing business was no foundation for starting a life in another country; that would take money, money Daisy simply did not have.

Daisy felt a fool for ever imagining that running away to Memphis would bring a joyous, happy ending. Clearly her mother would never even *meet* her own father, let alone build up any sort of relationship.

The realisation of the impossibility of the situation also made it startlingly clear that there could be no future for Daisy and Blue. Daisy cursed herself for letting her impulsive heart rule her head yet again. There was nothing to suggest Blue would even want her to move here, that deluded daydream was also all in her head. For all the sweet nothings he'd murmured in her ear, he'd known all

along this was a casual hook-up, she was only ever passing through. Blue wouldn't be short of female company once she had gone, she was sure of that. Once this trip was over in a couple more days, their holiday romance would be over too. The fantasy had to end, Daisy had to accept she must forget about Wes and Blue and go home.

Chapter Thirty

Daisy swapped the over-size sweater she'd worn for the chilly dawn secret mission at Graceland for her new black and gold Sun Studio t-shirt. She might not be in the right frame of mind, but at least she could dress the part. She spent the rest of the morning pretending to be a regular tourist as the group were taken on their final scheduled excursion to Memphis's Rock 'n' Soul museum.

She fake ooohed and ahhed along with Anita and Chance as they drooled over the country and western style outfits on display. One in particular did catch her eye: a tan two- piece with a large red rose motif across the back of the jacket and two more climbing up each leg of the flared trousers, it had echoes of the design on her cowboy boots. It was nothing to do with Elvis, however; it turned out to have been worn by Jerry Lee Lewis.

She was finding it hard to work up the correct amount of enthusiasm for all the sights, knowing that she needed to have a conversation with Blue later on that just might break her heart. It really was the ultimate irony, she realised as she mooched along, seeing the whole history of rock 'n' roll music laid out before her. A soundtrack of soulful music played constantly in the background as her mood descended into melancholy at the thought of never seeing Blue or Wes again. What she was experiencing was the very definition of 'the blues'. At least she could say her time in the American South was authentic.

Museum trip over, the group had the afternoon to do whatever they pleased. Some headed straight for the Beale Street bars, others wanted to return to the Peabody Hotel for a second look at those ridiculous ducks. Daisy resolved not to waste the little time she had left. She may be sad and blue, but that was no excuse for not ticking all the tourist boxes. She decided to take herself off on her own and return to the Graceland Exhibition. There were several things she'd missed seeing on the day the party had toured the mansion.

Opposite the Graceland gates was a site with museums dedicated to Elvis's fleet of cars and his personal aeroplane the Lisa-Marie and, of course, a selection of cafes, diners and gift shops. Daisy could easily spend several hours there pottering around.

As she wandered amongst the Cadillacs, Ferraris and numerous other vehicles on show, Daisy had to keep reminding herself that the man who had owned these amazing things and lived a lavish lifestyle in the mansion over the road was someone she was distantly related to. The fact was still too incredible to absorb.

She should feel thrilled, she *wanted* to feel excited about it, but there were too many other things going on, things that were so out of her control. *Nothing ever feels the way you think it will,* she thought to herself as she came to a shiny black car exhibited on a plinth in the centre of the vast museum.

Daisy didn't know much about cars, but even she could see that this one was a beauty. Low slung and angular, it had a real masculine, sporty vibe. The glistening black bodywork and polished chrome trims contrasted with the deep-red leather interior. It looked like an exclusive nightclub on wheels! The information displayed nearby said this was a 1973 Stutz Blackhawk. Wow, even the name was sexy!

Daisy gave a gasp as she read more of the printed blurb: the car had a claim to fame she had not been expecting. The Stutz Blackhawk was the very last car Elvis Presley had driven. Shortly after midnight on August 16th 1977, Elvis had been spotted driving through the gates of Graceland and he had been at the wheel of this very car.

It was upsetting and maddening all at once for Daisy. She'd idolised Elvis all her life, and now here she was, on his home ground, surrounded by the trappings of his life but despite discovering a direct link between them, she simply couldn't find a way to feel part of this world. She didn't think anyone would ever understand how she truly felt right now, not even Blue.

Blue had headed home to get his head down for a couple of hours after the dawn scattering of Teddy Price's ashes. Daisy knew he was due at work this afternoon and wouldn't finish his shift until much later tonight, so she'd timed the text message she'd sent him to be when she knew it wouldn't interrupt his sleep and he would be safely at work. She didn't want him calling so she would have to talk to him; she couldn't face that, not yet.

He'd taken her news about Wes in his stride. For Blue it was confirming what he already strongly suspected – Wesley Presley had been Rose Featherstone's lost love and that made him Daisy's grandfather. He'd thought as much. Reading Blue's rapid-fire responses over text, Daisy noted that Blue made no connection between the discovery of her heritage and their future together.

Wow, you really are a Presley! he'd written. *See you later to celebrate x*

There was nothing about making Memphis her second home or how this might lead to making their relationship more permanent. Of course not! They had only known each other a few days – Daisy felt like slapping herself on the forehead for her stupidity. She was the one who crashed into situations head first, blundering about like a baby elephant, not giving the slightest thought to other people's feelings and the consequences of her actions. Blue wasn't like that. Most normal people weren't like that.

Daisy knew she had to try and be less selfish in her actions. She'd jumped at the chance to come to Memphis without really thinking of how her mum was feeling. She'd just lost her own mother but Daisy had forged ahead with her plan to find out the identity of Lilian's father without stopping to check if that was what Lilian had wanted. Now she cringed at the idea of leaving her mum on the other side of the world so soon after losing Rose, while she re-invented herself with a new life here in Memphis. How cruel and self-absorbed. Now Rose was gone, she and her mum only had each other, it was time to come together.

The practical difficulties of a dream to move to Memphis had also begun to bite. She needed to knuckle down and rescue Blue Moon Vintage before she could consider any new career move. The shop could work, she was sure of it, but she needed to double her efforts, explore new avenues, diversify and work really, really hard. It wasn't that she wanted to prove Lilian wrong... She actually wanted to make her mum proud.

With this new outlook, Daisy began to reconsider her position on the choices Nana Rose had made in her own life. The words of an Elvis song floated into her mind: 'Walk a Mile in My Shoes'. What was it Elvis was saying in those lyrics? That if you could see the world through someone else's eyes, if you could walk in their place for just one day, you would understand their point of view. She'd felt as though she was following in the footsteps of Nana Rose the whole time she'd been here in Memphis. She'd even fallen for a handsome local man who just might break her heart. She still didn't know why Rose had not told Wes she was carrying his baby, but Daisy did now have a better understanding of how complicated life could be. You couldn't always make the choice your heart wanted, you had to use your head. Was that what a young Rose had done?

Daisy decided she had no choice but to continue to follow Nana Rose's example and leave Memphis far behind.

The Featherstone women weren't really rock 'n' roll after all, she realised with a sinking heart, they just liked some of the old tunes.

The rest of the day rolled by like a Mississippi paddle-boat. To a casual observer, Daisy might look like any other tourist, taking in the sights and shopping for gifts, but just beneath the surface her emotions were in turmoil.

Daisy had arranged to meet Blue at an all-night diner on the outskirts of the city once his shift had ended around 11pm that night. He'd offered to swing by the motel to pick her up, but she insisted on catching a cab there. She pulled out a range of outfits from the few clean clothes she had left before she set off, trying to work out what to wear. What was the dress code for a *last* date? In the end, she settled on a flared pale-blue knee-length skirt and a pretty white blouse dotted with daisies. Funnily enough, it struck her as an outfit Rose might have worn when she was young. Just before she left she stuck an oversized daisy clip in her dark hair; she could at least *appear* cheerful and carefree, she decided, even if that wasn't how she felt.

First to arrive at the old-style diner, she settled herself in a booth and ordered a coffee. The waitress left a couple of menus, but Daisy wasn't in the slightest bit hungry.

Blue roared into the parking lot on his motorcycle and ordered his coffee with a wink to the waitress as he wove through the tables towards Daisy. Damn, he looked good in that uniform! Daisy remembered the first time she'd laid eyes on him at the airport cab rank, his blue shirt fitting tightly across his broad shoulders, the tufts of sandy hair sticking up on the top of his head, the naughty twinkle in his bright blue eyes. He focused them directly on her now as he slid into the seat opposite. 'So, how ya doin'?' He sat watching her as she played with the buttons of her denim jacket across her lap. He seemed to sense her conflicting emotions.

Daisy had determined to keep her tone bright and breezy, there was no need to make a drama out of all this. It wasn't like she was going to break this guy's heart or anything, look at him for heaven's sake. He was hardly going to pine for her, a weirdly dressed whirlwind from Wales, when he could have his pick of any passing Southern belle. It was so presumptuous of her to have ever thought there could be more to her and Blue. It was a holiday fling, that was all, and there was nothing wrong with that. The fact that he was great-looking, kind, thoughtful and seemed more in tune with her than any man she had ever met before... well... there wasn't much point dwelling on all that now.

'I'm just swell!' Daisy grinned at she dropped the Americanism into the conversation. 'I mean, it's not every day you find out you're related to rock royalty now, is it?'

Blue narrowed his sapphire eyes a little and nodded slowly. 'Well, it's not your ever'day occurrence, I don't s'pose.'

Daisy tapped her fingers in time to the music playing through the speakers in the diner while Blue ordered himself shrimp and grits followed by a slice of apple pie. Clearly nothing was affecting his appetite.

She chattered on while he ate, talking about how Wes had revealed he had met Nana Rose at the Graceland gates and how he clearly had never known she had been pregnant with his baby.

'… and I have to say, I believe him.' Daisy was talking ten to the dozen while Blue forked shrimp into his mouth while listening attentively. 'You know, he said I reminded him of her very much. I think I must look a lot like she used to when he knew her, how mad is that?'

'That must be hard on ole Wes, poor guy.' Blue spoke quietly and it jarred with Daisy's excitable non-stop chatter.

'Yeah, I suppose… um, yeah.' Daisy remembered the tears that had welled in Wes's eyes and her heartfelt desire in that moment to try and help him feel that something good would come out of this mess, even after all the time that had passed. She shook her head to clear the thought and in doing so realised she couldn't let Blue believe she could be so heartless as to reveal herself as Wes's granddaughter and then simply vanish, even if that was what she now intended to do.

With a few stops and starts, she eventually managed to find a way to explain that she'd hoped Lilian would come out to Memphis to meet Wes straight away, but that it wouldn't be possible right now, too busy at work, too much still to sort out. Instead Daisy casually dropped into the conversation that she would be returning home as planned the day after tomorrow and then, she added, she would come back… at some point.

Blue put his fork down on the empty plate in front of him and wiped his mouth with a paper napkin. 'At some point?' He repeated the phrase Daisy had just used but she wasn't sure if he meant it as a statement or a question.

Daisy could barely meet his blue eyes. She nodded. She'd be back... *at some point*... of course she would.

Blue reached across the table and took her hand. 'I s'pose it's a helluva lot to take in for you and your mama.'

Daisy felt her fingers curl inside his hand and knew it was now or never. She had to make it clear to Blue that she had accepted this was a fleeting relationship – a holiday romance – and that was all. If he was hoping for one last night of passion before she left, he was going to be disappointed; she didn't trust herself to let things go that far and still be able to walk away. This ended now.

She twisted her fingers from out of his grasp and slapped a huge smile on her face. 'I would never have solved this puzzle without you, Blue, really, I can't thank you enough. I know how busy you must be at work and you've helped me so much. You'll be glad to see the back of me I bet, taking up all your time like this, what am I like?'

Blue cocked his head to one side and looked at her for a heartbeat before replying, 'It was a pleasure, all part of the service I'm sure.'

Bolder now, Daisy carried on, 'And showing me the sights like you did, it's really added to this whole holiday experience for me, so... you know... thanks.'

Her words were beginning to sound trite and false, even to her own ears, but Blue was a man of the world; she was sure he knew a brush-off when he heard it, and knew how to take it on the chin.

Just to make sure, Daisy drove her point home. 'I should be getting back to the motel now. We've got a big day ahead tomorrow, haven't we? I can hardly believe they are going to go through with it... it's so crazy!'

'Well, good luck to them, I say,' countered Blue. 'You only have one life, so why not go for it?'

Daisy busied herself pulling on her jacket, and she didn't look at Blue as she muttered a reply.

Ever the gentleman, Blue offered to give her a ride home but Daisy knew he lived in the opposite direction so was insistent on getting a cab back to the motel. She kissed him quickly on the cheek, a bit like how she had kissed him that very first time on the highway in Tupelo in front of the tour bus, and told him she'd see him tomorrow as arranged.

As the cab pulled out of the diner parking lot, Blue was also thinking about that day in Tupelo when fate had landed the crazy girl from the airport slap bang back into his life. He'd begun to believe there was no such thing as coincidence and that he and Daisy had been brought together for a reason. He'd never known anyone like her and he'd fallen for her in a big way. But it was now clear that Daisy didn't share his thinking. Perhaps they were just too different after all. As the cab pulled away, Blue raised his hand to give a mock salute just like he had that day back in Tupelo, then he turned his bike around and headed home, alone.

Chapter Thirty-One

L ilian barely remembered driving to Rose's house. She'd left work at the stroke of five o'clock, desperate to escape the curious looks Sanctimonious Sandra had been giving her all afternoon. Daisy's bombshell news was still causing aftershocks inside Lilian's brain. She had a real-life dad – BOOM! His name was Wesley Presley – BOOM! She was half-American and her mother had never told her – BOOM! BOOM!

Now she found herself sitting in her car outside her mother's house as though some invisible magnetic force had pulled her there. Why? How was coming here going to help in any way?

Lilian closed her eyes and tried to figure out how she really felt. She'd spent so much of her life burying her emotions that it was taking a huge effort to work it out. When Daisy had called and told her she'd found her father, Lilian's instant reaction had been to pretend she didn't care.

That attitude had stood her in good stead over the years, but of course it wasn't true, and it wasn't working now.

She was angry with Rose for denying her the right to have a dad, for never telling her the truth and, yes, she was angry with her for dying.

She was hurt beyond belief to think her dad had been living on the other side of the world and had never made any attempt to find her and get in touch. What sort of man turned his back on his own daughter?

When Daisy left for Memphis, she'd *wanted* her to uncover the truth. For a little while a flicker of hope had ignited in her heart. She'd soon put a stop to that. She knew first-hand that hope too often leads to disappointment, so she'd convinced herself there was nothing to find. No secret love of Rose's would ever be found and so she would never have to deal with a real live man claiming he was her father. But today Daisy had called…

The pain and the fury now boiled up inside Lilian and she opened her eyes and glared at the ordinary house standing in front of her. Was there something, anything, inside Rose's house that would help her make sense of all this?

Once inside the door, she flew from room to room, looking for… what? What was she hoping to find? She'd shoved the picture she'd discovered of young Rose with her Memphis boyfriend back where she'd found it in the scrapbook beneath the gramophone unit. She pulled the door beneath the record deck open now and let the cupboard spill its insides all across the carpet as she rooted through the papery debris until she found it again.

There he was. Wesley Presley, this must be him, it had to be. He was tall with a good head of hair, nice enough looking in an unthreatening way but he was no smouldering sex god. Maybe Elvis and him weren't that closely related?

The sight of Wesley's easy smile seemed to mock her. Fired up by the sight of his arm casually draped around her mother, Lilian set to work searching high and low for anything else that linked Rose to this smirking man.

She looked in the boxes on top of the kitchen units, in the old biscuit tins stacked in the cupboard under the stairs and even rifled through her mother's handbag. She searched through the shoeboxes piled inside the wardrobe in the back bedroom and then finally emptied the entire contents of Rose's bedside table. If Rose had kept a diary, Lilian was determined to find it.

She had no idea where the time had gone, but suddenly she noticed the sun was going down and long shadows were now creeping across the flowery bedspread where she sat surrounded by dog-eared books and crumpled magazines, heartburn tablets and handkerchiefs. There was no diary.

Eyes swimming with tears, Lilian looked around her mother's cosy, familiar bedroom, the embroidered kimono dressing gown hanging on the back of the door, the fluffy slippers still sitting next to the dressing table stool. Lilian's eyes rested on the framed painting that hung on the wall opposite Rose's bed. It had been there for as long as Lilian remembered: a watercolour of a large white mansion house, its white pillared portico just visible behind a line of tall trees. It was the house from *Gone with the Wind*, one of Rose's favourite films. Lilian racked her brain to remember the name. What was it...? It was something like a girl's name... Tara! That was it. She sighed and shook her head. If Rose had loved the Southern States of America so much, why hadn't she made a life for herself there? One where she married the man she loved, had a child and brought up a family that stayed together.

She stared at the painting of the house; she'd never taken that much notice of the picture before, it was just always... there. There was something about it that was bothering her. Now she thought about it, she couldn't remember exactly when her mother had told her the picture was of the house from the American civil war movie. In fact, had she ever said it at all?

Lilian sprang to her feet and stood right in front of the painting. What a fool she was. This house wasn't Tara, it didn't have anything to do with *Gone With The Wind* or Scarlett O'Hara. The picture was of Graceland.

All this time, the last image Rose had ever seen at night, the first thing that had greeted her each and every morning was this image of Graceland, the place that Lilian now knew linked Rose directly to the man who was her father.

With trembling hands, she reached up and lifted the picture off its hook on the wall and turned it over. There, tucked into the edge of a frame, was a yellowing letter with a Memphis address written in her mother's distinctive loopy handwriting. Across one corner was a bold-red ink stamp that read 'Return to Sender'.

As Lilian plucked the letter from its hiding place, a

second envelope that had been wedged behind fluttered to the floor. Reaching down to pick it up, she saw this letter had been torn open down one side. It was addressed to Rose.

The faded date stamp on the sealed envelope written in her mother's hand was impossible to read. Lilian laid it carefully on the bed and sat down beside it. She would start with the already open letter.

Jennifer-Jane's note was handwritten in tiny, exceptionally neat lines. It wasn't very long. The date at the top was late November 1960, a couple of months after Rose had returned from her visit to America, she would have known she was pregnant by then. The thick cream notepaper was expensive and headed with an embossed logo that read 'Walnut Grove House'. For all its fancy luxury, the frosty tone of the contents could not be mistaken.

Jennifer told Rose that her letter for Wes was being returned unread and unopened. She said that Wesley Presley was not interested in anything Rose had to say and wanted nothing to do with her or the baby she claimed was his.

I regret to inform you, Jennifer wrote, *Mr W. Presley refused to accept delivery of the letter you sent care of my address.*

He has made it perfectly clear to me that he accepts no responsibility for the unfortunate situation you find yourself in and has no desire to be involved.

I consider this matter now closed and I do not wish to be involved in any further correspondence from you in this, or indeed any other regard.

A hot flush of indignation washed over Lilian as she read the cold words written more than fifty years before. How dare Wes reject her mother in this way, and how cruel of Jennifer to end a friendship because she clearly didn't approve of what had happened.

But as she read through the harsh note again, she remembered what Daisy had put in her texts. She'd said Wes swore he knew nothing about Rose being pregnant. In fact, hadn't she also said something about him trying to contact Rose?

Lilian ran downstairs to find her bag and pulled out her phone. She flicked through the messages as she slowly walked back up the stairs to the bedroom. Yes, there it was. Daisy's texts stated Wes had gone to visit Jennifer-Jane but *she* had told him Rose wanted nothing to do with *him*. Daisy had also insisted that Wes was a lovely, kind and thoughtful man. Something here did not add up.

Picking up the sealed envelope addressed to Mr Wesley Presley c/o Miss Jennifer-Jane Jenkins, Walnut Grove House, Germantown, Memphis, Lilian felt the real truth was contained inside this letter. She instinctively felt she couldn't trust the words written by Jennifer. The young woman appeared to care more for her own position than for her friend Rose. She needed to find out what her mother had to say.

It was dark in the bedroom now and Lilian reached over to switch on the bedside lamp as she sat with her mother's letter to Wes still in her hand. She'd read it numerous times and instead of the words weighing heavily on her they'd made her feel somewhat lightheaded.

The mature approach her mother had taken had impressed her – no recriminations, no unreasonable demands. Despite being young, unmarried, pregnant and alone, Rose had been clear she intended to keep her baby. Not only keep it, love it and treasure it in a way that honoured the love that had created it. Lilian felt the warmth of her mother's love surround her now in the lamplight.

Rose had promised Wes she would raise his child with an understanding of their heritage and background, and yet she had asked for nothing in return.

Lilian's memories of all the times she had rejected the rock 'n' roll music Rose loved so much flooded into her mind. She remembered how often she'd ignored Rose's attempts to talk about Memphis and the Southern States. Rose had tried so hard, but had patiently accepted Lilian's dismissal of all of this. She had allowed Lilian to decide for herself what she liked and who she was. She had let her be her own person. Lilian understood this now for the very first time.

She thought about Daisy, how like Rose she obviously was, how they loved so many of the same things and shared the same traits. Lilian resolved to let Daisy be her own person from now on too. She was suddenly so grateful that Rose had had Daisy to share her passions with, how wonderful it must have been for her to find her granddaughter appreciated everything she held so dear.

Rose had even shared with Wes what she was thinking of naming her baby:

Something tells me it's going to be a girl, she had written. *Of course I could be wrong but if it is I think I want to name her after a flower. We already have our matching rose tattoos and I believe they bind us to each other more than any wedding ring could do. I like the idea of making our baby part of that special bond so I plan to call her Lily.*

Lilian had stifled a sob as she read that. It had always annoyed her so much that her mother continued to call her 'Lily' while she always wanted to be known as Lilian. What a blind idiot she had been.

Rose had signed the letter: 'With love from your sweet Rose' and Lilian knew without doubt that if this letter had ever reached Wes he would have found a way to be with his 'Sweet Rose' again and be a proper father to his baby daughter, Lily.

Had her mother really believed Jennifer when she said Wesley wanted nothing to do with her? Had she kept him a secret to protect her daughter from feeling as rejected as she did when she read what Jennifer said? Or was it Jennifer's reaction that made her think it was better to leave things as they were, concentrate on bringing up her baby and leave Wes to continue his life in Memphis? If her best friend could turn against her like that, were the odds against the romance from the start?

Whatever the truth, Rose had kept her love for Wes tucked away just like the letter that had been hidden behind the painting of Graceland. It was too late to ask Rose anything more about her side of the story, but it wasn't too late to talk to Wes and Lilian knew that was what she was now desperate to do.

D aisy stood on the steps of the tiny clapboard wedding chapel. The setting could not have been more beautiful, tucked away in picturesque woodland on the edge of the Graceland grounds. Daisy had only just discovered the place even existed. Who would have thought she would be standing here, at a hastily arranged wedding? The last couple of days had indeed been full of startling revelations.

She leaned on the white picket fence that surrounded the front porch and gently touched the sprigs of ivy and gypsophila that had been wound around the bannister of the front steps. But this wasn't *her* special day… She sighed and tried to ignore the ache in her heart and the nagging 'what if' thoughts in her mind. It wasn't nice to feel jealous, but she just couldn't help herself.

Suddenly the door behind her opened and Priya stepped out onto the porch. The two of them were dressed identically in blue and white floral knee-length prom dresses and both held neat posies of cream roses. Daisy had stamped her own unique style on the outfit by teaming her dress with the cowboy boots she'd bought in Tupelo – turned out Trixie was right, you could indeed wear them anytime, anywhere.

Priya grinned as she looked at her flowery twin and said, 'It's not my usual style but you did great finding these frocks. I feel like an extra from *Little House on the Prairie*.'

Daisy smiled ruefully in reply. She'd clocked the dresses hanging on a jam-packed rail in a little rundown vintage clothes shop she'd discovered when she first got to Memphis, never imagining for a second that she'd be wearing one as a bridesmaid outfit before the end of her trip!

They both turned at the growling sound of a car engine approaching, and an open-top pink Cadillac emerged from between the trees and cruised to a stop in front of the tiny chapel. Valentin, dressed in his very best white 'Elvis' jumpsuit, sprang from the driver's seat, a dazzling blur of rhinestones and tassels. He gallantly opened the door for his passenger and Anita stepped out of the car. Her lacy white frock also had a Fifties feel – with a fitted bodice and a full, flared skirt. On her feet were white pumps with a pointy toe and a kitten heel, her blonde hair was teased into a beehive style, and she carried a bouquet of dark red roses.

Sean clambered from the back seat of the car and stood awkwardly at the bottom of the three wooden steps. Anita took his arm and, giving it a squeeze, said, 'I'm so pleased you could stay long enough to give me away, Sean.'

Sean nodded. 'It's okay, my flight isn't until later

tonight.' He started to say how honoured he was to perform the role, but a beeping noise interrupted him.

'Is that a phone in your pocket or are you just pleased to see me?' teased Anita.

Red-faced and flustered, Sean pulled the phone out. 'Oh look, it's a text from Lynette, and she's sent a picture.'

Daisy and Priya hopped down the steps and peered at the screen along with Anita and Valentin. Sean tapped the message and smiling woman appeared holding a tiny red-faced baby. Lynette had added the message: *Have a lovely wedding day, y'all, love from Lynette, Harry and Baby Wesley X*

'Oh, I'm filling up,' said Anita.

Sean made sure his phone was set to Silent and they arranged themselves into formation. Valentin led the wedding procession into the chapel, followed by Anita on Sean's arm, Daisy and Priya behind them.

The 'Hawaiian Wedding Song' began to play as they walked towards where Chance was waiting for his bride in front of a rose-patterned stained-glass window, a replica of the ones found in the front hall of Graceland. Elvis's voice filled the chapel to its rafters as beams of coloured light reflected through the window and played across the floor around Chance's feet. He stood there resplendent in a tan-coloured Western-style suit with white piping and fringing.

Daisy felt Blue's eyes on her as they made their way between the pews but kept looking forward. She had a feeling he might see right through her if he looked too closely. This casual, carefree demeanour was tricky to maintain.

There were several guests seated alongside Blue and

Wes, including a few fellow tourists from the Graceland Experience. Some of the motel staff like Loretta, Carlton and George were there and also Todd and Howard, the tour guide and coach driver. This was certainly a first for them – they'd never had a guest meet and marry during one of their tours before... even in the Deep South!

Daisy and Priya slipped into their seats as Reverend Proctor addressed the tiny congregation, 'Dearly beloved, we are gathered here, in this special place on this beautiful day to witness the joyous union of these two people, Anita and Chance, two people who have travelled far and journeyed long to find each other and, in doing so, have truly found themselves...'

Daisy gripped the posy in her lap tightly and fought the urge to turn and look at Blue although the sense of him nearby was almost overpowering.

The service was simple and sweet, Anita tried to take in every last detail; all of her senses seemed magnified in the moment. The perfume of the flowers in her bouquet was strong and heady, the sound of Reverend Proctor's voice echoed within the clapboard walls of the chapel. She held on tight to Chance's hand and tried to focus on what the preacher was saying. When he asked if anyone present could show just cause why they should not be married, she held her breath until she thought her chest would burst. The moment passed without incident and within minutes Chance and Anita were proclaimed husband and wife.

Anita gazed up at Chance as they faced each other. His brow was slightly furrowed as he asked, 'Are you okay?' Anita stroked his kind, bearded face and replied, 'I'm thousands of miles away from everything I've ever known... and yet I've never felt happier.' Instantly his look of concern was gone and he leaned down to kiss her tenderly. Daisy gulped down the lump in her throat and prayed that Anita and Chance had all the happiness they deserved in their new life together.

Everyone burst into spontaneous applause as the happy couple walked back down the aisle and headed out into the afternoon sunshine to pose for photographs. Daisy and Priya fell into step behind Chance and Anita, closely followed by Blue and Valentin.

The newlyweds only had eyes for each other and paused in the doorway for yet another lingering kiss, which almost led to an embarrassing pile-up as the wedding guests were forced to an abrupt halt. Daisy couldn't help but laugh as Priya called out, 'Whoa' to warn those behind not to press forward, but then the laugh became a gasp as she spotted a familiar face standing in the clearing facing the chapel.

'MUM!'

Lilian was wearing a smart navy skirt suit and had one hand resting on the pull-up handle of a small black cabin suitcase. She looked like a lost air hostess.

At the sound of Daisy's voice, Lilian took a small step forward and briefly raised her hand as if to say 'Hi'. Daisy ducked around Anita and Chance as the rest of the crowd poured out onto the porch behind her. In two strides, she stood facing Lilian. Standing there in her flowery vintage dress and cowboy boots, Daisy was even more aware of how out of place her smartly dressed mother appeared. What was she even *doing* here?

'Mum? What are you even doing here?'

Lilian looked tired and Daisy realised she must have flown through the night, but she gave an odd little smile as she said, 'I thought you wanted me to come.'

'Yes… yes, of course… but …' Daisy had so many questions but this moment was still all about Anita and Chance and everyone was calling Daisy back to have a photograph taken on the steps of the chapel.

'Daisy, it's okay, you go…' Lilian nodded as she repeated the phrase she'd used at the airport when she'd seen Daisy off at the very start of this journey.

Daisy smiled back gratefully and said, 'It won't take long.'

Lilian watched as Daisy ran up the steps of the Graceland chapel and was absorbed into a colourful tableau of new friends.

Todd called for everyone to smile at the camera. The bride and groom at the centre of the group didn't need to be prompted, they shone with happiness. The rhinestones on Valentin's white jumpsuit dazzled in the sunshine as he struck his best Elvis pose on one side of Chance and Anita, while Sean shook off his shyness and attempted his own hilarious version on the other. Priya and Daisy were pretty as a picture in their blue bridesmaids' dresses on one side of the porch while on the other Lilian noticed a good-looking young man sneaking glances at Daisy. An older, white-haired gentleman, meanwhile, seemed to be looking directly at Lilian herself.

. . .

The wedding breakfast was held in the restaurant back at the motel. Loretta had overseen a partial transformation of the room where they usually ate their bacon and pancakes, and fresh flowers and white ribbons now decorated every nook and cranny in between all the Presley memorabilia. Dainty sweet and savoury snacks had been laid out on a long table covered in a white tablecloth and there was even an enormous wedding cake covered in sparkly cream frosting. It all looked delicious.

As soon as they'd arrived back at the motel Blue had appeared and turned on his easy Southern charm, offering to take Lilian's suitcase to Daisy's room and saying what a pleasure it was to meet her. Lilian had thanked him and then remarked to Daisy, 'What a thoughtful young man.'

Daisy quickly introduced Lilian to Priya and Valentin and explained that Sean would have to leave soon to make his flight home to meet his new baby. Lilian took this news and the sight of a Russian Elvis impersonator in full costume completely in her stride, much to Daisy's amazement. She grabbed some food and a couple of glasses of champagne, and steered her mother to a quieter table in the corner.

'I can't believe you're here.' Daisy couldn't seem to stop looking at Lilian; seeing her here in Memphis felt so strange.

'I didn't expect to arrive in the middle of a wedding,' Lilian said, looking around the room, taking everything in. 'Talk about a whirlwind romance, but I have to say, they do make a lovely couple.'

Daisy wondered if jet lag was having some sort of weird

effect on her mother. Lilian seemed strangely calm and somehow not as brittle as usual. She was gazing around the room with a look of wonder on her face. Goodness, she was even *smiling* at people.

Lilian caught the expression on Daisy's face and gave a little laugh. 'Look at you, I suppose you thought only Nana Rose was one for surprises, well two can play at that game, you know.'

'Oh, Mum,' Daisy said. 'Why didn't she tell us about Wes, about him being a Presley... about all this? How could she keep something like that a secret?'

Lilian sat with her head on one side and a thoughtful expression on her face. 'Maybe, in her own way she did try, she certainly never lost her love for anything and everything rock 'n' roll now, did she? It seems the clues were there, but maybe the real problem was... I wasn't willing to hear it.'

Daisy looked at her mother in complete amazement. She must have gone over and over things in her mind and was willing to believe that her own obstinate refusal to show any interest in what turned out to be her heritage had been a reason Rose didn't tell her the truth. It was a theory.

Lilian then began to talk about the lost letter she had found hidden behind the painting in Nana Rose's bedroom. 'Did you know that picture was of Graceland?' she stopped to ask midway through. Daisy shrugged and nodded. Of course she did, wasn't it obvious?

But when she told Daisy the unopened letter had been sent back stamped 'Return to Sender', Daisy almost fell off her chair. 'Just like Elvis's song!' she exclaimed.

Lilian reached for Daisy's hand then. 'I don't believe Wesley ever knew a thing about that letter and something tells me things could have been very different if he had. I think it was a certain Miss Jennifer-Jane who tried to make sure Rose and Wes forgot all about each other.'

Of course! It was all so clear to Daisy now. Rose and Wes truly loved each other, and, despite Jennifer's best efforts, they never did forget.

Daisy sat lost in her own thoughts for a while until Lilian bent her head forward and whispered, 'Isn't there someone rather important you want me to meet?'

Over by the bar, Wes had been watching and keeping his distance, but he crossed the room in a flash when Daisy beckoned him over. Suddenly, there he was, standing within touching distance of Rose's girl, his own daughter, Lilian.

'Wes, this is…' Daisy hesitated. What was the right way to introduce your grandfather to your mum? Amazingly, it was her mother who knew just what to say. She stood up, smoothing down her skirt with the flat of her hands.

'Hello,' she said, reaching out to touch Wes gently on the arm as she gave a warm smile. 'I'm… I'm Lily.'

Daisy gasped as she heard her mother call herself by the name Rose always used but her mum had refused to use for so long. Was it something in the warm Tennessee air that was causing this change? It seemed to Daisy that from beneath Lilian's previous frosty exterior a tiny bud called Lily was attempting to grow and bloom. The sudden name change might not mean much to Wes, but Daisy knew the significance; her mum was making a huge effort to fit in, not just in Memphis and with Wes, but with Daisy too.

. . .

As the afternoon wore on, Daisy found herself standing at the edge of the dance floor as Anita and Chance stepped out to take their first dance. Her mum had waved her away, telling her to enjoy herself, and Lily and Wes remained in their own little bubble, heads close together, talking intently, catching up on so many lost years.

Someone pressed a button on the juke box and 'Can't Help Falling in Love' started to play. Chance took Anita in his arms and waltzed her gracefully around the floor, her white dress flaring out as they whirled by.

Daisy was suddenly aware of Blue by her side. 'Shall we?' He held out his hand and Daisy let herself be pulled into his arms as more couples joined Anita and Chance on the dance floor. As they span around, Daisy heard Elvis sing about wise men and fools rushing in and wondered how anyone ever really knew what was wise and what was foolish. The feeling of being in Blue's arms felt so right, no one else had ever made her feel this way, like the very best version of herself. Leaving Memphis would mean not only leaving Blue and Wes, but also leaving this Daisy behind. The thought stopped her in her tracks and she stood still as the music carried on and dancers moved around them.

'I'm sorry, Blue... I can't...' A sob escaped and she made a dash for the door.

Lily found her daughter a little while later in the ladies' restroom. Daisy was attempting to fix her face so she didn't look like someone who'd just bawled their eyes out. Lily took Daisy's hands in her own and spoke quietly but with complete conviction.

'Daisy Featherstone, what on earth do you think you are doing?'

Daisy stared at her mum in embarrassment. 'What... what do you mean?'

'Now listen to me, my girl.' Lily was forceful now, and this was more familiar. 'You've come all this way, found my father, your own grandfather – a remarkable man, I must say – you've solved a mystery that has hung over this family for all these years and you don't seem to be happy about any of it.'

Daisy opened her mouth to speak, but Lily cut her off. 'Don't try to tell me I'm imagining things, I know exactly what's going on here.'

'You do?' Daisy couldn't see how Lily could, she'd completely lost track herself.

'Of course I do. You and Rose were always so alike, the things you loved, the way you behaved... but do you think for one single second I'm going to let you make exactly the same mistake as she did all those years ago?' Lily looked down on her daughter's bemused face and couldn't resist taking it in between her hands as though she was about to kiss her.

'Oh, Daisy, don't turn your back on happiness when you see a chance of it. Anita hasn't, now has she? She's taken her chance... with Chance.' Daisy couldn't keep up with her mum's train of thought; she was talking about Daisy's new friends as though she knew them herself. 'And Priya and

349

Valentin, they're heading back to Wales together, you know, she won't ever get back with that cheating lowlife Sid!'

'Wha...?' How on earth had Lily got the measure of the entire group in the space of a couple of hours?

Lily was still speaking, her face just inches from Daisy's. 'Now, Officer Cody seems like a real gentleman, not at all like those *boys* you hang out with back at home. But maybe he's too much of a gentleman to tell you when you are making a damn fool of yourself.'

Daisy's mind was working overtime now. Was her mother saying what she thought she was saying? What was she saying now? Good grief, she was still talking! Lilian released her grip on Daisy's face and turned to check her own appearance in the mirror. 'You've always been one for jumping in, feet first. How many times have I said it?'

Daisy shrugged, completely bewildered. She knew her mother was always moaning about how impulsive she was, how she never thought about the consequences of her actions. But why was she saying it now – because she *should* be impulsive, or because she *shouldn't*? She really wished she'd said no to that second glass of champagne, everything was so confusing.

'Now, Blue, as you call him,' Lily carried on regardless, 'it rather suits him, doesn't it? Those eyes! He's had a rather lovely idea... Such a kind, thoughtful man. Come along now, Daisy, Anita and Chance are about to leave.'

In a flurry of hugs and kisses, Anita and Chance were heading off to Beale Street to celebrate their union with a singing spot in the club where they first met. After an embarrassing misunderstanding, Priya and Valentin had agreed to join them, once Priya had reassured Val the invitation was to help *celebrate* not *consummate* their marriage.

'We're just going to watch them sing down at a club on Beale Street,' Priya explained to the much relieved Russian. 'Maybe we should sign you up for a few extra English lessons when we get back home.'

Evening was beginning to fall as Daisy and Lily arrived at the gates of Graceland. This had been Blue's suggestion and he was standing with Wes waiting for them. The tourists were long gone and the mansion grounds were quiet and empty. Cars flew past on the highway, but no one was taking notice of the little group of people gathered by the entrance to the Presley home.

Lily took in her first sight of the gates decorated with twin guitar players and metal music notes and then looked up to the white mansion beyond. It really was quite something.

Wes seemed a little nervous as he shuffled his feet on the dusty ground. 'So this is the very spot where I first met your momma,' he said to his daughter.

Lily simply nodded and reached for his hand, then she turned to Blue. 'Did you get some?' she asked.

Blue smiled, his eyes meeting Lily's then resting on Daisy as he pulled a blue and white plastic Graceland gift bag out of his pocket. 'As soon as I asked Anita for some of the red rose petals from her bouquet, she said yes straight away,' he said.

'We're going to scatter them here... for Rose. This was all Blue's idea,' said Lily, looking straight at Daisy.

Daisy felt her heart bloom with pride. Trust Blue! How did he always know just the right thing to do? Standing there on the spot where her Nana Rose had met Wesley Presley all those years ago, Daisy finally realised she did not want to make the same mistake her grandmother had and live her life without the man she loved. Whatever happened from now on, she knew that she and Blue were meant to be together. Jumping into a new life in Memphis might be the biggest risk she would ever take, but Lily was smiling and nodding, actually encouraging her daughter to dare to do this. Daisy hoped it would also give Lily a very good reason to visit often and get to know her newfound father.

On the way over in the taxi, Lily had told Daisy she knew things had been increasingly difficult at Blue Moon Vintage. Daisy had always been terrified of her mother finding out. She'd always thought Lily would gloat and say 'I told you so'. Instead, Lily had said mysteriously, 'Perhaps it's the right idea, but just in the wrong place?' She'd also told Daisy that Nana Rose had left her some money, not a fortune, but enough to pay off the shop's debts and give her some breathing space.

Now Daisy's mind was racing. Might she be able to open an antique clothes store in downtown Memphis? Could Blue Moon Vintage be a real success here? Might she eventually be able to convince Lily to tell Sanctimonious Sandra at the insurance company where to stick it so Lily could move over and help her run the shop? Maybe? Her mum and Wes had certainly struck up an instant bond and it was wonderful to see. Suddenly a world of possibilities opened up ahead of Daisy but... *Steady, one small step at a time.* She needed to get this right.

Blue was standing patiently with the Graceland gift bag in his hands. They each reached into the bag and took some of the red rose petals. Once they all had a handful they waited expectantly... What now?

Once more it was Blue who gave the cue. 'This is for you, Mrs Featherstone, ma'am,' he said, throwing his handful of petals into the evening breeze.

One by one, they all followed his lead. 'For you, Mum,' said Lily.

'For you, Nana,' said Daisy.

'For my Rose,' said Wes.

The petals swirled lightly in the air and landed softly on the Memphis ground. Wes looked at the upturned faces of his newly found daughter and granddaughter and his heart felt full. 'My sweet Rose is here at last,' he said.

Daisy took a small step towards Blue, just one small step but he knew what it meant.

'Well sure, I thought you were never gonna get here,' he said with a smile as he reached for her. 'But now you're here, I swear I'm never gonna let you go.' And when he kissed her, Daisy knew she was right where she belonged.

Read on for extract from Shake It Up,
Beverley

Beverley Wilson has always loved the Beatles but kissing a
poster goodnight isn't really an option when you're a fifty-
something mum of three. So when she decides it's time to
get back into the dating game, she turns to a dating agency
for help.

But the long and winding road to real love is littered with
dating disasters – the pantyhose pervert being the real low
point and in Bev's opinon it's all too much. But meeting
fellow Beatles fan Scott Smith changes everything…

Chapter One

I'd crawled on my hands and knees across my living room and pulled the curtains closed across the bay window from underneath, keeping out of sight. Of course, that only proved to the baying mob outside that I was indeed at home, and they immediately started shouting and yelling, holding cameras and phones above their heads and taking pictures of my little terraced house as though I was a movie star or a serial killer.

Of course I am neither of those things, but on that particular morning I woke to find myself a household name, a national laughing stock and the punchline to countless "jokes" doing the rounds on social media.

Me! Mild-mannered Beverley Wilson; completely ordinary in almost every respect. A Liverpool lass, a widow, single mother of three, and a part-time estate agent.

Well, I suppose that's not quite the full story. Life had been fairly humdrum and ordinary for the vast majority of my fifty-plus years, but that all started to change after my Geoff died. It's been over ten years now since he's been gone... I can't quite believe that... Ten years? Where did they go? Well, mainly into bringing up my three boys and trying to get through each and every day the best way I can, exactly what most women in my situation would do, is the short answer to that.

I can pinpoint the first time I ever decided to do something *extraordinary*, something unexpected and just for me. It was when I spotted this house was up for auction and decided to go for it. Downsizing made perfect sense once my middle son moved out to live with his girlfriend and the eldest was away doing his final year at uni. Once I only had my youngest still at home full-time – and knowing he wouldn't stick around much longer – meant this little terrace was just the job, but it wasn't simply the financial advantages of running a smaller home that swayed me to do it.

I'd gone along to the auction at The Cavern Club down on Mathew Street clutching the particulars for 72 Western Avenue, Speke, in my hot little hand. The Cavern was renowned for being claustrophobic and clammy back in the day, when The Beatles were just a bunch of local lads playing to a Swinging Sixties crowd rammed like sweaty sardines into the basement club. Apparently, it stank to high heaven! I'd missed out on that scene – born a little too late to be one of the lucky Liverpudlians who could honestly say they'd been there – but there I was now, about to try and grab my very own piece of Beatles history.

I don't know how I found the nerve to raise my hand and bid the way I did. It was like an out-of-body experience. One minute I was Beverley Wilson, anonymous lifelong Beatles fan, the next I was the owner of Paul McCartney's childhood home and had been dubbed "Beatles Bev" in the report of the auction in *The Liverpool Echo*.

People are often surprised that I was able to afford a home once lived in by a Beatle. They hear the word "Beatles" and instantly presume it must have cost millions, but really it's just an ordinary little terrace in a Liverpool suburb. It's not ordinary to me though.

This place isn't the more famous Forthlin Road home where Paul lived as a teenager and started to write songs with John Lennon in the back room. That house is kept as a museum, not lived in and used as a regular home like this one. That was part of the attraction to me though. I mean, think about it... Paul McCartney actually lived here with his little brother, Mike, and his parents, Jim and Mary, and now it's my home. I truly get a tingle up my spine every time I walk in the door.

Once I'd sold the family home I'd lived in with Geoff and the boys I was easily able to afford this place and I've never regretted it. Yes, I needed to relocate to make a fresh start, but I'll be honest, the house really was the ultimate prize for an avid collector like me. Over the years I've amassed an amazing collection of Beatles memorabilia, from signed original posters and programmes, to limited-edition lunchboxes and rare Beatles perfume bottles, plus other stuff you can't get for love nor money these days. I can't claim all the credit though; the bulk of the early items used to belong to my big sister Deb. I treasured it once it all became mine, and have added to it religiously over the years.

Life settled back into comfortable obscurity once the flurry of interest in me buying the house died down. But suddenly that all changed and I found myself being hounded by the bloody press, who were beating a drum solo on my front door that would put Ringo to shame. I attempted hiding under the window, trying not to listen, but they kept on yelling at me.

"Mrs Wilson? Come and talk to us, Mrs Wilson…"

"Come on, Bev, it'll only take a minute. You might as well talk to us. We're gonna print the story anyway."

"Mrs Wilson, Beverley, love – you need to tell your side of the story. Talk to us, Bev, it'll make you feel better."

"Bev – is it true you've got a yellow submarine tattooed on your arse?"

That did it!

I told them all to sod off and leave me alone … and just for the record added that I did NOT have a yellow submarine tattoo on me arse, or anywhere else, for that matter. Also, I've never rummaged through George Harrison's rubbish bins. What a disgusting allegation; it was just a good viewing spot, that was all. Oh, and while we're at it I do NOT sleep with a lock of Ringo Starr's pubic hair under me pillow. Bloody *Daily Star*!

They all buggered off eventually, but not before they'd made a right mess of me rhododendrons.

I knew they'd be back though... It was obvious they weren't going to leave me alone that easily. It wasn't even this bad when I worked part-time at The Beatles Story down on the dock. I was well chuffed when they said I could train up to drive the yellow duckmarine tour bus. You'll probably remember the way that all ended ... at the bottom of the Albert Dock! It wasn't my fault – that damn thing was hard to keep afloat, you know – but probably the least said about that the better, that's what the lawyers advised anyway.

The only thing I was really guilty of was wanting to stop being so safe and careful in my middle age. I was never like that when I was young, but life can do that to you, can't it? What was it John Lennon used to say? *"Life is what happens when you are busy making other plans."* So I simply decided it was time to shake my life up a bit.

It's always given me a thrill living here in Paul McCartney's childhood home. I've loved The Beatles from the first moment I saw them but it was always Paul for me. You know that feeling you get when you're young and you suddenly discover someone – a singer or a movie star – who makes your heart flip and your palms sweat? Well, that's how Paul made me feel; always did and always will. But even I knew we weren't likely to end up together, and after so many years on my own I started to think there might be someone out there – a real, live man – whom I could love and be loved by. Does that sound like I've lost my mind? Is it really so terrible that I wanted to meet a living, breathing bloke, and not simply share my life with a fantasy ... or a ghost, or a memory?

In some ways I think I was chasing those feelings you only get when you're young – when the world is still waiting to be discovered and all your mistakes have yet to take place. I wanted someone to make me feel like a teenager again. Bit of a tall order, I know. In the end, I've found myself riddled with insecurity, feeling like the whole world is against me, and I'm constantly in a terrible mood – so as far as experiencing a teenager's life, job done, I suppose!

I think part of the problem was the fact that I'd only got Harry still at home and the moment was fast approaching when he'd be off, too. That empty-nest syndrome is a right kick in the teeth, isn't it? You spend your best years ricocheting between toddler tantrums and history homework only to wake up one day to find they're off with barely a backward glance. I mean, that's fine – totally, completely fine – as it's what you've spent years working your fingers to the bone to create: independent adults ready to make their own way in the world. Marvellous. But let's be honest here, it's also just like someone has cut your heart out with a rusty old knife.

So that's how I found myself, Beverley Wilson – "Beatles Bev" – brought quite literally to my knees hiding from the gutter press. That lot just loved to write the most bloody outrageous lies about me. I went from being a woman who usually feels invisible in me own house to someone they talk about on daytime TV! They had a phone-in, for cryin' out loud! A bleedin' phone-in! People I've never met ringing in to give their opinions on MY life! Cheeky bloody beggars.

Chapter One

You wanna know how it all started? How someone who always believed that "All You Need Is Love" realised she "Should Have Known Better" and wished she could just "Get Back" to "Yesterday"? Well, read on...

Chapter Two

Four months earlier...

It had been a very ordinary Thursday in the estate agent office and I had just one last appointment in the diary. I double-checked the address of the property and made sure I'd got the right set of keys before I left Gratwick & Griffiths. I figured I'd be able to shoot straight off home from there once I was done.

It was only when I was halfway to Allerton that I realised there was not very much to be gained from an early dart. As usual, there would be no one at home waiting for me; no one to share a glass of wine with while cooking tea; no one to laugh with when a contestant on one of those teatime TV quiz shows demonstrated they didn't know their Shakespeare from their show tunes.

I know I was probably idealising day-to-day married life – I've got mates who do nothing but moan about their husbands – but sometimes it's having someone to do nothing with that's the thing you miss most. Like when you're sat watching telly and you just get a grunt of uninterest because you're wittering about wallpaper and they're pretending to be fascinated by the latest fracking debacle on *Newsnight*. Well, you don't half miss it when there's no one there grunting.

Harry was hardly ever home in the evening either. You can't blame him, he's eighteen and always off somewhere or other, often with his guitar slung over his back. That's one thing I'll take some credit for; Harry has picked up a real love of music from me. Not that he thinks I have any actual musical taste, of course. Or any taste at all. Apparently, the only thing I'm an expert in is being a complete and utter embarrassment. And I nail that without even trying. Seriously, the way he reacts to me singing along to the radio I might as well do a full-on Lady Gaga and pop on a meat dress to nip to the post office… I'd give it a go just to prove a point but I lean more towards a veggie diet these days.

I pulled up outside the house I'd come to value, a white-painted semi with a small overgrown front garden. There was a driveway big enough for one car behind a pair of low metal gates but I parked my car on the road. I wanted to take a few pictures and I didn't want my trusty VW Polo making an appearance in those.

It was a nice house on a pleasant street but it looked a bit unloved. I knew how it felt.

The owner of the house had been an elderly lady who'd lived there alone until she'd recently died. Mrs Malkin's family dropped the keys into our office a few days before and asked if we could give them a valuation. I'm used to doing viewings at properties without the owner being present as most people ask us to show prospective buyers around – I think they'd rather not hear any rude remarks about their interior design choices – but it was unusual for me to be inside a house completely on my own.

As I let myself into the front hall, and felt the door push against a small pile of mail on the mat, I suddenly felt a little apprehensive about being there. I gave myself a shake and a bit of a talking to; there was no point freaking myself out when there was a job to do. I intended to have a good look round, take some snaps, make a few notes, and with luck I'd be home in time to impress absolutely nobody with my extensive general knowledge whilst simultaneously shouting at the TV and cooking pasta.

I moved from room to room looking past the old-fashioned furniture and dated decor. I was concentrating on the room sizes, how the house was laid out and what features it had that a buyer would be looking for. I decided the first thing a young couple would want to do was knock through the two downstairs reception rooms to open the ground floor up and make it a much more usable space. The kitchen was a decent size, with room for a breakfast table but no separate utility area, which a lot of people ask for these days.

I opened a door I suspected might be a walk-in pantry but was pleased to find it had actually been converted into a downstairs cloakroom with a toilet and small handwashing basin. That was a bonus.

Upstairs, the two smaller bedrooms had a distinctly unused air as the beds were made up not with duvets but candlewick bedspreads. I felt a twinge of sadness for the old girl who'd lived there. How long had it been since anyone came to stay with her, I wondered? The cold rooms were overfilled with large pieces of dark wood furniture, cumbersome dressing tables, and wardrobes that looked like they held the secret entrance to Narnia. I edged around the bed in the back bedroom as there was hardly enough room to move, and tugged open one of the wardrobe doors. It squeaked loudly on its hinges and I was instantly hit by a strong, musty smell; clearly no one had looked in there for a very long time. As I peered inside I almost laughed out loud. There were a couple of huge fur coats hanging from the rail, just like you would find inside a Narnia wardrobe. I resisted the temptation to clamber in to see if I could also find a lion and a witch.

The sun had started to set and the bright afternoon had given way to a gloomy half-light in the empty house. There was just the old lady's bedroom left to assess now and I was conscious I was putting off the moment when I had to step inside. I can't remember now what I was so worried about.

As I turned the handle of the master bedroom door, I was aware I had the lyrics from the song "Eleanor Rigby" nagging at me inside my head, begging for an answer to the question of where all the lonely people in the world do come from. I had no idea what Marjorie Malkin's life had really been like, but the sense I was getting as I poked around her home was that in her old age she spent a lot of time there on her own. I knew that her son, who seemed to be the only family she had, lived on the other side of the country – that's why he and his wife left the keys with me for the valuation – and he'd made it plain they wanted to sell up quickly. No one had even started clearing out the old dear's belongings; they probably intended to employ one of those house-clearing firms to come in and give one price for taking the lot. I had an image in my mind of poor old Marjorie being just a face at her own window, sitting in her drab, draughty house day after day, watching the world go by without her. I wondered how many people had gone to her funeral ... or if, like Eleanor Rigby, nobody came?

That morbid train of thought was really giving me a spooky sensation. I hesitated on the threshold of Marjorie's bedroom and steeled myself as though I was about to confront the ghost of the old lady herself, sat up in her bed, furious with my intrusion into her home.

The bedroom door swung inwards and I stepped forward onto the tufted Wilton patterned carpet. The dark curtains were partially closed across the bay window so it took a moment for my eyes to adjust, but the sight that suddenly materialised sent a shockwave of horror through me as I shrieked in fear and stumbled backwards.

A stark, pale face with a shock of white hair was staring straight at me through a pair of glittering eyes in deep, dark sockets.

My heart hammered in my chest and my hands fluttered to find the door frame so I could steady myself. What horrific nightmare was this?

As my breath came in short gasps my eyes never left the evil glare that was being levelled at me. Then sense slowly dawned. It was not a cadaver or a ghost. The unblinking gaze I had been confronted with was that of a large porcelain doll sitting upright, her legs sticking straight out in front of her from beneath the ruffles of a Victorian-style white lace dress. She was propped in the centre of the pink satin eiderdown, her blonde hair fanned out on the pile of pillows behind her.

I shuddered in relief and swept my eyes around the rest of the bedroom from the sanctuary of the doorway. There were dozens of similar dolls all around the room, sitting in groups on a bedside chair, on a dressing table, even on top of the wardrobe. They were everywhere I looked. They varied in size and colouring but all shared the same blank expression and slightly accusatory air of the first doll.

My sympathetic feelings towards poor old Marjorie Malkin morphed into irritation as I wondered why on earth anyone in their right mind would collect such an array of creepy dolls like these. How had she slept at night surrounded by so many pairs of staring eyes? As I moved towards the window to open the curtains and let in a little more light and sanity, I was aware of how those eyes followed me around the room. It was enough to freak anyone out.

I took my notebook from my bag and resolved to pull myself together as I began to write down the dimensions of the room and some of the original features I was able to spot in between the dozens of dead-eyed dolls: a small fireplace, original coving, an ornate ceiling rose above the centre of the bed... As I scribbled the details as quickly as I could I noticed my fingers were still trembling. I'd be lucky to be able to read half of those notes back later.

I gave the room one last look around. The collection

might end up being worth quite a bit of money, but I decided I'd be glad to never see a porcelain doll again for as long as I lived.

I'd taken a single step towards the hallway when there was a sudden and distinctive sound of breaking glass from downstairs. I froze immediately and racked my brains for what could have caused such a noise. Could something have fallen in the kitchen? I hadn't spotted anything that looked precarious when I was in there; in fact, the work surfaces were fairly uncluttered, unlike the rest of the house.

I was holding my breath but before I had chance to exhale, a further noise confirmed what I now know my subconscious had been dreading; the distinctive rattle of the handle on the back door to the garden and the shuffle of a footstep entering the house. It was almost like I could sense rather than hear the invasion of another person into the property. Someone had broken in.

My body took over while my mind stayed on pause. Instinctively, I took a silent step towards the bedroom door and pushed it gently shut. As I heard the intruder beneath me move into the dining room I moved quickly to the far corner where there was a gap between the wardrobe and the wall just big enough to wedge myself into. I pulled my mobile out of my cross-body bag and dialled 999.

I honestly have no clue how long I was standing, pressed up against the floral wallpaper, terrified and trembling. The noises from downstairs left me in no doubt that Mrs Malkin's home was being thoroughly ransacked. I hadn't heard any voices but I couldn't be absolutely sure there wasn't more than one thief on the premises. I didn't want to know. The eyes of the dolls now seemed to be staring at the closed door of the room we were all trapped inside; like me, they were waiting to be discovered at any moment.

Three sharp bangs from below thudded through the house and my body simultaneously. Were the intruders smashing the place up? Then, out of nowhere, a deep, loud voice yelled, "POLICE!"

Still I couldn't move, I stayed exactly where I was, frozen to the spot, literally shivering with fear.

The police officer who found me a little while later guided me out of the bedroom and down the stairs, talking to me all the while like I was a small child.

"Just a couple of kids," he said. "They didn't get away with anything as they dropped the bag of stolen stuff in the garden when they ran. They're on their way down to the station now."

I sat, still shivering, on the chair in the front bay window where he'd perched me, while from the kitchen he kept up a running commentary that was meant to be reassuring. He boiled the kettle to make me a cup of tea and informed me there'd been a spate of break-ins in the area. He added that I'd done a great job of calling the cop shop while the little buggers were still in the house.

"Caught 'em red-handed, thanks to you," he said with a friendly grin as he handed me a china mug, adding, "I put a couple of sugars in, to help with the shock." And then, I can't be absolutely sure – my faculties had been numbed by the whole experience – but I could have sworn the detective constable actually winked at me.

I sipped my tea then and took a moment to look at him properly.

DC Collins, he'd said his name was when he introduced himself, was rather good-looking. Fit, both in the athletic and the fanciable sense. He was wearing a very smart dark grey suit, white shirt and a navy-blue tie. His black leather brogues were polished and shiny, but he looked like the sort of guy who would be more comfortable in a rugby shirt or a knitted Aran sweater and walking boots. I've never been one for the great outdoors but if a hike up a hill with DC Collins was followed by a pub lunch at a country inn beside a roaring fire, I decided I might be persuaded.

I snapped out of my fantasy to notice DC Collins's dark eyebrows were furrowed slightly as he looked at me in concern.

"Are you okay?" he asked.

I stuttered a reply, and my fingers fumbled for the cup of sweet tea I'd placed on the side table next to me. I couldn't work out whether I was all of a dither owing to my recent brush with crime while trapped with the creepy doll collection, or if it was the close proximity of DC Collins.

It was definitely highly unusual for me to feel attracted to a man in such a way. Perhaps I just don't get out enough, but I really couldn't remember the last time I'd fancied someone. In fact, I'd go so far as to say I really felt there was some sort of connection between me and DC Collins. It could have had something to do with the fact he'd just come to my rescue, like a knight in shining armour, or it could simply have been down to his lovely broad shoulders and the distinct twinkle in his dark brown eyes that he was using to great effect on me.

I looked down and felt relieved I was wearing my second best pair of black trousers – they fit me well and together with my leopard-print shirt and black ankle boots I didn't look too bad, all things considered. I ran a hand through my blonde hair and hoped it wasn't too much like a bird's nest. I also wished I hadn't left my black leather jacket in the car; it would have given my outfit a more modern vibe. People tell me I don't look my age, and I'm damn sure I don't feel it, but I wasn't sure how old DC Collins was. He could easily have been several years younger than me; it was hard to tell.

I fluttered my eyelashes as I sipped my tea and gave him my best smile. "I'm good, thanks to you," I said with what I hoped was a note of flirtation in my voice.

He gave me a warm smile in response but then said something that to this very day chills me to the bone.

"Have you lived here long?"

The question hit me like a kick in the guts. He thought that I lived there, in that old lady's house, with swirly patterned carpets, floral wallpaper and old-fashioned furniture! There were even antimacassars on the armchairs and doilies on the nest of tables. No one under the age of eighty-five would have such things and … oh my God, the dolls! He'd found me hiding upstairs and so must have seen the macabre spectacle of those ghoulish dollies in every corner of what he had clearly presumed was *my* bedroom! What kind of batty old woman did he think I was?

"I don't... This isn't ... my... I don't live here," I finally stammered, sounding more than ever like a doddery old dear. Seriously, could this day have got any worse?

It took a little while to sort out the confusion but DC Collins eventually understood my role as an estate agent and even seemed to find it all quite amusing that he at first assumed I was the lady of the house.

I was struggling to see the funny side of the mix-up. Just as I was casting myself in the role of femme fatale and entertaining the idea of attempting to seduce a hunky, darkly handsome detective, I discovered he actually saw me as a decrepit grandma with a passion for porcelain playthings. I know I am out of practice with the opposite sex but that didn't just take the biscuit – it took the whole damn packet of Jammie Dodgers!

Luckily, a neighbour from next door came to my rescue by popping round to see what all the commotion had been about and offering to board up the back door. Thank goodness I didn't need to stick around any longer.

As I made my hurried excuses for a quick exit, DC Levi Collins handed me his card in case I remembered any further details to add to my statement. I shoved it into my bag and in a final act of utter madness told him I had to dash as I had a belly-dancing class to get to. Belly dancing? Where that notion came from I have absolutely no idea, but I was so desperate for him to see me as a vibrant and youthful woman instead of a wizened old hag. By the look on his face, I think I only managed to revolt him more and who could blame him; the thought of me gyrating my pelvis in diaphanous harem pants would be enough to scare off even a beefy busy used to confronting drug-dealing gangsters.

I left DC Collins looking rather bewildered standing on Mrs Malkin's driveway. Once in the safety of my car I punched Julia's number into my phone and talked to her on hands-free as I made as quick a getaway as was possible whilst being closely watched by an officer of the law.

"Jools, I'm heading home to drown myself in booze. D'ya fancy coming over?"

Julia is a good friend, the best mate anyone could have. She didn't wait for further explanation. Instead, as always, she cut straight to the point and answered, "Hold on, girl, I'm on my way."

Available now in paperback and ebook